6 Days in January

A Novel

"Mr. O."
Thanks for the
love, Man!!!
your lady's gonna
love this!!!

6 Days in January

A Novel

WILLIAM FREDRICK COOPER

SBI

Strebor Books
New York London Toronto Sydney

Published by
SBI
Strebor Books
P.O. Box 6505
Largo, MD 20792
http://www.streborbooks.com

This book is a work of fiction. Names, characters, places and incidents are products of the author's imagination or are used fictitiously. Any resemblance to actual events or locales or persons, living or dead, is entirely coincidental.

Originally published in trade paperback in 2003.

Cover Design: www.mariondesigns.com

ISBN 0-7432-9614-1
LCCN 2003112279

First Strebor Books mass market paperback edition October 2006

1 0 9 8 7 6 5 4 3 2 1

Manufactured in the United States of America

For information regarding special discounts for bulk purchases, please contact Simon & Schuster Special Sales at 1-800-456-6798 or business@simonandschuster.com

Praise for *Six Days in January*

"*Six Days In January* is an eye-opener into the inside of one sensitive but strong Black male who strips his soul bare and rebuilds his character from the ground up into an indestructible edifice that any woman worth her mettle would love to meet."

—Emma Wisdom, *Chattanooga Courier* (August 2002)

"*Six Days In January* is a wonderful story, emotion filled from a man's point of view... It was a pleasure and honor to read."

—National Best-Selling Author Donna Hill

"William Fredrick Cooper's a very different voice, a powerfully dramatic voice and a voice to be reckoned with. Move over, Carl and Eric: Sir Fredrick is coming through."

—National Best-Selling Romance Writer Gwynne Forster

"*Six Days In January* is an easy read—sure to dangle readers on the edge of literary ecstasy. Make room,

Omar, Eric and Carl; William Fredrick Cooper is sure to be around for many years to come."

—T.C. Matthews, co-founder of Profilic Writers Network

"William Fredrick Cooper is a fresh new voice who gives voice to what the African-American male is thinking today. This is a book that I think will appeal to many whether you are male or female, black or white, as love is the same everywhere. He's a dynamite writer."

—Suzanne Coleburn, the Belles and Beaux of Romance

"*Six Days In January* is a beautifully written novel. I applaud Cooper for having the talent and the bravery to paint such a vivid story for public consumption."

—*RAWSISTAZ* Review by Shonell Bacon

"*Six Days* is a story that screams reality. Buy this book. Read this book. Open up your hearts and listen to William Fredrick Cooper."

—Cheryl Faye, author of *A Time For Us*, *A Test Of Time* & *First Love*

"William Fredrick Cooper definitely knows how to pull at the heartstrings. This is a must-read and when you finish, you'll want to hug someone dear to you."

—Darrien Lee, author of *All That and a Bag of Chips* and *Been There Done That*

"*Six Days in January* is an emotionally complex story with an unforgettable main character: a man whose unbridled romanticism leads him through many trials in his search for love."

—David McGoy, *Black Reign News*

Dedicated to Marlin Reed

A good guy who left us too soon.

Rest in peace, buddy.

"If the world was created in seven days,
then a brother can change his life in six."

—TIMOTHY CHAPPELLE

Chapter One

SNOWY MOONLIT EVENINGS

Day One

He didn't know which was worse, the bitter cold raking against his dark skin or Della's icy words just moments ago. Echoing softly in his heart, and though wishing the wind would blow them away and the winter chill along with them, he couldn't deny their truth.

Nothing's worse than getting put out at one in the morning on the coldest night of the year, he decided while making his way to the subway station. Face stinging and ears burning from the extreme weather, William McCall wondered how he had gotten there in the first place. Della wasn't supposed to forgive him this time. She'd been "through with his shit" over a month ago after calling his Brooklyn apartment one morning in early December and hearing the voice of another woman—a woman whom she insisted was his ex-wife, a woman he'd divorced two years prior.

"But it wasn't her," he'd persisted, "she's just a friend."

Although honest that time, the issue hardly mattered to her anymore. Fed up with all the crap she'd ingested at the hands of this man, she no longer had the strength to weed through his lies in hopes of finding the truth.

But this was a snowy, moonlit Thursday evening in mid-January, one of those blustery, sub-freezing days in New York City where a cold, empty bed is so hard to bear alone. Doing computer consultant work at a midtown Smith Barney office, nothing awaited Della Montgomery at her Bronx apartment except post-holiday bills. So when William called her office that morning sounding desperate—as though he'd learned his lesson—she'd accepted his invitation to have drinks after work.

Heading to an after-work watering hole in lower Manhattan where they'd first met a year ago and had frequented often since that fateful night, William found her sitting at a dark, red-bricked bar nursing a Heineken. Della was dressed provocatively in a blue dress, revealing a tight, aerobically carved frame. Her thin braids complemented an unblemished tan shade, making her appear younger than her thirty-nine years. She still feels as if she must impress me. *That's a good sign*, he thought as he approached her with flowers in hand.

"I'm so glad you decided to meet me," he said, handing her the bouquet while offering a kiss that she accepted with her cheek.

"It must be a new year," Della replied, aggressively grabbing the arrangement as she crossed her sculpted stems. "You actually made it here at the time you said you were going to. I'm surprised you were able to find such beautiful flowers on such a cold day. Then again, you're at your best when you're being cold."

Grimacing at her bluntness, he thought, *maybe this wasn't such a good idea.* "Ouch, that hurt. You didn't decide to meet me here just to read me my rights, did you?"

Della offered a sarcastic smile. "No, it's because I missed you so much."

"Well, I'm glad to see you, anyway." William ogled her and her beauty filled him up. Her full, inviting lips were sensuous and her eyes, although serious, were warm, sparkling and dove-like, soaring with radiance. "You look extraordinarily beautiful. I'm really glad to see you. Did you get my package last month?"

"I did, but I didn't open it." Della wasn't being truthful at this point. At first she'd thought of sending it back but after the holidays, she'd given in. Upon reading the card, she'd played the accompanying love tape every day for a week, but there was no way she was going to let him know that. Just last night, she'd held the teddy bear and cried, wondering why William couldn't be so sweet and thoughtful all the time. Acknowledging his tender side, it seemed he only showed how much he cared when he'd hurt her, and was tender only when they made love.

Still, the thought of his December package softened

her to the point of wanting to strip this slim, athletic thirty-four-year-old man from his blue double-breasted suit. As he looked away to get the bartender's attention, she detected disappointment in his tone when he ordered a Long Island Iced Tea. Realizing that she was supposed to be annoyed with him, she guarded her own vulnerability once he returned to her. "I meant to; I've just been busy," she explained. "I went away over the holidays, and…"

"Where'd you go?"

"To the Bahamas, with my girlfriend, Toni."

"Where'd you stay?"

"At the Nassau Marriott Resort. You know, the hotel with the casino."

The sparkle returned to William's eyes.

"Did you meet Dexter?"

"Plenty of them, but I wasn't looking for one. I was actually trying to figure out why men are so fucked up."

Like a drop of water lingering on the tip of a melting icicle before falling to the ground, William paused ever so slightly, then, prepared for the confrontation he'd briefly sidestepped upon his arrival. "Della, I don't know how else to say I'm sorry…"

"I don't want your apologies, William. I just want to know how you can be so fucked up? Be totally honest with me. Do you enjoy playing games with people's emotions? Do you find pleasure in hurting women?"

"I was honest with you. That wasn't my ex-wife."

Sipping from her beer and realizing that she was being drawn in, Della wanted to resist the temptation to question him. She couldn't. "Well, who was it, then?" Before his lips formed an excuse, "No, forget it, don't tell me. I don't even want to know. It doesn't matter if she was your ex-wife, or your friend. You lied to me, William. I thought I was the only one, and maybe I was a fool to think that. But you proved me wrong."

During the ensuing silence, William tuned in to R. Kelly's "Down Low" on the jukebox. *Everyone's talking about creepin', having sex on the DL, fuckin' on the sneak tip*, he thought. Amused at the irony, he mumbled, "Maybe I shouldn't listen to the radio so much."

"What did you say?"

"Nothing."

The bartender finally returned with his drink.

"You can't think of anything to say?" Della's tone jolted him.

"What else is there to say? I tried calling you. I sent you a package explaining everything and you ignored me. What am I supposed to do? I never said I didn't have a past or a life outside of my life with you. I'm really sorry about what happened that day, I really, really am. But I can't apologize for you not being the only one in my life."

He turned away from her to take a swallow of his drink.

Della crinkled her forehead. Her emotions rising, she began regretting the agreement to see him, having heard his, "I got divorced recently, so I don't want to be tied down" speech too many times before. "Look. I'm not asking you to marry me or anything. I just want to be loved and respected and that means honesty about who you're dealing with. But it seems like that's too much to ask from you, or any man, for that matter."

"That's not true. What do you expect me to do, make a mad dash to the phone just in case it's you who's calling? What was I supposed to do? You have a right to be upset, and while understanding you may not have liked what happened, there are some things that just go with the territory."

"Is honesty part of your territory? Or am I just supposed to accept being disrespected by some heifer? What's her name, anyway? The fuckin' wench!"

"Now, why does she have to be all that?"

✪✪✪

As he crossed the Grand Concourse and made his way down the icy streets, William thought of the hodgepodge of truths, half truths, untruths and deceptions that had painted a murky picture for Della hours earlier—an illustration that became more blurred with each question, each answer and each drink. As candid with her as he could be, but not at the risk of what he wanted, in short, he'd told her what she needed to know.

The woman he'd been with was "a friend," but he was no longer seeing her. In fact, he hadn't seen her since the day she'd spewed venom at Della over the phone. He liked her, he conceded, but she was too demanding and insecure. Reminding him of his ex-wife—in a bad way—he'd stopped seeing her because what he shared with her wasn't worth the loss of Della's companionship.

Having spent the holidays alone, he'd been really down about having hurt her. He was fairly certain that he'd really lost her this time, a point emphasized as the conversation continued. "And I just wanted to see you to let you know all of these things, for whatever it's worth. I know I'm almost out of rope when it comes to my word, for it means almost nothing to you. But I still have to speak my peace, because no matter what happens, I still care about you."

The words rang familiar to Della; they echoed the ones in his holiday card. Already knowing the details of his alibi, she wanted to hear it directly from him. Anyone could write a letter. But probing his eyes that night at the bar, she remembered the heartfelt words he'd expressed to her in his card. Della never questioned William's ability to treat her right, only his willingness and commitment to doing so. Maybe staying away had been just what he'd needed to see what he was risking. Still, the fact that she feared what he'd say if she asked for a commitment from him created an uncomfortable silence as they sat together; William, not knowing anything else to say to mend fences, and Della, trying to resolve questions and issues that his presence provoked. William breached the quiet with a truce.

"Look, Della. I'm just glad to see you. Let's not dwell on what happened anymore. I know it was wrong. I just wanted to see you, share some memories and have a good time. I missed you."

They continued to talk things out, drink after drink and eventually, they tired of the back and forth waffling and began to enjoy themselves. Knowing he was glad to see her—he could hardly take his eyes off of her—Della felt soothed by his presence. After another drink, the night continued with a dinner filled with steamy flirtations at Jezebel's, an old-fashioned Cajun restaurant in midtown. From there, they took a cab to her second-floor Bronx apartment on University Avenue. Then, after some wine and listening to Will Downing, she was ready to forgive him.

✪✪✪

"Get off of me, you fucking bastard! Get your dick out of me!" Della pounded on William's chest and shoulders until he backed off.

"Della, please, I'm so sorry. I don't know what I was thinking. It must have been our conversation earlier," he continued. "Please forgive me; I didn't mean anything by it."

"You are one fucked up individual, William!" Della screamed as she stormed around the bedroom in a fury. "How could you? Every single time I give in to you, I feel more and more like a fool for listening to your trifling, sorry ass. But, not anymore. Get the hell out and stay the fuck out of my life!"

William stood by the bed, naked, his erection subsiding. "Baby, please, don't get hysterical. Calm down. You need time to think this over."

"Hysterical? You've stepped over the line too many times before...but to call me another woman's name! Is Barbara the bitch you told me all about? Your friend? Well, she can have you, because you can't do shit for me!" Della made her way to the dresser, turned on the bedroom light and started emptying belongings he had left at her house on the floor.

Watching her in silence, he couldn't stop his eyes from blinking as Della's tirade moved from the dresser to her bedroom closet. A pile of clothes, underwear and toiletries from prior visits was accumulating on the floor. *The sex with Barbara wasn't even that good,* he thought. When Della was finished, she slumped to the floor and started crying.

Up to this point, he hadn't moved. But now, still naked, he staggered over to her with drunken tears of his own forming in his eyes. "Della, I'm sorry. I don't know what else to say." Now seated next to her, he tried to rest his head on her shoulder.

Della angrily moved away and began stuffing his belongings in a blue duffel bag. "That's the problem with you, William. You never know what to say. Then again, you always seem to know exactly what to say. But you know what?" She paused to sniffle and wipe the tears from her face. "I just wish this had happened before, because I should have done this a long, long time ago. This past year has been such a waste of my time, trying to get your black ass to act right and treat me the way I deserve to be treated. All I wanted from you was honesty and respect, and you can't even give me that. You never have. You're a fuckin' dog, like so many of you sorry ass black men." She started sobbing again.

"Della, I care about you, you know that. I'm just going through a lot, right now. That conversation we had earlier had me thinking about her, that's all. You have to believe me when I say she doesn't mean anything to me."

Blankly staring off and ignoring all pleas, Della recounted an incident she'd observed earlier that day while traveling to work. She saw a teenager outside the D-train station trying to get this young sister's attention while attempting to be cool in front of his boys, communicating his attraction to her with all of this "Yo, baby" shit. The young girl had ignored him, so he called her a bitch and threw a snowball at her.

"Later on in life she's going to run across guys like you; always full of shit," she continued. "Always looking for that next piece of ass. Never knowing how to treat a woman, only trying when things go wrong." She paused, shaking her head in disbelief. "I don't believe some of you brothers today." Lifting herself from the floor, Della sorted through the remains of the heap to find his suit. "Just looking at you is starting to repulse me, William. Please hurry up and leave."

"But you can't believe how sorry I am," William implored, as his clothes were being thrown at him. "It will never happen again. I promise."

"You're right about that. You are sorry, and you're damned straight, this shit will never happen again. Now, hurry up and leave." Della left the bedroom, refusing to let him see her cry anymore.

William got dressed and picked up his briefcase, leaving the duffel bag she'd packed in the middle of the floor where she left it. Entering the living room, he found her on the couch, her knees pulled up to her chin with her arms wrapped around them.

"Della, please accept my apology."

"Let me give you some advice, William. Stop apologizing so much and start acting like a real man. Now, get out."

"Please, can't we just start over? Nothing like this will ever happen again. Della, please. Look, I can start here." Pulling a Tootsie Roll from his coat pocket, he remembered how she loved the small chocolate candy.

The peace offering would not work tonight.

Della rose and walked to the front door. "Start by learning how to love someone besides yourself." She opened the door. "Good-bye."

Drunk, defeated and dejected, William walked past her without turning around and made his way to the elevator.

Della stepped into the hallway.

"And you can continue by learning how to fuck!" The door slammed.

✪✪✪

Now, walking through lazy snowflakes and swirling winds this Friday morning, William McCall wondered how he had gotten there; not back into Della's life or even into her bed.

Still feeling the lingering aftershock of Della's lambasting of the black man, William realized that he'd become the negative stereotype often stamped on his brothers, and was mortified. In the past, it had been he who'd cried from being left in pain; it had been his feelings that were always taken for granted. He recalled a time that seemed so long ago, when the thought of William McCall being a dog was so unfathomable, so farfetched, it would have made anyone who knew him scoff in amusement.

Stung by Della's words, he'd never wanted to be considered in such a negative light. But after all his lies, all his broken promises and all of the mortgaged dreams they were supposed to share, he knew she was right.

In fact, from the moment they'd begun dating, Della had exuded tolerance to a fault. Exhibiting patience more durable than Egyptian pyramids, William felt she'd understood his patience, albeit, grudgingly. Unreturned phone calls were analyzed with prudence. His sabbaticals during their acquaintance were forgiven. Even the many times he'd told her "something came up" were accepted without much of a fight, for there was no official commitment, no concrete definition to the union. All these actions had been accepted as part and parcel of dating William. Restraining all objections to these unspoken rules and rarely articulating discontent, Della had been incredibly compliant.

However, tonight had been the final straw, for William's selfishness now bordered on blatant disrespect and total disdain for her feelings. Della's leniency now eroded, much like a river wearing down a sturdy mountainside, she refused to put up with his irrational behavior another second.

I can't really blame her for throwing me out, William mused while reaching for his MetroCard at the train station. *I wouldn't put up with my recent actions, either.* Feeling as though one woman would never be enough to satisfy his cravings, until tonight he had never confused his sex partners. Whichever woman he was with, he'd always wanted them to feel like the chosen one.

He reflected on that time when he'd been so different...but had he been a better man? Still considering himself a good black man, he knew he had a lot going for himself. A young, intelligent legal professional at Goetz, Gallagher and Green, one of New York's prestigious firms, he had a secure income, as evidenced by a closet full of suits, shirts and footwear. He spent hours at a midtown Bally's working to strengthen his lanky frame and an affinity for sports contributed to his fitness. Proud of his sinewy build, his narrow hips, lithe yet powerful legs and moderately built chest declared him, without words, an athletic sort. With smooth, clear mahogany skin, ivory teeth, a bald dome and a gold hoop earring in his left lobe, he could pass for Jordan, if he were a half-foot taller. Witty, articulate and polite—after years of being perceived as uninteresting, boring and not sexy, labels that are an albatross weighing on any halfway decent brotha—he was considered highly desirable. But he had reached a crossroad in his life where he was growing into a man he couldn't possibly be proud of. He wasn't strong, not in the ways he needed to be. He'd never been, not even in the past when his compassion and sensitivity were construed as weaknesses. The bitterness and pain of years past had hardened him, but he still was not strong.

Dwelling on a time where innocence and naivete were apparent, he remembered a cold night in February many winters ago, when he'd fallen in love. He thought he'd loved many times before—too many—but it had always been a fickle, pristine kind of energy. But years ago, on a snowy, moonlit evening just like this one, he'd stumbled and fallen upon a love that had changed everything, and felt the heartbreak that would make even the most hopeful romantic cynical.

Chapter Two
WATCHING AND HOPING

February 1987

"Yo, Will, they're waiting on us, man. Come on!" Carlton Butler yelled in the reception area bathroom.

"I'm fixing my tie."

"If we're not at the bar by six-thirty they're goin' without us."

"Carlton, you need to chill, man. It's only a quarter to," William replied, coming out. "You know, you guys don't have to do this. It's not like I'm disappearing off the face of the earth. I'm only gonna be eleven blocks away."

"Yeah, but it won't be the same without you here. The office will miss your enthusiasm, man. Besides, who am I going to brag to about my sex life? Who's going to handle my work while I'm off bullshitting with secretaries?"

"Fuck you, Carlton," William responded, retrieving their coats from a nearby closet.

This Friday evening marked his last day working

as a messenger at Smith, Anderson & Friedman, a midtown law firm on Manhattan's eastside, and some of his closest co-workers were sending him off in a fashion deemed appropriate to them—by partying. Carlton and William were to meet up with the others at an Irish pub, where they would guzzle drinks and rave about his new position as Litigation Court Clerk at Robinson, Burton & Luftkow, then proceed to the Copacabana between Madison and Fifth Avenues to continue the revelry. *All of this for a twenty-year-old,* he thought as he walked with Carlton to meet up with the rest of the crew.

"The man of the hour is here," Carlton announced as they entered the bar.

"Shh, man. It's not like that," William retorted.

"Come on, Will. We love you, man," Gil slurred, toasting his glass along with Kim, Sandra and Serafin. All of them had a head start on the occasion and were now eagerly awaiting the sounds of the Copa.

"Hurry up, get him a drink," Kim said.

Serafin then ordered William a Long Island Iced Tea. "Ever try this, man? It'll put some hair on your cojones."

When the drink arrived, William chugged it down, to the amazement of everyone at the table. They were thinking of him as a novice because of his youth.

"Damn, Will!" Kim shouted. "I thought you were wet behind the ears, man."

"Not when it comes to these," he explained, blushing. "I had tons of these at Saturday dorm parties at college."

His five hosts were equally amazed when he ordered and guzzled a beer before they departed to their next destination. Time passed at the bar with all of them wishing him success at his new place of employment. Feeling that he was wasting his intelligence as a messenger, Carlton Butler, a black law clerk working for a retired judge, saw William's potential and acted immediately.

Taking him under his wing during the last six months at the firm, Carlton tutored him on the law process, nuances of court filing procedures from his legal assistant's perspective, and offered tips on professional grooming and attire. Upon hearing of an opening at another firm, he got William an entry-level position there through inside contacts that paid thirteen-thousand dollars a year. "Anything's better than the hundred fifty dollars a week you're making now as a messenger," Carlton had reasoned.

William was grateful for the opportunity.

Additionally, all were hoping this amiable young man would find success in his future relationships with women. They'd all heard about Tami, his ex-girlfriend, and the drama she'd subjected him to during a tumultuous off-and-on relationship. Sandra, thirty something and happily married, brought this to William's attention en route to the nightclub.

"You know, you're too sweet to be by yourself. How come no one's snatched you up? I'm telling you, if I wasn't married I'd act just like those silly girls your age. I'd bat my eyes and try to get the time of day from you."

Trying to sound convincing, William stated, "Look, I'm really not lookin' to get into anything now. Tami was a trip and a half. I need to lie low for a while."

✪✪✪

William's heart, however, screamed otherwise, for he wanted someone in his life to share ardent feelings of passion he yearned to express. It had been almost two months since he and Tami McDaniels parted ways, the relationship ending once and for all when she and her girlfriends jolted his psyche by questioning his virility.

They'd reconciled for the last time back in September of 1986 after it was revealed to him that, not only had Tami lost her virginity to some guy she had gotten involved with after a prior breakup, but was impregnated by him as well. Informing Anthony of her expectancy, he'd left her to fend for herself.

William had taken her to get the abortion, then, comforted her afterward when she cried with guilt. Offering platonic support at this juncture, amorous feelings they used to share swiftly resurfaced in his heart. With reciprocal yearnings coming from Tami, they attempted a relationship one last time. However, that proved to be an exercise in futility.

Overly sensitive to the whole abortion ordeal, William never pressured her for sex. Tami and her girlfriends had other inferences for his lack of intimate advances.

Rose Wilson and Carla McDowell, two of Tami's associates who'd attended Staten Island's Curtis High School with William (Tami had been enrolled in nearby Port Richmond), had always wondered about him as they labeled her choice of suitors odd, for they'd never seen him with a girlfriend back in those days.

"All he ever did was sit with the white guys and talk about sports," Rose had commented.

Unaccustomed to dealing with a person so accessible, kind and dependable, William was considered weird. He wasn't the type of guy who would greet her and her friends with a "Yo, whassup?" salutation, like Anthony did, so his emotional display while viewing *The Color Purple* at Tami's house heightened, then confirmed their collective suspicions.

Rose and Carla had never seen a man cry before,

and in solidifying Carla's words—"I hope I never see that happen again. He's too weak, a little light in the ass for me"—they failed to recognize, respect and understand his sensitivity.

Reminiscing on these sparked another recollection. He'd spent Thanksgiving Day with Tami at her sister's house in the Rosedale section of Queens. After dinner and a few drinks, the conclusion Tami and her friends had come to was revealed during a heated conversation in the kitchen.

"William, you don't have to do the dishes for my sister."

"She'll be in here all night. It's the least I could do for her hospitality. It won't take me much longer."

"I need to ask you something," Tami said as she took a seat. "Do you find me attractive?"

William shot an incredulous look at her. Enamored with her smooth, cocoa-butter complexion, round face and light-brown eyes, he'd always complimented her on her beauty, not to mention the compact, curvaceous shape that accompanied a sassy, street-tough disposition he'd never had. "What are you asking me? I wouldn't be with you if I didn't."

"Then why haven't you...?" Tami paused. "Why haven't we...?"

"What?"

"Had sex yet?"

William sighed. "Tami, it's not that I don't want to have sex with you. It's just that with you having the abortion and all..."

"It's been about five weeks."

"Let me finish. I didn't want to pressure you into doing something you're not ready for." He'd assumed he'd been reassuring.

"And what was the reason before the abortion?"

"You were a virgin, weren't you?"

"So what!" Tami snapped. "That doesn't stop you from kissing me all over my breasts and leaving hickeys all over the place, now does it?"

Feeling tension bubble under his skin and sensing the place for this discussion was elsewhere, William didn't reveal his inner reservations about having intercourse with a virgin or, in this instance, someone very close to being one. His theory was that after a woman loses her virginity to a man, they unconsciously suffocate them. Besides, William wasn't the teaching type. Instead of voicing this, he said another truth that entered his mind at that moment.

"I never wanted to pressure you. I always felt when our relationship reached that level, it would just happen."

Tami wasn't having it. "Yeah, right. I've been ready for a while. You can kiss me and caress me all over, yet you can't make love to me? Don't feed me this shit! Me and my girlfriends think either you're scared of pussy, or..."

"Or, what?"

"Or, that you like men."

William almost dropped a plate.

"What are you talkin' about, Tami? I'm no faggot!" Seething now, he shook his head. "What are you coming to me with this for? I don't believe this crap. I can't believe that you and your girlfriends have sat around and..."

"Whenever we're around them, you never act like you have me in check. I like my man to be aggressive. I want him to put me in my place once in a while."

"I'm supposed to act like I have you in check? Nobody owns anyone in relationships."

"Yeah, but you don't even get jealous when I talk to other guys. While we're on that subject, whenever I introduce you to my male friends, you act all soft and shit, saying hello like a little bitch!" She wasn't done. "And ever since Rose and Carla saw you crying watching that video, they've been wondering what's up with you. They were glad we broke up over the summer and I started dating Anthony."

At this point the people outside the kitchen were wondering what was happening, for they heard voices rising with each statement. Astonishingly, no one came to see what the commotion was about. The discussion evolved into an embarrassing, no-holds-barred argument about William's sexual orientation.

Furious by this point, he got up in Tami's face and started yelling, "Do you see the shit you got yourself into with this Anthony? He knocked you up and jetted! And is Rose happy with her boyfriend Roy? Hell no! He treats her like shit! And from what I hear, the reason why Carla can't find anyone worth anything is that she gives pussy away like it's water. Fuckin' slut!"

"Don't talk about my friends like that," Tami hollered back.

"Fuck your friends! How the hell are you gonna sit there and let them brainwash you like this? You know damn well I'm not gay! I can't believe you actually agree with them." William paused to collect himself. "I guess stupidity travels in threes." As he sat down in a chair, Tami stormed through the kitchen door.

Although peace was made that evening, things were never the same between them. They continued to see each other for two weeks afterward, however, in William's heart the relationship ended with that altercation. Feeling he'd handled the delicacy of Tami's situation correctly, the reward for his effort had been three classless women's emasculating beliefs about his carnal desires. Instead of being lauded for patience, he was unfairly labeled as effeminate.

Showing apprehension in meeting anyone else

shortly thereafter, he concentrated on his studies. When finals were over at NYU, the college he attended at night, he exhibited signs of his readiness to return to the dating game. As a matter of fact, he completed some card and candy shopping for his annual Valentine's Day send-off to friends and family on that last day of employment. Two weeks before that he'd gone solo to the Palladium, a popular nightclub in lower Manhattan, to hone his dance moves. Although withholding his intentions from his colleagues, he was ready to meet that special woman.

✪✪✪

They arrived at the Copa around seven-thirty feeling better than when they'd left McAnn's. Oblivious to the light snow flurries, the group stopped in Central Park to take pictures with William and to get high on the weed Gil had purchased for the occasion.

"You can't have any," Kim barked at William while Carlton, Sandra and Serafin sparked and smoked. "You're too young."

After the photo shoot, the celebration reached a zenith of sorts as the group presented William with a three hundred-dollar gift certificate to a local sporting goods outlet. "Get those Air Jordans I keep hearing about," Sandra said. By the time they reached the Copa, William was fighting back tears. Maybe I should reconsider leaving, he pondered as he entered the nightclub, still choked up by his friends' generosity.

"I got first dance with William," Kim called as she checked her coat.

"Who do you want to dance with first, sugar?" Sandra interjected.

"I want to dance with another one of those Long Island Iced Teas," William said. Gil, Serafin and Carlton laughed as they, too, checked their coats.

After sharing one last drink together at a long table slightly above the club's extended, strobe-lit dance area, Sandra reminded everyone of the reason they were all at the Copa. Taking his cue, William grabbed her hand and led her to the dance floor.

During the week, the club normally catered to the predominantly Latin crowds by playing salsa and merengue grooves. Fridays were mixed so the DJ rocked his jams accordingly. Lisa Lisa's "Can You Feel the Beat" was ripping through the club when they started dancing. Sandra did a good job of getting his attention when she started doing the Snake.

"I didn't know you could do that dance," he bellowed over the music.

"My daughter showed me that. I needed to learn something. You can dance your ass off."

After playing a series of salsa records, the DJ then proceeded to put on Colonel Abrams' "Trapped." It had taken about thirty minutes, but now William was a slave to the rhythms of the Copa. Sandra danced to a few more songs, then asked him to venture back to the table where they'd been seated. He obliged, but grabbed Kim's hand.

"Damn, William, you have so much energy," Kim said excitedly. He smiled, took her to the dance floor and continued bouncing to a couple of house songs.

It was during the latter of these that he turned his vision to the left of his dance partner and was magnetically drawn to a caramel-colored beauty dancing nearby. About five feet seven, with beautiful almond-shaped eyes, the fitted black and white checkered dress she wore revealed well-placed curves, coordinating perfectly with her white boots. Hypnotically moving to the pulse of the music, she commanded William's attention; he experienced difficulty taking his eyes off this woman. Spellbound with infatuation, he adored the way she danced with her partner, a chubby fellow with glasses, and felt compelled to share at least one dance with her. However, he wondered if she'd come alone, or was involved with the person she was dancing with.

The query his mind posed was immediately answered

when the two left the dance floor in separate directions. Watching her every step as she walked toward her Hispanic girlfriend, William could see that every movement of this woman exuded a confidence that belied her youthful existence, every stride long and sure, graceful yet purposeful. When Kim eventually tired of dancing with him, he walked her back to the area where the party of six were seated and started thinking of a way he could dance with that fine young woman who had so captivated him. Beginning his walk over to the table where the two women were seated, he saw two other men nearing the ladies and stopped short. As William and the woman made eye contact for the first time, she looked disappointed that he didn't continue his stroll.

Returning to his group, William came across Priscilla Anderson, a long-legged woman he'd met clubbing at a spot called the Area over the past summer. Remembering how she loved to dance, he immediately grabbed her hand.

With Phyllis Nelson's "I Like You" now playing, William intentionally directed her to a spot on the dance floor where they could be viewed dancing by the woman whose interest he wanted to garner. He showed many sensuous moves from his repertoire during this song and the ones following—spins, shakes and hip grinds by the two, body waves and pelvic gyrations. It seemed that Priscilla and William became one as they danced provocatively to the musical selections.

Feeling this mystery woman looking at him, he next took his statuesque dance partner onto the stage above the club dance area so she could get a better look. Priscilla seemed caught up in the moment also, for she made a comment about "just sitting down and watching you, because you move so well."

William just grinned and said, "I'm just feeling the grooves."

Twenty minutes passed and Priscilla finally tired. William took her to the bar, walking past the table at which the object of his desire and her friend were seated. As he strolled by them, they were alone enjoying their drinks and talking. William overheard their conversation.

"He's a good dancer," the woman in the checkered dress said.

"So ask him to dance," her friend responded.

Priscilla, hearing these comments as well, smiled and said to William, "I think you have a couple of admirers. The one in the black and white dress wants to dance with you."

William looked at her as if he needed her approval. He needn't have bothered.

"Don't worry, sugar. I'm off to change after I finish this drink," Priscilla declared at that moment. "Larry Levan is calling me."

Sure enough, ten minutes later she kissed him on the cheek. "Take care, sweetie," she said, scurrying to prepare for a rendezvous at the Paradise Garage, the ultimate all-night house music spot in the city.

By now, William's co-workers had dispersed, each person choosing to go their separate ways. With Priscilla's departure, he was flying solo, as well.

Back on stage once more, this time by himself, he noticed that his beauty had moved to a space near the dance floor. After a couple of songs, he sat down on the edge of the platform indecisively. An hour had passed since he'd first spotted this woman dancing, but time had come and gone and he still hadn't conquered the internal demons that prevented him from taking the initiative for this much anticipated dance.

Reminiscing on that trip he'd made a couple of weeks prior to the Palladium, William remembered being watched by a strikingly beautiful woman for what seemed like an eternity while dancing on a stage above the dance floor. Thinking she too was interested, he'd finally mustered the courage to come off the platform, walk across the crowded dance floor to ask for a dance.

She'd turned him down.

Then about five minutes later, he saw her on the

dance floor with "the guy of her dreams." This individual, a muscular, copper-skinned brother, towered over her, and the look on her face let him know that he'd swept her off her feet.

There was eye contact between William and that woman once more before the evening ended. Standing to the left of the coat check area with a few of her friends as he approached to retrieve his coat, she suddenly turned to her friends and said, "I enjoyed turning that one down 'cause he looks like midnight and ain't that good-looking."

Then, they all laughed.

Replaying that bitter experience as he sat on the stage, William's eyes darkened with the memory of that rejection. *Will it happen again if I approach this woman? Will I have to face that kind of embarrassment again?* These thoughts were coupled with intense self-doubt. *Am I too dark? Not tall enough? Am I too skinny? Or, not fine enough to dance with?* These fears assaulted his mind as he contemplated his next move.

Chapter Three

NO RINGS...FAIR GAME

The wee hours were a disaster for William. Not only was he unceremoniously kicked out of Della's home and life and into the winter of a first-month Friday morning, he just missed the train that would take him to his Brooklyn apartment. "Talk about Murphy's fuckin' Law."

Parking himself on a wooden bench in the middle of the deserted subway platform, he looked to his right and overheard a young sister telling a brother who was trying to talk to her that she was already involved with someone. The young brother's response to her was, "No one owns you." He added, "You don't have any rings on your fingers."

With a combination of irony and disgust, William shook his head. Looking intently at the couple involved in the verbal exchange and noticing their youth, he wished he could march up to that brother and tell him about the time in his life when he'd spoken those exact words to a woman and the results that followed his brashness—the good, the bad, and the ugliness—of it all. Instead, those words conjured up thoughts of that formative lesson that began one evening, years ago.

✪✪✪

Fuck this! What's the worst she could say? With a steady groove now thumping through the speakers, William jumped off the stage. He wanted to dance with this woman and, hook or crook, he would.

Like Tony when first mesmerized by Maria in *West Side Story*, fate introduced itself to him at that point, for a path directing him to her magically appeared on the congested dance floor. Nearing her, he almost tripped on his tongue as he reveled in her beauty. She had a small nose, yet its keenness was alluring. Her heart-shaped lips were properly highlighted with a minimal amount of red lipstick. Petite, heavenly structured breasts pressed against the front of her dress, and her sculpted legs were lean and appealing, much like the rest of her lovely appearance.

"Excuse me, but can I share one dance with you before your boyfriend steals you away?"

"Sure."

William took her hand and together they glided onto the dance floor. It was beginning.

After only a few minutes of dancing, nothing else surrounding these two individuals mattered. Within the confines of the Copa, a shared dream world was under construction; the process jump-started with a simple compliment.

"You are so flexible," the woman said.

William smiled. "No one's ever told me that before. Do you come here often?"

"No. I was about to leave my girlfriend here all by herself. My head's killing me."

"I'm sorry to hear that, but it's a good thing you didn't. I've wanted to dance with you all night but I was scared you were going to say no."

"Say no to a great dancer like you? I'd be crazy," the woman responded.

"I also thought that the guy you were dancing with earlier was your boyfriend."

As the comment drew a giggle from the woman, a song came on that neither of them cared for so they walked off the floor.

"You know, you look kind of young. How old are you?" he asked.

"Twenty."

"The drinking age just went to twenty-one. Let me get security," William said, playfully gesturing to a bodyguard that wasn't there. "Excuse me. She doesn't belong in here."

"You're a jokester, huh? How old are you?"

"I'm twenty as well."

"Then you don't belong in here either! Security! Security!" They both started laughing.

"Listen, can I at least buy you a drink before you leave?"

"Sure."

So as the woman took a seat at a table near the dance floor, William walked to the bar. Hearing her encouragement, "Hurry back so we can get further acquainted," had him thinking, this must be a dream, as he ordered two screwdrivers.

To his surprise, upon his return he found his ex-boss, Carlton, seated in his chair, attempting to keep his newfound interest company.

"Damn, Carlton. Can't a brother get a woman a drink without you trying to step on his toes? Where did you come from?"

Quickly rising, Carlton mumbled something like, "My fault, Will," then went on his way.

"He's a creep," the woman said to William, taking her drink from his hand. "Thanks, honey. That guy was talkin' about how he would love to take me home with him. You know him?"

"Yeah. He was my supervisor before today. We're cool, but around the office he has a reputation with the ladies."

"Certainly it can't be a good one."

"From what I hear, it's not."

"I can tell. He's a Superfly wannabe with his Afro and yellow shirt opened like it's the 1970s. Who does he think he is, Huggy Bear from *Starsky and Hutch*?" William struggled to contain his laughter as she continued. "Is he like that all day?"

"Yeah, I'm afraid so. Every day, he would come in bragging about a different score and how he'd turned this one and that one out between the sheets. I found it funny because a secretary I know who dated him told me he has a case of SITS. I asked her what that meant and she said he sucked in the sack. Get it?" The woman's laughter rang out loudly, sending an involuntary chill down his spine. Brushing it off quickly, he continued, "I'll miss him, though. Today was my last day at that job."

"Really? What type of work do you do?"

"Well, before today I was a personal escort."

"Bullshit," the woman said, giggling again.

"Seriously, I was a part-time messenger, part-time docket clerk at a law firm. I'm moving on to another firm so I can become a court clerk full-time."

"I'm an administrative assistant at Met Life."

"A secretary, huh? That's cool."

Once more she smiled.

William extended his hand. "You know, we've been

talking a while now without introductions. I'm William McCall."

"I'm Andrea Richmond. It's spelled like Andrea but pronounced 'ahn-DRAY-uh.'"

"That's unique. What are you, from France or something?"

"Very funny. I guess my mom wanted me to be a little different."

"So she should have named you Shauntifa, or one of those other pseudo African names everyone seems to name their children these days."

They shared another chuckle as William lifted his glass.

"I'm just teasin'. Well, Andrea, here's to meeting you."

As they toasted, he noticed a diamond-chipped name ring on her left hand. "I see your boyfriend has good taste." Getting no response, he asked himself, *well does she or doesn't she?* Vocally, "Andrea, what sign are you?"

"Aries. My birthday is April fourth."

"Really? I'm a Gemini. My birthday is May twenty-first. Actually, I'm on the cusp between Taurus and Gemini. So if you don't like Geminis, then I'm a Taurus. I use them interchangeably."

Again, Andrea giggled.

And for the next half-hour or so, the couple jumped

from topic to topic like old friends. Their chat was filled with mirth and sincere animation, and both seemed to have a premonition that something unique was about to happen in their lives, something inextricably binding. William's initial fears of rejection were washed away as they talked about life. He was eerily comfortable with her, as if he'd known her forever.

Apparently, Andrea shared the feeling, for she grabbed his hand whenever she got excited during their discussion. He noticed, however, that whenever he hinted about her availability, she'd quickly drop his hand and change the subject, as if she were attempting to delay bad news.

Eventually, she tired of his tap dance and with slight irritation, threw down the gauntlet. "You know, why don't you just ask me if I have a boyfriend?"

"Well, do you?" William asked, anticipating the inevitable.

"Yes, I do." She looked dejected, as if resigning herself to her unavailable status.

"Are you happy with him?"

She wouldn't touch that one, but the sullen look on her face told him everything he needed to know.

"Are you engaged to him?"

"No."

"Well, since you have no ring on that left hand,

that means you're fair game, especially if you're not happy with him. You're entitled to do whatever you want to do."

In the years that followed, William would often look back on that uncharacteristic statement and wonder where it had come from. His answer? On that particular evening, he'd met a young woman he was enchanted by, and her beauty, charisma and attraction engulfed his presence, blinding him to future consequences. Having a wonderful feeling around this woman—an electric, explosive sensation he'd never known before—that energy made him a bolder, more confident person. Making statements he'd never been known to make and taking risks he'd never been known to take, he'd become a gambling man, a man who'd stepped beyond his normal, self-imposed boundaries. *Sometimes, love does these things to a man.*

Upon uttering those words to Andrea, he'd noticed an eager look in her gentle eyes that sent signals of curiosity, signals he interpreted as, "yes, I'm willing." Seeing a certain mystique she wanted to become acquainted with; a certain something she yearned to get closer to, mutual perception told him them they would be spending considerable time together that evening.

Right at that point, Janet Jackson's "Control" remix

blew up the spot. Excitedly grabbing Andrea's hand and rushing her to the dance floor, William had a ball simulating movements from the video. They looked crazy, yes, but they were looking crazy together. Sharing a good laugh, the two went on for about twenty minutes, then returned to their seats.

"Damn! Do you know the steps to all the videos?" Andrea asked.

"No, I don't. I'm just a huge Jackson fan," he said while pushing her chair in. "I love Michael and Janet. What type of music do you like?"

"R&B mostly. But lately I've been listening to a lot of house music. That sound is thumpin'!"

"Do you like love ballads?"

"Do I?" Andrea exclaimed. "I live for them. Especially Luther Vandross. That big man can sing to me anytime."

"He's not so big anymore. He's lost stupid weight, about seventy pounds."

Andrea's beautiful eyes widened.

"Really?"

William nodded.

"I just picked up his *Give Me the Reason* LP. It's real good."

"I heard."

"I'll tape it for you, if you want me to." William's intuition screamed he would see this woman again after this evening. I have to see her again. Acting on this hunch, he gave her his address and phone number.

Waiting half an hour for her to reciprocate, though he detected apprehension during this time, he knew he was going to get the number. When you find true love, he thought, destiny takes over. Sure enough, fate intervened and she gave him her digits.

After taking her number, Andrea fully expected him to venture off. She began tossing out judgmental statements like, "Men are after one thing, and nothing else." She even attempted to hasten his departure, stating, "You know, now that you have my number, you could go dance with the rest of your admirers."

William ignored such nonsense. Yes, he'd obtained her number, but the feeling now permeating his soul transcended more than this one evening. The woman had him walking on air. Now he wanted her to join him among the clouds.

While they continued their discussion about life and other interesting subjects, Andrea's friend finally came over. Andrea was about to apologize for being gone for so long when her friend—a leggy, Puerto Rican beauty—shook William's hand and said, "Thanks for helping her get rid of her headache. I think she just wanted to dance with you. I'm Vikki."

William smiled as he returned his attention to Andrea. "A headache, huh?"

"Well, I did have one," she replied through her blush.

"I'm William. Would you like a drink, Vikki?"

"I know you're not expecting me to say no," was her response, so William sauntered over to the bar once more. Andrea was gone when he got back.

"She went to the ladies room and told me to tell you not to go anywhere," Vikki announced.

"I like your friend, Vikki."

"So, tell her."

He wouldn't have to, for at that instant the DJ slowed things down and artificial smoke floated across the dance floor as Gregory Abbott's "Shake You Down" wafted through the low-lit nightclub.

Spotting Andrea coming from the bathroom and motioning her toward the dance floor, William shared a secret with her. "You're going to have to guide me through this. I never shared a slow dance with anyone before."

Grabbing his hand firmly, Andrea looked deep in his eyes and said, "Baby, you're in good hands."

Holding her close during this song and the ballads that followed, William couldn't keep his hands still. Andrea felt so good in his arms. Soon this slow dance turned into a deep, passionate grind. Incapable of resisting her own carnal impulses, Andrea caressed the arches in his slender frame before blowing into his ear. Slowly, but surely, she was falling under the trance already gripping William.

Finally, as the set of melodies ended, both thought inwardly, not a moment too soon, while leaving the dance floor holding hands.

"You two looked like lovers out there," Vikki said as they seated themselves. William blushed.

"Look at that, Andrea. He blushes."

Andrea smiled upon hearing that. Unusually quiet for the minutes subsequent to the slow dance, she felt guilty about developing affection for him. Normally able to curb wayward desires for other men, the week before meeting William, Andrea had had a talk with her mother. Realizing that Andrea was having problems with her boyfriend, during the discourse, Mrs. Richmond told her, "You're too young to be with one person. You need to start seeing other guys so you won't get hurt." She closed the conversation by telling her daughter to "protect yourself because I know firsthand how men can be." Now, one week later, she'd met a guy who seemed to be smitten by her, and she found herself flowing with the moment. Snowy evenings can be strange, she thought.

By now, the two had had enough of all the fast music. Vikki hadn't, so she went on her way, leaving Andrea and William at the table to enjoy their solitude, for they were cocooned in their tiny world of two.

Nearing their table was a man selling red roses by the half-dozen. Reaching into his pocket, William quickly and discreetly purchased a bouquet, then tapped her on the shoulder. Her attention in that brief moment had been directed elsewhere, so when Andrea saw the roses she was pleasantly surprised.

"My God, what did I do to deserve this?"

"Nothing. I'm just glad I met you this evening." He paused. "Andrea, will I see you again after this evening?"

"Definitely. You'll be seeing plenty of me." If only they'd had a little foresight.

For the next hour or so the twosome sat at the table, fingers and palms threaded together, romantic minds synchronized in anticipation of the next set of slow musical selections. Sure enough, the DJ obliged them by playing Anita Baker's "Sweet Love." Andrea looked at William as the first chord played and nothing else was said as they walked toward the dance floor.

The building passion between the two ignited into flames of desire. From the beginning, their dance was a sensuous cuddle, the petting deeper than before. William could hear Andrea's arousal through her panting. Instead of blowing, she now nibbled on his left earlobe. She had finally joined him on the cloud he'd been floating on since their meeting.

The collection of love songs culminated with Melissa Morgan's "Do Me Baby." Struggling to contain himself while dancing with this woman, William was on the verge of overheating. During this song, she whispered something to him about how good his warm body felt against hers.

Gazing into her eyes with passion, William attempted to kiss her.

"No, please don't," Andrea pleaded weakly. On this night, guilt and better judgment emerged victorious over emotional, passionate instincts—barely.

"I understand," William responded. Arm in arm, they left the dance floor. At the table, the two waited for Vikki to finish taking a guy's number, then they all went to get their belongings from the coat check. Andrea noticed all of William's bags and inquired about the contents.

"Chocolate hearts. For Valentine's Day."

"You think you have enough girlfriends?"

"I don't have one, if you want to know the truth. These are for friends and family." Seeing a cynical look from both ladies, he continued. "Seriously, I'm not dating anyone. While we're on that subject, Andrea, when are we going to see each other again?"

"When do you want to?"

"Let's go out Sunday. I want to go to the Bronx to get some sneakers, the red and white Air Jordans everyone's talking about. Wanna go?"

"Sure."

So the first date was set. Once outside, they parted company with Vikki and went to the subway together. Andrea lived in Brooklyn, as well, in Sheepshead Bay, so they traveled part of the journey home together on the D train.

When the train was approaching the Union Square Station, William offered to ride to Andrea's stop. "It's not safe for a woman to be traveling on the trains alone this late at night," he said.

"No, I'll be okay," Andrea responded.

"Are you sure? It's really not a problem."

"You're just the perfect gentleman, aren't you?"

"Well, if I had a car, I'd drive you home. Hey, I'll ride with you to Canal Street." The doors opened up at Fourteenth Street, William's transfer point.

"Go home, baby. Call me tomorrow. Good night."

Giving her a quick hug, William got off the train. *Sunday, huh?* he thought as her train pulled off. *I wish it wasn't so far away.* The train hadn't been gone thirty seconds, yet he missed Andrea already.

✪✪✪

Ironically, it was the iron horse labeled D that William would take from Della's house these years later to his Brooklyn apartment. He thought of the coincidence as the train entered the Fordham Road Station.

When seated, his mind drifted back to the initial ride to Sheepshead Bay to meet Andrea for their date. He remembered how he'd purchased a stuffed Garfield doll and a blue sweater right after he'd spoken to her the day before. The excitement he'd felt when the train approached the Sheepshead Bay Road station, the anticipation racing through his bones once he boarded the B36 bus that took him to her neighborhood, and, upon seeing her, the smile he'd never beamed for any woman, were all vivid in his memory. That first date, he now recalled, had been special.

✪✪✪

That Sunday was overcast and unseasonably warm for early February. The 1987 NBA All-Star game was to be televised from Seattle, prompting William to appreciate the impression Andrea had made on him two nights earlier. Only something or someone special can pull a brother from his All-Star game.

Getting off the bus at the corner of Nostrand and

Avenue W, he noticed Andrea walking toward him. Wearing fitted black jeans and a red wool coat, her beauty made him tingle all over.

"Hello, stranger," Andrea said as she welcomed him with a warm hug. "I couldn't wait to see you again."

"I felt the same way." He handed her the box with the stuffed animal. "Please forgive me for not wrapping him properly."

Once she saw the animal was Garfield, she enthusiastically thanked him with another embrace. "I love Garfield! You're so sweet."

"You ready to go hang, sweetie?"

"Let's do this," she responded, posing in a mock b-boy stance. Sharing a hearty laugh, they crossed the street and got on the bus headed to the subway.

During the bus ride and the ensuing train trip, they picked up where they'd left off at the Copa. After chatting about their childhoods—Andrea had two older brothers and a younger sister, and William had come from a family of six, he had five brothers—next came their educational backgrounds. He'd told her about his studies at NYU and how he'd thought of majoring in political science but had settled for the liberal arts program after finding out that they only offered politics. Andrea had the plan of taking night classes in the fall at Hunter College in Manhattan.

Then came their past experiences with the opposite sex. Listening intently to Andrea when she told him how her father had left the Richmond home when she was three and never looked back, she also mentioned that her mother still harbored bitterness toward men and instructed her to protect her emotions at all times. "For the most part, I have," she continued, but admitted to him that in spite of her age, she was one for long relationships because she wanted something enduring, something lasting.

"How long have you been dealin' with the guy you're dating now?" William asked.

"Two and a half years."

William cringed. "Have you ever cheated on him?"

"No."

"So why are you out here with me today?"

Andrea paused. "There's something about you." In future years, that statement would come to haunt him. But at this point, how could he know that?

As the D crossed the Manhattan Bridge, William changed the dating plan.

"Do you mind if we go to the Bronx some other time? I mean, how am I going to take a woman out on the first date to get sneakers?"

Andrea giggled. "You have a point there. What are we going to do, instead?"

"I'm in the mood for a record shop; how about you? I know you want Luther's new album."

"Are you a man after my heart, or what? You know I can't say no to Luther. Or, to you, sweetie."

She sure knows how to make a guy feel like a million bucks, William thought. So instead of traveling north, they took the train to the Canal Street Station. There, they leisurely walked hand-in-hand to the Tower Records store in the East Village.

Inside, the couple gleefully shopped, selecting vinyl albums and remixes while dancing down the aisles to the jams mixed by the store DJ. Andrea got Luther's new album, as well as Janet Jackson's LP once William found out she didn't own a copy. For his own collection, he bought the "Shake You Down" single and the Melissa Morgan album containing the song "Do Me Baby." Left with an indelible impression from the slow dances shared two nights earlier, by obtaining these records he told her, "I'll always remember the impact of our first evening together."

"Believe me, you'll never forget about me," Andrea announced while leaving the store. She could have been a seer.

Next for the couple was dinner at a trendy barbecue joint on Eighth Street.

"Baby, I wanna know why in the world no one's scooped you up for themselves?" Andrea asked as they seated themselves in the crowded, checkered-floor establishment.

"Well, I was seeing someone off and on last year, but it didn't work out. She thought I was too soft." As William revealed Tami's insinuation, Andrea shook her head in disbelief.

"Then let her continue to date those slugs that just want to fuck her. That girl's a moron. Let me get this straight, she had an abortion, y'all got back together and she thought you were a faggot because you wouldn't sleep with her right away? Are you serious?"

Nodding yes, William continued verbally, "I had my reasons. It wasn't time for it to happen. Plus, I had this thing about not sleeping with virgins. She was one when we started dating."

Without him having to go further, Andrea nodded her head with approval. "I know exactly what you're going to say. Once the cherry is gone, sometimes the woman views the man who took it as larger than life. An eternal bond forms."

"Exactly."

"I can relate to that. I thought..." She paused. "Well, let's just say I know the feeling." Hearing the bulletin made William smile, for she'd answered a question that would've come up down the road. Besides, he mused, she's been dating a guy for two years, so I know she had to put him on.

"You aren't scared of having sex, are you?" Andrea teased.

William eyes widened as he almost choked on his turkey burger.

"No! I'm just not as forward as… What are you asking me?"

"Well, I had to ask. From the way you move those hips dancing, you don't look like you're scared of anything."

"I'm not. It's just that I have to really care about someone in order to give myself to them. My feelings get involved."

"You know, I never heard a guy say that before. Admit it; most of y'all are dogs that do your thinking with the little head downstairs."

"Andrea, my mother is a woman of principles and she taught me to respect women. I try to uphold her teachings. It's not always easy because I want things, like everyone else, but I'd rather be a gentleman, get to know someone, grow to care about her, you know, the whole nine yards." He paused. "Let me ask you something, do you devour a steak when it's put in front of you?"

"Come again?"

"The anticipation of sex can be like a steak dinner, Andrea. Many men want to go right for the meat first, as opposed to savoring the entire meal."

Andrea got it. "Tell me about it. Instead of slicing it correctly, putting sauce on the entrée to enhance the flavor, eating the vegetables and partaking of the wine, they'd rather eat the meat, like depraved lunatics."

William smiled. "That's my point. I want my woman to respect me. Then when it finally does happen, it'll really mean something."

"Wow! How many McCall men are there, again?" she playfully asked.

"Five of us. However, none are like me, sweetie."

Continuing their dinner, they ribbed each other about their childhoods, how poor their families were and things of a trivial nature. When the check arrived, Andrea offered to put in her share of the bill. William wasn't accustomed to that, so he paid in full.

"Didn't I ask you out on this date?" he asked her.

"William, you're just too much. The next time dinner's on me, you got it?"

He nodded as he aided Andrea with her coat; he loved this woman's style.

Outside again, he grabbed her hand and fixed her eyes with a heated stare. Wanting to kiss her right then and there, William couldn't pull the trigger as fear became a roadblock once more. He was that afraid.

"Andrea, before the night is over, can I give you something to think about?"

"What do you have in mind?" she replied, knowing his intentions.

"I don't know. Something."

Andrea turned her face away from his, hiding her disappointment in his bashfulness. Continuing their walk toward the subway, Andrea began talking about her boyfriend.

"You know, Derrick called me this morning. He wanted to go out today."

"His name is Derrick, huh? If you had to be with him I could have taken a rain check." *What are you saying, you idiot?*

"No, William, I had to be with you. You've been on my mind ever since you got off that train Friday night. When you called me yesterday, I got goose bumps."

"Couldn't you hear how nervous I was over the phone?"

"Yeah, I could. There's just something about you. You're not like most guys. You seem to be more in tune to a woman's feelings than most guys your age. Don't ever change."

✪✪✪

Don't ever change, she said.

As the D train roared through the Bronx and into Manhattan, William completed his recollection of that first date. No matter what thoughts sailed through his mind—their viewing of the movie *Platoon* at a Times Square theater, the shared sundae afterward, how Andrea, not William, had cemented the beginning of their surreptitious relationship by kissing him and the "mmm, not bad" response that followed—he kept returning to that statement. Recalling the innocence he'd felt after their long kiss good night when she'd said, "I'll tear you apart when we make love," and how he'd excitedly written his best friend, Steve Randall, in Delaware at two in the morning to tell him all about her and how special she made him feel, a smile creased his face. Yet, it quickly disappeared when he thought of how much he'd changed since that overcast Sunday. Thinking of that date, then of the events of this snowy, moonlit evening in January where he'd been branded and fitted for a dog collar like many of his fellow brothers wore, William could empathize with Della, but he now felt bad for himself, as well.

With the train nearing the Columbus Circle station, he silently made a pact. *Before I get acquainted with any other women; before I attempt to satisfy any craving I may have; and before I get involved with anyone and hurt another one of my sistas, I have to check myself. I've gotta find out why shit keeps going wrong.* A soul searching session began.

Chapter Four

A BELIEVER?

"Della, please don't hang up on me!"

"William, you're full of shit and I don't ever want to talk to you again."

"You gotta believe me when I say what happened tonight never happened before. I feel awful. Please forgive me."

"Yeah, I forgive you, but I won't forget. By the way, have you checked your messages? Everything I wanted to say has been said to your answering machine."

"Don't do this, Della. I just want to smooth..."

"Look, I gotta go. My company's here."

"Della..."

Click. Just like that, the conversation ended.

After arriving home and sorting through his mail, William took a shower. While standing under the spray, the need to make peace with Della overwhelmed him. So he called.

Incensed by her rudeness, he looked at the clock on his bedroom wall. Two-fifteen. Wondering who

Della would be entertaining at that time of the morning, he dialed her number again. After four rings, the answering machine came on.

"Thank you for calling 555-7213. Unfortunately, I'm not available to take your call right now, so please leave a message at the tone."

When her machine beeped, William let loose. "Yo, I don't appreciate the way you got off the phone with me. Fuck you, Della! I'm sorry I ever met you, you bitch!" He slammed the receiver down so hard that his own messages automatically began to play.

"Message received 10:00 p.m.: Yeah, this is your homegirl Lisa. Hopefully things worked out with Della this evening. You're not at home, so if it's not too late when you come in, call me."

That Lisa, he mused. *She's always there when you need her.*

"Message received 1:12 a.m.: William, you are lower than low. I mean, how could you? You don't know how close you came to being physically injured in my house. But I know what to do now. I hope you have a nice evening, because I will."

With the insinuation in Della's message, he now battled jealousy. *Who in the hell would she be seeing this early in the morning?* His confidence shattered, the blame for William's sad state could be found in his bathroom mirror, that is, if he bothered to look.

Emotionally out of sync, he pulled a bottle of vodka from a kitchen cabinet and headed toward his living room, dimming the lights and putting on his stereo. Vaughn Harper was wrapping up WBLS' "Quiet Storm" with Janet Jackson's "Funny How Time Flies." The song brought his mind back to a moment in his life when he'd felt confident, secure and self-assured. That had been a time when he'd felt, for the first time, what it was like to belong to someone else.

✪✪✪

William's first week at his new job was a hectic one, and Andrea had had to work late every night, so they had to wait until Saturday—Valentine's Day—before they could see each other. Instead, they spent the week after that first date burning up the phone lines with lively chatter. Thinking of the hiatus as a blessing in disguise, William realized it gave him sufficient time to prepare something artistic for her arrival. Working diligently, he purchased a two-pound chocolate heart, a stuffed red devil, a beautiful Valentine's Day card and a bottle of Moët champagne for the occasion. The fact that he'd never shared this day for romantics with someone special fueled his efforts to make the day memorable for him and his new love.

Her entry into his life excited him so much he barely slept the Friday night before. Even his grandparents, who he'd been living with since starting college, were anxious to meet her since he'd talked up a storm about her and how special she made him feel after only knowing her a week. They were happy for him, but their joy for William turned to caution when he informed them of her status. Sensing their displeasure, he told them that she was unhappy in the relationship, assuring them that everything would work out in his favor. It was the first of many times he would have to defend his feelings for Andrea.

The first thing he did that Saturday morning was to call her for confirmation.

"Hello?"

"Good morning. This is William speaking. Is it possible that I can speak to Andrea?"

"This is she."

"Andrea? How are you on this day made for love?"

"Fine."

"Are you coming over today?"

"Yeah, but I can't stay too long. I, uh... I'm supposed to be hooking up with my girlfriend Vikki later and hanging out with her."

"Your partner from the Copa, right? Tell her I said what's up."

"William, I'm really sorry about not being able to stay a long time."

"Well, at least we'll see each other for a little while. I'm really looking forward to holding you in my arms. I've missed you, sweetie."

"Really? You're just too much."

"I'll meet you at Fourteenth Street at around three. How's that?"

"You better make it four."

"All right, Andrea. Four. See you then."

"Bye."

Hanging up the phone, he could barely conceal his excitement. Just hearing her voice caused him shortness of breath. Anticipating her presence made time drag. Images of the kiss they'd shared on their first date still lingering, the mere thought of seeing her again made his heart palpitate. *Sometimes love does these things to a man.*

Wanting to be punctual, William arrived at the Union Square station at three-thirty. During the wait, he thought of something his mother had told him about women. While living with her on Staten Island they'd never talked about his love life; in fact, because of her religious beliefs—Eunice McCall was a devout Jehovah's Witness—he wasn't allowed to have a girlfriend in her house. However, once he'd moved to Brooklyn with his grandmother, his mother finally began to discuss women and relationships with him.

She'd told him, "If a woman always keeps you waiting, you're going to have your hands full dealing with her."

Entertaining this notion briefly after waiting that first thirty minutes, William dismissed it.

He shouldn't have. Four o'clock came and went with no sign of Andrea. Deciding to give her an hour before calling her house, he walked down to Tower Records and splurged on some albums, returning to the station around five.

Still, no Andrea.

"Fifteen more minutes," he mumbled. "Fifteen more minutes, then I'm outta here."

In 1987, with the exception of the F train, which traveled along Sixth Avenue, all the uptown trains entered Manhattan through Broadway, running along the express tracks commencing at Canal Street and running to Fifty-Seventh Street, with stops at Fourteenth Street/Union Square, Thirty-Fourth, Forty-Second and Fifty-Seventh Streets. Fourteenth Street is where William spent the next half-hour watching trains go by. First, it was the B train; then an N train; then the D; another N; another D; then a B.

At least they change in sequence of arrival, he sighed, becoming more depressed with each passing train and minute.

By five-thirty, William was exasperated. Rushing upstairs, he attempted a call to Andrea's house in search of answers. He got none, for her phone line was busy. Confused, his emotions were in a flux, torn between the worry that something had happened to her and the fear that he'd been stood up by his dream date. These worrisome thoughts embedded in his brain, William decided to stay for thirty minutes more.

The time passed quickly, and still Andrea was nowhere to be found. William's heart was crushed. All week he had prepared for what should have been the most romantic day of his life, and now this.

How could she do this to me? All she had to say is that she couldn't make it. Resigned to this belief, he walked dejectedly to his L train.

In the seconds before his Canarsie-bound train approached, anxiety tortured William as he thought of returning to the platform Andrea's train came on. The loud rumbling and eventual sight of a gray, graffiti-decorated locomotive rolling into the station brought a swift decision. *Fuck it. She's not coming.* Boarding his train, out of nowhere his sadness was dissolved by a familiar voice.

"I wouldn't do that if I were you." It was Andrea. Holding the door so that she could come aboard as well, the two shared an extended hug, followed by a long kiss.

"William, I'm so sorry."

William's agitated disposition vanished with her apology and instead of inquiring about the unusual delay, his response was, "That's okay. I'm glad you could make it."

"Don't you wanna hear why I was late?"

"Not now. Are you ready to have a good time?"

"Sure am. I've been waiting to see you all week."

"Are you hungry?"

"No. I ate something before I left. I just want to get to your place and chill, if you know what I mean."

The devilish smile accompanying those words had William blushing as the two played catch-up for the duration of the twenty-minute ride.

Arriving at his house, Andrea met William's grandparents who were on their way to a Valentine's Day party. Upon completion of the usual introductions and subsequent parental interrogation of Andrea, he quickly whisked her upstairs to his room.

"I'm sorry I can't entertain you downstairs in the basement. It's not finished being renovated," he mentioned before opening his bedroom door. "Besides, I find it a little more intimate up here. I like the privacy."

"Mmm. I can see why." She gasped with surprise when she saw the stuffed red devil perched on the neatly made bed. "He's so cute! I think I'm going to call him William."

"I hope I'm a little bit cuter than he is." They both chuckled. "Andrea, I'll be right back."

She shot him a "don't leave me not even for a second look" as he continued.

"I'm going downstairs for a moment. While I'm gone, you might want to look under the pillows. There's something that might interest you underneath."

Retrieving champagne glasses from downstairs, William quickly returned and found her seated on his bed, suffocating the stuffed red devil with her hug. Beside her lay the card and the chocolate heart.

"William, you are truly amazing. No one's ever done this for me before."

"Valentine's Day is the holiday of romance, isn't it?"

Andrea nodded her head as he handed her a tall, thin goblet. "Okay. What do you want from me?"

"Nothing," William responded while pouring champagne. "This is something I've always wanted to do on Valentine's Day. Would you like to hear some music?"

"Sure. Put on Luther for me."

To Andrea's delight, he obliged by putting on the *Never Too Much* LP obtained while he was waiting for her. Bringing a huge smile from her by lip-syncing the lyrics to the title track, when the selection ended she gave him a rousing ovation.

"Bravo. Bravo. What's your next song for me?"

"It's your turn."

Andrea's face wore a mask of mock fear. "What do you mean, my turn?"

"You gotta sing for me."

"I can't."

"Yes, you can."

After a pause Andrea sighed.

"You really want me to do this?"

William laughed. "Nah, you don't have to." Andrea feigned relief. "But I do want to share a slow dance with you," he said after a sip of Moët.

"Baby, you don't have to ask for that. I noticed in your bag Sheila E's new jam 'Hold Me.' That song is fierce!"

"Would you like to hear it?"

"Please put it on." A seductive expression now appeared on Andrea's face, a heated, come-hither stare. Feebly trying to ignore her glance as he put the record on, William succumbed to the spell she cast the moment he gazed into her dreamy eyes. The first chord played and, immediately, she stood up and said, "Please share this dance with me."

William held his hand out and engulfed her in a secure, comforting embrace. By the song's first chorus, their dance resembled the ones shared that night their paths first crossed. Andrea, aroused by the moment, softly sang the lyrics into his ear.

Sounding better than Prince's protégé, her sensuous whisper had parts of him standing at attention.

"Andrea, is this how you feel about me?"

"Let me show you." They shared a deep kiss and by the record's end, both were panting heavily from the flames of amour raging around, then through them.

Andrea suggested that he put on a slow-jam tape.

"What makes you think I have any?"

"You're too romantic not to, sweetie."

This woman responds to everything, William thought, fulfilling her request by finding a tape he'd made a few weeks prior to their introduction.

"I think you'll enjoy this one."

"I enjoy just being here with you," Andrea retorted, returning to his bed. "And from the looks of things, I can tell you enjoy me being here as well," she continued, alluding to his noticeable erection.

William blushed.

"Baby, why do you blush so much? You've had girlfriends before."

"One," he mumbled nervously while starting the tape.

"Tami. That's right, the Thug-fucker." Passion took a respite as they both howled at that one. "Seriously, William. You mean to tell me you and her never chilled like this?"

"No, we didn't."

At this point, Luther was serenading the two with "Make Me a Believer."

"She always thought moments like these were too geeky."

"Really?"

By now, William was accustomed to Andrea's disbelieving looks.

"Well, it's her loss and my gain," she added.

Pausing briefly as he sat beside her on his bed, a burst of confidence went through William as he stared into her eyes.

"You want to know something? This is my favorite Luther song. Andrea, can I make you a believer?"

"How do you plan on doing that?"

"Let me show you."

Smiling, William's mouth met hers once more, and for the next hour, the two were lost in each other's arms. As their bodies became entangled on the bed, he fantasized about what it would be like to make love to this woman. Moaning in pleasure as her soft, moist lips and tongue slowly yet expertly ran across his neck, the warm, cherry taste of her mouth collided with his hunger for affection. As the couple locked legs and moved their bodies in unison—just the way he'd visualized when she'd captured his attention at the Copa—the sudden urge to feast on her completeness was so strong that his urge to tickle, touch and taste every inch of her frame startled him.

Knowing Andrea shared the mutual sentiment of this erotic coupling, his gentle kisses alerted her senses and had her moaning, "Oh shit" over and over. With his tongue plunging deeper into an eager mouth, together they continued their horizontal dance as if they'd been put on this earth to make out with one another.

Any lingering doubts as to how Andrea was feeling at this juncture were erased when she shouted, "Ooh, William" as the core of her trembled uncontrollably. Tingling with satisfaction from her best Valentine's Day present, she planted kisses all over his neck. "Damn, William. It felt like..."

"I know, Andrea," he interjected, feeding her a champagne-dipped piece of chocolate.

"I take my statement back," Andrea declared, struggling to regain her breath. "I think you'll tear me apart."

William smiled. "I'm glad you enjoyed yourself."

"I can't wait for the real thing. Let me ask you something. Why didn't you go further?"

"It's not time yet. We've just met."

"You're heaven sent, aren't you?"

"Nah, sweetie. I'm just someone trying to do the right thing."

"William, don't ever change."

"You have to go, don't you?" William asked.

Andrea had a look of disappointment on her face. "Yes, I'm afraid so. I'm sorry for not hooking up with you earlier. I promise I'll stay longer next time."

"Can you share one last dance with me before you go?"

"For you, my valentine, anything." With that, William got off the bed, stopped the slow tape and put Janet Jackson's "Funny How Time Flies" on his turntable. Kissing fervently throughout the tune as they shared a slow, sensuous dance, they concluded their romantic interlude with a long embrace.

✪✪✪

I never did find out why she'd kept me waiting that day, remembered William as the selection ended the "Quiet Storm." Smiling he recalled various rendezvous following that one. They'd had many wonderful moments like that one in the beginning. Like the day they'd taken Andrea to Staten Island to meet his mother. His entire family had taken to her like a sticky caramel apple, for she brought out facets of William's personality never realized. With the exception of his prom night, they'd never seen him with a woman before. Tami, his ex, had never wanted to meet his mother.

Feeling proud that her son displayed the chivalrous qualities she had instilled in him, before they'd left that evening, his mother had pulled him into her bedroom and told him, "She seems like a real winner, son."

"Ma, I can't believe she likes me. I mean look at her; she's beautiful, intelligent and she's..."

His mother had interrupted him. "William, you have a lot to offer so stop selling yourself short. You're a very special guy; I think all my sons are, and I don't want to see you hurt. Take your time, son, and believe in yourself. If you don't, you'll get taken advantage of. Don't act like it's all about her. It's about you as well. Be a better man to her than your lousy father was to me."

"Don't say that, Ma."

"It's true, son. You know the things he did after you and Andrew were born were..."

"But you can't change what's done, Ma."

"You're right, William." As he turned to leave the room, Eunice grabbed his hand. "Here, son, take this."

To William's surprise, she'd given him a balled-up twenty-dollar bill. "Ma, I work, you know."

"Just take it. Get her something nice," she'd instructed him while receiving a hug.

"I love you, Ma."

"I love you, too, son."

As he left the room, William remembered glancing

back at his mother as she sat on her bed and seeing her wiping tears away. Although he wasn't her oldest son, she'd always known he would be the first of the McCall men to be stung by the love bug. On her lonely nights between boyfriends, a young William would always join her pity parties and rest his head in her lap. Together, they found comfort and the affection they desperately craved as they listened to love songs in a dark living room.

Of all of her boys, Eunice sensed that he, too, might face the perils that accompanied that uncontrollable passion for he was most like her, in that her heart was her weakness, as well as her strength. Eunice McCall was an intelligent woman—somehow while raising six kids, she found time to attend a couple of semesters at college—but naïve and uneducated concerning matters of the heart. Having loved each man that had come and gone in her life as if they'd been her first love, she, too, had issues concerning self-worth and the need for affection. Unfortunately, her suitors had exploited her vulnerability time and time again.

Eunice McCall knew first-hand of the painful lessons that went hand in hand with this emotion, yet William's first voyage into the depths of love made her proud. Her son had evolved into a man before her very eyes.

Then there'd been the time William and Andrea shared a candlelight dinner at the South Street Seaport after she'd experienced a particularly difficult day at work. Having had a heated altercation with her supervisor and fearful of losing her job, she'd called him in tears at day's end. Using her despondency as a springboard to action, he'd invited her to the movies, where they took in *Mannequin*. At its completion he'd asked her if she had ever seen the nighttime beauty of the Seaport and hearing a negative response, he took her there. By evening's end, Andrea's spirits had been lifted tenfold.

That's what love is all about, being there for someone when they're down, William reflected while swigging from the Absolut bottle. The vodka was serving its purpose; he stumbled over to an extensive CD collection and searched his section of favorites. Fumbling with a Phyllis Hyman disc, he loaded it into his system, then remembered her singing about the joy and pain of love as "Meet Me on the Moon" played.

"Sing to me, Phyllis! We'll never be unhappy as long as we have each other," he shouted, staggering back to his black leather sofa and into his thoughts of Andrea.

✪✪✪

Things were going well with Andrea. Conversing on the phone for hours daily and convening at least one day every weekend, William was sure to greet her with all of his affection whenever he saw her. One weekend would be spent dining and the following one would be spent in the confines of his room under a romantic-colored light, listening to aphrodisiacal music and telling each other their intimate desires. Their petting sessions deepened with each passing encounter, for the two were harmonious with their passions.

One particular instance was the week before Andrea's twenty-first birthday. Having already purchased a gold nameplate and necklace for her special day, William was so anxious that he couldn't wait until then to give them to her.

As usual, they met at their designated meeting point, Fourteenth Street. And, true to form, Andrea was over an hour late.

"William, you have to forgive me for always running late."

"That's okay, Andrea." Somehow, once she'd appeared the irritation at her lack of punctuality instantly disappeared.

"So, Romeo, what are you going to do to me... I mean, what are we going to do at your house today?" Andrea flirtatiously asked.

"I've got a surprise for you, Crumbcake."

"That's so sweet! You even have a nickname for me. You're just too much, William." Hearing her excitement over his using a pet name made him turn his face away in embarrassment. "There you go again with that bashfulness."

"I can't help it. You do this to me."

"It's weird. How can someone so shy be so sex... Forget it. It's hard to explain."

So during the rest of the ride to William's house, they continued chatting, alternating their conversation between the events of their lives with their own intimate innuendoes. When they were walking through the front door, he sent her upstairs ahead of him.

"Don't be too long, honey," Andrea said with a wink.

Twenty minutes later, William poked his head into his room.

"What kept you?"

"This." Opening the door completely, he watched her facial expression shift to amazement as he brought in two food trays, then two glasses.

"This one is for you," William announced, placing a tray on her lap. "And this one is for me."

"You can cook, too?" Andrea excitedly asked.

On her plate was a piece of honey roasted chicken, corn on the cob and small portions of collard greens and Spanish rice. Accompanying the meal was a glass of homemade fruit punch.

William put his head down and shyly uttered the

obvious. "Yes. I watched Ma and Grandma throw down for years and I worked with chefs at a Jewish sleep-away camp during my high school summers." He raised his punch glass. "Well, I hope you enjoy it."

He didn't have to wait long for a response, for she made her sentiments known after sampling the chicken. "You cooked this?"

William nodded.

"It's fantastic."

While she devoured the rest of her food in record time, William just sat there watching her pay tribute to his culinary skills, waiting until she had completed her meal before he partook of his.

"That was wonderful," Andrea commented.

She thought something was wrong when she saw his nearly full plate. "William, you barely touched your food. Here, let me be of assistance." She attempted to feed him some rice with her fork and after the first try, they chuckled.

"Stop it, Andrea. You're beginning to make me feel like a baby."

"You are. You're my baby." She then gave him a peck on the cheek.

This woman is one of a kind, William thought.

After the two took the trays downstairs, washed the dishes and freshened up, they rushed upstairs like two young kids raiding an unguarded candy warehouse. There, William unscrewed the regular light bulb in his wall lamp and inserted a red one. Next, he went looking for some music to put on. Popping in another one of those slow tapes, he moved to his bed.

Andrea noticed a subtle change in William's persona as he sat beside her, as if the unspoken role of intimate predator had changed at that moment. He was a hungry panther now, ready to devour his prey.

"William, I think you should put the regular light back in," she said jokingly. "You have this look on your face like you're going to tear into me."

"No, I don't." Although those were the words that fell from his lips, the wicked, impish gleam in his eyes said otherwise. "Andrea, have you ever listened to Marvin Gaye's *I Want You* album?"

"Ooh, do you have that? My girlfriend Karen keeps telling me about that album."

"I have the cassette."

"Then what are we listening to this for? Put it in."

"Do you really want me to put it in?"

Andrea turned a deep shade of red.

"Just put the tape in."

He did just that and as he returned to his space, horny stare still affixed on her, Andrea decided to meet his aggression head-on.

"Are you trying to tell me something by putting this tape on?"

"What do you think?"

"Well, then come get me, baby," she said, lying back on his bed.

He didn't hesitate.

Marvin's erotic melodies echoed through the moment as the two indulged in each other's momentary cravings once more. Under normal conditions, the romantic rendezvous consisted of nothing more than fully clothed fondling. Something was in the air that particular evening and both parties sensed this session would go a little further.

Andrea wanted to explore, so through his denim jeans she began stroking William's throbbing member. Approving of her actions, he caressed her while devouring her mouth. As he unbuttoned her red blouse, she made no effort to stop him from going further.

"Please suck them," Andrea cried meekly.

Eagerly but gently, William complied, cupping her breasts and slowly running his tongue around pouted, berry-sweet nipples in small, concentrated circles. Her receptive, pleasure escalating responses increased his arousal. Waves of gratification engulfing her, the warmth of smooth, rich hands touching her body sent rivulets of sensations through Andrea.

"Ooh, yes, just like that, William," she moaned.

These reactions only heightening his curiosity as

to what it would be like to be in the valley of this woman, William wanted to please her in every way possible.

Ever so tenderly, he kissed her body, beginning at her forehead, then venturing to soft, delicate earlobes. After pecking her cheeks, he bit her lips softly, then tugged at her chin with teeth like hard candy. After licking her neck and firm, supple breasts, next he ran his tongue in a circular motion in and around her navel.

"Yes, baby, please do it like that," she purred, clenching a fist at her side as if that would conceal her convulsive motions. Reaching then grabbing his trim waistline, Andrea arched her body upward, truly enjoying what this young man was doing to her. Finally, as he attempted to unzip her jeans, Andrea stopped him by pulling his head up to hers.

"I'm not ready for that yet." She paused to catch her breath. "I'm sorry."

"I understand." William quickly camouflaged what he was feeling at that moment. Hungry to go further, his body and soul were left aching yet another day.

"Do you eat things downstairs the way you sucked on my breasts?"

To that, he just smiled. "You'll just have to wait and see, won't you?"

"If you do, then what am I going to do with you?"

William shrugged as he made a request. "Close your eyes, Crumbcake." When she complied, William went to his dresser, opened a drawer, pulled out her birthday present and placed it around her neck. "Now, open them."

"Oh, my God!" she screamed, covering her face.

"I know your birthday isn't until next week, but I couldn't wait. I hope you don't mind."

"Thank you so much! Oh, William, thank you. You are so incredible. This is just too much. What did I do in this lifetime to get blessed with someone like you?" she said, wiping the crystal drops of joy from her cheeks. "You have such a giving heart. Please, don't ever change."

William shook his head. "You know, that's the third time you've said that to me. What do you mean by that?"

"Just don't ever change, that's all," Andrea repeated, as if she knew something about men that William didn't know, some transformation that he hadn't heard about, some lesson he hadn't learned yet in his dealings with women.

✪✪✪

Years later, alone on a couch and drunk on vodka, Andrea's words finally registered. *If I'd known what she meant at that time, I would have kicked her out of my house*, William thought, looking at his watch and noticing the time. Twenty minutes to five. Shit! I gotta get some sleep. With that, he stumbled to his bedroom, leaving Phyllis Hyman miles from earth, all alone yet again.

Chapter Five

A SUDDEN WIND CHANGE

"Yo, Lisa! I apologize about not returning your phone call last night. I had a rough one, girl."

"Yeah, right. You were gettin' your groove on with Della. That's okay, though, because had I been gettin' done I wouldn't have answered the phone either."

"Hold on. Hold on." Restraining a giggle by shaking his head, William briefly placed the receiver down on his office desk that Friday morning. He could always keep it real with this woman. Replacing it at his ear, he told her, "Nah, on the real, I fucked up royally. I called her Barbara during sex. At her house."

Lisa paused. "Damn. That's messed up. What made you do that? I mean, were you thinking about the good times you had with her? Was Barbara's honey that good?"

"I don't know what happened. Yeah, I messed up."

"Did she kick you out?"

"Yep."

"I would have done the same thing, you dog!" Lisa

replied jokingly. "Just kiddin'. Seriously, you know shit's dead there, right?"

"I don't know about all of that. Maybe if I..."

Lisa boldly interrupted, "Maybe if you nothing! That shit is dead! Done! You begged to see her and then once you do, you fuck it up. Hello-o? Earth to William. You better start putting those feelings away. She's not taking you back anymore."

After a brief silence, William responded, "Thanks for the reality check, Ms. Strickland."

"Shit, you know me. I call a spade a spade. Listen, corporate America's callin' me and I've got bills to pay. Let's do something tomorrow."

"Sounds like a plan. I'll holla at ya'. And Lisa, thanks for lettin' me bend your ear."

"What are you thanking me for?"

"For being you, as always. I needed to rap about things and you were there for me."

"Save the Hallmark moment for Della, William. You'll need all of them trying to get her back." After a hearty laugh, Lisa got serious for a second. "You know how we do, William. I've stretched your cute ears so much I'm surprised you don't look like Baby New Year. Or Dumbo. Hee, hee. Let me go. Peace."

"Peace." After hanging up, William counted his blessings. *Not many brothers have homegirls like Lisa that they can rap to about anything. Sure glad we kept in touch after I left Robinson, Burton & Luftkow.* Fondly recalling gales of laughter shared during lunch, and drink dates after work, he recalled that people on the job had thought they had something going on. *Goes to show how small-minded people are to think that a man can't genuinely befriend a beautiful woman without sex becoming an issue.*

Olive colored and possessing an hourglass figure like Halle Berry's, in some ways Lisa Strickland was the kid sister William had never had, the one woman he trusted with all his dirty laundry about failed relationships and one-night stands. She in turn had found a confidante in him, revealing her fears, man problems and secrets during regular gift-shopping runs for friends and family.

Instinctively, almost through telepathy, their connection deepened during times of despair. When William's divorce became final a few years back, it was Lisa who'd been his rock, always encouraging him to put the past behind him and learn from the experience. And when she encountered difficulties with Roland Harris, her half-stepping, womanizing boyfriend, he'd talked her through many a lonely night. In fact, before making that call to Della, he'd consulted Lisa the night before. *Fighters in this game of life recognize other fighters and I'm glad she's here,* he thought. *I wish she could've been there at another time when I really could have used her humorous insight.* He was referring, of course, to a time when a certain young woman had held his heart by a string.

✪✪✪

In the days leading up to Andrea's birthday, William and his Crumbcake shared interesting phone banter. Being as she had received her birthday present the previous weekend, she wondered what was up his sleeve for the following Sunday. When posed with the question he'd simply told her, "I want nature to run its course between us." Asked what he meant by this, he'd vaguely replied, "Let's just wait and see."

But deep down, William knew exactly what he wanted to transpire on that day. He wanted intimacy to progress to another level between them. Each date ended with his wishing he could spend more time with her. Time goes too fast when we're together. Each kiss left him desiring his queen more and more.

Wanting to remedy both disappointments simultaneously, he decided he would be her birthday present. *She already has my heart. Why not my body and soul, as well?*

On the Friday night before they were supposed to meet, he put together a slow tape of seductive music just for the occasion. Fantasizing about Sunday, the mere thought of making love to Andrea had William fighting involuntary spasms while curling his body in a fetal position along his bed. Missing the sultriness of her smile, he longed for her touch and yearned for the pillow-like texture of her lips. Envisioning holding her body against his masculinity, kissing every inch of her, every contour and crevice, he thought of how a teasing, hypnotic creature between his lips would dance a dervish upon an erect clitoris, sending intense, euphoric shockwaves through her.

The fantasy of pleasing her now running rampant, he dreamed of how wonderful it would be to enter Andrea's drenched canyon and the pleasure he would give her with his erect staff. With the urgency of each stroke he would transfer the heat of his love to her. Receiving each thrust of his passion, he thought of the delicious feeling she'd be left with, for his Crumbcake would speak in unfamiliar voices of pleasure. Ascending to and descending from their sexual peak together, he saw her moaning his name in complete ecstasy, and how he would hold her endlessly afterward, telling her he loved her so.

The next day, after picking up a white, strawberry-topped birthday cake from a neighborhood bakery, he passed a lingerie store, looked in its window and murmured, "Oh, what the hell!" Minutes later, he emerged from the store with a box containing a black silk evening robe, and then from an adjacent wine store he purchased another bottle of champagne. He wanted to make this a birthday to remember… for both of them.

After another sleepless night of anticipation, the big day arrived. He called her house at ten to confirm their plans.

"Hello?" The voice of an older woman was in his ear.

"Good morning. This is William. Is…"

"Oh, so you're the gentleman I've been hearing so much about lately. You're pretty famous in this part of town."

"Really?"

"You better believe it. My daughter talks about you all the time."

William was excited. "Mrs. Richmond? I finally get to speak to you?"

"That's Ms. Richmond. I'm divorced."

"Okay, Ms. Richmond. I wanna say that Andrea is a beautiful person. She's been like a breath of fresh air. You've done a wonderful job with her."

"Are you done buttering me up?" Ms. Richmond joked.

"Yeah, I guess so. I hope to meet you some day."

"Likewise. I finally have a voice associated with your name. Now all I need is a face."

"I look like Billy Dee Williams, drinkin' that Colt 45." He heard Ms. Richmond laugh in the background. "I'm just joking," he admitted.

"A jokester, eh?"

"Wanna hear something creepy? Your daughter said the same thing to me on the night we met."

"Brilliant minds think alike, William."

"I take it you're an Aries, as well."

"No. I'm a Gemini."

"So am I! I'm May twenty-first!"

"I'm the twenty-ninth."

"Now, I really have to meet you." They both laughed. "Ms. Richmond, is your daughter available to come to the phone?"

"Dearie, I'm sorry. She, um... She stepped out. I'm sure she'll be back momentarily."

"Would you please have her call me when she gets back? I just wanted to confirm our arrangements for today."

"She's supposed to be seeing you today?" Ms. Richmond sounded surprised.

"Yes. I wanted to give her a birthday present."

"Oh, I see. Well, I'll have her call you when she gets in."

"Thank you. It's really been a pleasure talking to you."

"Same here. You have a good day."

"Bye."

Wondering if Andrea had forgotten about their plans, William didn't entertain the notion too long because he was focused on continuing his preparations for her arrival. His grandparents had gone away but had left the keys to their dining room. There, he spent the next two hours cleaning and decorating. He put up a huge, white "Happy Birthday" sign and some balloons. *Red is her favorite color. And wouldn't you know it, the dining room is red*, he noted, observing the carpeted floor. Fate works in mysterious ways. He was right about that.

When he was almost finished, he heard his phone ringing so he sprinted upstairs to answer it. "Hello?"

"Hi, William." It was Andrea. She sounded weary.

"Happy birthday, Crumbcake! How are you?"

"Besides being a little cranky, I'm okay."

"Had a rough night?" Hearing no response, he continued, "I'm a little sleepy myself. I couldn't get any rest last night. But don't worry, though. You can sleep all you want once you get here."

"That's what I'm calling about. I won't be able to make it today."

William's heart almost sank through the floor.

"Baby, don't tell me this."

"I'm sorry. I'm just too tired. I was out late last night."

"I've got some goodies over here for you, honey. Please don't disappoint me."

"I got my birthday present from you last week, didn't I? By the way, my girlfriends think that it's way too soon for you to be giving me a necklace."

"What do you mean too soon?" Taking exception to the statement, William jumped all over her. "Andrea, you don't suppress true love. You're not supposed to restrain how and what you feel for a person. You do what's in your heart. What am I supposed to do, take it back from you because they don't feel it's time for you to have a necklace?"

"That would be ridiculous."

"Of course, it would! Your friends, whichever ones said that, sound like idiots!"

"Don't call my friends idiots!" There was an awkward pause between the two.

Finally, Andrea reached out.

"Our first argument."

Another pause, then there was laughter from both of them.

"Yeah, I guess so. Listen, I apologize for that tantrum. It's just that I've already been through that girlfriend, eye-in-the-sky bullshit before."

"I'm not Tami, William."

"I know that, Crumbcake. It's just that you were the last person in the world I would expect to heed someone else's opinion of the do's and don'ts of getting to know someone. So much for that. Are you gonna meet me at Fourteenth Street or what?"

"What type of goodies did you get me?"

"Meet me and you'll see."

Pausing for a second, she made her decision. "Okay, you've convinced me. How's three-thirty sound?"

"That's perfect. See you then."

"Bye."

That yes didn't sound emphatic, he thought while hanging up. *I guess I'm going to have to make my baby feel special from the very second I see her.*

So when he arrived at their meeting place at three-fifteen, William held a bouquet of red roses. Crumbcake's gonna flip when she sees these.

Andrea wouldn't see those flowers until five-thirty; some two hours after the arranged time.

Finally arriving, she immediately tried to downplay her tardiness with sweet talk. "Hi, honey. Nice flowers." She kissed him. "You're so precious."

"Uh-huh."

"Baby, I have to apologize again for being so late."

This time, William's annoyance didn't diminish.

"You know, if you didn't want to come over, you shouldn't have let me talk you into it. You should have just said no. I could've dealt with that a whole lot better than you arriving two hours late. Damn!"

"You're lucky I even came," she responded sarcastically.

Infuriated by her nonchalance, William snatched the roses from her hand, a move that completely surprised her.

"Look, nobody's holding a gun to your head. You could turn around and take your never-ready-on-time ass home!"

Andrea was stunned. Quickly regrouping, she stood up to his ultimatum. "You're right. I don't have to be here. And I don't have to take this shit, either!"

She stormed up the stairs and to the opposite subway platform. William walked to his L train platform.

After about ten minutes of waiting for his Canarsie-bound train, he went to the platform where Andrea was, seeking a halt to the crossfire. Happy to find her still there, he extended the roses to her once again.

"Look, baby, let's forget about all of this bullshit and celebrate your birthday the right way."

Maintaining her glacier-like stance, Andrea decided she wanted him to beg just a little more. "I'm going home. This 'never-ready-on-time ass' can get some rest there."

"Andrea, I'm really sorry for that outburst. It's just that I wish you would've gotten here earlier so that we could spend more time together." He nudged her. "Come on, Crumbcake. You have to admit, though, your new label was very creative."

Andrea smiled reluctantly. "You're just lucky you're so damn cute. Let's go."

Hearing that, William breathed easily again.

Once seated on the L train, Andrea inquired, "What type of surprises do you have in store for me today, William? You already gave me the roses."

"You'll see."

Resting her head on his shoulder, she tried to coax him some more. "Come on, sweetie. The suspense is killing me."

"You'll see," he reiterated, smiling at her knowingly.

The train ride passed quickly as Andrea forgot about her pseudo-death by anticipation and dozed on William's shoulder while he spent the time reading. Being the excitable person he was, he exhibited great self-control in staying calm about what he wanted to happen.

It was also fear that kept him silent. In a little over two months Andrea had made him feel as if he could move mountains; she'd brought the very best in him to the surface, traits he'd never known he had. The caring, loving spirit cavorting within his soul for so long arose with storm-like delirium, manifesting itself in a barrage of amorous affection through corny jokes, radiant smiles, hugs and kisses. Whether it was a trinket offered as a token of his affection or the caring display of exemplary treatment, he felt he couldn't give enough of himself to this woman. Now, he hoped to show her the magnitude of his emotional growth by making love to her.

Upon their arrival at his home, William asked Andrea to wait for him in the dining room. Scaling the staircase to his room, he paused to hear her response to the decorations as she opened the door.

"This is beautiful."

He smiled, then continued his flight upstairs.

She was seated on his grandmother's long, white sofa when he approached her in the dining area carrying a large black box. Around the box was a huge red bow and taped on top was a birthday card.

"Andrea, this is for you. Happy Birthday, Crumbcake. I hope you like it." With nervous hands, he gave her the gift.

As she opened the box containing her evening robe, William watched intently for her reaction. The next few moments, he thought, would tell him everything he needed to know about what would happen later. The seconds passed slowly as she removed the ribbon, read her birthday card, then lifted the lid while a myriad of thoughts raced through his mind. *Will she like it? I hope I'm not being too forward. What if this scares her? Oh, shit! Will I ever see her again? God, I hope I don't get rejected. Damn, just take the thing out for crying out loud!*

Upon viewing the robe, Andrea lit up the room with an approving smile. "When can I put this on?"

William was elated. Feeling like he'd won the lottery, he had great difficulty maintaining his composure, yet somehow he managed to say, "You wanna wear this tonight?"

"Don't you want to see me in it? Where can I change?" Andrea wanted to get into the evening wear just as much as he wanted to see her in it.

"Hold your horses, honey. I've got something else for you."

"Something else? Damn! You're good at bombarding a woman's senses, aren't you?"

"Just stay right here, I'll be right back."

Andrea sucked in her breath when he rushed out of the room. *If she loves what's happening now, wait until after we…*, William thought with a smile while dashing away.

Five minutes later, he returned with her birthday cake and dimmed the dining room lights, causing her to shake her head. Placing it on the glass table in front of her, he lit the candles and made an atrocious attempt at singing a familiar tune.

"Happy birthday to you. Happy birthday to you. Happ… Ah, fuck it!" William changed up. "Seriously, I think this occasion calls for another one of those lip syncing moments."

"Go for it!" Playing along, Andrea fainted on the couch like an awestruck teenybopper as William put on Stevie Wonder's rendition of "Happy Birthday" and did his thing. By the time he'd completed the skit, Andrea was doubled over in laughter.

"You're not a well person," she said between breaths as William joined her on the couch.

"You'd better catch your breath. You have candles to blow out."

Andrea pulled herself together, made a quick wish, and blew out the candles.

"William, you're an incredible human being," she announced with a forkful of cake in her mouth. "I've never seen anyone like you. Please don't ever..."

"There you go again. Let me ask you something. Is there any other way to show a woman who's swept you off your feet how much she means to you?"

"There is one other way, you know." Projecting a sensuous look that indicated only one thing, Andrea rattled him.

"I, um... I think you need something to drink." At that instant William bounced up and ran away, once more to her chagrin. Minutes later, he reappeared with two champagne glasses and the bottle of Moët.

"Champagne and birthday cake. Not a bad combination," Andrea said as he popped the cork.

"Would you like to make a toast, Crumbcake?"

"Yeah, I would. Here's to meeting a whirlwind. William, the Whirlwind." She paused to sip the bubbly. "It has a nice ring to it, doesn't it?"

"Yeah, it does."

"Listen, can we take this party upstairs?"

"Sure. Just let me tidy the place up a little bit. Want any more cake?" Andrea shook her head no. "I'll wrap up the rest so you can take it with you."

"I'll meet you up there, sweetie."

"Sounds good. Give me ten."

"Take your time."

While she took the champagne upstairs, William cleaned up the dining area and washed the dishes.

Ten minutes later he opened his bedroom door and was taken aback by what he saw. Already comfortable in his domain, Andrea had taken the initiative to put in the red light. He glanced to his left and saw the blue jeans she'd been wearing, as well her bra and her beige sweater, nicely folded in his guest chair. She had slipped into the black evening robe.

"Do you like what you see?" was the question posed as she stood up and modeled the lingerie.

Speechless, William sat down on his bed. A voluptuous smile spread to her face as she completed her pirouette and sat beside him.

"I guess the silence means you do."

Clearly unnerved by her assertiveness and the surprise of the moment, only after gulping hard and clearing his throat did he collect himself.

"Andrea, you look even better in it than I ever imagined."

"For a second there, I thought you became a mute. Well, I guess the Ebony Fashion Fair moment is over." She reached for her clothing.

"No, no." William grasped her hand firmly. "I mean, please don't."

"My, aren't we persuasive all of a sudden," Andrea declared, smacking his hand away. "So, maestro, what are we going to listen to today?"

"I made a tape just for the occasion. It's entitled 'The Message.'"

"Mmm," Andrea cooed fondly. "Please put it... Wait! Let me rephrase that. Can I please listen to it?"

"Press the PLAY button on the second cassette deck," William directed, pointing to the stereo.

Andrea complied and instantly the room was filled with Lillo Thomas' "Show Me." Recognizing the first chord, she shrieked.

"I can't believe it! You actually started a tape with a song I introduced into your life."

"Yeah, I kinda like this one." As William listened to the tune he noticed Andrea nodding her head ever so slowly to the rhythm of the song. At the first chorus, she turned to him while singing the lyrics.

When he started to look away timidly, she instinctively grabbed his hand.

"Baby, please don't blush. You do this to me. It feels so good being here with you. You make me feel so good inside."

"I'm glad you feel that way."

For the rest of the song, the two just sat there holding hands. Then, as the tape glided into Major Harris' "Love Won't Let Me Wait," Andrea's feathery touch sent an aching sensation racing through William. At the point where Harris crooned "*...now move a little close to me...*," he moved closer to her, causing a mutual giggle.

The laughter stopped when William retook her hand and slowly ran his other one over the front of the silk robe. Breathing heavily from the warmth traveling through her veins, Andrea closed her eyes and allowed her gaze to wander to his waist. Locking eyes one more time, they shared a peck, then another, then another. Then they turned their inhibitions loose once more.

From the very beginning, the intimate foray carried more fervor than all the previous ones combined. Each kiss deeper than the one that preceded it, each maneuver more aggressive than the one prior; it seemed both parties knew where this romantic interlude would culminate, for the passion between them was white-hot.

William wanted Andrea in the worst way. Moaning softly as her gentle, practiced hands ran down the small of his back, he fought hard to control the urgency he now possessed below. Warmed by an incomprehensible, yet pleasurable instinct and succumbing to this hunger, his kiss now became a tender plea for satisfaction.

Andrea was losing control also. A frenzied lust running through her skin, she loved the imaginativeness of his caress. Weakening from the romantic syncopation, saying things in voices she'd never heard from herself, wanting to be held by this man tighter and tighter, on this day, at this moment, she didn't say no to anything.

She didn't say no when he removed her evening robe and told her how beautiful she looked, her caramel silhouette caught and muted by soft, red lights. She didn't say no as his warm mouth met her breasts and nibbled on her swollen nipples; didn't say no when he kissed down cottony thighs and between her legs. In fact, she whimpered as her hips matched the tempo of his active tongue, then his nose. She didn't say no when he made her sample her own ambrosia while kidnapping her lips once more with a loving peck. His tongue re-engaged with hers, he ran it across her teeth, tickled the corners of her red petals and warred aggressively with the brim of her face. Not saying no when

William quickly undressed himself, she didn't say no as they pressed their warm bodies together under his floral sheets and continued foreplay in the nude.

William paused slightly before exploring the warmness of her flesh once more, moaning softly while slowly guiding her hand over the hardened muscle at his groin. Tracing her fingers across the tip, Andrea moved her hands over this rigidness nervously, refusing to gain courage as they returned to his chest.

Herb Alpert's "Making Love in the Rain" now embraced the mood, and by some uncanny coincidence it actually began raining outside that evening. William noticed these things while touching his lips to hers once more. Feeling the gasp of indrawn breathing as her body tensed, he thought she was preparing herself for entry. Everything seemed to be building toward what was about to happen next, what was supposed to happen next.

"William, I... I can't. I'm sorry. I'm so sorry." Andrea sat up on his bed.

"Andrea, what's wrong?"

"I... I... I just can't do this." Burying her head in her hands, she started sobbing.

William was numb. He wasn't angry, just numb. Turning off the tape that contributed to his numbness, an awkward silence filled the room for fifteen minutes. Not knowing the words to say that might comfort her, he placed his arm around her shoulders as she continued to cry. Although it was disappointing to him that the moment of making love to the woman of his dreams would be put on hold yet again—hey, I still have my fantasies, he thought—his immediate concern was Andrea's condition. Soon, the arm around her shoulder turned into an affectionate cuddle and after she stopped crying, there was more silence. Finally, after what seemed like an eternity, William threw out a life preserver.

"Do you want to talk?"

"No. I'm just sorry. You think I'm teasing you, right?"

"No, I don't. I actually thought the robe may have been a little too forward. What do you think?"

"No, it wasn't that."

"Am I rushing things?"

"No. Everything seemed to be so right."

Stinging from the response, his mind questioned, everything seemed so right? What do you mean, everything seemed so right? Baby, I'm in love with you. Everything doesn't seem so right. It is right, because I love you. Somehow, when he attempted to verbalize his thoughts they came out, "If you don't mind me asking, then what stopped you tonight?"

Frowning, Andrea gave him a very sad look. Her

eyes were telling him words she couldn't say; the look told him everything, everything he didn't want to know.

"No!" he yelled. She bowed her head in shame. "No!"

William jumped off the bed and began pacing around his room like a lunatic. He had lost that winning lottery ticket he'd obtained just a short time ago.

"I thought you weren't happy with him?"

"I never said that." As much as he didn't want to admit it or remember it at this juncture, he knew Andrea was right. On the night they met, she'd never told him that she was unhappy with her boyfriend. It had never come from her lips.

"Damn!" He removed her clothes from the guest chair and sat in it. "Were you with him last night?"

"He's my boyfriend. What do you think?"

A sudden, uncomfortable chill passed through him when she said these words. Unable to think of anything to say that could make this truth go away, he couldn't do anything to ease the excruciating pain in his heart. For two months he'd ignored it; in fact, judging from his actions, it wasn't a stretch to say he might have completely forgotten about it. But today, on what was supposed to be the most emotionally fulfilling day of his life, William McCall received the harshest of reminders. The woman he'd fallen in love with was someone else's.

✪✪✪

As the negative image ran its course, William now regretted his lack of poise over what eventually followed. Remembering how he'd wanted Andrea to leave after his disappointing discovery, he'd had to take the long trip back into Manhattan with her. That ride back from the city had been agonizing. Recalling how he'd lost control—blankly staring into a space only he knew about while muttering, "What am I going to do now?" at least a dozen times on the train ride home—he also remembered how his sleepless nights of anticipating love evolved into sleepless nightmares of torment from that night onward. He used to stay awake at night thinking about what she might have been doing with that other man; wondering if he'd done the same things William had done, only better. He speculated on what her reactions were when that other guy kissed her, held her and made love to her. Instead of "her and me" they had quickly become "her and him and me."

His thoughts were suddenly interrupted by the ringing of his office phone.

"Can I help you?"

"You have something at reception," the voice said, giggling.

"I'll be right out."

Approaching the area, he saw a couple of sisters standing by the reception desk, laughing hysterically. He heard one of them say, "You go, girl," and upon hearing those words the receptionist and one of the women that was standing there exchanged high-fives.

What could be that funny? he wondered as he neared them.

To his horror, he quickly found out. Della had dropped off the duffel bag he'd left at her house the night before but had added her own gifts to it, as well. A half-dozen dead roses were hanging from the bag and the contents of the duffel bag were faded; having been soiled with bleach. William turned the bag around to face a note:

Thanks for the memories. Please find two admission forms to Intercourse 101 at the bottom of this bag, Mister No-Can Fuck. Della

"Had a rough one, huh?" the receptionist asked, making no attempt at concealing the humor of her findings.

One of the women announced with glee, "Welcome to the twenty-first century. We're not taking any more shit from you lame-ass men."

"Good for y'all dogs," the other woman chimed in with rancor.

Remarkably, William remained calm in the face of this verbal humiliation. Taking the duffel bag back to his office, he ignored the many baffled looks of surprise on the faces of his colleagues. Once there, he closed his office door and placed it in his guest chair. As he went around to sit behind his desk, he knocked over a Stevie Wonder cassette that was there. Picking it up and holding it for a second, he thought, *I guess you were right, Stevie. All in love is fair.* Emotionally drained by both Della's assault on his manhood and the unpleasant memories of Andrea, William slumped into his chair, miserable.

Chapter Six

NOBODY REMEMBERS SECOND-PLACE FINISHERS

Day Two

"Lisa, are you sure you don't want to see a movie? We could do that, or go to the Café in downtown Brooklyn to listen to open mike."

"Nah, man, it's too cold to be driving around. Besides, I'm getting tired of some of these spoken word artists. Every man takes the mike, raps about us being his queen and shit, and come to find out he has three kids by three different women he opened up with his words."

"Another way of running game on a sister, huh?"

"Yup. Say what you think she wants to hear, get the pussy, and keep it moving."

William chuckled. "So, my Nubian princess, the mother of all life..."

"Uh-oh. Not William, with the Def Poetry Mack. Let me find out!"

"You're sick, Lisa."

"I know. I should stop hatin', right?"

"Yeah. You should." William paused. "Lisa, you want to come over for dinner?"

"That sounds like a plan. I'll bring some DVDs from Blockbuster."

"Cool."

"What do you want to see?" she asked.

"I'll leave it up to you. Just don't be funny and rent *Waiting to Exhale*. I've experienced enough black male bashing over the past couple of days to last a lifetime, so you know I don't want to see any in cinema form."

Lisa chuckled. "How about *Jungle Fever*?"

"Very funny, pal. You telling me that I should be dating white women?"

"Most of y'all do whenever you come into money anyway," she countered. "I'm just kidding. I'll think of something. William, you better not kill me with your cooking."

"Who do you think I am, Thelma from *Good Times*?"

Both of them erupted in laughter.

"Lisa, have I ever?"

"How should I know? You probably had one of your girlfriends cook that Thanksgiving dinner you brought to me."

"Nah, I did that all by my lonesome. I'll be cooking turkey ziti tonight."

"Mmm, sounds good."

"Want a cheesecake with strawberry topping, too?"

"Hell yeah!" she exclaimed. "I'm surprised you still look like Pookie from *New Jack City* with all the cooking you do."

"A brother's gotta stay in shape these days."

"I hear ya. So, Black Lalane, what..."

"You have a name for everything, don't you?"

"I try. What time should I grace your presence?"

"About seven. I live on the corner of Cortelyou Road and East Sixteenth Street. A gray brick building. My apartment's over a drugstore, right on the corner. Three seventy-eight is the building number. You need directions?"

"No. I know Brooklyn pretty well."

"That's unfortunate. I was going to tell you to buy a compass."

"Smart ass. I'll see you at seven."

"Okay. Peace."

The rest of the Saturday went by quickly as William cleaned his apartment and cooked in preparation for her visit, completing the meal just as she rang his intercom. Perfect timing, he thought, buzzing her up to the third floor. When his doorbell rang, he opened the door, greeting his buddy with a loving embrace. Removing her black wool coat and noticing the tight black jeans gripping her tight, round bottom, he said, "Damn, girl, I never knew you had such a future behind you."

"Shut up and stop looking at my ass!"

They shared another hug while laughing.

"On the real, thanks for coming by," William intoned.

"Thanks for having me," Lisa said, walking into his living room.

She was immediately drawn to the black leather furniture, topaz-blue carpet, his white marble wall unit and his collection of black art along the wall above his stereo. But the painting that captured her attention most was Ernie Barnes' "Sugar Shack" mural. First seen during the opening segment of the '70s sitcom *Good Times*, the painting also graced the cover of Marvin Gaye's *I Want You* album.

"You have a very nice place here. I see why all the women want to stay over," she commented, giggling.

"Kill that noise, Lisa," William countered, snatching the Blockbuster bag from her. "Let's see what we have here."

Lisa blurted out the titles before he opened the bag. "There's a bootleg copy of *The Best Man* that I purchased a few days ago, and *Brown Sugar*."

"I guess it's Taye Diggs night at the McCall house, huh?"

"Don't hate on a fine brother doing his thing."

William smiled. "Yo, you did good."

"Would you expect any less from a girl like me? Now where's that ziti? Your homegirl's ready to get her eats on."

William escorted her to the kitchen and sat his cream-colored, brown-eyed friend in front of a hot plate of meaty pasta.

"Aw, ain't this sweet. You're the perfect gentleman," she observed.

"I guess I'm making an attempt at cleansing myself." He seated himself at the opposite end of an oval-shaped, wooden dinner table.

While partaking of the meal, Lisa began the discussion they knew would take place sometime during the evening. "So, have you heard from Della?"

"Nope. Well actually, yes. Yesterday she returned a duffel bag I had at her house with bleach all over my shit and left it at the reception area."

Laughing hysterically, Lisa almost choked on a portion of the ziti in her mouth. "She really did that?"

"See for yourself." William got up, hurried to his bedroom and, seconds later, returned with the faded bag.

Laughing even harder now, she doubled over.

"She also added a half-dozen dead roses and a note saying that I couldn't fuck," he continued.

Regrouping, Lisa wiped her brown eyes. "Well, can you?"

For the first time in recent memory, William blushed. "I plead the fifth."

"I know the receptionist got a charge out of that."

"She had the audacity to call two other women to

the area. Once I got there, they serenaded me with some woman of the new century crap."

"That must have been enjoyable."

"You can imagine how I felt. I've never been more embarrassed in my life, Lisa."

"Do you have any plans on contacting her anymore?"

William shrugged his shoulders. "Who knows?"

"By the way, this ziti is outstanding."

"Thanks. I put three cheeses in it. Cheddar, mozzarella and ricotta."

"Looks like we're going to be breakin' wind all night, especially after the cheesecake," Lisa quipped.

"You're a trip, girl."

"William, what was it with Della that made you see that other chick? What was her name again?"

"Barbara. You wanna know the truth?"

"Spill it."

"I don't know. Greed, I suppose. I didn't feel secure being with her. All of Della's male friends were past boyfriends that either slept with her or wanted to."

"Were they really friends, William?"

"Tell me about it, Lisa. Ex-boyfriends only remain friends for as long as the possibility of pussy still exists. I know this, you know this, but Della?" He sighed. "That crap bothered me. Especially this one dude, Jerry, she was screwing at one time. He used to call her house when I was there and hang up without leaving a message. That, or she wouldn't talk to him in my presence. What is it? Do all women now have Emergency Dick just in case shit goes wrong with men they're seeing?"

"Did you ever tell her how you were feeling?"

"No. I just became nonchalant about the whole relationship. I always thought she was fuckin' around on me, especially because we went to bed on our first date. I mean, how many other guys did she do that to?"

"Did you make her feel wanted?"

"Truthfully? Sometimes. But after I saw that she had all these other acquaintances, friends, whatever you want to call them, I saw her as a good-time girl."

"What's that?"

"A good-time girl is a woman we men never take seriously, except late at night when our dicks are hard and we're in need of a booty call. We lie to them and say we want something serious, but more often than not it's said during pillow talk, because we know she's not the type we bring home to Mama. These types of women think they have everything together in their lives, and they're the first to claim they only need a man for this or that." William shook his head before continuing. "They don't. They're so love starved they fail to realize how easy they make themselves for the wrong type of man, the one that has a killer instinct."

"Guys like you, right?" Lisa joked.

"Don't go there."

"My bad, William. So, anyway..."

"So, anyway, these women keep making the wrong choices in men, because they're usually older and they don't want to be alone, and feel like time is running out on them. A lot of them say that all they want is physical companionship, but they are really lying to themselves. They're looking for love in all the wrong places. The funny thing is, some of them know it, too, and resign themselves to being what they are.

"A man never wants to commit to this type of woman but always wants her accessible, because the sex is so damn good. And chances are she will be, because she has too much baggage for anyone to stay around long in her life. It's like a sure thing, an automatic piece of pussy. All we do is call them out of the blue, take them out, show 'em a good time and it's on. I began viewing Della this way, so instead of treating her like that, I stopped hanging around her."

"But you kept going back," Lisa argued through her laughter.

William confessed. "It might have been because of the sex. That shit was good. It always is with a good-time girl because they've slept around so damn much they know what they're doing."

"That's fucked up, William."

"I'm just teasin'. I cared about her, don't get me wrong." Noticing her plate was empty, he asked, "You want any more?"

Lisa nodded yes, so William got up and refilled her plate, as well as his own.

"It was like I was torn between my feelings for her and my lack of trust for women, period. That's when Barbara entered the fray."

"And messed it all up," Lisa quickly pointed out.

"Yeah. She was just one of those things. I met her at a party. She talked all this shit about how she would turn me out in bed, and when push came to shove, she didn't represent."

"Be nice," Lisa admonished.

William did his best Joe Friday impersonation. "Just the facts, ma'am. Just the facts. I did all the work in bed, all the fucking time. She was one of those 'lay there do nothing' types. No rhythm whatsoever. All it was about was banging. In and out. In and out. I felt like a robot with all the mechanical sex we had."

"Some women like it like that."

"All the time, though? It was so workmanlike."

"If it wasn't good, why was she over here the day Della called?"

William shrugged.

"Greed. The male ego. I don't know."

"Stupidity is what I'd call it. You should have kept it real with Della."

"The funny thing about all this is, on one hand Della had all these male whatever you wanna call 'ems, and on the other she wanted a commitment from me. I just didn't know where she was coming from, so I kept my options open. And I sure as hell wasn't going to jump into any competition for her heart."

"And why not?" Lisa argued. "Sometimes we sisters want to be treated special. We want to feel wanted and needed by our brothers."

"And men don't?"

"She was with you, right?"

"That doesn't mean a damn thing these days. A lot of sisters today are fed up with black men and are starting to act just like us in that we're only supposed to fill a certain void. You wanna hear something crazy?" Lisa nodded. "On my way home from work yesterday, I overheard a woman braggin' to her girlfriend on the train about how she steps out to screw an ex-boyfriend at night while her man's at work The reason? The ex has a bigger dick. Ain't that something? But the kicker is that the other woman mentioned she was fucking someone else's man, that they had an understanding."

"We had good teachers," Lisa cracked.

"Does putting two wrongs together make a right solution? This isn't algebra where two negatives equal a positive. If you want variety, then get a damn dildo!" William sighed. "You know what that crap tells me? It tells me that some women today can make you feel like you're the be all and end all and be out fuckin' Stanley's brains out tomorrow. It would be ludicrous to say all women are like that, but a lot of y'all possess the same type of ruthlessness as..."

When he stopped short, Lisa finished the sentence for him. "As men, right?"

William nodded. "Dating today is like war. Everyone's out for him or herself with little or no regard for the feelings of the other party."

"You sound bitter."

"No, I'm not. I just know. I just know."

"You don't know shit," Lisa joked.

"Yeah, I may be stretching it a bit. But I do know how special a person can make you feel at one moment, then pull the rug out from underneath you." William rose from his seat. "I'm tired of sounding like Deacon McCall, with all this preaching. Let's go watch a movie."

Lisa echoed the sentiment and after putting away the leftover ziti and washing the dishes, they headed to the living room where the next few hours passed by with Lisa and William viewing the two movies and conversing about life, love and their pursuits while eating cheesecake. At the conclusion of *The Best Man*, William looked at his watch. It indicated twelve-thirty.

"Lisa, you're welcome to stay the night if you want to," he offered while walking to the kitchen.

"You want some of this?" she joked.

"Some other time, pal. On the real, it's cold out there and I know you don't feel like driving all the way back to Queens."

"True."

"Besides, I haven't made my cinnamon and spice pancakes for breakfast in a while."

"Where are you going to sleep?"

"With you, in my bed."

Lisa made a face that said, yeah, right.

"Seriously, I'll sleep out here," he said, pointing in the direction of his living room. "If you need something to slip into, there's a pair of flannel pajamas under my pillow."

"I'm not going to find anyone's garter belt or handcuffs hanging from a bed post, am I?"

"Good night, Lisa."

As she turned away from William, he grabbed her hand and planted a wet one on her cheek. "Hey, thanks for being there for me. I needed your company tonight. Good lookin' out."

Lisa smiled. "That's what friends are for. Good night, William."

Watching her full hips and brown, shoulder-length hair sway fluidly as she walked down the corridor leading to his bedroom, he thought, *Damn, she's beautiful, inside and out. I wonder why she's not hooked up with a caring brotha. Oh well.*

Returning to his living room, he dimmed the lights while reaching for his headphones. Placing a Barry White CD in his stereo, he searched for the song "I've Got So Much to Give" and pressed the repeat button on his disc player. That song would put him to sleep that morning, but until then, William's memory took another trip back to a time where he had so much to give, yet his love was unrequited.

✪✪✪

There comes a period in every relationship when you step off the cloud of infatuation you've been riding on and begin to see the object of your affection for who they really are. At about the same time, you take off the rose-colored glasses you've been wearing and start to assess your situation realistically. At that juncture you usually begin to make decisions that are in your own best interests. But what happens when you fall in love for the first time and have to do both simultaneously? The conclusions can be confusing if you're unsure of yourself.

Exhibit A: William McCall.

Slapped in the face by reality on Andrea's birthday, William had to make a decision about whether to continue to seeing her. Every time he passed a floral arrangement in a store window he thought of how special it would be for Andrea to have it. Walking into card shops, he found the cuddliest, softest stuffed animals and thought of how she would enjoy holding them. He'd breeze by a box of chocolates and memories of that Valentine's Day resurfaced. Her presence had enlivened him so much his face would express exhilaration, mirroring joy and happiness. Andrea had unlocked the door to William's soul and an abundance of love that had lain dormant behind it came bursting out, adding something to his life he'd never known before. William liked that something.

Yet the fact that she wasn't his tormented him unceasingly. As special as she had made him feel, she'd been doing the same for someone else, if not more so. He didn't want to relinquish the love he had for Andrea, yet he was not happy being her other man.

Those next few weeks after Andrea's birthday had brought heartache into William's life like he'd never experienced. The phone conversations between the two that usually lasted hours became terse, and every time he extended an invitation to Andrea for a date, she either told him she had something to do or canceled just hours before they would meet. By intentionally avoiding him, she'd hoped the growing feelings between the two would eventually dissipate.

Her actions gnawed at William's psyche; not only did he battle insomnia, but his appetite disappeared. Eating one meal a day instead of three, his grades began to slip in school, as well. In his first two semesters at NYU, he'd made the dean's list, no small feat for someone working full-time and going to school at night. But love now ruled his life and, for better or worse, it affected him.

Needing to reach out, in the midst of his emotional turmoil he called his best friend, Steve, in Delaware, who, a couple of years earlier, had experienced a similar situation. Perhaps he can give me some help, William thought while dialing his number.

"Yo," Steve answered.

"What up, Black?" William responded, using an affectionate term they'd called one another for years.

"What's up, Black? I was just thinking about you, and the fact that your punk ass hasn't been down here since you met that Andrea chick. By the way, how did her birthday turn out?"

"Steve, she loved the robe, man. We had a real nice time, too. But..."

"Uh-oh." Steve Randall knew his pal like the back of his hand. After all, their friendship went back to the seventh grade, when William first moved into his neighborhood on Staten Island and needed directions to the principal's office that fall. Originally forged around sports talk, as that year went on and ones followed, their bond became much more, having reached the point where they could finish each other's sentences. So when Steve heard that "but," he knew his bro wasn't doing too well.

"What happened, Black? Did you punch that clock?"

They both laughed.

"C'mon, man."

"On a serious tip, did it happen?"

"Nah, man. We were close. Very close. But she couldn't. She had..."

"The other guy on her brain."

"Yep. She couldn't bring herself to do it."

"Cut her off, Black." Hearing no response from William, he snickered. "Nah, I'm just teasin'. What are you going to do?"

"Steve, I haven't the slightest idea. I haven't been able to sleep, man. I keep thinking about her with that other dude."

"What's his name again, Derrick?"

"Yeah."

"Black, I can't make up your mind for you, but I

will tell you this, if you decide to compete for her, the odds are stacked against you. The fact she was with this guy two years before she met you ought to tell you something. She may have kissed you, made you feel special, and the whole nine. But she's still with number one. If she entertained the notion of leaving him, she would have had sex with you. Derrick is still number one in her heart. And in competition for a woman, number two always loses to number one."

"I think I love her, man."

"Did you tell her this?"

"Of course not! But I've made it kind of obvious, don't you think?"

"Yeah, you have." Steve sighed. "Ask yourself this. Do you want to settle for always being number two? You do all these wonderful things for her like you have and she's not giving you any? I know it's not all about sex, but stop and think for a second. Do you think she would be giving you the time of day if he were doing the things you're doing for her?"

"I don't know, Black."

"She couldn't be that selfish, now could she?"

"I don't know."

"Do you want to be just her ace in the hole?" Hearing an extended pause, Steve hoped his reality check hadn't worked in an adverse way. Although William was a caring, considerate person, there was also a competitive streak in him that Steve came to know, having firsthand knowledge of this on the basketball court. William, though not of the same talent level as he, always gave him tough battles when they opposed each other in neighborhood skirmishes, largely because of his determination. Steve saw in him a steely resolve, a relentless, never-give-up attitude he unspokenly admired.

But love is different, Steve pondered during the break. *Surely he'll do what's best for his heart.*

Finally, William spoke.

"I don't know, Black. I just don't know. What did you do when you were in that situation?"

"That decision was taken from me. Kelli was engaged, so I already knew the score. It was just one of those things, a last fling for her, I guess."

"I can't do that. My feelings get involved, Black."

"Then you should consider that before going all out. Like I said, number two always loses to number one."

"I know. I just don't know what to do, man."

"If I were you, I'd just chill for a while."

"And let her forget about me?"

"Now you know that ain't gonna happen," Steve snapped. "Just the same way you're on the phone with me, she's probably on the phone with her girlfriends talking about the mess she's created. Give yourself some credit, Black. You have her open just as much as she has you sweatin' her, but she's handling it better because she has to. She has Derrick's needs to tend to."

"Now if Derrick weren't around we wouldn't be having this conversation."

"Yeah, but he is. And from the way it sounds, you're in love with his girl. All I can say is that whatever you do from here, proceed with caution, Black. I don't want to see you get hurt. The damage could be irreparable."

"Steve, I can't begin to tell you how much..."

"Shut up, Will. You sound too much like your boy Michael Jackson. She's out of my..."

"Fuck you, Steve."

"Fuck you, too, Black. I gotta run. This graveyard-shift post office gig is kickin' my ass."

"Handle it, Black. Good lookin' out with the advice."

"Just remember, number two always loses to number one. Strive for that top spot, bro. I'll catch up with ya."

"Peace."

Hanging up the phone, William thought about what Steven said about not settling for being the ace in the hole, and how he craved that top spot; in this instance, Andrea's heart. He wanted her for himself—to be his woman—the idea of having feelings for another as strong as they were for her seemed contemptuous.

His mind was made up.

Receiving permission to use his grandmother's credit card, the next phone call he would make that evening would be to 1-800-ROSES. Andrea would find a surprise when she arrived at work.

The next day at work, he heard from her. Overjoyed upon receipt of her floral arrangement, they had a short discussion, during which they agreed to meet to clear the air and talk about their future together. They decided to meet for lunch the coming Sunday.

Sunday came upon him quickly and, as usual, he'd neither eaten nor slept the night before. However, this time it didn't go unnoticed. For two weeks Edith Hall, William's youthful seventy-something, Indian-featured grandmother, had observed his deteriorating condition quietly. Noticing dark circles under her grandson's eyes and recognizing a slight weight loss—abnormal symptoms for a reasonably healthy twenty-year-old—she decided to confront him before he left to meet Andrea, motioning him into her apartment and into the kitchen.

"What's up, Grandma?" William inquired, seating himself.

"You have a few minutes for your grandmother, don't you?"

"Yes, I do."

She immediately became intrusive. "Baby, you look like you haven't been sleeping. Are you having troubles with your studies?"

"Nah, Grandma," William lied.

"Well, I can tell you haven't been gettin' any sleep. How are things with that Andrea girl? I haven't been seein' her with you lately."

William lowered his eyes to the kitchen floor and sighed dejectedly. "We're having problems."

"Well, I could have told you that was going to happen," his grandmother stated matter-of-factly. "That's why you don't rush into situations like that. She's a phony, son."

William raised his head in shock. "Grandma, don't call her that!" Then realizing whom he was talking to, he softened his tone. "I mean, she's not a phony. She's just confused."

Edith's opinion of Andrea was unwavering. "Personally, I think the girl's using you. But if you feel as strongly as I'm thinking you do, then all I can tell you is to hang in there.

"She's not using me, Grandma." He got up and walked into the hall leading to the outer doorway.

"I hope not. You enjoy yourself, today."

"Thanks, Grandma."

En route to the subway, William thought, *I understand how Grandma feels. She has my best interest at heart.*

But in this case, I have to go with what I'm feeling. Before the day ended, he would realize that such a decision wasn't so smart.

✪✪✪

Instead of meeting at their usual checkpoint, William and Andrea made arrangements to meet in front of the American Cafe in nearby Chelsea. Arriving at twelve-thirty, one half-hour before their arranged meeting time, he'd purchased a stuffed rabbit for her on his way there. Three weeks had passed since he'd last seen her, so he wanted to make up for lost time.

After waiting an hour outside for her arrival, William angrily muttered, "Late again," and went inside the trendy restaurant to be seated, leaving a message with the maitre'd just in case Andrea came inside and inquired of his whereabouts.

Another half-hour passed and there was still no Andrea. During this time, a black waiter came by his table a couple of times to take his order. To save himself from immediate embarrassment, William ordered a Sprite each time. After requesting the second one, he decided to give her another half-hour.

The time elapsed swiftly as he sadly sipped from his soda. At that point the waiter approached his table and said, "She isn't coming, is she?"

"No, I guess not," William responded unhappily. "Can I have the check, please?" The waiter obliged. As he waited for change, he stood up and put on his black windbreaker. To his surprise, the waiter came back to him with not only some change, but an Alabama Slamma on his tray.

"This one's on me, pal," he said, startling William with the drink. "Any brother who waits two hours for a woman who doesn't show deserves a free drink." William and the waiter, a honey-complexioned older brother who appeared to be about thirty-something, simultaneously sat down. "Don't worry, pal. My break starts in a couple of minutes. Let me ask you something. Is she worth the trouble?"

"I'm still trying to figure that out right now. I mean, she makes me feel so special."

The waiter interrupted.

"They all do. And when they feel like they have you where they want you, acting like a complete wimp, they flip the script." Those remarks made William wince. "By the way, my name is Wallace."

"I'm William."

"Are you in love with her, man?"

"I think so. But she has a boyfriend," William stated. The drink had him telling all at that juncture. "I thought she was unhappy with him."

Wallace shook his head. "Then why are you seeing her? There are plenty of available women in this city.

Why are you limiting yourself to chasing forbidden fruit?"

"I don't know. I guess you can't control who you fall in love with."

Drawing laughter from Wallace, William gave him a quizzical look. "Did I say something funny?"

"Yo, if I were you, I'd be just trying to fuck her. She's having her cake and eating it. I'd bet any amount of money she hasn't given you a whiff of the pussy." William didn't respond verbally, but the look on his face said it was true. "Haven't you ever heard of the five F's when it comes to women?"

"No. What's that?"

"I was like you once, young and dumb. After I got hurt a few times, I adopted a killer instinct, a philosophy all men should utilize when need be. Women aren't attracted to that good guy shit; they're excitement-craving challenge fiends who like the unknown. Hell, it's been like that since the beginning of time, when Eve ate from the damn apple. You have to have intrigue, mystery, always keep them on their toes, not knowing what to expect from you. You find 'em, fool 'em, feed 'em, fuck 'em and forget 'em. Those rules serve me well. You get more pussy that way, too."

William was bewildered. "Nah, man. I can't do that. Let me ask you something. If she's getting everything she wants from this man, then why is she going out with me?"

"You have to answer that one on your own. If I was in your shoes, I'd be going for mine. Fuck the dumb shit! There's no future there. And even if, by some miracle, she does come to you, what makes you think that she won't cheat on you?" Noticing that the look on William's face was worse than it had been before they sat down, Wallace sighed as he got up from the table. "Listen, if you really love her, then dig in and fight for her. Just don't let her play you out like this anymore. Good luck."

"Yeah, man. Thanks for the drink."

Leaving the restaurant, William's emotions were in chaos. He had never been stood up on a date before. Wanting to forget about ever agreeing to see her, he didn't even bother calling Andrea's house for an explanation.

Wallace's words, as harsh as they sounded, gave him an alternative to ponder. Should he suppress the fondness he felt for this woman and make it strictly a dick thing? Momentarily entertaining Wallace's view of putting his needs before a woman he dated, he quickly dismissed the idea with disgust. *That's just not me*, he concluded. Possessing feelings in his heart for Andrea that transcended lustful cravings, he thought of her night and day and of things he could do to delight her the next time he saw her. He would dig in and fight for her, as Wallace put it, however, the battle would commence another time; the rest of this day would be spent trying to ease the pain of being stood up.

Chapter Seven

IF ONLY FOR ONE NIGHT

Day Three

Rising early that Sunday morning after a restless night, William greeted Lisa with breakfast in bed. The delightful aroma of bacon, scrambled eggs with cheese, cinnamon and spice pancakes and orange juice brought a smile to her face as she turned over.

"Damn, this service is better than IHOP."

"I thought you might wake up starvin'. I know you don't eat much at home. All you have is bread and water in your fridge."

"Very funny. That's why you're tryin' to kiss my ass because the breakfast you made sucks."

"Ooh! Nice comeback. By the way, you look good in my flannel pajamas."

Lisa smiled as she started consuming her meal. "Damn! This is good. You sure you're not gonna ask me for some pussy?"

"Why would I want to kiss you now, with that awful morning breath you have?" William laughed at her while getting up off the corner of his bed. "Seriously, you gotta eat up. I want to go see if I can get some Knicks tickets. They have a matinee game against Tim Duncan and the San Antonio Spurs. I hear they still have seats available at the Garden. Do you wanna go?"

"Can't," Lisa replied between smacks, glancing at his bedroom wall clock. "I have a lunch date. Damn! It's ten-thirty! I'm supposed to be hooking up with him at one-thirty."

William immediately returned to his position on the corner of his bed. "Oh, so you held out on a brotha last night. You know that's not fair. Who's the lucky guy?"

"His name is Augustus."

"Nice name." William smirked.

"Shut up. He's from St. Maarten. I met him at a party a couple of weeks ago. He seems like a nice guy. He's been sweatin' me for a date, so I figure a Sunday lunch for starters."

With concern in his voice, William butted in. "Lisa, are you ready? Have you given yourself enough time to get that sucker Roland out of your system?"

"It's just a lunch date, William. Besides, I haven't heard from that fool in over a month."

"But you know how love crazed he had you. You could have fit the Brooklyn Bridge through your nostrils. And the way he stood you up at that Toni Braxton concert a couple of months ago was foul."

"Yeah, I'm kind of lucky you weren't screwin' anybody that night," Lisa joked. "Seriously, you got to Radio City Music Hall with the quickness and even took me to dinner afterward to cheer me up. See, you're not as bad as these women make you out to be." Speechless, William looked at Lisa. "You're kind of quiet, pal. Did I embarrass you?"

"The only reason I came to your rescue that night was because I wanted to see if Toni got her boobs done. Ha, ha, ha!"

"Ha, ha, ha! Fuck you, William," Lisa mocked, eliciting laughter with a dead-on mimic.

"Seriously, Lisa, are you going to be okay today?"

"Yeah, I'll be fine. He seems to be a nice guy."

"Don't we all, at first. Don't we all." William rose from the bed and walked toward the bedroom door, then out. "There's a washcloth and towel on the toilet seat for your shower, lotion in the medicine cabinet and I have extra toothbrushes under the sink."

"Damn! You put the drugstore out of business!"

"I heard that!"

After breakfast, Lisa hastily showered and prepared herself to go. Once ready, she found William in his living room, sitting Indian-style on his sofa, watching *SportsCenter*. To the left of him was her coat.

"Are you trying to kick me out? Is this what you do to all your women?"

"Nah, just you," he replied as he aided her with her coat. "I thought you might be in a hurry."

Now ready for departure, Lisa faced him.

"William, are you going to be all right? When you called yesterday morning, you didn't sound like yourself. I mean, I can cancel, if you want me to."

He looked at her like she was crazy. "You're not serious, are you? You better go meet that man and have a nice time." They walked toward his apartment door. "Let me know how everything goes," he added while opening the door.

"Even if I get some and the sex is whack?"

"Get out, girl! Thanks for coming by."

Shutting the door after Lisa's exit, William giggled. "Damn, she's funny," he said aloud.

Alone again, he picked up the phone and called the Madison Square Garden ticket office. Just as he presumed, he would have to go there to get Knicks tickets. While in the shower, he thought of Lisa again, sincerely hoping all would go well on her date with Augustus. *With a name like that he better treat her like a queen*, he mused, feeling she deserved the red carpet treatment after dealing with Roland's bullshit. *That asshole is a nut job. Anyone who stands a beautiful person like Lisa up is one beer short of a six-pack, a couple of sandwiches short of a picnic. I know what it's like to spend a romantic evening at a concert without your loved one.* He paused in his thinking to change that; though slightly. *In actuality, she'd been there. But, not with me.*

✪✪✪

William, recuperating from being stood up by Andrea that Sunday, took a trip to his old neighborhood to cure his ills. Arriving home that evening, he found a note on his room door from his grandmother. She had found out that tickets to Luther Vandross' *Give Me The Reason* concert would be available that Monday morning at Madison Square Garden. William didn't have any credit cards at the time, so he knew he would have to get up pretty early in the morning to stand in line outside the Garden box office.

Sure enough, when arriving at the arena at four that morning, hundreds of people were already waiting. The ticket office wouldn't open until eight, so he would have to endure four hours of people trying to jump ahead of him in the line, as well as the abnormally cold spring morning. But the possibility of taking in this event with Andrea was the motivation William needed in mustering the patience to endure all the bullshit associated with getting tickets.

Eight o'clock finally came and he purchased four tickets, two for him and Andrea and the others for Steve and his college sweetheart, Jackie. The ordeal had been worth it because he ended up with fourth-row seats. He rushed to his job that morning so that he could share the good news with Andrea, immediately calling her upon reaching his desk.

"Legal Department," Andrea answered.

"Hey, Crumbcake! Guess what?"

"William! I'm really sorry about yesterday. I had..."

"Don't worry about that. I've got fourth-row tickets for you and me to see Luther. Please come with me."

"I can't commit at this point," Andrea responded. The concert was six weeks away, so she couldn't make concrete plans, not while she had Derrick to appease. "Let's just wait and see. Do you want to hook up tonight for dinner?"

"Sounds like a plan to me. I'll meet you at your job at five-thirty," he responded. Maybe it was selective amnesia or a knock on the head or something, but William's reaction to Andrea's request showed that he had forgotten about her no-show just twenty-four hours earlier. Blinded to all negative occurrences of the past few weeks—those brief phone calls, cancellations of ready-made plans—all of that was ignored by William. He was going to see his Crumbcake and that was all that mattered.

The day went by quickly as he anxiously waited for the moment when he would see his love. Five o'clock couldn't have arrived any sooner. William rushed to make himself presentable in the men's bathroom at his job, wove through the rush-hour crowd at Grand Central Terminal, purchased an assortment of carnations and made a bee-line to Andrea's work site some twenty blocks south of his.

Butterflies fluttered in his stomach as he went through the revolving doors leading him to the Metropolitan Life building lobby. Once inside, William glanced at his watch. Five thirty-five. He looked to his right and to his surprise, saw Andrea standing nearby wearing a gorgeous blue ensemble, waiting for him.

"Shocked ya, didn't I?" she said after a lengthy hug.

"Yeah, you did." He handed her the flowers and pointed to a female security guard stationed across the lobby. "Could you give these to that security guard over there?"

"Very funny. So, where are we going to eat?"

"Let's try the American Cafe," William suggested sarcastically, evoking an apologetic grimace from Andrea as they went toward the revolving doors.

"We can go there, if you like."

"Nah. I couldn't go back there, even if I really wanted to. I was there for two hours yesterday."

"William, I'm really sorry about not calling ahead of time to cancel. But I was out with..." Her voice trailed off as they went through the doorway.

Walking to the Twenty-Third Street train station, William responded with irritation in his voice. "I figured as much. Let me ask you something. If you aren't unhappy with him, as you put it so creatively the last time we hooked up, then why did you agree to see me today?"

"There's just something about you," Andrea answered.

"Can you elaborate?"

She shrugged her shoulders as they put their tokens through the turnstiles of the Park Avenue South subway.

"No. It's an indescribable feeling. There's just something about you. It's not about what Derrick's doing wrong. It's about what you're doing right."

"And that is..."

"There's just something different about you. That's all I can say."

Instead of pressing the issue, William dropped the matter as the downtown Number 6 train entered the station.

During the train ride and ensuing dinner at their favorite barbecue joint, the couple behaved as if their problems were nonexistent. The conversation across the dinner table was filled with hilarity and flirtation. William felt whole now that Andrea was in his presence again.

Judging from Andrea's enthusiastic behavior, she had truly missed his humor, charm and generosity. He knows all the right things to say and do, she thought as William complimented her on her beauty and exhibited chivalry. *He treats me like I'm a goddess or something*, she marveled. Having dated Derrick almost three years, Andrea felt his love seemed forced, superficial and shallow, like he was more concerned in having arm candy than in tailoring their relationship to her real needs. Already feeling as if something was missing, William had come along with his endless cupboard of natural affection and she'd been powerless to resist him.

In William's eyes, she was the pulse of his existence. The way they carried on, playing footsie under their table and exchanging long, seductive stares, one would have never known that three weeks had passed since they'd last seen each other. The various patrons surrounding them in this atmosphere were banished from their private world the minute these two were seated. Hadn't she kept this man waiting for two hours in a restaurant yesterday? It didn't matter, for idle affections simmered anew as they left the restaurant holding hands and kissing.

On the ride to her neighborhood, William proudly showed Andrea his Luther Vandross tickets, eliciting an excited reaction from her.

"I can't believe it! He's coming to New York in June!"

"Yeah. I can't wait for him myself. My boy Steve wanted us to come with him to see him when he opened the tour at the Philadelphia Spectrum, but I told him that the only real place to see Luther is at Madison Square Garden. Besides, there will be so many after-concert parties we can all go to afterward."

"Yeah, we could," she replied, lowering her eyes to the subway floor.

"Does Derrick like Luther?"

"No. But if I wanted to go bad enough..."

William cut her off. "Now you see, you should be going to see Luther with someone who loves him just as much as you do. Since meeting you, I've bought all of his albums I was missing. Now, I have them all: *Never Too Much; Forever, For Always, For Love; Busy Body, The Night I Fell in Love;* and his latest one, *Give Me The Reason*. You really should be going with me to that concert."

"We'll see. We'll see."

She didn't have the heart to say it at that juncture, but deep down Andrea knew William was taking a shot in the dark with his request. Knowing his pleading was futile but not woman enough to be straight with him, she knew that when Luther came to New York in June, if she were to go see him, it would not be with William. Despite her current disappointment with him, Derrick was still her boyfriend, her number one.

This would be a point reinforced during the next few weeks through another series of broken promises, postponements, canceled engagements and brief, rushed telephone conversations, all to William's great consternation. After promising to share his twenty-first birthday with him, Andrea had called and told him that she'd be out of town on that particular weekend.

William didn't have to guess with whom. Number two always loses to number one, he kept thinking, drowning his frustration in two bottles of Asti Spumante all by his lonesome during those days. He decided he'd tolerated enough of Andrea's inconsistencies.

Yet every time he neared this breaking point and wanted to give up his love for her, something magical transpired that enlivened his flagging spirits, renewed his hope. On the weekend before the concert, they arranged to meet at their usual Fourteenth Street place. They were supposed to meet at two-thirty, yet William arrived at two. To his astonishment he found Andrea waiting.

"I must be dreamin'," he muttered as he neared her. "I must be dreamin'."

"What was that?" she said after greeting him with a kiss.

"Nothing. I'm just shocked to see you here so early. Actually, I'm more than shocked. Flabbergasted. Bewildered. Stunned."

"Okay, okay, I see your point. So where do you want to go, sweetie?"

"Let's go to Central Park," he said as the uptown N train sped into the station right on cue.

Arriving at the park's entrance, William, noticing that the beautiful blue sky had darkened considerably, asked Andrea if she still wanted to enter the park in spite of the threat of rain.

"Let's go anyway, baby." Her insistence produced a radiant smile from William and for the next hour or so the twosome went frolicking through the park, sharing a giant ball of cotton candy while watching people bike ride and roller skate. After playing games of tag and hide-and-seek, they slowed as they approached the charming Bow Bridge in the heart of the park.

"This is nice," Andrea said, appraising the surroundings. Turning left, she saw the skyline of the West Side of Manhattan overlooking Central Park West and its blossoming greenery. Straight ahead and to the right was a lake surrounded by the park's magnificence. Fresh spring scents filled the air and the trees, while not yet laden with the green foliage of summer, were budding. The natural splendor surrounding Andrea clearly compensated for the gray sky above.

William stood silently by and observed these sights, as well. Enjoying the tranquility and rapture of the moment, he wanted to share something else with her. Now, right now, I have to tell her I love her.

"Crumbcake, there's something I have to tell you."

"What is it, honey?" she asked attentively, unable to interpret the nervous look on his face.

"I think... I think I'm..." He was so afraid to say those three powerful words.

"What is it, baby?" In that precious moment William felt a raindrop. God had either decided that an hour of gray skies without precipitation was enough time for the two to admire His creation, or that it wasn't time for him to tell Andrea that he loved her.

"I think we'd better get going. I felt a drop of rain."

"Okay, but can we find a pretzel stand and get

something to snack on before we leave? I'm famished."

"Sure." As the heavens opened up a little more, the would-be lovers hurried through the park. Nearing its exit, they stopped at a hot dog stand.

"Let me have two," William told the merchant.

"No, get one. We'll share it."

"Okay. Let me have one."

A glow that could have cleared clouds away shone with William's smile as they shared a hot dog, and not because of the temporary easement of hunger. It was the thought of sharing the little things in life with the woman he loved that meant so much to him, the fact that Andrea wanted to share. *That's what love is all about. Sharing and caring. Perhaps she really does see what I see.*

✪✪✪

I knew by the end of that day she'd been feeling the love I was feeling by that point, thought William while boarding the Manhattan-bound Q train. Seated, his mind sifted through the chronology of events that had him convinced of that.

He remembered how, after leaving the park that afternoon, he'd spotted a stuffed teddy bear with a blue scarf and a red snow cap out of the corner of his eye in a drugstore window along Seventh Avenue. Politely asking Andrea to wait under a nearby building scaffold while, "I take care of something," she'd ended up waiting about ten minutes while the manager inside went deep into his storage inventory to find his last one. Surprising her with the gift, William recalled the warm smile on her face and how she'd hugged the stuffed animal upon receiving it.

He also recalled the shocked look on her face when he'd suddenly broken into a run in the steady downpour in search of an umbrella for the two of them while leaving her to stay dry in the Eighth Street station. Coming back to her soaked, but with umbrella in hand, she'd asked him, "Why did you do it?"

"I didn't want you to get wet out there. You could catch a chill."

That had been one reason. Never mind the fact that he could have gotten pneumonia. More prominent was the fact that he'd been in love. At that instant, he would have done anything for Andrea. He would have given her the shirt off his back, dived in front of a moving train, jumped off of the Empire State Building if she'd asked him to. *Sometimes love does these things to a man.*

He also remembered how after they'd had dinner and gone back to his place, they'd marched straight up to his room without much conversation, put in a red light, a tape into the deck, and embraced each other ferociously.

His manhood began to harden as he fondly recalled how her parted lips had moved insistently across his. Their kisses had been fierce and urgent as they'd remained secluded in that romantic haven for the next two hours. His warm breath had sent shivers through her as his tongue burned a trail down her spine, and she'd groaned from the feelings he'd induced. Plunging his vibrating tongue into her succulent, swishy-sweet center, sending heated ripples through her body as he sampled her treasure, he smiled when recalling how wonderful it had been to taste the overflowing juices from her well of desire.

Damn, William. I like that, sweetheart, she'd moaned.

He could still hear those words as if she'd uttered them just yesterday. Hearing the sweet timbre of her voice change as the throes of passion overtook her had only increased his arousal, as his clever fingers explored her slippery wetness while his tongue licked and flicked with hunger. Taking her clitoris between his lips, he flattened his oral instrument and fluttered it until he felt her little rosebud jump.

Ooh, baby... Yes, she'd cried as she gripped the blue sheets on his bed.

Remembering how he clamped his arms around

her soft thighs as he swirled his oral snake inside of her with all the love he could muster, the gratifying feeling of her firmness wriggling, thrashing, then trembling in complete satisfaction as she bucked against his mouth was indescribably unforgettable.

My God, I loved pleasing that woman. Still tasting the orgasm that left her years ago on his tongue, the rigidity in his pants began to wane as he thought, *all that five days before Luther.*

When he arrived at the Garden, William was disappointed to find that the remaining tickets available for the matinee game had been sold out. Instead of turning around and heading home though, he went up the street to a local bar for a couple of beers. After his first glass, his mind wandered away from Tim Duncan, Tony Parker, Keith Van Horn, Allan Houston and the Knicks-Spurs contest shown on the pub's television. His thoughts turned, once again, to Andrea.

✪✪✪

"Damn, Andrea! Why can't you go to the show with me?"

"William, you already know why. Derrick got tickets for tomorrow night's show through his sister. So you know I have to go with him."

"Of all the nights to get tickets for. They add three additional shows because the tickets went so quick for that first show, and somehow he gets tickets on the same night that I do."

"Do you have someone else to go with?"

"I guess I'll have to find someone now."

"William, I'm really sorry about this."

"What are you sorry about? You didn't promise me anything. I guess I was hoping for a miracle. Listen, you have a nice time, okay? I'll talk to you next week."

"Enjoy the show."

"Yeah, you, too," he murmured in disappointment. As William hung up the phone that Thursday night, he buried his head in his hands, uselessly attempting to stop the pounding headache brought on by her bad news. Sounding brave while talking to Andrea, the thought and eventual reality of her going to that concert with Derrick hit him like a ton of bricks. She would be attending the concert with him on the same night as he would be there alone, if he couldn't find a last-minute substitute to go with him.

Desperate, he searched for a replacement, first calling his aunt who couldn't get off from her night shift as a nurse at Coney Island Hospital, then his ex-girlfriend, Tami, hoping she might be free. She got a good laugh over the prospect that William could be dateless since she, too, would be there...with a new man. Finally, he came across Monique Rivers, his high school prom date.

While dialing her number, he reminisced about the crush he'd had on her during high school. Enchanted by her spice-colored skin, sculpted eyebrows and light-brown bedroom eyes, he tried in his own clumsy way to be appealing, cool, exciting, fresh; things he saw in boys she'd dated through those years; traits he'd never possessed.

When she was finally available during the latter portion of their senior year, she'd mentioned the senior prom to him and he'd leapt at the idea of escorting her there. In an effort to win her heart, he'd begged his grandmother and older brother for money four days before the prom and watched them generously withdraw funds from their respective accounts to take care of everything. He also recalled the anguish he'd felt when she burst his bubble on prom night by telling him that they could only be friends, with no further explanation.

He was about to hang up when... "Hello?" the soft voice answered.

"Hello, Monique."

"William?" She sounded surprised. "Oh my goodness! How are you? I haven't heard from you since last year. What have you been up to?"

"Nothing really. How's your family doing?"

"Grandma's fine." (Monique stayed with her grandparents.) "She asks about you from time to time. My grandfather wants to know why you stopped visiting us."

"I don't live on Staten Island anymore. I never told you?"

"No, you never did. Where are you now?"

"Brooklyn. I have a room upstairs over my grandmother's house. The commute's easier for me."

"Are you still in school?"

"Yeah, I am. My grades are slipping a little bit though."

"You'll be fine. My grandmother thinks you're very bright. 'Articulate' and 'polite' are the words she uses to describe you."

"Tell her I said thanks. Monique, I need to ask..."

"You know, Cheryl and I were talking about the prom just the other day. She and my other girlfriends thought you were the perfect prom date. They just knew we would come back as boyfriend and girlfriend."

"I thought we might, too," William admitted. "I guess it wasn't meant to be."

"But you know how most girls in high school think. If you're not the coolest guy in school or on the football team, then they don't want to have anything to do with you."

"I was kind of popular," William countered. "I was in the chorus. And I got lead parts in school plays."

"But it wasn't like being on the football team. I was always a sucker for an athletic type of man."

"I was athletic."

"But you weren't on any school teams. Also, you were kind of nerdy and my friends thought you were too white for me. We used to laugh at you."

Tell me something I don't already know, William mused as he heard her chuckle, before continuing. "I mean, you never wore any of the name-brand clothing everyone else wore. For crying out loud, you had Michael Jackson on your name-belt. We thought you were weird."

She's got me there.

"Plus William, you weren't one of those fine guys we were chasing after."

Just as William thought, this call wasn't a good idea. She continued.

"But looking back on some of the things you used to do, I found your gestures flattering. I mean, how many girls in high school had boxes of chocolates left on their desk in classes before they arrived? William, that was so sweet. How did you get the money to always do that?"

"My older brother gave me a ten-dollar allowance every week from his job at the hospital."

"I used to think those things were silly. But now that

I'm a little older, I realize a lot of these knuckleheads out here can learn from you. Don't ever change, William." Upon hearing Monique utter that statement, he just knew she would come through. All he had to do was ask.

"Monique, do you like Luther Vandross?"

"Who doesn't? You know he's at the..."

William interrupted her thought, saying, "I have an extra fourth-row ticket to tomorrow's show. Do you want to go?"

"I'm already going. My fiancé is taking me to Sunday night's show." The fiancé part startled him.

"I'm sorry. I didn't know you were seeing anyone. At least, you hadn't mentioned it the last time we spoke. Who's the lucky guy?"

"His name's Rodney. I've known him for a long time. He's been around the family for years. We got engaged in January. I'm getting married in August."

"Congratulations," William mumbled, shocked by the news. But what Monique said next supplied the coup de grace.

"I'm so happy to have found him. He's such a sweetheart. He's tender, strong and compassionate. He's just like you. I mean he's just like you."

There was a pregnant pause on William's end; not pertaining to the fact Monique was engaged. It's the fact that she was to marry someone just like him when, if she'd paid attention years earlier, she could have been with him. Finally, the politically correct thing to say came to mind.

"Monique, I have to admit, I was caught off guard by your announcement, but I'm happy to hear that you have found happiness. You deserve it and I hope you and Rodney receive only the best in your life together."

"What a sweet thing to say," Monique responded in a voice that sounded more condescending than genuine. "So, are you hooked up with anyone yet?"

"I don't have a girlfriend, Monique."

"So, why the extra ticket to the concert?"

"I thought I had a date, but the person backed out at the last minute."

"That's life," Monique said. "I'm sure you'll find someone."

"Yeah, I hope so. Listen, I gotta run."

"Thanks for calling."

"Not a problem," William said graciously. "You take care, okay?"

"Bye."

After hanging up, William went to the nearest convenience store and picked up a 40-ounce bottle of beer, his way of coping with two disheartening developments. First, he would have to sit among eighteen-thousand snuggling romantics in a packed arena while the woman he loved would be in the arms of another man. That was agonizing enough. But the fact that he'd called another woman he'd once been fond of to find that he had won the battle, yet lost the war left him inconsolable that evening. While he'd been putting positive traits on display for Monique years prior to her engagement, she hadn't appreciated them, although she had made a mental note of them. When it came time to find a permanent suitor, a person to share her life with, she'd found someone just like him.

✪✪✪

Monique was in Utah now. *Her husband had gotten an offer from a brokerage house out there that he couldn't refuse, so… Man, that was some phone call.* A somber feeling engulfed William as he reflected on that low moment, then, on the events that followed. He remembered the embarrassment he'd felt for being the three that made a crowd when he'd hooked up with Steve and his girlfriend with no date of his own, and how the sight of couples holding hands and walking arm-in-arm had only added insult to his injury. He endured the miserable experience of sitting next to the only empty red chair in the Garden while Luther serenaded the capacity crowd with love ballads for two hours, and also recalled how he thought of Andrea when Luther sang "If Only for One Night." Oh, how he'd wished he could've been in Derrick's shoes for just one night.

That had been a bad stretch, William concluded while slowly drinking his beer. He also recalled how he'd continuously asked himself, "Does love get any worse than this?" numerous times throughout that lonely subway home. He received the answer to that query all too soon.

Chapter Eight

CONFUSED LIVING

Only one message was on William's answering machine when he arrived home late that Sunday afternoon. Assuming it was Lisa with the happy recap from her lunch date, he pressed the retrieval button.

"Message received at 1:30 p.m. today. This message is for William McCall. This is Jerry Lovette, Della's friend. I wanted to have a word with you. I've been rappin' with her and the recent developments between you two have her very upset, so despondent that I asked for your number so I can pick your brain a little. She's my friend and it really bothers me to see her in this state. Anyway, give me a call at 718-555-6822."

I can't believe this woman. Why in the world would she give this asshole my phone number? What do I have to talk to him about?

There was no way he would call someone who used to have relations with the woman he was seeing.

About an hour later, however, his stance mellowed. *It might be good to talk to another man about what's going on*, he surmised while dialing the guy's number.

"Hello," the husky baritone voice answered.

"Is this Jerry Lovette?"

"Who's this?"

"This is William."

"William! I didn't think you'd respond to my phone call."

"I wasn't going to," William shot back. "I don't know what you're trying to accomplish by playing mediator."

"Chill, brother, I'm just helping a friend out. We've been talking ever since Friday."

"Were you in her company early that morning?" When he got no response from Jerry, William became annoyed. "That's what I thought. I don't know why I even bothered calling. You two idiots deserve each..."

"First off, I'm no idiot," Jerry answered indignantly. "And secondly, the fact that I took the time to call you should tell you how bad this woman is hurting right now."

William was on the defensive. "Thursday night was a mistake. We were talking about Barbara during the course of the evening and it slipped."

"I'm not referring to that, man."

"Oh," William said, curious to know his meaning.

"Della really loved you. Couldn't you see that?"

"How could I see that with people like you always

calling her house and hanging up? How would you feel if someone you were seeing was constantly barraged with phone calls from someone she used to fuck? Wouldn't that give you pause? And what about those guys she's always telling me who want to get with her? Jerry, don't feed me this shit!"

"She kept them all at bay, William, me included," Jerry confessed. "She used to rap with me about how these guys continually asked her out when you weren't with her. And she even admitted to me how tempted she was on occasion. But she wouldn't do it. You wanna know why? She wanted you to say some of the things they were saying to her. She wanted you to do some of the things they were offering to do for her. Life it about choices, William, and she chose you, man."

"So why didn't she ever tell me these things?" William sighed. "That's the problem with people in relationships these days. Instead of confronting their mate and addressing a problem so it can be solved, they take it outside and tell their friends who can't do shit about anything." He heard a sigh from the other end. "Jerry, how old are you?"

"Forty-three."

"I'm thirty-four."

"I've been where you are, brother: Young and confused. Della's the type of woman that needs someone to put her on a pedestal, someone that will be all about Della, someone that she can build something with. She was hoping you were the one that would fit the bill, and from what I hear you had a lot going for you. But you lacked direction. Brother, with a woman like Della inspiring you, that would've come in time."

William detected a subtle change in how Jerry spoke of him and Della as he rambled on. *What does he mean had a lot going for me? He's speaking in the past tense. This asshole's talking like she doesn't want me anymore,* he thought, restraining the anger now building inside while he listened more attentively. "William, all Della wants from a man is..."

"I know. I know. Love and respect."

"And a commitment, William. Commitment. Are you willing to give her those things?"

William paused. "I don't know, Jerry."

"Do you love her, man?"

"I don't know."

"If you don't, don't be ashamed to say so. There's nothing wrong with that. You met a sister, had a nice time, but weren't ready for the commitment part. Don't beat yourself up over it." Jerry seemed anxious, as if awaiting this concession from him. Instead, he became the recipient of William's controlled ire.

"Jerry, let me ask you something. You were seeing her at one time. Why didn't it work?"

"Well... I, um... You see..." Now it was Jerry's

turn under the bright lights. Slowly, this conversation began to resemble a chess game. Initially, Jerry's scrutiny had William on the defensive. William castled to protect his king, in this instance, his vulnerability with regard to his feelings for Della. And with one question, he'd put Jerry in check. Now it was his turn to retreat. After an extended pause, Jerry finally responded. "When we were seeing each other, I was just like you, tryin' to be a mack. And I made..."

"Take caution in what you say from this point forward, Jerry," William replied, perilously close to his boiling point.

"Let me finish..."

"No, I don't want you to finish! You don't know me well enough to be calling me a mack! You don't know anything about me, much less the roads I've traveled to be steppin' to me with this playa-hatin' shit. I cared for Della. I still do."

"You're not the only person who does."

William wasn't trying to hear him.

"Who gives a fuck about your damn feelings? If she loved me as much as you're telling me she did, you should've had the decency to stop calling her house so goddamn much!"

"Who in the hell are you talking to like that? When you and she had problems, she would call me and I went out of my way to never say anything bad or disrespectful about you. I always told her to try to force her way more into your life, the parts your dumb ass wouldn't let her into. She felt like you were hiding a whole other life from her. But I wouldn't expect you to understand any of that."

"What do you want, a medal for being her PR guy?"

"No, I don't. Della deserves a man, not a boy. She loved you, man, and you blew it."

"Don't tell me what I blew, you fuckin' jerk!"

By this point, both men had finished attacking one another and had reached a stalemate. Jerry, in stating what he felt was the truth to William, had clearly gotten under his skin. And William, in an attempt to get Jerry to admit his interference, had uncovered his feelings for Della. An unnerving uneasiness brought a silence that lasted for what seemed like minutes. Is he reloading, William wondered. Instead of firing more ammunition himself, William broke the tension by extending an olive branch.

"Look, man, we're getting nowhere with this male pissing contest. We sound like two spoiled brats fighting over a toy."

"Della's no toy, William," Jerry quickly noted.

"I know that. It was just an analo..." William sighed. "Look, Jerry. Why don't you and I meet over drinks tomorrow night so we can air our differences like men?"

"I agree."

Hallelujah! We're finally on the same page, William thought as Jerry continued.

"Where do you want to meet?"

"Where do you work at?"

"I'm at a marketing firm at 1633 Broadway, on the corner of Fiftieth Street. The Paramount Business Building. I get off at six. Do you work in midtown?"

"I'm right down the street from you at Broadway and Forty-Seventh."

"Oh, I see. What type of work do you do?"

"I'm a toilet cleaner," William sarcastically stated. "Jerry, does it matter?"

"I was just curious. Della needs to be in good hands, you know what I'm saying?"

Once again, William bit his tongue, opting not to say what had first come into his mind. "I work at a law firm."

"In the mailroom?"

"What if I did? What the fuck difference should it make to you?"

"Della needs to be..."

William again lost his patience.

"Look, are we going to do this or not?"

Jerry sighed. "Okay. Meet me in my lobby at six. What do you look like?"

"I'm about five-eleven, slim, bald and brown-skinned. I'll be wearing a black leather coat and carrying a black Coach briefcase."

"Sounds good. Listen, William, I apologize if I messed up your evening," Jerry said, feebly attempting to sound sincere.

"Don't apologize, pal. You're the one buying tomorrow. I'll see you then."

"Yeah. Bye." Hanging up, then going into the kitchen to nuke Saturday night's leftovers, William did a poor impersonation of Jerry. *"Della needs to be in good hands." Why are men so damn competitive? Everything's gotta be a dick measuring contest.*

Finished with dinner, William grabbed a bottle of Chardonnay and headed toward his living room. Turning the stereo on, he went deep into his CD collection and pulled out Phyllis Hyman's *Prime of My Life* disc. Inserting it into his system, he went to selection number eight and pressed the REPEAT button on the stereo. The song was "Living in Confusion." Not knowing why, the ballad was his favorite song ever recorded by that beautiful, tragic artist.

Listening to Phyllis belt out the lyrics to her song and remembering the many nights he'd seen her at Sweetwaters, the Blue Note and other jazz clubs throughout the city, William felt the late singer's agony over her search for better times. Visualizing the stunning beauty she'd possessed, not to mention the emotional intensity that came from a voice that sensuously blended power and delicacy, she'd been a gift from God. *These scantily clad, tone-deaf heifers the media focused on nowadays can't sing for shit. All they do is look pretty, shake their asses and get in trouble. And they call themselves divas. Please.*

The last minute and a half of the song had always sent chills through his slender frame, for Phyllis' heart-rending vocal improvisations were an unrecognized scream for help. *All she'd ever wanted professionally and emotionally was to be loved and appreciated. Somehow she'd known that would never happen,* William inferred sadly. *I guess that's why she left it all behind.*

Understanding that her trials and tribulations had led to self-destruction, he knew firsthand what it was to be "always goin' through changes" as Phyllis so eloquently, yet tragically put it. Knowing what it was like to be "living in confusion," he understood how it felt to desperately seek approval from others because of insecurities and low self-esteem, only to find, by some cruel twist, he was never good enough. Knowing what it was like to have a love life in utter turmoil, William could relate to Sister Hyman's pain regarding matters of the heart as he sat on his leather sofa that Sunday evening.

✪✪✪

What could be worse than the humiliation of sitting

alone at the Luther concert? He knew he had to get past that, but how?

Thinking about it now, there was only one thing on his mind as far as Andrea was concerned. *I have to leave her alone.*

Tired of hearing her excuses, he'd also grown weary of constantly having his feelings hurt by this woman who claimed to care so much for him. Fed up with being the number two man in Andrea's life, he had an even bigger problem, however; he couldn't bring himself to tell her about his disenchantment. How could he tell her that he didn't want to have anything else to do with her when he walked and talked and breathed her? Despite all the pain she'd caused him, he couldn't bear the thought of not having her in his life.

Do I want to be alone again? With a sigh he thought, *but I'm already alone, aren't I?* In spite of the fact that she had brought so much heartache into his life, she was the best thing to ever happen to him. *Girls had never seemed to be interested in me. It made me wonder if something was wrong with me*, he mused. In Andrea's company, however, he'd felt sensational; she made him feel so special that complications instantly vanished with one heated gaze from her, his world splashing into a warm sea of contentment.

William's first attempt at extricating himself from

his self-deprecating relationship with her would be at their favorite barbecue joint two weeks after the Luther concert. While they were seated, William informed her of his decision. Andrea didn't take the news very well. Shooting sad looks at him throughout the meal, she told him repeatedly how she would miss his smile, his charm, his sensitivity and his sensuality.

His heart skipped beats with her admission, causing William's knees to tremble. Maybe I'll give it another shot. No one had ever paid attention to his smile before, or at least told him so, and no one had ever complimented him on his charm or, for that matter, his sensitivity. *Shit, Tami thought I was a faggot because of that*, he thought. And no one had dared mention his sex appeal, for everyone else had thought of him as prudish. Hearing all of this from Andrea had done wonders for his confidence.

It also caused him to stop thinking logically. I can't stop seeing her, not if she sees me in this light. Who else would? By evening's end, William had put his gut feelings on hold. The night ended predictably, with the two sharing passionate kisses at her train station and Andrea asking him to call her tomorrow.

As per her request, he did call her that next day and with that phone call came more pain. Wanting her to accompany him to Staten Island that weekend to meet Steve, who hadn't yet traveled back to

Delaware, she supposedly came down with a cold a couple of hours before.

"Okay, maybe dinner next weekend," William suggested.

She couldn't. She had plans with Derrick.

Frustration with Andrea ultimately boiled over on a steamy Thursday afternoon in July. She was going to Myrtle Beach for the weekend and William had put in for a day off to spend some time shopping with her before the trip.

The day had started well, as they shared familiar ardent moments, exchanging smooches and acting like two lovebirds. Then, at the Macy's Herald Square store, the romantic tenor changed dramatically while she was trying on bathing suits.

"Does this look good on me, honey?" Andrea asked, slightly opening the door to her small changing booth.

Seeing how she filled out the red and blue bathing garment, William blushed. "Andrea, you look fantastic. Gosh, I'm going to miss you. I wish I was going with you to Myrtle Beach."

"There'll be a time for that," she assured.

"Really?"

"I hope so. I really get tired of doing things with Der..." She stopped herself, but not before she'd said a mouthful too much.

And William picked up on it.

"You're going away with him again, aren't you?"

Receiving no answer from Andrea before she quickly shut the changing room door, he knew the answer. For the rest of their time spent in Macy's and the other stores they visited, William indicated this to her through his silence.

Andrea just kept on shopping, as if nothing had happened.

Then the couple met up with her friend, Vikki, at Washington Square Park. Vikki felt the chill instantly.

"Damn, y'all have an argument or something?"

"Nah," Andrea insisted. "William's feeling unappreciated, that's all."

"Got that right," William echoed.

Taking a quick trip through the Square, the trio took a seat in the center of the park to enjoy the comedy of CP Lacey. About twenty minutes into his routine, Andrea spotted Taimak, the handsome karate star from the movie *The Last Dragon*. Sitting directly across from the trio, she excitedly acknowledged his presence.

"Vikki, look! There's the guy from..."

"That karate picture, right?"

"Yeah, girl. That boy should thank his mamma every day for making him so fine," Andrea said.

"Perhaps you can take him to Myrtle Beach, Andrea," William sarcastically snapped.

"Ouch," Vikki quipped, excusing herself to get a hot dog.

Andrea flashed an angry glare at him. "How dare you embarrass me in front of Vikki? What in the hell is wrong with you?"

"Your going away with Derrick again is the fuckin' problem."

Andrea paused before responding. "The trip was planned before I met you. I wish I could get out of it."

The look on William's face was one of disbelief. "Yeah, right. I bet when you were in the store trying on your outfits, you were thinking of him."

"I was," she admitted.

"But you're with me right now!"

"When I'm with him I think of you, and vice versa. You wouldn't understand."

"You're damn right! Why am I even sitting here wasting your time and mine?" Moving to get up, Andrea grabbed his arm to stop him. "You do everything with Derrick," William stated. "What am I here for, window dressing?

"William, please don't leave," Andrea pleaded.

At that instant, Vikki returned. "What's going on here? Are you guys fussin' again?"

Andrea tried to downplay the spat. "William's feeling unappreciated again."

He started to say something, but changed his mind.

Too furious to elaborate on the intensity of the spat, William rose and walked away, muttering, "I gotta step for a few."

"And where do you think you're going?" Andrea called out. She heard no answer. "William! William!" Still no response. He continued walking toward the western exit of the park.

"Aren't you going to kiss Andrea bye?" Vikki yelled. "Are you coming back?"

William stopped.

"Let her get someone else to kiss her bye! She's good at that!" he yelled back, causing people in the park to shoot perplexed looks at Andrea as he continued his stroll.

About twenty minutes later, he returned to the park and found the two women still seated at the circle where he'd left them. The comedy routine was over and the two were engaged in conversation with a tall, light-skinned gentleman who seemed to be interested in one of them. Instead of exhibiting jealousy, William strolled over to the trio.

"Yummy, yummy, girl," he said, taking Andrea's hand, kissing it.

Andrea and Vikki giggled.

"You're not a well person," Andrea said.

"Shit, you contributed to this madness."

Vikki butted in, saying "Reggie and I are going

over to Panchito's for a drink." William extended his hand to Reggie. "Are y'all coming?" Vikki asked.

Andrea and William gave each other a look that indicated they had issues to resolve.

Andrea answered for them. "We'll meet you guys over there."

"All right. Don't be too long," Vikki said as she and Reggie rose from the bench.

"We won't," William replied.

As Vikki and her acquaintance headed toward the west exit of the park, William took Andrea's hand once more. "Baby, we have to talk."

"I know."

When she got up, the two walked toward the park's arch. Along the way, William began to break it down as he stared into her pupils seeking truth.

"Andrea, to know that you're going away with Derrick again is tearing me up. I don't know how much more of this I can take."

Andrea cast her eyes downward. "I understand, William."

The duo stopped as they reached the arch above the park's exit.

"No, Andrea, you don't understand. Baby, I'm in love with you. I love you so much, Crumbcake, that it's driving me crazy. My every thought is of you, holding you, protecting you, loving you and making you happy. I've never had this feeling before. I realize that the timing for this is inappropriate, with you going away with Derrick and all, but I can't hold this in any longer."

Andrea's face remained unchanged during his outpouring. Somehow, she'd been expecting this. Having not heard such candor from him in the weeks leading up to this humid evening had given her ample preparation time. Her energy repressed for the moment, she was unwilling to reveal how happy she was to hear him finally say these words to her. She couldn't disclose the warm smile that appeared when talking to her mother or anyone else who would listen, about how special William made her feel. Her relationship with Derrick was barely making it through its terrible twos. All we do is argue and have sex, she thought.

At first, her tryst with William had been a pleasant escape. However, the more she'd submersed herself in this comfort zone, the more the definition of their companionship became blurred. Not only was he more than she'd ever dreamed a man could be, but the thought of their tongues mingling made her body tingle. Unable to remove her thumb from the emotional leak in her dike, she couldn't confess to him how feeling his heartbeat as he drew her close made her want to sing; that his touch turned her to liquid satin. She didn't want her feelings to burst forth with the truth; that her heart was terribly confused. Stepping over the line drawn at the edge of a cliff—that of control and reason—she'd teetered and fallen and was now hanging on by a fingernail. That fingernail screamed Derrick's name whenever she thought too much about the prince before her. That fingernail was her reality, although the "fictional hero" in front of her looked awfully good. That reality kept the truth from escaping her lips, and all she could muster was, "I don't know what to say."

"Andrea, I'm not expecting you to say or do anything. I just wanted you to know why I reacted the way I did earlier. I just hope you don't hate me for saying all of this."

"I don't, William. You're a very special person. Don't ever change."

William turned his face away upon hearing those loaded words.

"You want to go meet Vikki?" she then asked.

"Yeah. Let's do this."

Off they headed west, their destination being a little Mexican hole in the wall in the heart of Greenwich Village. Entering Panchito's, both were stunned to see Vikki alone in a dark, secluded booth sipping an Amstel Light. As they approached her, they could see the annoyance on her face.

"Where's Reggie?" Andrea inquired.

"You know, that guy forgot to go to the bank." William shook his head as Vikki continued. "He wanted me to buy drinks for both of us. Ain't that some shit?"

"I don't see anything wrong with that," William said.

Andrea and Vikki both looked at each other and laughed. "I just met the brother, William," Vikki retorted.

"So what? If he promised to go to the bank afterward, then what's the big deal?"

"You are so naïve, William," Andrea announced. "Do you know how that looks to us? Like this brother was trying to get over. Vikki, how long has he been gone?"

"Fifteen minutes," Vikki said as she looked at her watch.

"He's not coming back," Andrea stated.

Deep down, William hoped the brother would prove them wrong. *If he doesn't, then I'm done for.* His intuition telling him what the topic of discussion would be if Reggie didn't come back, William sat silently drinking his Corona, hoping against hope as the two young women continued talking.

Fifteen more minutes passed, and there was no sign of him.

Andrea tapped him on the arm. "See, I told you. Men are so predictable, aren't they?"

"Guys make hollow promises all the time," Vikki added.

"Maybe he was embarrassed," William answered. Sighing, he continued. "Look, ladies, everyone's not like Reggie."

"You could have fooled me," Vikki said.

"Where are all the good brothers?" Andrea asked.

"Yeah, where are they?" Vikki repeated.

Initially, the topic of men hadn't fazed William, but as the two continued with their collective opinions, his irritation with Andrea stewed once more. Understanding how Vikki felt at the moment—her angry state being justified by Reggie's actions—William continued to listen to Andrea bitch and moan and wondered if he really meant anything to her at all. *This woman's using two men, and she's got the nerve to be bitching about brothers.*

The conversation shifted to the Myrtle Beach trip and Vikki expressed excitement about leaving New York for a few days.

"Yeah, I'm kind of looking forward to it myself," Andrea added.

"Vikki, who are you traveling with?" William asked.

"No one. Maybe I'll get lucky and meet a Southern honey."

"I hope so. Derrick already thinks you'll be hanging around us the whole time we're there, like a sixth toe," Andrea indicated.

Hearing Derrick's name once more, William's face appeared forlorn.

Vikki noticed the look and asked a pointed question. "William, how do you feel about Andrea going away this weekend?"

He took the bait.

"I think the fact that Andrea is talking about the trip she's going on with Derrick in front of me is very selfish. I also think..."

Andrea angrily interrupted. "Listen, you knew when we started seeing each other that I had a boyfriend, so I don't want to hear this shit!"

"If you appreciated me, I wouldn't be hearing this shit! And if I would have known how self-centered you can be at times, I wouldn't be dealing with you, period!"

"Well, there's nothing holding you here!" Andrea fired back.

Vikki, trying to play peacemaker, said, "Come on, you guys. Calm down. There's no need to create a scene."

It was too late; William had already lost it. "Did anyone in this fuckin' place ask for a third person's opinion?" he snapped at her.

"Don't talk to my friend like that!" Andrea insisted.

"Fuck you, Andrea!"

"Fuck you, too!"

By now, people at the adjacent tables had heard the

shouting. The waiter was about to intervene when the two squabblers realized the venue was inappropriate. Just as quickly as it had been ignited, their anger subsided. There was a silent pause between the trio.

Finally, Vikki broke the ice. "Well, at least I found out that you guys aren't lovey-dovey all the time."

Andrea and William both smiled gingerly.

"Hey, Vikki, my fault. I shouldn't have told you to mind your business. I'm sorry," William said.

"That's okay. Listen, you two have some things to talk about. I'll be in the ladies room." Vikki got up, leaving them alone.

"Andrea, what's happening to us?"

"I don't know, William. I don't know."

"We never used to argue."

"I know." After another awkward silence, William continued the dialogue. "Where do we go from here?"

"Well," Andrea said, "I think it's time to do what needs to be done."

Giving a brave smile, she reached over the table and initiated a passionate kiss.

She's going to give herself to me, he decided. "Andrea, are you sure that you want to do this?"

He misread the signal big time.

"Yes. It's time. I'm tired of hurting you. William, I don't think we should see each other anymore."

William's face, seconds earlier brightened by Andrea's

kiss, instantly became pallid. His heart now heavy and his insides churning with excruciating pain, the special feeling that only Andrea could give him was torn away.

But wasn't this what he'd really wanted a few weeks ago? Hadn't he grown weary of the repeated disappointments that resulted from his relationship with Andrea? Hadn't she just given him the reprieve he'd been too afraid to ask for? Although in his mind he knew this was the best thing for him, his heart couldn't bear the reality of Andrea's decision. He tried to disguise his pain by sounding brave.

"Andrea, is this what you really want?"

"Yes."

There was another pause.

"Well, could we share one more date? I don't want our last time together to be remembered like this."

Andrea hesitated before responding.

"Sure."

At that instant, Vikki returned to the booth and asked if they were ready to leave.

William, still in a stupor from the conversation, nodded his head yes. Andrea wanted to stay a little while longer.

"Please stay," she implored.

"C'mon. Don't be a spoiled sport," Vikki said.

"Nah," William said, rising slowly. "I'd better be going. I gotta work tomorrow."

After reaching into his pocket and placing thirty dollars on the table for the bill, he gave Vikki a hug, kissed Andrea on the cheek, and headed for the exit.

"Call me later!" Andrea shouted.

William turned, gave her a halfhearted smile and headed home.

✪✪✪

She had me spinning around, William thought, reflecting on that somber moment as Phyllis echoed the words. Remembering his mangled emotions and comatose state on the L train home that evening, and how he'd stayed up all night listening to sad songs, William could only smirk at the irony. *Phyllis, the more things change, the more they stay the same.*

Chapter Nine
GOOD-BYE

Day Four

When William got to work that Monday morning, he had three messages on his voice mail.

The first was from Lisa. "Lunch was cool," she noted in her bulletin, "but his true intentions surfaced later when Augustus propositioned me."

"Damn, at least he could've waited until they had become acquainted," William muttered. "Well, she won't be using that phone number anymore."

The next message was from his supervisor, Michael Garvey, and had to do with motion papers he needed filed at Federal Court. Additionally, he wanted William to attend a luncheon while he was downtown, one of the requirements of his position as Assistant Managing Clerk. *He's been adding to my responsibilities lately*, he thought, referring to the fact that he was appointed to supervise the firm's court research systems six weeks prior to this request. *I wonder what's up.*

The last message was from Jerry. *Why did Della*

give him my work number? Jerry wanted to meet for drinks at six-thirty instead of at six. *I guess he really wants to talk.*

While going through the course routed for him: the court assignments and legal research, the mundane luncheon and follow-up evaluation with his boss, William's mind drifted between the matters at hand and the forthcoming encounter with Jerry. The more he thought about the impending meeting, the less sense it made to him. *What do we have to say to each other?* he wondered. He thought of backing out, but Jerry hadn't left a job number where William could reach him. Nice move. That way, I look like the asshole if I don't show.

Finally six o'clock arrived, and at that instant William cleared his desk and headed toward his showdown with Jerry. Knowing he would be early, William used the extra time to prepare himself for what lay ahead. Pensive during the four-block stroll, William thought of questions that needed answering. *Why are we meeting like this and what do we hope to accomplish by this? If you still care about Della, then why call me? What do you have to offerthat I don't, and what makes you think she's better off with you? You dated her once upon a time, fucked up, and now you want to play prodigal son? What makes you think she's gotten over me in four days, idiot? Are you trying to see if the coast is clear? By the way, you never explained all of those hang-ups.*

Relishing the moment, he likened himself to a young gunfighter, preparing for his *High Noon*. Reaching the front of 1633 Broadway, William's six-guns were loaded and ready. He'd have to wait twenty minutes before firing away though, because it was only ten after six. After killing five minutes in the lobby store buying Tic-Tacs, he decided to wait outside and savor the relatively mild January evening.

Popping a mint in his mouth, William looked across the street at the theater marquee where *Cats*, the longest-running Broadway musical in history was playing. Glancing to the right of the playhouse, he noticed a Japanese sushi bar and tourist store had replaced the entrance to what used to be Hawaii Kai, a Polynesian restaurant. *I wonder what happened to that place*, he thought.

Suddenly, without warning, his eyes began to water. He'd trained himself not to cry through the years. However, given his present emotional state, this time seemed harder than most to control his feelings. Having dined at the restaurant only once in his life, he could never bring himself to go back, no matter how many times he wanted to.

William retained an emotionally devastating memory of the only time he had eaten there. Often recalling that day, despite how he tried otherwise, the hurt felt the same each time. Even now, over a decade and a half later, *it's still so hard to say goodbye*, he thought.

✪✪✪

Predictably, William did not call Andrea that evening when he arrived home; in fact, he couldn't bring himself to call her for another two weeks. Struggling with the reality of not seeing her anymore, the fact that they agreed to see each other one last time compounded his misery. How do you say goodbye to a woman you're still in love with?

During those two weeks, the answers came. Serving papers one Tuesday morning, he passed by the Ambassador Theater on West Forty-Ninth Street. *Dreamgirls* was playing. Remembering how his mother had seen the musical four years prior and how she'd raved endlessly afterward, William returned to the playhouse that evening and purchased two tickets for the show a week from that Saturday.

A couple of days later while in White Plains doing research, he was walking through the local mall during his lunch hour and noticed a store called Forever Yours. Seeing the romantic accessories from the outside, he decided to check it out.

The store sold all sorts of things for the incurable

romantic. William passed racks upon racks of cards that said, "I Love You" and aisles of heart-shaped candies. They even sold edible underwear, which brought a smile to his face as he examined a pair. Also catching his eye was the erotic lingerie for women, items such as crotchless panties, red garter belts and fishnet pantyhose. Wincing with regret after envisioning Andrea in these garments, he thought, *the things I would've done to see her in those.*

Walking to the back of the store he observed a man painting airbrush designs on T-shirts. He smiled, made a mental note to himself and vowed to return. On the MetroNorth train back to the city, William found the answer to the question that had plagued him. *You leave through the same door you entered.*

As painful as saying goodbye to Andrea would be, William was determined to show her how much he loved her one last time. If he wasn't going to see her after this day, he wanted to make the night unforgettable, for he knew no other way.

As the days swiftly passed and as that fateful Saturday drew near, William became increasingly depressed. His mind was constantly on Andrea; the fact that he had to relinquish his love tore him up. He would come home from work, screw in a blue light, turn off his phone and listen to sad music. Unable to dredge up the energy to clean his room, clothes were strewn all over the place. Every couple of days his grandmother would come upstairs and order him to tidy up, but he just didn't have the will. He had no motivation since love was leaving his life, and the funk that came with this eventuality was all-consuming.

On Thursday, he summoned enough strength to call Andrea. She agreed to meet him one last time at her train station and after telling her about the *Dreamgirls* tickets, she mentioned that she'd already seen the play but would be happy to see it again. He asked her to dress her best.

"I will," was her response before she asked, "William, are you sure you want to see me again?"

He immediately went on the defensive.

"I guess the fact that we haven't spoken in almost two weeks gave you time to get me out of your system, huh?"

"No... I missed you. And I'm kind of scared that..."

Fuck! Why'd she have to say she missed me? Why now?

William's heart bled once more. "Does this really have to be the last time we see each other, Andrea?"

"Yes."

There was another pause as William tried to compose himself.

"The play starts at eight. Could you be at the train station at five? I'd like to get something to eat before the curtain rises."

"Sure. I'll see you then."

He wasn't ready for the call to end.

"Listen, I have to go upstate to pick up something that morning, so if I run a little late, be patient with me, okay?"

"Okay. Take care."

He continued his stall.

"Andrea, I just wanted you to know that I'll always love you and I'll never forget you."

Andrea sighed. "I know, William. I know." There was yet another pause. "Well... I guess I'll see you Saturday."

"Yeah. Saturday."

As he hung up the receiver, pain permeated his soul. *This isn't going to be easy.*

Unable to sleep that Thursday or Friday night, he was so pensive and uncharacteristically quiet at work that his coworkers thought he'd had a death in his family. Speaking barely above a whisper all day, the sadness for what he had to do robbed him of his jovial spirit and his usual vigor and vitality.

I've got to be strong, he repeatedly told himself. *Show Andrea the traits that made her care; the warmth, humor and compassion she's going to miss.* Trying to convince himself that she loved him, he decided, *that's why she's doing this.*

"Then why do I feel so bad about tomorrow?" he grumbled to Steve over the phone that night at home. "Why does it have to be this way?"

Listening to his buddy's lamentations for nearly three hours and trying to be a big brother although the two were the same age, Steve was direct, but consoling. "Sometimes if you really love someone, you set them free. Andrea's doing this for your own good. I'm sure she loves you, man," he rationalized.

Desperately wanting to believe this, the pain William felt prevented him from seeing anything positive about his situation.

"Sometimes you have to do the things you don't want to," Steve reiterated. "But there'll be other Andreas."

William couldn't believe this; the thought of ever loving anyone else the way he loved Andrea seemed incomprehensible, absurd.

The phone call ended with Steve's attempt at humor. "Punch that clock tomorrow, Black."

William laughed bravely. "Yeah, I wish I could. Maybe I wouldn't feel like shit about all of this."

"On a serious tip, you don't want to do that. It would only make matters worse. If you're as good as you say you are, she might get whipped."

"That's the idea." Again, the two laughed. "Hey, man, thanks for being there."

"Call me Sunday, after it's all over. Be strong, Black. There'll be others."

"I hope so, Black. I really hope so. Peace."

"Peace."

Talking to Steve had eased the misery for a bit but as he sat in his room that night and listened to his music, Andrea dominated his thoughts. Recalling the many times he'd held her soft hands, never wanting to let go; the memory of her titillating kisses sent chills up his spine. While thinking of how perfectly she filled his arms and how their lips, minds, and bodies perfectly intertwined during sensuous moments, a haunting memory of her favorite fragrance, Poison, tormented him. Her beautiful smile had lit even this dark moment, albeit briefly. "Damn," William groaned deep into the night. "Damn."

Awakening at seven o'clock Saturday morning, he was out of the house by eight as he wanted to be in Westchester County by ten so he would have plenty of time to emotionally prepare himself for the inevitable.

Riding the MetroNorth line upstate with his mind in a fog, he decided Andrea would receive an airbrushed T-shirt as a parting gift, although he didn't know yet what inscription it would bear. His first thought was of having "Crumbcake" written in black and layered on a red heart. Too simple, he concluded. Wanting to say goodbye, he next considered a broken heart with his name on it. "Too dramatic," he muttered to the empty seat beside him. Having to bid adieu to his sweetheart was awful enough this day, but he leaned more toward describing the beauty of their brief relationship.

Entering the mall, a light bulb went on in his head. "A Hawaiian sunset," he told the artist while handing him a long white T-shirt. "Put two people holding hands, walking into the sunset, with palm trees to the left of them. Up in the right corner put 'To My Crumbcake. Always and Forever.'"

"In script?" the designer had asked.

"Yes."

"Are you sure you want me to do this shirt? It may take a while. About two hours."

William looked at a clock overhead. It was ten-thirty. Calculating the time quickly, he answered, "Yes," and left the store.

Time passed slowly as he skimmed through a couple of sports books purchased from the Barnes & Noble bookstore on the level below. When the time came for him to pick up his shirt, he noticed a crowd in front of Forever Yours admiring a T-shirt that was hanging in the window. The background of the design was a deep shade of yellow and overlaid with a beautiful sunset. The silhouettes of a man and woman walking hand in hand along a brown, sandy beach with palm trees in the distance completed the stunning airbrushed motif. Near the right shoulder of the shirt, was the inscription: *To My Crumbcake... Always and Forever.*

"The best shirt I ever did," the artist said.

William didn't say much as he gave him an additional five dollars with the fee. Leaving the mall and venturing back into the stifling July heat, he shook his head at the irony. *Even as she leaves my life, she gets the very best of me.*

Arriving home, he found his grandmother waiting in his room. She was quite perturbed. "Boy, don't you ever let this room get sloppy like that again!"

The clothes that had accumulated during the course of two weeks were folded in neat piles. His bed had been made, the furniture polished and the windows opened to give the room some fresh air.

William lowered his head in shame. "I'm sorry, Grandma."

"What the hell is wrong with you? Is it that girl again? Are you still courtin' her behind that dude's back?"

Biting on his bottom lip in an attempt to maintain his composure, he told her, "Today's the last day I'll be seein' her." A single tear trickled down his cheek as he looked at his grandmother.

His sadness struck a chord with Edith Hall, and instead of facing an "I told you so" stare, William received her sympathy. "You'll be fine, son," she said, rising from the bed and kissing his forehead. "You'll be fine."

As she left the room, William noticed the time.

Twenty-five minutes to four. Gotta hurry. No time to be feeling sad.

He rushed downstairs for a quick shower, then hurried back to his room. Donning a suit he'd purchased for special events—a gray one with pale-pink pinstripes—he brought out the color of the muted lines with a pink shirt, a pale-pink paisley tie and a matching pocket square. After a splash of cologne, he was good to go.

When he came downstairs, he saw his grandmother by the front door. "You look nice, son." She noticed the T-shirt and grabbed it from his hand. After a gander, she gave him an approving smile. "You never stop giving, do you?"

"I might as well die with my boots on, Grandma," he replied, smiling halfheartedly. "I got that one from you."

"I know." She placed a fifty-dollar bill in his suit pocket. "I won't be here when you get back, so I figured you might need to eat tomorrow," she said, knowing that William wouldn't use it for food. "I'll be in Philly tomorrow."

"Thanks, Grandma." Giving her a quick kiss on her cheek, he told her, "I gotta run. I'm supposed to be meeting Andrea in an hour."

"Enjoy the show."

Stopping in his tracks, William glanced back, wondering how she knew about his plans.

"I saw the tickets while cleaning up," she explained.

"Thanks, Grandma." With that, the young Napoleon was off to face his Waterloo.

✪✪✪

William was a nervous wreck as the D train approached the Sheepshead Bay Road train station. For two weeks he had tried to think of an appropriate place to have a farewell dinner with Andrea, but he'd come up with nothing. And today, with his head spinning from fractured emotions, he was still without suitable dinner plans.

I don't even know what she's wearing, he pondered as the train entered the station.

You'll get through this, he told himself as he moseyed down the stairs leading to the waiting area. *Don't be mushy. Act cheerful.*

Turning to his left, he saw a woman talking on the telephone by the concession stand. Wearing a tight yet elegant white dress that revealed her well-proportioned figure and white high heels, her hair was done in long Shirley Temple curls. From the back she was a sight to behold. What an incredible sexy woman, he thought, although he still hadn't seen her face. Seconds later, however, William gulped as the woman turned in his direction.

God help me. It was Andrea.

As she approached, he noticed the redness of her eyes, as if she'd been crying. Maybe she, too, was finding it difficult to say good-bye.

"Had a rough night, huh?" William commented after a long hug.

She played it off well. "Allergies. So, Mr. McCall, are you ready to do this?"

"Not yet." He handed her the shirt.

After looking it over, Andrea bowed her head slightly. "This is beautiful." Raising her head slowly, he saw that her eyes were misty. "William, you're incredible."

To avoid further tension, she grabbed his hand and started toward the subway turnstile.

"Wait," William said. "You look extraordinary. I can't have you riding the train in that outfit. Do you wanna cab it to the city?"

Andrea shook her head. "No, we don't have to do that." She led him in the direction of the train station exit. "C'mon. Let's go."

"Where are we going?"

"You'll see."

Outside, Andrea hailed a cab and instantly one arrived.

How could they turn her away looking the way she does? William thought.

"Where are we going?" he asked again.

"You'll see."

The two sat silently as the cab motored into Andrea's neighborhood. She asked the driver to let them out at the corner of Bathchelder and Avenue W in the heart of Sheepshead Bay.

"There's an express bus that comes at this corner," Andrea said as they got out.

Turning left, she noticed a stocky, dark-skinned man coming toward them. "Do you wanna meet one of my brothers?" she suddenly asked.

"Sure."

"Hey, girl," the man said while kissing her on the cheek.

"Jarred, I'd like you to meet someone. This is..."

He cut her off while extending his hand. "William, right?"

"Yeah," he replied.

"Man, this girl doesn't stop talking about you. She should be with you full-time, not that sucker she's with."

"That's enough," Andrea interjected after a gentle elbow to his ribs.

"Hey, listen. It was a pleasure meeting you," William replied, shaking Jarred's hand again. "I wish I would have met you a whole lot sooner."

Jarred shot a strange glance Andrea's way before responding. "Why? What's up?"

"Well, it's just that..."

"Wouldn't you know it, the bus is here," Andrea interrupted.

The trio looked left and, sure enough, a white Command Express Bus was only seconds away.

"Hope to see you again," Jarred added as Andrea pulled William toward the bus stop.

"Yeah. I hope so," William responded, knowing their paths would not cross again.

The bus arrived and the couple found seats near the back of the bus. As it pulled off, William turned to Andrea. "Your brother's cool."

"Yeah, he's all right. He's heard a lot about you."

"You just can't keep your big mouth shut, can you?" he joked.

"I guess not."

"Well, at least I know I meant something to you."

William's comment reminded them of why they were meeting today, and an uneasy interval of silence ensued. For the better part of the bus ride, it remained like that. Instead of the usual jokes and laughter they normally shared, a thick undercurrent of sadness filled the air. The reality of the moment left the two visibly uptight, as evidenced by the nervous compliments that passed between them. Each of them made overt attempts at not hurting the other's feelings. Knowing any mistakes made today would be lasting, the silence was almost palpable.

Finally, as the bus began its run through Manhattan via Avenue of the Americas, William attempted to ease the tension. "Andrea, I'm going to miss you."

She gave him a look that told him she wanted to say so much to him, but all that came out was, "Ditto."

The bus turned right, onto Twenty-Third Street, and he asked a question about the musical they would see later. "How is it?"

"It's incredible. The music is outstanding. Jennifer Holliday sings her ass off!" She then smiled at him, knowing what his next question would be. "And yes, the choreography is fantastic."

Laughing, they finally began to act like they always did when they were together. One last time.

Minutes later, the bus reached Thirty-Fourth Street. William looked at his watch. Six-thirty. "Andrea, wherever we eat, it's going to have to be quick. The show starts in an hour and a half." Then as it occurred to him that he didn't make any dinner plans, he panicked. "Oh, damn."

"What's wrong, baby?"

"No dinner plans. I didn't make any reservations anywhere. All this running around today and I forgot to make dinner plans. I wanted everything to be so perfect today."

"Relax, William. I know a place right around the corner from the theater."

"Really? Nice bailout, Crumbcake."

Smiling and standing as the bus approached Fiftieth Street, Andrea rang the bell to get off. "This is our stop."

Seconds after disembarking, a yellow cab pulled up to them. The cab driver rolled down the passenger-side window. "West Side, right?"

"You got it," the couple said simultaneously, looking at each other and giggling.

As they entered the back seat, the cab driver, a forty-ish black man, explained his sudden stop. "You two look fantastic together. I just had to be the one to take you guys where you're going."

"Thank you," Andrea said.

"How long have you two been dating?"

William looked at Andrea. "Almost six months," he responded, taking her hand affectionately.

"Are you in love with her, man?" was the next question.

William hesitated slightly.

The cabby egged him on. "C'mon, man! What are you scared of?"

What are you scared of, William? Finally, he had the necessary boldness to face the issue. "Yes. I am." He held her hand tighter as he spoke with more conviction. "I love this woman more than I do myself. My sun rises and sets with thoughts of her."

Andrea looked flustered.

"How do you feel about him?" the cabby persisted.

William looked over at her; how do you feel, was etched all over his face.

She didn't respond.

"Bashful, huh?" the cabby said.

"Yes," Andrea said.

William turned his face away, obscuring the pain of her Houdini-like escape.

The cabdriver added one more thing before changing topics. "It's so refreshing to see two young black people in love. Hold on to that feeling, kids. By the way, where are you guys headed?"

"Fifty-First and Broadway," Andrea stated.

"What restaurant is over there?" William asked.

"You'll see."

So as the ride continued, William and the driver talked about sports while Andrea sat quietly.

Upon arriving at their destination, the driver introduced himself. "My name's Rich, guys."

"I'm William. She's Andrea." He paid the fare.

"Andrea," Rich said, "you've got a good brother here. Hold on to him."

"I know. You have a nice evening," she replied.

"Likewise."

As the cab sped away, William turned to Andrea. "So, where do we go now?"

"Follow me, honey."

Walking about fifty yards from where they exited the cab, they approached a restaurant that upon initial appearance, looked smaller than the black and white Hawaii Kai sign outside. However, once they entered, William was pleasantly surprised to see that what looked like a dive from the outside was actually a moderately sized place of beauty. They were greeted by an Asian hostess, who immediately draped them with leis.

"Andrea, the place is beautiful!" he exclaimed while surveying the establishment.

Conscious of the Samoan ambiance this place had from readings of Polynesian culture at NYU, William noticed the straw-like decorations and palm trees that were adjacent to the performance stage and was impressed. The waitresses breezed by candlelit tables wearing hula skirts, the busboys had on *Hawaii Five-O* floral shirts, and faintly audible in the background were the simulated sounds of Oahu shores. It was a truly exotic atmosphere.

"Are you two staying for the show?" the hostess asked.

"Nah, we have a play to catch," William said, looking at his watch. It was five after seven.

Once seated, he complimented Andrea on her choice of restaurants.

"I came here the last time I went to see *Dreamgirls*," she responded.

"You didn't go with..."

She wouldn't let him finish. "I came here with my mother, William," she admonished, then began her farewell address. "You see, this is why we can't see each other anymore. The fact that I'm with Derrick bugs the hell out of you and I'm tired of hurting you."

"I think you're scared."

"Scared of what?"

"Scared of allowing yourself to love me." William became bolder. "Let me ask you something. If you had to choose between Derrick and me, who would you choose?"

"Don't ask me that."

"I'm asking you! Derrick or me?"

Andrea hesitated slightly. "The only reason... I've been with... I'm not going to answer that. You have a better heart, that I can tell you."

"If I have the better heart, then why are you with him?"

"I've been with him almost three years," she said meekly.

"That's not answering my question," William insisted. "What type of work does he do?"

Andrea sighed. "He's the youngest executive at a bank."

It was William's turn to sigh. *I had to ask.* "That means he makes good money, right? Does he have a nice car?"

"Yes, he does. He has a white Cougar."

"So you're with him because of his financial resources, aren't you?"

"Of course not! You don't have a ride. And I'm seeing you, aren't I?"

"Not after tonight." A short lull followed William's bluntness. "How old is he?"

"Twenty-four. He's an only child. Spoiled as hell, too, used to getting his way. You and he are exact opposites. He's so self-absorbed, and you're so humble."

Hearing all of this only added to William's frustration, but he continued his inquiry. *Might as well find out every reason why she won't leave him.* "What does he look like?"

"He's about six-four. Light-skinned."

William paused once more. Disappointed, he paid little attention to the remaining chat about Derrick.

"Like I said, you guys are different in every way."

"Andrea, if you love him so much, then why was I in your life at all?"

"There's just something about you."

Annoyed at hearing the phrase yet again, William took a minute to give his order to the waitress before renewing his assault. "Andrea, what is that something? You keep saying that."

"It's hard to describe."

"And I guess after tonight, I'll never know."

That comment elicited no response from Andrea. Dissatisfied with seeing that confrontational conversation was useless and eschewing further argument, by the time their entrees arrived they again displayed amorous tendencies. Temporarily, their last supper resembled times of their not too distant past. Andrea fed William bites from her pu-pu platter while he reciprocated with his assorted seafood dish. As they shared a tropical drink called a headhunter, the waitress came over with their check.

"You guys look like you really love each other," she said, the remark sapping the liveliness they'd built and returning clouds of dread that signified the true purpose of this date.

As she walked away, Andrea leaned across the table and gave William a peck on the cheek. "I'm really going to miss you," she said.

William sighed as if conceding the inevitable. "I'm going to miss you, too, Andrea."

As he got up, he saw tears welling up in her eyes.

"Allergies, huh?"

"Yeah. They're a killer," she responded.

"C'mon. We're running a little late."

Returning to a hazy summer evening's twilight, William looked at his watch. It was ten after eight.

"Andrea, do you still want to go see *Dreamgirls*? We're late. We can go elsewhere to have drinks if you want to."

"William, it's right around the corner."

With that, the couple walked briskly to the theater.

✪✪✪

"We haven't missed very much," Andrea whispered as they seated themselves in the maroon velvet seats of the dark playhouse. "I think it started a little late. Thanks again for bringing me."

"Shh. I want to take all of this in."

This was William's first trip down Broadway via musical and he wanted to rid his mind of all anxieties for the next two or so hours. Even the imminent goodbye would have to take a back seat. Little did he realize, that idea would have a mind of its own.

The narrative of *Dreamgirls* traces its origin to Chicago, where three talented young women establish a singing group called the Dreamettes. Forming a promising trio, and building a trusting bond of friendship while moving their act to New York, the girls attract the interest of a sharp agent named Curtis Taylor, Jr., who recognized potential in the group almost immediately and signs them up. From there they become the Dreams, a Supremes-inspired force in the music industry.

However, some musicals often have a subplot. Such was the case here.

The agent, Curtis, fell in love with one of the Dreams, Effie White, the character portrayed by Jennifer Holliday. Viewing this underlining theme, William couldn't help but notice the irony. The first act reached its climax with Curtis shifting his affections elsewhere, a move which led to Effie's removal from the group. Walking into her dressing room at the end of that scene, she found the two loves of her life—the Dreams and Curtis—taken away from her, just like that.

Effie, deeply and defiantly in love with this man, goes berserk, ranting and raving through the scene, then launching into the signature song of the performance, "And I Am Telling You I'm Not Going."

As Jennifer raged through this song with power and pain, a strange feeling came over William. Connecting with Effie's futile, desperate pleas, he envisioned himself on that stage, scratching and clawing, kicking and fighting, doing all he could to make Andrea love him—doing anything to stay in this woman's life. As she sang, "He's the best man I've ever known...," the impending reality of an uncertain future set in as he looked Andrea's way.

I don't want to go…

Crystal tears of hurt flowing down his cheeks with emotions inspired by Effie's agony, he thought of life without his Crumbcake. All those corny jokes, those hugs and caresses, all those barbecue dates, those passionate red-light moments, all that would be gone after tonight. Just like that. As Effie filled the theater with a lonely feeling of an abandoned dream, William's heart, too, was breaking along with every word.

When the song ended, the lights came on for intermission. Andrea looked over at William, who had regrouped just enough for her not to notice what had transpired.

"Excuse me," he politely told her, then bolted to the men's room.

When he returned to his seat, Andrea tried to interrogate him. "William, you weren't crying, were you?"

"No.

"I don't know. I heard some sniffling."

"That was the woman in back of me."

"Oh."

Minutes later, the second act began.

Effie, alone with child, started on the long, grueling comeback trail, eventually revitalizing her career with a song entitled "One Night Only." Jennifer belted out this song as well, and as she reached the chorus, Andrea grabbed William's hand tightly. Maybe the gesture communicated to him her emotions, as well. Maybe she does care, he thought as the house lights came up, signaling the end of the play.

Outside once again, William asked Andrea if she wanted to go anywhere else. Hearing the "no" from her signaled the beginning of the end.

I've got to know if she loved me.

"Andrea, do you love me?"

Hearing no response, her silence was like a knife piercing his back. He asked a second time. Still, there was no answer. The knife twisted deeper.

As they reached the corner of Fifth Avenue and Forty-Eighth Street, Andrea finally ended her silence. "I can't answer that question. I'm sorry."

William threw his hands up.

"Let me ask you something. Do you think of marriage when you're dating someone? When I look at you, I see forever. That's the way love is. That's the way it's supposed to be."

"You don't fall in love and have it end happily ever after, William. I know I'm not going to marry you."

"So why date someone if you can't see yourself with them forever?"

Andrea paused before responding. "Well, no one

likes to be alone, and everyone wants to be treated special."

"So you're telling me you use whoever you're with until the right one comes along? I'd rather be alone than do that."

"I didn't make the dating rules."

"Are you saying you used me?"

"I didn't say that."

"You didn't say that you loved me, either. Do you love me, Andrea?"

Andrea was quiet once more as the express bus pulled up.

They took seats in the middle of the vehicle, and the reality of the moment finally set in, hushing the couple. These would be their last moments together. Andrea sat in her window seat, intentionally directing her attention to the streets while William just sat emotionless, all energy depleted, oblivious to everything. Wanting to put his arm around her but unable to gather enough strength, it was like he'd been injected with Novocaine, his body was so numb.

The bus sped along Fifth Avenue, then Broadway, passing many diverse and incandescent areas that made the Big Apple a brightly lit melting pot never totally asleep. As they approached the Brooklyn-Battery Tunnel, a voice from deep within told William to hold her hand one last time, and he clamped on to her with a vise-like grip. Andrea, still avoiding eye contact, squeezed his hand right back. She too, understood the gravity of the moment.

While time seemed to accelerate once in Brooklyn, still there hadn't been a word said between them. As the Command bus went from Coney Island Avenue to Cortelyou Road, then onto Ocean Avenue, William held her hand even tighter. When Andrea finally mustered the nerve to look at him, he looked away.

Be strong, his inner voice coached as the bus entered Andrea's neighborhood. *You'll make it through this.* He wanted to believe that so bad, but the devastation of his shattered love turned this bus ride into a death march. Knowing there would be no stay of execution on this night, the hurt he felt was like none he'd ever experienced. This was the worst moment of his life.

The bus turned left onto Avenue X. Only a few blocks remained. Last good-byes would be in a few minutes.

Andrea mentioned to William that he should get off at Nostrand and Avenue X, "So you could catch the B36."

William looked at his watch and saw it was five minutes to twelve. Summoning his last ounce of love from an emotionally tapped reservoir, he looked at her with a brave smile.

"I guess we both turn into pumpkins at midnight."

She didn't laugh.

"William," Andrea said with water eyes, her voice cracking, "don't ever change."

Don't ever change, she said.

Those words awakened him from his limp state and a defeated, crushing feeling was hurled deep into his soul, causing his bottom lip to quiver and his body to stiffen, before slumping over like an unhinged marionette. Finally succumbing to the tidal wave of pain he surfed for so long, William surrendered to the emotional wipeout when he broke down, crying as never before.

Andrea placed his head on her shoulder and began stroking it gently.

"I'll never forget you, William. I'll never forget you."

Raising his head from her delicate frame, he controlled his sniffles, kissed her passionately one last time and got up, refusing to look back. Upon stopping at a red light at the corner of Nostrand and Avenue X, the bus doors opened and William quickly got off, walking to the bus stop some twenty yards away.

As the light turned green and the Command bus went by, William wanted to look at Andrea one last time. Her face was pressed against the window, straining for one last look at him as the bus disappeared from view.

Wiping his eyes, he noted the time, two minutes after midnight. A new day had begun. Then as if the gloom of the moment had to be reinforced one last time, the dark skies opened up.

With no shelter anywhere and caught under a steady torrent, he waited about ten more minutes, hoping a cab, bus or something would come along. Fate had other plans, however, for it worked overtime to make the pain unbearable. With no transportation in sight, his gray suit soaked and his heart now broken, William McCall began the long journey home by walking to the train station.

✪✪✪

Blinking away the sheen of tears that accompanied the memory, William glanced at his watch. Seven o'clock. Jerry still hadn't come downstairs, so William assumed he wouldn't make their meeting. *I guess he didn't want to pay for drinks*, he mused while walking away from the building and back into darkness of winter.

I wonder if Justin's still serves smothered turkey wings.

Chapter Ten

SO MUCH FOR SMALL TALK

Justin's, an en vogue, upscale bar/restaurant owned by Sean "P. Diddy" Combs, was unusually crowded for a Monday evening as William seated himself at the long, burgundy oak bar overlooking the lounge area, the establishment's hub.

After ordering and drinking half of his Long Island Iced Tea, William walked past a group of young, professionally attired women en route to the restroom, one of whom gave him a wink, then turned to her girlfriend and announced, "That guy in the olive suit looks like Michael Jordan. I want his number."

William blushed. *If they only knew what it was like for me years ago when I couldn't buy a date*, he thought, continuing his stroll to answer nature's call.

Upon his return, he found another Long Island Iced Tea next to his unfinished one, prompting him to motion to the tall, auburn-colored woman working his side of the bar.

"Excuse me, did one of those women over there order this for me?" he asked, directing her attention to the middle of the bar at the group of women staring his way.

"No. Your admirer's seated over there." Grinning slyly, she pointed to the left. "The woman over there thinks you've got it goin' on. I told her I think she's buggin', but she wouldn't listen," the barmaid joked.

William directed his attention to where the woman had pointed and saw a gorgeous, brown woman wearing a taupe dress sitting alone at the other end of the bar, drinking a Margarita. Lifting his glass in her direction and mouthing, "Thank you," she acknowledged his gesture with a seductive smile.

"Aren't you goin' to kick it to her?" the meddlesome barmaid asked.

"Can a brother finish a drink before gettin' his rap on?"

"I guess so," she said, suppressing her amusement. "Though I admit, I didn't figure you for the type that would need liquid courage."

"You're funny."

As the barmaid tended to her other patrons, William finished his first drink, then lifted the second one and drifted over to the woman who'd generously supplied it. *Just make small talk. You don't need any more drama in your life*, he mused, passing the ladies now throwing daggers of envy in her direction as he neared her.

"I didn't think you'd come over," the woman responded as he pulled up a stool.

"To be candid, I don't know how to start this conversation. No one's ever sent me a drink before."

The woman looked stunned.

"As handsome as you are? I find that incredible."

"It's true." He paused to admire her beauty. "Why are you here by yourself on a Monday? Is the job that bad?"

"No." She paused. "Well, actually, I was supposed to be meeting someone here." Reading the look on William's face, she continued. "My ex-boyfriend. We're trying to work things out."

"Is it that bad?"

"Yeah, it is."

"How long have you been waiting for him?"

After she looked at her gold Cartier watch, she said, "About an hour."

William shook his head disgustedly. "He should have been here by now. Well, at least you gave him the opportunity to right what's wrong. By the way, that's a beautiful dress you're wearing."

"You're not saying that because I bought you a drink, are you?"

"Of course not! I've always preferred earth-toned garments. And from what I can see, you're workin' that dress, sis."

"Thank you. So do you have a name, mystery man?"

"William. William McCall." He offered his hand. "And you?"

"Janet Collins. So Mr. McCall, where's your girlfriend?"

William paused slightly before responding.

"What makes you think I have one?" Beaming flirtatiously now, he thought, so much for small talk.

"You wouldn't be here on a Monday night if you weren't stressed out by one."

"I guess I can't use football as an excuse, because the season is just about over," William joked. "To be quite honest, I was supposed to be hooking up with this guy to talk about the woman I screwed up with. He's a friend of hers."

Janet looked puzzled.

"That's original. Why do your dealings with her concern him?"

"Who knows? He used to see her a long time ago. Now, they're just friends."

It was Janet's turn to shake her head. "You know the word friend has a broad definition in relationships these days, William."

"Tell me about it." He took a swallow of his drink before resuming. "Yeah, I think he's still tryin' to get with her."

"If that's the case, why in the world would he want to meet with you?"

"I'm the one who suggested it. We were supposed to meet in his lobby and go from there, but he never showed. The more I think about it, I'm glad he didn't. What could I have said to him?"

Janet nodded in agreement. "Sounds to me like he wants a status change."

"I hear ya."

Commiserating for the next half-hour about relationship pitfalls, Janet was surprised when William told her about his failed marriage.

"You mean to tell me a nice guy like you couldn't make it work? Was she a good woman?" she asked.

William nodded.

"Very good."

"So, what happened?"

"I just wasn't ready. I had too many issues at the time."

Sensing that he was uncomfortable with the topic, Janet shifted gears.

"William, how old are you?"

"Thirty-four." Janet raised her eyebrow as he continued. "I take good care of myself. I play in touch football leagues downtown in the fall and basketball leagues uptown when I'm not doing that."

"I see," she responded, looking him up and down appraisingly as her forefinger traced the salty rim of her Margarita glass. "You look good in that olive suit."

William blushed as she grasped his slender arm.

"Aren't you kind of slim to be playing football, honey? I mean, I watch it on television and I see those jarring hits..."

Surprised, William interrupted. "Two-hand touch is different, though in my league you can use forearms. Wait a minute, you watch football?"

"Of course! Though I must admit, it's been kind of hard watching now that my Dallas Cowboys haven't done much recently."

Excited now, William acknowledged her comment. "The Cowboys are my team also!"

Reciprocally interested in learning more about one another, they continued their conversation over dinner in Justin's elaborate dining area. William satisfied his urge for smothered turkey wings along with macaroni and cheese, and sweet potatoes while summarizing the Della saga.

Janet sympathized with him, but admitted that, "I would have thrown your ass out, too, if you'd uttered another woman's name while you were sexing me up."

"It was an honest mistake," he argued.

"Doesn't matter." His plea for exoneration was denied in the Collins court.

Judge Janet, he soon discovered, was forty-two, which William found unbelievable. Returning her coquettish stare, he loved her full, electric smile and her feline-like eyes. About five-six with smooth, sandy brown skin, she had thin, elegantly sculpted eyebrows, auburn-tipped locks, the cutest dimples, and a little button nose to boot. He also found her slim waistline and firm body enticing. "You look fantastic," he told her.

"I'd better. I spend two hours every other morning in the gym."

"And brotha man takes you for granted? Please. The sisters my age don't look half as good as you. A lot of them just let themselves go, for whatever reason."

"Well, it's good to run into someone who appreciates the effort I put in." Janet then proceeded to tell him her history. She was a senior manager at Farberware, "the place that makes all those damn pots," she razzed. The company was located in the Bronx, the borough she also resided in. Her sun sign was Scorpio. She'd graduated from Cleveland State with a degree in business management, had thought of pledging crimson and cream in a graduate chapter but didn't because she'd never found the time with her busy schedule, and had never been married. She'd thought this boyfriend was the one until she learned, about a month ago, that he was screwing her best friend.

And I thought I had it bad, William mused while listening to her story. He commended her for trying to work things out, in spite of her friends' and family's beliefs that she was crazy for doing so. That was her reason for being here, although, she admitted, "I'm having a much better time of it rappin' with you."

"Thank you."

"You appear to be so nice. I can't imagine you going through changes like you are."

"I'm trying to sort out the reasons why now. It's like being a chemist in a hi-tech laboratory. You continually mix formulas hoping to concoct the right potion and you keep blowing shit up all the time."

Janet laughed. "I'd take my chances with you. You can't be all that bad. Just learn from your experiences, that's all. Try not to make the same mistakes over and over again. And don't be like so many of our brothers out there in that they lose the art of communication, holding so much of themselves in you never get to know them."

"Can you blame a person that's been hurt so much?"

"Women get hurt all the time."

"But it's different with men. Our sisters network and communicate about their hurts. Men are trained not to. We're not supposed to show any vulnerability, especially as black men. We struggle with denial of our emotional vulnerability every day. That theory alone fucks with us, 'cause if we indicate pain, we're considered soft by some women—wimpy, weak, not manly enough. Yet, at the same time, our sisters beg for sensitivity from us. It's a catch twenty-two."

Janet paused, as if to change the topic. "Let me ask you something. Do you drive?"

William lowered his head. "No. I have a fear of driving I'm trying to break out of. When I was twelve, I was riding with my grandmother on the Belt Parkway. We were by the Pennsylvania Avenue exit and we passed a really bad accident. Two cars were totaled, and I saw paramedics carrying body bags. It freaked me out."

"How old are you again?"

"Thirty-four."

"Get your license, William. What line of work..."

Becoming defensive, William interrupted. "Before you go any further, let me ask you something. You're not the type of woman who falls in love with people based on appearances, are you?"

"What's that supposed to mean?"

"Do you have it in the back of your mind that any man you date has to fit a certain description, talk a certain way, drive a certain type of car, be in a certain type of field... Need I go on?"

"I see your point. No, he doesn't. But he has to bring something to the table."

"Does everything have to be based on materialism? Instead of basing judgments on substance and integrity, so much emphasis is put on financial worth."

"Women need security."

"What about building together, establishing a solid

foundation? Why do I have to give the appearance that my ducks are all in a row before a woman steps to me? Why can't we do that together?"

"Because our single mothers told some of us not to get involved with anyone who can't take care of you, even though, for the most part, we can do it ourselves. Besides, what if the woman's foundation is already solid, you know, she has her own home, her own ride, is financially independent? Why shouldn't she want someone who, at the very least, can offer her something of his own?"

"That doesn't make sense, Janet. Why is it that a black man is supposed to have it all together before we can get a date? If I struggle to accomplish everything on my own, then what do I need a fair-weathered woman for?" William sighed. "Can't a brother be accepted by a black woman for his heart?"

Janet sighed. "I can't answer for every sister. But I will say this. In this day and age you have to have more than your heart to offer a woman. Love doesn't conquer all anymore, like it used to. I know that sounds unreasonable, but it's true. I mean, we all have to live in this world and the world doesn't give a damn about how much I love you or you love me if the rent's not paid, or there's no food on the table, etcetera."

Sadly, William agreed. "I'm beginning to find that

out. I feel like love is taking on totally different dimensions. Everyone has a hidden agenda, a motive for being with a person. Check this out. In the elevator at court today, I heard this woman say that she's going to do a background check on her next boyfriend to make sure he has good credit. That's crazy!"

"I can see why she would do that. A lot of y'all have fucked up credit. I'm not gonna start a relationship with a guy who I know can't balance a checkbook. As far as I'm concerned, that's a sign of immaturity."

"Yeah, but, Janet, do you see my point about how men and women put everything else before love when it comes to dealing with one another?"

"I see your point, but do you see mine? How many men do you know making a hundred thousand dollars a year who are trying to get with a woman who doesn't have a job? Why should women who have their stuff together be short-changed all in the name of love? Should we lower our standards? Women today want someone to share our lives with, not someone to provide for us. And until the man of our dreams comes along, why shouldn't we strive to accomplish things on our own? What are we supposed to do, sit at home, and be satisfied with whatever nine-to-five job we can get until we meet a man we can build something with?"

"I'm not saying that, Janet, but nobody even gets

involved for love anymore. What if my credit's suspect, are you gonna tell me at the end of the first date that a second date is contingent upon my credit report from TRW? Who thinks about that when you're feelin' romantic energy?"

Janet laughed.

"That's so true."

"So, Janet, you have to really ask yourself this: Are a lot of our women falling in love with me because I meet particular standards, as opposed to the person I am?" Janet was silent as he continued. "As I said, no one gets involved for love anymore."

"Love is in the eye of the beholder, William. It means different things to different people. Some people... No, a lot of people measure it in money and success. Why do you hear so many women using the phrase 'love don't pay the bills'? Because everyone feels they can struggle on their own. To live comfortably, you want someone who has something.

"Why do you think women pay more attention to a man that's self-sufficient? If he has a nice apartment and car, they figure he's more responsible and better than the guy at home with his parents at a later age. It's all part of that growing process, the ability to take care of yourself."

Janet had said a mouthful, but William countered. "That's bullshit, Janet. Does the fact that I don't drive mean that I'm financially insolvent, or irresponsible? What if there are circumstances that keep me at home until an advanced age?"

"Circumstances like what?"

"Having to take care of an elderly parent?"

"Okay, I see your point."

"Again, Janet, some of our sisters have the tendency to look at the fabric of my suit opposed to the fabric of my character. And sad to say, that's what messes them up repeatedly. Sometimes, I want to scream, 'Fall in love with me, not a damn standard!'" He sighed before continuing. "Janet, have you ever noticed that a man is never truly prosperous without the aid of a supportive woman? More often than not, you can always tell by the way that an apartment looks whether the man is involved, or in love. Unless, of course, he can afford to have maids come into his home to tidy up.

"So much has changed. Whatever happened to the day where you could say hello to a woman on the street and not catch an attitude? Whatever happened to the time when women were emotionally nurturing? Where's the love a lot of our parents shared? As I said, love takes on different meanings nowadays."

Janet responded. "Some equate sex, or good sex, with love. They feel if the sex is good, everything else will fall into place. The perception of love varies,

William, from woman to woman, and from man to man. And there are plenty of women who are still emotionally nurturing and who smile when a brother greets her on the street with respect."

"How about you, Janet? Does Mr. Right have to be this perfect man?"

"At this point in my life, all I expect from a brother is honesty and respect. If he can't give me that, I don't have time for him. Can you give me those things, William?"

Her candor left him momentarily speechless and he blushed as he responded. "Now, you know I can't answer that right now."

"Why not?"

When he wasn't immediately forthcoming, she mumbled behind her drink, "Well, can you give me a good screw?"

"What was that?"

As Janet turned away to conceal her embarrassment, William grabbed her hand. "C'mon. What did you say?"

"Nothing," she said and pulled her hand away.

"I heard what you said. You said something about screwin', didn't you?"

"If you heard what I said, why are you asking me?"

"'Cause I wanted to see if you had the courage to repeat it."

Janet hedged a bit before continuing. "Hasn't there been a time in your life when you met someone that had you feeling comfortable, desired and secure, like you've known them forever?"

"I feel that way right now," William said, taking her hand again. "C'mon, let's get out of here."

"Wait. I have..."

"Let's go."

After splitting the bill, the two left a generous tip for the barmaid who'd played matchmaker. The woman smiled when she saw they were leaving together.

Helping Janet with her coat, William followed her through the revolving doors, then flagged down a taxi on Sixth Avenue. Surprised I got one so easily, being a black man, he thought while opening the door for Janet.

"Where are we going?"

"You'll see." He directed his attention to the cabdriver. "Take us to Central Park South."

"William, it's almost ten-thirty."

"So. Do you have a curfew?"

"Whatever we do, you're escorting me home, right?"

"Do I look like the type of man that would leave you stranded?"

"You can never tell these days."

William scoffed at the notion.

"Let the evening play itself out, then judge for yourself what type of man I am."

For the rest of the ride, the tipsy twosome enjoyed the lights of the city in silence. When they arrived at William's requested destination, he paid the six-dollar fare and after the couple alighted from the cab, his arm went around Janet's shoulders. After walking a few yards east, she noticed the horse-drawn carriages.

"I never rode in one of those before."

As she pointed to a red carriage and the white horse harnessed to it, William flashed her a smile. "Do you think it's too cold to take a trip in one now?"

Janet looked excited, as if she'd been jolted with a current of electricity.

"Are you serious? We're going to..."

"Shh," William said, gently aiding her into the carriage. "Did anyone ever tell you that you talk too much?" He laughed as he boosted himself in. "You'd better bundle up. It's gotten nippy out here."

"Where to?" the driver asked.

"The West Side. Down Broadway."

"You got it."

Starting their journey into the brisk January night, the couple snuggled under the complementary blankets and enjoyed the trip. As they approached

Forty-Eighth Street along Broadway, William pointed right, showing her a huge, blue skyscraper adorned by a dazzling electronic stock-market billboard.

"That's where I work."

"Damn. I miss working in the city," Janet said as he pointed to his left and brought Caroline's Comedy Store, then the Virgin Records Megastore, to her attention. "All the bright lights, the night atmosphere. I just miss it."

Hearing her comment brought William full circle.

"Janet, I can't believe you came all the way from the Bronx and that okey doke stood you up."

"Yeah, ain't that somethin'? For a million dollars I'd pay to know what he's thinking right now."

William nodded slowly. "I admit, we still take some of our sisters for granted, but the playing field is leveling out. The problem of mistreating one another has become more a human problem than a gender one. People don't know how to treat each other anymore." He paused. "Janet, have you ever wondered why men, especially our brothers, do such fucked-up shit sometimes?"

"No. I'm always too busy licking my wounds," she joked.

"I can't speak for all those generations before ours, but I can say this about some men today. We have hearts, too, and when they get damaged, the repercussions can be devastating because of our difficulty in handling emotional turmoil."

"Can you elaborate?"

"All it takes for some of us is to experience the pain of being hurt, slighted or rejected and we'll do whatever it takes not to ever feel vulnerable again. With some of our brothers, all it takes is one time. Just one time. Once that pain is experienced, we change forever. Withholding our hearts from future relationships, we trust no one with our innermost thoughts. How many times have you heard women say, 'How come my man won't open up to me?'"

"Too many."

"We suffer in silence, Janet. Can I tell you a story that illustrates the emotional pain we hide from our sisters, the pain a black man carries when his heart is broken?"

Janet nodded.

"Janet, I recently found out that a psychology professor I had years ago in college came home from work one day to divorce papers from his wife, a woman he lived all his days for. Not only was she leaving him, but she also announced to him that their year-old child was not his daughter."

"How is he dealing with his pain?"

"He's not. He's dead. He stepped in front of a speeding train."

Janet gasped.

"Did he talk to anyone?"

"From what I was told, it was his second divorce."

"Wow."

"Janet, that's the worst case scenario. Our hurt manifests itself in so many ways because we can't handle emotional injury. As I said before, we withdraw." He paused. "I've heard that some men even seek other avenues for their affection."

Janet chuckled in amusement. "Really?"

"Yes. Yes. Don't laugh. Just as some women completely fed up with men turn to lesbianism, some men cross the street of homosexuality. It's rare, but it happens."

"Don't forget about the ones who come into a lot of money and start dating interracially," she noted. "They don't even give us a chance."

William nodded again in approval. "That, too. And finally, there's the dog. These are the brothers who develop the 'get them before they get you' philosophy while embarking on a vengeful rampage through the world of women. Most often, these self-centered individuals are ambivalent and indifferent, unwilling to show a glimpse of their hearts. Funny thing is, some of us have no clue why we're out there like that. It's not the right attitude to adopt, but try to understand why it's done."

"So what's your story?"

"I'm trying to figure that out right now."

"Try 'none of the above.' There's still hope for you."

"That's good to know."

They shared a comfortable silence for the next few minutes until Janet asked, "If you can acknowledge that men don't talk to one another about their emotional pain the way women do, why don't you take the initiative to begin a dialogue with other men about the things that hurt you?"

"We don't talk about our pain with other men because we don't want to appear weak," William reiterated.

"Yes, but are you all so pigheaded and egotistical that you're willing to continue down the same dead end of emotional dysfunction just to save face? If you're all carrying the same burden, why won't one of you stand up, like a man, and say, 'Enough!'?"

"Well, I guess therein lies the paradox, Janet. We know what needs to be done, but no one's willing to take that first step because of how the other brothers may perceive them, so instead we do nothing and the cycle goes round and round. Society has us fucked up in so many ways, huh?"

Janet shook her head.

"So how can you expect sisters to change their ways if you brothers won't?"

William shrugged.

"That one I can't answer. But, I will say this: If

neither gender makes a change, our relationships will continue to get worse. Something must give, because we need each other."

"Do we really, William?"

"Yes, Janet. We do. Everybody needs somebody."

As the carriage stopped in front of the ESPN Zone Sports Bar, William tipped the driver, then helped his date from the carriage.

"Janet, do you have any plans on seeing your boyfriend again after what he did to you tonight? What's his name anyway?"

"Thomas. I don't know."

"If you do see Tom again, ask him if he's ever been hurt before." Reaching into his pocket, William handed her one of his business cards. "I'm interested in hearing the answer."

Janet looked bewildered. "I thought you were interested in me?"

As they entered the Times Square train station, William paused before answering. "To say that I'm not attracted to you would be a lie. I mean, look at you. You're a beautiful woman, and, more importantly, you have a wonderful spirit."

Janet's face reddened as they put their tokens in the turnstile and headed toward the Bronx-bound No. 2 train. He continued speaking when they reached the platform.

"Janet, you have the loveliest eyes. They're like rubies. Quite enchanting. And your sensuous lips are begging to be kissed. Let me oblige." Lowering his mouth to hers, he tenderly pecked them causing her face to flush once more. "But it wouldn't be right for either one of us now."

"Even for tonight?" she asked meekly.

"Do you really want a momentary diversion?"

"I don't want this evening to end like this," she responded with a sexy nervousness.

"It's not. I have to see you home."

William turned and, as if on cue, a faded, red locomotive clanked into the station. Smiling, he grabbed her hand while boarding the train.

Time passed quickly as the train flew up the West Side, then east and into the Bronx. So much for small talk, William thought as it rolled onto the outer, elevated tracks.

Janet had left the door of temptation ajar; all he needed was to walk through it and a night of temporary fulfillment would be his. But, somehow that word temporary didn't sit well with him.

Aren't you trying to get away from that? Aren't you trying to correct your situation with Della? You just told Jerry how much you care about her. For the past few days, you've been searching your soul; struggling to find out why you've become the man you now are. Wouldn't it be hypocritical to succumb to your physical longing after you've just preached about how no one cares about love anymore?

As much as he wanted to leap into the chasm of opportunity, his conscience would not allow him to take advantage of the alluring prospect he now faced.

Finally, the train reached the Bronx Park East station, Janet's stop.

"Would you like to come home with me for a cup of coffee, William?"

The charming way in which the offer was presented made it all the more tantalizing, as evidenced by William's deep sigh.

"Janet, I'd love to...but it wouldn't be right. We're both in need of affection and making love to you right now would only add to the confusion." He gave her a warm hug.

"You love her, don't you?" Janet said, referring to Della.

"I'm not sure, but it's more than that, much more. One day I'll tell you all about it. I promise."

"Will there be a next time?"

"I gave you my card, right?" She pulled it out of her coat pocket. Taking it from her, William scribbled his home phone number on it, then returned it. "Hold on to that. Call me sometime."

"You can count on that," she stated, planting a

kiss on his cheek. "Thank you for the wonderful evening."

"What are you thanking me for? I should be thanking you. You're the one that sent the drink over."

"Yeah. I forgot about that. William, don't ever change."

Where have I heard that before? he thought, glancing over her shoulder and noticing the Manhattan-bound train approaching the station.

"You going to be all right from here?" he asked.

"Yeah," she answered with a demure smile.

"I'd better get going." Returning the kiss, he jogged to the stairway leading to the underpass.

"I'm gonna call you," Janet yelled to him as his jog turned to a sprint.

Barely catching the returning train, William felt invigorated as he sat down despite the fact that he was slightly out of breath. Having thoroughly enjoyed Janet's company, he wasn't sorry they had graduated to more than mere small talk, but he was proud of himself for not allowing the situation to get too deep because he really didn't want to exploit her vulnerability. He realized that in those few short hours they'd spent together, he'd come to value her company and although while not in dire need of companionship, he remembered a similar time in his life when he'd seemed desperate to substitute for a love lost.

Chapter Eleven

ALONE

July 1987

Life without Andrea began on a rainy Sunday morning. William's grandparents were in Philadelphia visiting relatives, so it seemed fitting that on this day of mourning he would be alone. Arriving home at two in the morning, drenched from the steady downpour outside and drained from what had transpired the previous evening, he'd cried himself to sleep.

Getting up at eleven that morning, the very first thing he did was call in to work. "An emergency came up" was the message he left for his boss. He would call back on Monday with the particulars. Then, it was downstairs for breakfast.

Barely tasting the bowl of Fruit Loops he'd prepared, William forced himself to eat, then went back upstairs to retrieve an old milk crate filled with vinyl albums and remixes. He headed to the unfinished basement where he found an old turntable and equalizer, two huge speakers, a vintage furniture set and a panel of mirrors. There, William's road to recovery commenced.

Spending the remainder of the day there, he passed the first few hours on the couch listening to nothing but love songs. Ballads from Whitney Houston's "Didn't We Almost Have It All" to Klymaxx's "I'd Still Say Yes" conjured up memories of Andrea for William as he wondered if she, too, was grieving like he was. Racking his brain over the thought, he venomously mumbled, "She's not. She's probably fuckin' Derrick today, telling him how she'll love him forever." Instantly his despondency turned to animosity. With that mood change he switched to dance music.

For the next five hours he danced. Moving to the music in this room full of mirrors was his way of momentarily liberating himself from the hurt. About nine o'clock that evening, he headed back to his room and fell on his bed, exhausted and sweaty, having danced 'til he dropped.

Monday came and William called in again, telling his boss, "A close relative is sick and I have to travel out of town this week."

"Take as much time as you need," was the considerate reply.

"Thanks," William responded.

That was the last phone call he made the entire week.

He stayed in his room for the next six days, in the same blue pajamas, coming downstairs only to eat, to relieve himself and to periodically talk to his grandmother, who was very consoling and understanding. She cooked his favorite meals that week; on Tuesday, they had chicken and noodles with cream-style succotash; Thursday was London broil; and on Saturday afternoon, she interrupted his Luther Vandross marathon by presenting him with her special pineapple-topped cheesecake. She gave it to him with a message, "If you fall off the horse, don't be afraid to get back on."

"Thanks, Grandma."

William went through the whole gamut of emotions during this stretch. Smiling briefly whenever he thought of a wonderful moment spent with Andrea, he quickly developed resentment when he realized his present state: alone.

At times he would miss her more than others; and he felt the urge to call her. Just hearing her voice, he thought, would do wonders for his spirits. Or would it? If he made the call, the minute he heard her voice he would tell her how tomorrow would be painful without her beside him. He would tell her she was the greatest thing that ever happened to him in spite of everything and how he'd give his life for one more magical moment in her presence. As much as it tormented him, he resisted the temptation.

Sunday came and William realized that he couldn't go on like this. With rancid breath and a pungent odor from a body not bathed in a week, the thought of Andrea still affected him, but he knew that somehow, he had to move on. Heeding Grandma's words of the day before, it's time to saddle up again, he concluded, finding the necessary mettle to strip out of the pajamas and run a bath for himself.

There'll be other Andreas out there, he tried to assure himself. Or would there?

✪✪✪

His first date took place some two months later. With thoughts of Andrea still prevalent, he, nevertheless endeavored to focus his attention on the evening classes that he was scheduled to take this fall semester, since, due to his emotional turmoil, his spring GPA at NYU had slipped dramatically. He'd been unable to concentrate since Andrea had monopolized his thoughts during his futile but wholehearted attempts to love her. Time to refocus, he thought.

It was evident, however, from the first week of classes that William had no motivation; his mind was still fixated on his lost love. Wondering if she had started school as she had claimed she would this fall, he was also curious about her relationship with Derrick.

In the midst of all of that, a woman on his job gave him a flyer to a Sadie Hawkins event sponsored by Chocolate Singles Networking at the Palladium. Although it was to take place on a school night, William decided to go anyway. Arriving that Tuesday evening at eight-thirty, he checked his coat and ordered a Corona before moving to the crowded dance floor. With Babyface's "I Love You Babe" remix thumping overhead, he began grooving, albeit a bit self-consciously since he had no partner.

After dancing to that and the next song, he was tapped on the shoulder by a chestnut-complexioned woman in a form-fitting black spandex dress with an abdomen so firm it looked as if she'd spent every day at Bally's. She was as tall as him in the red heels she wore, had beautiful brown eyes and luscious, violet-colored lips.

"You wanna dance?" she asked.

"Sure."

Almost immediately, the DJ began throwing down with house music. Marshall Jefferson's "House Music Anthem" was followed by Liz Torres' "Can't Get Enough." William and his dance partner wore the songs out, then walked to the lounge area and had drinks. Her name was Tracy Harmon and she was a secretary at a downtown law firm. She'd come to this function with her girlfriends, but, according to Tracy, the minute they hit the door, they'd gone on a manhunt.

"And what about you?" William asked.

"Me? If I meet someone, fine. If not, then I won't lose any sleep."

Good answer, he thought.

They continued their lively chatter for an hour and he gave her his work and home phone numbers.

"Call me. Maybe we can hook up and go out," he told her.

"Sounds good."

They shared one last drink together but when William was about to leave, one of Tracy's friends came over.

"Ooh, he's cute," she said to Tracy, then mumbled something about hoping for her sake that he had financial qualifications, as well.

"Shut up, girl," Tracy said.

William introduced himself to her, then kissed Tracy on the cheek and headed for the coat check.

On the L train home he thought of Tracy's friend's remark. Wondering how she could hang out with someone so tactless, he soon learned the meaning of the old "birds of a feather" credo.

He waited three weeks to hear from her. Finally, he assumed she had lost his number. His insecurities rushed him, transforming initial feelings of understanding to annoyance. I thought we'd had a decent conversation. At least, she seemed interested to me. I guess her friends don't think that I make enough money to merit consideration. How do they know?

Completing his self-deprecation, William succumbed to the reality that Tracy had rejected him.

One Thursday night after he'd gotten home from school, he picked up the ringing telephone to hear, "Hello, William?"

"Speaking."

"It's Tracy. How are you?"

"Fine. I thought you forgot about me."

"I apologize about not using the number sooner. It was in my other purse."

"That's okay. I figured you had other priorities."

"Anyway, I wanted to know what you were doing tomorrow night."

"What do you have in mind?"

"Well, would you like to take me out?"

Arching his eyebrows in shock, William jerked the receiver away from his ear. He waited to hear from Tracy for twenty-one days, and when she finally called, it's to find out if he wants to take her out.

Catching him at a time when his self-esteem was

still lacking because of his nonexistent social life, and still reeling from his breakup with Andrea, he was eager to find someone else.

"Sure," he hesitantly responded. "Do you want to eat by the South Street Seaport?"

"That sounds good. Listen, you should bring your car into..."

"I don't drive, Tracy."

She paused.

"You don't have a car?"

"No, I don't. I hope that's not an inconvenience to you," William responded humbly. "If it is, then I understand."

Tracy sighed. "What time do you want to meet me at my job? I work right by the ferry, at One New York Plaza."

"I should be there by six. I get off work at five-thirty. I'm coming from Grand Central."

"You work all the way up there?"

"Tracy, I told you that when we first met."

She sighed again.

"I guess I forgot. I'll be in my lobby at six."

"Sounds good. I'll see you then."

"Bye."

Damn, Andrea didn't even sound that selfish, William thought after hanging up. *Let's just hope the date goes a little better.*

Unfortunately for William, it didn't; in fact, the conversation over the phone was ten times better than the actual date. Moving quickly through the Seaport, Tracy kept talking about trying to find a financially secure man who could take care of her and pay her bills. She rambled on about what other criteria he had to meet.

"What about working together with him and taking care of each other?" William asked.

Tracy wanted none of that, reiterating that she wouldn't want to live from paycheck to paycheck with anyone; she could do that by herself.

"And he'd better have a car," she added.

"Nothing comes overnight," he replied.

"Well, he has to have that up front. All this traveling by train..."

"What are you, too good for us peasants who ride it?"

"Look at me. Do I need to be on the train on dates?" Removing her tan trench coat and revealing a skimpy blue and white dress that hugged her great figure, she answered, "No, I don't think so," before William could respond.

"So why are you out here with me tonight?"

Tracy paused. "Well... I do make exceptions every now and then."

William smiled at her response; for a brief moment,

the Tracy he'd met two weeks ago appeared before him, replacing this self-absorbed impostor. Hoping this faux diva imitating a woman with integrity would disappear over dinner at a seafood restaurant, he discovered otherwise.

On and on Tracy rambled about herself and the luxury she coveted, the furs, steady cash flow and cars she demanded her men supply her, ignoring his arguments for self-sufficiency and independence.

Shit, I wonder which one of her dates bought her that dress, he wondered.

Then she talked about the night they met. As she bragged to him about how she and her girlfriends were getting drinks from guys after he left, William decided this date was unsalvageable, lingering now only for the education.

"Have you heard from any of those guys since then?"

"I was supposed to hook up with one of them tonight. I mean, tomorrow night," she said, smirking.

"I see," William said, graciously ignoring her faux pas, but soon realizing that he was only a stand-in for the evening, and that pissed him off! Restraining the hostility he felt, the rest of the evening consisted of trivial conversation on his part. Tracy was definitely not the one for him.

Neither were Carolyn nor Linda, women he'd met in his night classes. Selfish, sassy and bitter, Linda harbored bitterness because of three failed relationships, and William couldn't get past the chip on her shoulder. Every time they conversed on the phone, he was the recipient of rudeness. The last straw came when she called him by an ex-boyfriend's name. An explosive argument ensued and culminated with William's exasperation surfacing in uncharacteristic fashion.

"Look, Linda, I'm not any of the men that hurt you!" he yelled.

His tone shocked some sense into her. Or had it?

"Hmm, I like a man that can stand up to me," she replied.

"You think this is a game?" He paused. "Listen, you need time to heal." With that, he clicked off the phone.

Carolyn was hung up on her son's father, a married corrections officer. William found this out the hard way. After accepting his invitation to a New Year's Eve party being thrown by one of his former colleagues, she'd kept him waiting by the phone that night for her to return his call. The clock struck twelve, and William brought in the year 1988 alone in his room.

Further complicating matters was his continuing nostalgia for Andrea. Granted, the three women he dated all had personality quirks that turned him off, but he wondered, had he given them a fair shake? While attempting to acquaint himself with these ladies, he had fondly remembered what he'd shared with his Crumbcake. Subconsciously hoping one of them would replicate the good times and fill the tremendous void created by her absence, he concluded that dating cold New York women was useless. This left him discouraged and feeling worse than he had in July when the two of them parted company.

William's solitude continued with drinks on a Thursday night in mid-January. He had just completed his last exam at NYU and was happy that the semester was finally over with. His grades slumped so severely, that he elected not to register for spring classes. This decision caused his grandparents displeasure since they had assumed all was well with his studies. William was truthful when he revealed that the burden of working full-time while attending school at night was taking a toll on him, but he opted not to tell them the real reason—lost love. Drifting across the street from his job to an Italian restaurant, he took a seat at the vacant bar and began to drown his sorrows with a pitcher of beer.

Halfway through his second glass, he was tapped on his shoulder.

"You must be feeling down, drinking that pitcher all by yourself. Do you mind if I join you?"

The woman looked like a business professional despite the fact that her black suit sensuously framed her voluptuous physique.

"Of course not," William responded.

After obtaining a beer mug from the bartender, the woman immediately began her interrogation.

"So, what brings you here on a Thursday night?"

"Tonight was my last night of finals at school."

"Well, you sure as hell don't look like you're celebrating."

"I have things on my mind."

The woman giggled as he wrinkled his forehead. "You're too young to be so serious. How old are you, sweetie?"

"Twenty-one," William answered, sipping from his beer glass.

"Why, you're just a baby." She gave him the once-over. "Humph! The things I would do to you. So, what's your name?"

"William." Smiling weakly, he offered his hand. "And yours?"

"Gladys. Gladys Miller." Shaking his hand, she concluded that his weak grip indicated insecurity. "Baby, you can grab my hand stronger than that. So, what type of work do you do?"

"I'm a court clerk at a law firm."

"I kind of figured you for something like that. You dress like an attorney, a paralegal or something like that."

"Thanks for the compliment." Noticing she was a quick drinker, he instinctively refilled her glass.

"Thank you, William. You're so sweet."

"Not a problem."

"You know, I bet your girlfriend must be really proud of the fact that you work and go to school. You seem to have a good head on your shoulders."

By the phrasing of her sentence, William easily figured out what she wanted to know, and concluded that the beer was acting as a truth serum.

"I don't have a girlfriend."

Gladys' almond-shaped, brown eyes lit up like a robber's being handed the keys to a Lexus. "Why not, sweetie?"

"Bad luck, I guess."

"Don't worry. Your luck is about to change."

What could she mean by that? Although he didn't mind her company, he really wasn't attracted to Gladys. She was an older woman whom he figured he could talk to, and maybe get a little insight into the female psyche, although she wasn't a bad-looking woman. Her hair was cut in a short bob giving her a youthful look; her full lips, high cheekbones and broad smile complimented satiny, milk chocolate skin. He just didn't look at her in a sexual way. *My mother's her age,* he thought while consuming beer and conversing.

"You're not bullshitting me about not having a girlfriend, are you?" Gladys asked.

William shook his head, then became more forthcoming. "I was in love with someone, but she belonged to someone else."

"From the looks of things, you had it bad for her."

"Yeah. I did."

After sharing that second pitcher with her, William noticed the time. It was eleven o'clock and he had to go work in the morning. Gladys wanted to go to a club downtown, but he declined.

Leaving the restaurant together, Gladys asked for his work number, got it and in return gave him a business card. She worked for a local Chase office as a Vice President. On the back of the card she'd written her home number.

"This is the first card I've ever gotten from a woman," William commented when walking with Gladys to her train.

"I told you that your luck is about to change," she replied. After waiting with her for the No. 7 train to Queens and receiving a kiss on the cheek, William was still perplexed. What could she mean by that?

The very next afternoon, he received a phone call from her during which she extended him an invitation to accompany her upstate for a weekend at the Concord Resort by Kiamesha Lake. Surprised by her aggression, he hesitated initially.

"Gladys, I, um…I barely know you."

"Does it bother you that I'm twice your age...and then some?"

Again, William paused. Her age had nothing to do with it; he just wasn't interested in that way, not while his heart was elsewhere.

"What's the matter, honey? Are you still in love with that girl? What's her name again?"

"Andrea. I can't get her off my mind."

"Going away with someone as sexy as I am would help," Gladys boasted. After a brief silence, she sighed. "Listen, I'm not asking you to marry me or anything. I just thought that you might be ready for a good time, that's all."

William wanted to tell her that he only wanted her companionship as a friend, but expressing this, he thought, would hurt her feelings, so he tried to buy some time.

"When do you plan on going?"

"I can go at any time. It's a complimentary stay, and I didn't want to take the two-hour drive upstate to Kiamesha alone. And once I met you, I figured why not?"

Although flattered by the compliment, William knew if he were to say yes, he would be agreeing to everything that went with the invitation. In short, he knew she'd expect to be rewarded sexually for her thoughtfulness.

"Gladys, I'll have to get back to you."

"Don't take too long, dearie."

She saw to it that he wouldn't. The following Monday, she was asking him, "How'd your weekend go?" and letting him know the offer was still on the table. Two days later she called again to see, "How's your week at work going?"

The very next day, William's boss received motion papers filed at the State Supreme Court without proper proof of service. The court rejected the papers and the attorney handling the action was livid because of the oversight. The papers had to be resubmitted, costing a prestigious client considerable time and money. William had inadvertently submitted the papers with the court a week before without noticing their lack of service. Although he'd received a severe reprimand from his boss, his job had been spared because he was an outstanding worker.

Dejected over the error, he was about to leave for lunch when his phone rang. It was Gladys calling again to find out if Saturday was a good day for him to travel upstate. He really wasn't in the mood to talk about any plans, so he ended his procrastination.

"Gladys, I don't think I can go with you. I'm sorry."

"What's the matter? Are you scared of Mommy? I don't bite, baby."

"I barely know you," William responded. "Besides, I enjoy..."

"You're not turning gay on me, are you?"

That question shook him up.

When he didn't respond, she again asked, "You're not gay, are you?"

Still, William was silent.

"Are you sure Andrea wasn't Andy?" Gladys taunted.

Finally, he answered.

"Are you going to be home tonight?"

"Sure. But I may..."

"I'll call you," he said sternly and abruptly hung up.

Angered to the point of a headache, for the rest of the day all he could think about was Gladys' stupid remarks about his sexual preference. This was the second time his manhood had been called into question by a woman. *This time I have to do something about it*, he vowed.

Returning home that evening, he dimmed the lights in his room and put on some slow music. Two hours later, after a couple of wine coolers from the corner bodega, he decided to make the call.

"Hello?"

"Gladys? This is William."

"I thought you weren't going to call. I was about to give up on you."

"When I say I'm going to call somebody, I try to

follow through." *Enough of the bullshit.* "So, Gladys, where do you want to meet Saturday?"

From the ensuing pause, he felt her excitement. "What made you change your mind?"

"Well, I was thinking, maybe I do need to get away. Maybe the trip will do me some good."

"Believe me, it will, sugar. Mommy will take good care of you." It was obvious that her hormones were now dictating her dialogue. "Have you ever been with an older woman?"

"No. Is there a difference?"

"You'll find out," she cooed.

"Gee, I don't know if I'll be able to handle you. You sound so experienced."

"Don't worry. I won't hurt you."

Any other time, William would have been intimidated or shamefaced by Gladys' assertiveness. Not this night, however. "It's been a while, Gladys."

"That'll make it more enjoyable."

"I hope so." He paused. "So, where do you wanna meet?"

"You tell me."

"I'll come into the city. Let's meet at Fifty-Ninth Street, by the Queensboro Bridge. Be there about two. I wanna get a haircut before we hook up."

"You're not gonna stand me up, are you?"

"No. I'm coming."

"You'll be saying that Saturday night," she said, giggling.

"We'll see. What type of car do you drive?"

"Look for a red Honda Civic. You know what they say about women and red, don't you?"

"No. I don't."

"That they're sluts in bed, and after this weekend, you'll know. See you Saturday."

"Bye."

After hanging up, William shook his head. *I hope I know what I'm getting into.*

Two and a half years had passed since he'd last given himself to a woman. That experience was an education in itself; a summer romance with a camp counselor while working at a sleep-away camp. Possessing a deep crush on Rhonda—a law student from England—and knowing he wouldn't see her again after the summer, he'd felt she was deserving of taking his virginity.

After the tryst, however, he'd made a vow of celibacy, opting to save himself for the right one. His noble idea would go by the wayside once he entered Gladys. That bothered him.

Another troubling thought was that sleeping with her would be a violation of his love for Andrea. Despite the fact that she was in an intimate relationship with someone else, and he hadn't heard from her in months, he still dreamed of her being his next one. Remembering her touch, her kiss, the outline of her sensuous body, their slow, imaginative movements along his bed and how he'd blanketed her rich, caramel hue with his tender, chocolate arms, he realized that by sleeping with Gladys he would be relinquishing his fantasy. With this thought, he wished he was in better control of his ego and hadn't consented to Gladys, but it was too late now. He had something to prove, and by accepting her invitation, he'd already said yes.

✪✪✪

Saturday morning came quickly and William packed for his trip. Into his large blue duffel bag went a box of lubricated condoms purchased from a pharmacist the day before, his blue bathrobe, two pairs of nylon boxer shorts, a pair of black jeans and a few tapes of slow music. After borrowing fifty dollars from his grandmother—he told her he'd be hanging out with a co-worker for the weekend—and getting a Caesar haircut, William went to face the music.

From the minute he took off his coat and stepped into the red Civic, Gladys fawned over him. Planting a disinterested kiss on her cheek, William complimented her on the black leather pants she was wearing.

"Leather turns men on," she flirted. She noticed his stone-washed gray jeans and white Kamikaze-designed sweater. "You don't look so bad yourself."

He smiled uneasily.

"Thanks." Then a sigh. "So, are you ready?"

"Sure am. Did you pack any con…"

"Yes. I have a box of them."

"You may go through all of them," she joked.

He grimaced. Glancing down to the floor of the car, he noticed an empty Spinners cassette case. "You a Spinners fan?"

"I was listening to them on my way here. You wanna hear them?"

"Sure. Why not?"

So as she pulled off, Gladys filled the vehicle with "Love Don't Love Nobody," singing the lyrics at the chorus.

"My mother loved Phillipe Wynne, the lead singer. It's a shame he's no longer around. Do you know he passed away while singing this song on stage?" William asked, more comfortable with this subject.

"What do you know about these jams? You're just a baby!"

"Gladys, please…"

For the first hour of the ride, up the FDR Drive and

through the Bronx via the Major Deegan Expressway, they talked about the music from her era. Gladys was impressed when William talked of his love for the Philadelphia sound of Gamble & Huff; the music of the Stylistics, the O'Jays, Harold Melvin and the Blue Notes, Billy Paul, Phyllis Hyman, Teddy Pendergrass, and, yes, the Jacksons.

"Did you know MFSB was the house band that played on all their tracks?" William mentioned.

"I see you know your music," Gladys declared, whizzing through the toll leading to the New York Thruway.

"Yeah, I do. I also love Marvin, Barry, Sam Cooke and Otis Redding. You name it, I love it. I grew up on it. It's a passion of mine."

"What are your other passions?"

"Sports. I love baseball, basketball and football."

"Can I share something with you? Do you know I'm forty-four and I've never been to a basketball game?"

Hearing her age stunned him.

"Wow! You're forty-four?"

"I told you I could be your mother."

"Age is nothing but a number, Gladys." She smiled at that. After stopping at a Roy Rogers service area in Middletown they continued conversing. Gladys had been divorced for five years and had a son in his junior year at Tuskegee Institute.

"He must be very bright," William noted.

"Yeah. He is."

"How old is he?"

"Twenty."

That made William pause to reflect on the fact that she had a son his age.

"Gladys, don't you feel a little uncomfortable about sleep...about going away with someone your son's age?"

"No. I don't," she responded without hesitation. "Most guys my age are full of shit, anyway. They sit around bragging about how good they are and are too set in their ways. Most of them have the 'done lap' disease."

"What's that?"

"Their stomachs done lapped over their belt buckles."

William laughed as she continued.

"They suffocate you in bed and they can't even get their dicks all the way in, they're so damn fat! Plus, you have to pull teeth to get your pussy eaten. I told a guy once that if he didn't go downtown, he couldn't get any."

William shook his head as she continued. "Meanwhile, guys like you are firm, virile and active..."

"That's not always the case," he interrupted.

"In your case it is," she said, rubbing his thigh with her free hand, then making her way up to his zipper.

William slapped her hand away, then blushed.

"Mmm, I hope it's big enough," she moaned.

Finally, the car passed the Monticello signs and they neared the Kiamesha exit.

"Are you sure you're not mad at me for taking you away from Andrea?" Gladys asked with a trace of sarcasm.

"No."

Up to that point he hadn't thought of her but once Gladys reminded him about Andrea, guilt arose. His first instinct screamed at him to run home; he'd rather be there, wishing he could be with his Crumbcake. But it was too late.

They arrived at the Concord about five o'clock, around the time winter twilight colored the sky. Both were impressed by the long circular driveway leading to the hotel's white, mansion-like entrance.

"Can I help you with anything?" a parking attendant asked.

"Nah, that's okay," William answered while removing the two large duffel bags from the trunk. "We don't have much."

Gladys took a cassette radio player from the back seat.

"We have to park your car for you," the attendant said.

"Go for it," Gladys replied.

While waiting for him to return with her keys, she

looked nervously in William's direction. "Are you sure you want to do this? We can turn around and..."

"We're here, right?"

"You know what I'm beginning to think? You're not as innocent as you appear."

"I never said I was innocent."

The attendant came with the keys and a parking ticket and the couple entered the hotel lobby.

Alone in a waiting area while Gladys took care of the registration, William took a good look at her. *She's not a bad-looking woman, a little big, but she was fun to talk to on the way up and she does have a cute smile.* He was trying to convince himself that sex with this woman was something he wanted as much as she did.

Once the registration clerk handed Gladys the white card key, she walked briskly to the waiting area with this weird look on her face, like she could do him right there in the lobby.

"So, honey, are you ready for school?"

"Yeah, I guess so," he responded, concealing his indecision again.

They boarded the elevator.

"I have two bottles of Moët in my duffel bag along with my clothes," Gladys announced.

"That's nice. I brought a couple of tapes."

"Ooh, I can't wait to hear them."

They ascended to the tenth floor.

"It's room 1007," she said as they stepped off the elevator.

Entering the room, William immediately dropped their bags and went in search of an ice machine. He had to venture to the ninth floor for ice since the machine on their floor was broken. Completing the task, he returned to their room to find Gladys had already made herself comfortable in their surroundings, for she was stretched out on the king-sized bed watching television.

"I must admit, the room is classy," William said as he placed the bucket on a table near the window, then admired the red and pink carnation-print drapes that covered it. "The floral arrangement on these curtains is tough."

"Most guys don't pay attention to the scenery, honey."

William turned to her. "So, what do they pay attention to?" he asked, already knowing what her answer would be.

Gladys rose from the bed, stepped up to him, and pinned him against a wall. With a smile, she replied, "They pay attention to…," then swallowed his lips with a kiss, before adding, "…the matter at hand."

"And that is?"

"Fucking me correctly," she whispered. "Can you do that, baby? Can you tame Mommy?"

She nibbled on his neck, causing an involuntary moan to escape his lips.

"Mmm, Gladys. Let's…um, shit… Let's pop one of those bottles of bubbly."

"You just put them on ice, sweetie."

"Let's just have one," he said meekly. "Please?"

"Okay." So while she retrieved a bottle, he grabbed the hotel-supplied cups from the bathroom.

"Here's to tonight," Gladys toasted.

"Yeah, tonight."

After they consumed the first bottle, she was ready. Torn between tipsiness and nervousness, William told her he wanted to shower first.

"Go ahead. We have all night," she said calmly.

While showering, he tried to erase Andrea's image from his mind. Although curious about what lay ahead, he really didn't want to do this. Considering telling Gladys that he couldn't go through with his charade because of his devotion to Andrea, he figured, *she'll think I'm crazy for still being in love with her. Worse yet, she'll think I'm gay. It'll confirm what she initially thought.*

Will it be love or manhood? Which would he choose?

He chose manhood, the clincher coming while gargling. Thinking of Andrea's trips with Derrick upset him, then his mind flashed to both Tami's and

Gladys' inquiries regarding his virility, infuriating him further.

"You're not drowning in there, are you?" Gladys yelled.

"Just a minute." He put on red nylon boxers and opened the bathroom door. Gladys walked by him flaunting her violet bathrobe and concealing something else from his view.

"My turn," she said, kissing him.

"Take your time."

While she was in the shower, William gulped down some of the second bottle of champagne she had opened while waiting. The more he consumed, the more he thought of her sexual query, and the more aroused he became. "I'm gonna turn this woman out," he mumbled as he put in a seductive tape and flopped back on the bed.

His excitement turned to surprise when Gladys came out the bathroom. She was wearing the same type of black evening robe he had purchased for Andrea for her birthday. It just doesn't look right on her, he thought, mustering the gall to compliment her as she snuggled beside him.

Ready for the World's "Love You Down" was now playing. As William reached over her to turn off the lights, Gladys pulled him on top of her, attempting to kiss him. He pulled away.

"Not yet," he told her, pressing an index finger against her lips, then giving her a peck. She wanted to taste his tongue, but again he pulled away.

"You're a tease, huh?" she asked.

"No. We're going to do this my way."

William leaned forward as if he was going to kiss her again. Gladys tried to meet him halfway only to meet resistance a third time.

"Say please."

"Please, William. Please kiss me."

When he finally consented, she reciprocated hungrily and from this point on, the need for love and affection William had long suppressed erupted like a volcano.

For him, making love was like dancing; everything done to a certain rhythm, a particular cadence; even in the initial stages of foreplay. As he gyrated his hips against her pelvis, he hoped Gladys would follow his lead and was disappointed that she simply lay there, panting heavily as he made his way down her robust frame. His head now at her bosom, William cupped her full breasts and fluttered an oral cape along her pointed nipples, causing tremors to rumble through her.

"Sss...Oh, William..." she moaned, pulling his head back to hers while stroking the hardened flesh between his legs. "Mmm, it is big enough. Please put it in."

Already? Ignoring her urgent plea and proceeding to more lush pastures he found that she was already soaked when he camped at the trimmed hairs of her loins. Gladys arched her hips forward and grabbed the sheets as he stimulated her orally.

"Yes... Yes... that's it. Ooh, William... Eat Mommy's pussy good... C'mon, baby, eat it good for her."

Playing her body like a cello virtuoso as he settled his mouth and tongue between her thick, spread thighs, he found a rhythm as he concentrated on giving her intense pleasure.

"You like the way it feels?" he asked as his fingers traced her lips.

"Oh, God, yes!"

Gladys hadn't been prepared for him to be so good with his mouth. With each glorious roll of his tongue, her clitoris throbbed with an aching need to be sucked.

Alternating between munching on the swollen, sensitive outer folds of her vagina and total immersion in her warm, watery channel, William stuck his fingers as far inside her canal as they could go while licking her with maddening skill. Soon, he found her pearl. Tickling and teasing it with gentle flicks from his brim, he drew her into the heat of his loneliness with his hunger. Breathless, greedy cries escaped her.

"Lick it good, baby. That's it! Just... like... that! Oh shit! Mmm, William... you... do that so... nice."

Gladys' body aflame with passion, her breaths became shorter as he sank his tongue deeper into her secret place. Bucking and shuddering, she arched herself, pushed her steamy pussy forward and humped his face.

"C'mon, Gladys, let it go. Let it go!" William barked as her body stiffened, then went limp. Gasping in pleasure as spasms tore through her, the woman who was supposed to be the teacher had been taught.

"Oh, William… I'm coming so hard!"

The vibrations Gladys felt were followed by uncontrollable shakes, then the shuddering aftershock that follows an intense orgasm. Descending from her sexual plateau, Gladys pulled his head back to hers and smothered him with affectionate kisses.

"Damn! Who taught you how…"

"Shh," William urged. "I'm not done."

Melting her once more with a kiss and deciding he was going to make Gladys beg for him, he again teased his way down her body, skillfully kissing around her ample breasts, grazing her nipples with lazy fingertips, then with the edge of a firm tongue. He bypassed her sweetness and while caressing the inside of her right thigh, he kissed down her legs.

Donna Summer's "Love to Love You Baby" was

halfway over when he made his way back to her honey, sliding a finger, then two, in and out to the rhythm of the song. When Gladys cried for something bigger, William reached for a condom.

Fitted now, he again kissed her.

"Are you sure you want me?" he teased, really asking himself that question. Was he sure he wanted to go through with this? Thinking of how Andrea would feel if she knew what was happening, he also thought of what might be said by Gladys if he stopped now.

Entering her swiftly, Andrea's ghost remained with William. Hoping Gladys would move like her, or move period, she was, instead, like a dead fish. He quickly resigned himself to the fact that he would have to do all the work.

"Give it to me, baby. Fuck Mommy good!" she ordered him.

"Move with me," he implored, rocking his hips slowly.

Her face contorted by his rhythm like a monster from the "Thriller" video, Gladys was in her own world and hadn't heard a word he'd said.

"C'mon, Daddy, fuck me good. Fuck Mommy's pussy good. C'mon, baby, do it good."

He wanted to take his time and make love. She wanted it hard and swift. He wanted to be gentle and tender. She wanted to get fucked. Reluctantly, he fulfilled her request.

With each forceful thrust, William plunged deeper into her triangular pleasure zone, first from the missionary position, then from behind. Ramming himself in and out of her hard, then harder, Gladys gasped for air as she pulled the bed sheet off the mattress, then grabbed the corner of the headboard to keep from going through the wall. Ripples of heat and electricity roared through her as he hit her G-spot, throwing her over the edge.

"That's it, William...This pussy...This pussy... is... all...yours," she moaned while panting. "It's...all... yours... Daddy. Fuck it, Daddy. Fuck it. Fuck it."

When he slowed the tempo slightly, Gladys' insatiable appetite urged an increase.

"Harder, dammit! Fuck me harder!" she demanded as her body convulsed wildly.

Pounding her backside in silence, William had mentally removed himself from the action at hand. Eventually, he reached a climax by imagining Andrea's supple body beneath his. As his ejaculation left him, he felt as if part of his soul was stolen from him, not willingly given out of love. The fact that he couldn't get it back left him nauseated, guilty and unfulfilled.

The scene was repeated later that evening and early Sunday morning. Gladys had a wonderful time.

William couldn't wait to get home. Feeling ashamed, he realized that he didn't have to prove his virility to anyone, and he had given this woman exactly what she wanted—a good time. *Shit, I even ate this woman on the first go-around,* he fretted. *Who knows how many times she's done this.* However, the fact that he had betrayed his love for Andrea bothered him most of all.

Merely cordial for the remainder of his time with Gladys, he, nevertheless, consented to the "one last piece" Gladys wanted as she pulled the Civic over on the Thruway. He allowed her to climb aboard his semi-erection— he wasn't turned on by her any-more; the Moët had worn off—and bounce up and down. He aided her orgasm by moving slowly, stop-ping as soon as she'd cum.

He was tired of this woman.

She drove him to his house and told him that she was looking forward to doing that again.

"Yeah, I am, too," William lied.

"You were fantastic."

"I'm glad you enjoyed yourself."

He gave her a kiss on the cheek, then left the car.

"Call me for a sequel, baby," Gladys called after him.

"I will."

William never saw Gladys again. Despite her periodic requests for a rendezvous, he finally told her one day over the phone that he wanted to make love to someone he loved, not fuck someone to get a nut off.

"I understand," she responded, "but one day your needs will supercede your wants. Just wait and see."

As William found out years later, Gladys' words would prove prophetic.

Chapter Twelve

HERE WE GO AGAIN

Day Five

Arriving home at two-thirty from the impromptu date with Janet and too wound up to sleep, William watched the last half of *SportsCenter* in his living room after listening to his phone messages. Jerry had called with a lame apology about standing him up earlier.

"Maybe another time," was the way it ended.

Jackass, he thought. *There won't be a next time.*

There was also a message from his mother, saying she hadn't heard from him in weeks and wanting to know all was going well with her second oldest son.

"She'll find out tomorrow," he announced, deciding right then and there to take Tuesday off.

After tossing and turning for about five hours, William got up at eight and made a call in to work requesting a personal day, then hesitated slightly before dialing his mother's number, telling himself not to bear his present emotional turbulence while pressing the numbers on his touch-tone phone.

"Hello," the pleasant voice answered.

"Ma?"

Eunice McCall was happy to hear his voice.

"William! How are you, son?"

"I'm okay, Ma."

"You sure don't sound like it."

She's gotta be psychic. "I'm doing fine, Ma. I'm off today, and I wanted to know if you wanted some company."

"Well, I was going to go out in field service, but I think I could skip a day. Jehovah won't mind," she said, reminding William of her religious requirements.

"I'm not going to get you in trouble with the elders if you skip..."

"Son," she interrupted. "Come on."

"Okay, I'll see you in a couple of hours. You need me to bring anything?"

"No. Do you want lunch?"

"Yeah. You could..."

"William, yeah is a grunt."

During the brief pause, William felt like he was ten again. His mother felt her sons were being disrespectful when they used words such as "yeah" and "nah," always reminding them of this with stern admonishments.

"Yes, Ma. You could."

"Okay. I'll see you about eleven then."

William felt like calling her back and canceling but from the way it sounded, she was looking forward to his visit.

As he listened to his portable CD player on the Staten Island ferry, the commuter craft adjoining the boroughs of Staten Island and Manhattan, he considered talking to her about Della and asking for help. "Jehovah's Witness or not, she's still a woman," he concluded while reflecting on his upbringing.

Eunice McCall, to William, epitomized the strength of a black woman. Having raised six kids on her own, the men in her life had never seemed to be right for her. This was evidenced by a failed marriage to William's father, and subsequent unsuccessful relationships that produced children. By cheating on her, physically abusing her, and mistreating her in other fashions, they'd given her more than ample reason to harbor bitterness toward men. Instead, she used her long suffering experience as a tool.

From their early years on Hawthorne Street in the Flatbush section of Brooklyn, the McCall boys—Andrew, William, Allan, Michael, Shawn and Ivory—were always the most courteous, benevolent and helpful kids on the block. They each displayed their own brands of chivalry—for example, assisting struggling women with groceries—and they never accepted money for their favors; their mother wouldn't have allowed it. When other adults scolded them, they never talked back. Raising six sons without emotional or financial support from their fathers or the men she'd dealt with, and doing the best she could with public assistance, Eunice McCall wouldn't have had it any other way.

Even as they moved to Staten Island, and her sons entered adolescence, she was unrelenting. She taught them all how to sew and cook, and every Saturday they were required to do housework. They scrubbed walls throughout the six-room project apartment, bathrooms, and all floors were mopped and waxed to a high shine. When their chores were completed, she studied an edition of *The Watchtower* with them. When her last relationship ended, she began attending meetings at nearby Kingdom Hall, adhering to the strict principles that came with being a Jehovah's Witness. Her sons were not allowed to run the streets with abandon, for she was known for quoting from the Bible, "bad association spoils useful habits." It wasn't that she thought their friends would have a negative impact on their lives, but Eunice McCall was wary of her boys succumbing to outside influences, especially from women.

Because of Kingdom Hall guidelines, dating was

prohibited unless one was preparing for marriage, meaning teenage girlfriends were off limits. This was not to say William hadn't tried. During his intermediate school years he'd received telephone calls from a couple of girls whom Eunice promptly informed, "He can't have any girlfriends." Those pronouncements provided several embarrassing moments come lunchtime the day after.

After boarding the S44 bus which took William to his old neighborhood, he remembered how his mother had changed once he expressed the desire to take Monique to the senior prom. That had triggered something in her.

From that day forward, Eunice began to talk about the importance of treating women properly. Always eager to give chivalrous advice, she stressed to him how men should treat women like their mothers and put them on a pedestal; how little things such as holding doors, pushing in chairs, helping them with their coats and showing respect in public were constantly overlooked. Perhaps these were things she'd always wanted and never received from the men in her life.

The fact that she tried desperately to instill these values in her sons so they wouldn't become irresponsible womanizers left William indecisive. When his heart was noble and pure, he displayed the lessons his mother had taught him. Unfortunately the pain of being unappreciated left behind wounds that remained unhealed; bitter memories of pain at the hands of women that William had failed to address until recently.

Maybe bringing Della up isn't such a good idea, he thought.

The bus left him at the corner of Cary Avenue, a block away from the West Brighton Apartments where he'd spent his adolescence. Walking down Broadway, then left onto Castleton Avenue, he couldn't help but notice the changes in the area. Neighborhood stores from his youth were gutted and barricaded with wooden panels. Drug dealers decked out in goose down bubble jackets, baggy jeans, and construction boots stood at the project's fenced walkway, braving the winter cold.

Anything for a fast buck, he thought as he zipped past them.

Before he approached his building, however, he heard a familiar voice from his past.

"Yo, Will!!"

Turning around, he faced a muscular, pony-tailed man. "Tony?"

The man in question nodded and William gave him a brotherly hug.

"Oh shit, man! How are you?" Tony McDaniels was

Tami's little brother. He wasn't so little anymore, a point not lost on William as he continued. "Damn, man. What you been eating, dawg?"

"Nothing, man. Just working with the weights."

"I hear ya. For a second there, I thought Rambo was coming to get me."

"You still got those white jokes, huh?" Tony cracked.

"Yeah, man." William paused. "So, what's crackin'?"

"Nothin', man. I've been lifting and going to college at night."

"Cool. Get that degree, man."

"I'm tryin', though it seems like they're trying to keep us out of school by raising the tuition every semester, as well as the bus fare."

"Nobody ever said making something of your life would be easy, Tony. Continue doing our race proud, man."

"Thanks for the big-up, Will."

"How's Tami doing?"

Tony paused.

William was baffled. "What?"

"My sister's a lesbian."

"C'mon, Tony. You're joking, right?"

"I wish I was, man. After dating a few losers and having a couple of seeds, she turned out of frustration." He paused. "Every time she would break up with one of them, my moms would bring up your name."

Damn. She always thought I was gay, William mused. "Word?"

"Yeah, man. She said you were the only one she ever dated that was about something, trying to make your life better."

That news was startling enough, but what came next left him speechless.

"My moms told me she wanted me to be like you, man, a real nice guy. And every time I fucked up, she mentioned your name."

"I... I don't know what to say."

"Don't say anything, man. I just thought I'd tell you that you provided inspiration for me to be a cool cat like you."

"I'm still tryin', dawg."

"I hear that." Suddenly their moment was disturbed by a honking noise. "Yo, man, I gotta run. I'm still living with moms, man. You've got the number?"

"I'd have to look for it."

"Do that, Will. Stay in touch."

William wiped a tear away as he watched Tony run up the walkway, then continue to the woman behind the compliment he'd just been given.

Entering the brightly lit lobby, his nostrils were assailed by the pungent odor of urine and grime. The scent intensified once the elevator door opened.

"Seven floors," he mumbled, holding his breath upon entry.

Jumping off the elevator and expelling his breath in relief, he walked to apartment 7B and knocked. Seconds later, a short, chunky, brown-skinned woman with thick glasses, close-cropped brown hair and high cheekbones opened it. Wearing blue, stone-washed denim and a matching blue blouse, she could pass for William's older sister.

"How are you, son?" Eunice McCall asked, greeting him with a warm hug.

"I'm okay, Ma."

"Are you losing weight, boy?"

"It's the job, Ma," William answered.

Looking at his facial reaction, his mother knew otherwise. "Right," she responded while walking to the kitchen.

As he entered, William was surprised to see lunch spread elegantly across a table covered in white linen. Noticing the steam rising from a white bowl, he asked, "Your homemade chicken soup?"

She nodded.

To the right of the bowl was a turkey sandwich with a large portion of macaroni and cheese.

"Ma, you didn't have to do all of this."

"Shut up and sit down, boy," she said, smiling broadly.

William obliged.

"So, how are you, son?"

"I'm fine, Ma."

"When's the last time you heard from your no-good, lying-ass womanizer of a father?"

William didn't answer.

"Do you still have his phone number in your desk at work?"

"Yes. I do."

"Has he called you since you took care of him after the heart surgery a couple of years back?"

Again, William paused. "No, Ma."

"See, I told you he's still no good. He's been that way ever since his girlfriend showed up on my doorstep with one of your half-siblings. You were three at the time. You and Andrew were the only ones out of his six kids who stayed with him up at the hospital. What about your half-brothers and sisters, the spoiled set?"

"The twins live far away, Ma. Mason lives in Dayton, Ohio, and Marlon is overseas. Mason came to see him once, for a little bit."

"What about Dalia? She lives in Yonkers, right?"

William nodded.

"What was her excuse?"

"She's afraid of hospitals."

Eunice stuck out her chest. "Now, what did I tell you years ago? If anything happened to your father, you and your brother would be the only ones there for him. His other kids have no moral fiber."

"Ma, could we change the subject, please?"

"Sure."

Moments later, his mother asked an uncharacteristic question. "So, son, are you dating anyone? How's your love life?"

William's eyes grew wide.

"No comment."

"Come on, now. You have this look on your face like you wanna talk about something. The last time I saw it you told me about your divorce."

She's gotta be psychic, William thought once more. But he said, "Nah, Ma. Everything's okay."

His mother paused before responding, as maternal figures do when knowing their son is being deceitful. "Okay, if that's what you say."

Burying her head into the *Awake* magazine she'd been reviewing prior to his arrival, her coolness compelled William to tell her all about what happened with Della. The happy mood Eunice had created had disappeared because by the time he'd completed his tale, her disappointment was clearly visible. Remarkably, she remained calm.

"William, how do you feel about what you did to this woman?" she asked.

"Like sh… Like crap, Ma. It's the first time something like this ever happened."

"If you didn't want to commit to her, you should have told her and been on your way."

It seemed that his mother had aligned herself with Della.

"It's not that I didn't want to commit to her. It's that... Forget it."

"Forget what? Forget what, William?"

"You wouldn't understand."

That response increased her coaxing. "Try me."

William paused, sighed, and blurted out what was on his mind.

"I'm scared of getting hurt, Ma. I'm terrified. The women out there are..."

Before he'd finished, his mother had rolled her eyes, gotten up from the table, reached into the refrigerator for a soda and sat back down.

"That's a first. I've never heard that before," she said.

William detected annoyance in her tone as she continued.

"After all the years my ancestors were raped in slavery by white men, all the years black women have been left to raise children on their own, all the years men sold us dreams which turned out to be horrific nightmares, all the years my sisters have gotten their heads knocked in by abusive men, men are scared of getting hurt by women."

"Times are different, Ma. Because of what men in generations before ours have done and because of some of the standards society deems necessary—

you know, the successful career, house, two kids and a dog philosophy—women have no patience with us these days, no resiliency, no staying power. Instead of nurturing, growing and developing together, they expect you to come into a relationship with so much these days it's incredible."

"I disagree, son. I disagree."

"Ma, for every one sister that has the old-fashioned virtues and is willing to work in order to build something, you have ten who expect you to be available, moldable, college-educated, financially secure, established in your career, expensive car-driving, tall, handsome, cool, family-oriented, God-fearing, yet in possession of a bad-boy streak, loyal, compliant, decisive, thinking what she's thinking, feeling what she's feeling, well-endowed, willing to go down on them and not be reciprocated in return, tolerant of any sexual hang-ups, gentle and forceful in bed, simultaneously, while they do nothing..."

"William, I get it."

"Ma, it's tough for both sexes now. In a society that preaches the quick fix solution to all problems, no one has embraced this philosophy more eagerly than the black woman when it pertains to our brothers. If we don't fit a certain standard, they make us feel like we're not good enough.

"It's getting to the point where brothers also come

into relationships with armor on. Not only are we dealing with a woman who wants it all, but with messed-up dispositions as well, like every brother on planet Earth has let them down. Everything said to a man they don't have to respect is done with rudeness, like the very sound of our voice is irritating. Who feels like dealing with that all the time? Ma, there's a big difference between being a strong woman that carries an attitude like luggage, and a woman with strength that won't tolerate the improprieties of a man."

"Do you know the difference, William?"

"Yes. I do. A woman showing strength doesn't announce to the world that she's strong; she lets her actions speak for her. Through true tenderness she appreciates her man, yet is willing to make drastic changes if her needs aren't met and she does so respectfully."

William sighed, then continued. "I don't blame our sisters for being angry, because brothers haven't always carried their weight. But to be shot down so quickly and so rudely nowadays because you don't fit a specific image they covet; that hurts. Black men are frustrated, too. We hurt, too, Ma."

"So seeing more than one woman at a time is the way to keep from getting hurt?" Eunice sarcastically responded. "Look, son, everyone gets burned in the game of love."

"Some more than others," he responded between bites of his sandwich. "Ma, it kept happening to me. I tried to do the right thing, things you instilled in me, and I continually kept getting my feelings hurt." William's eyes become moist. "Nothing works. I don't know what to do now. Why doesn't anything work?"

As he dabbed at his eyes in attempt to halt flowing droplets, the tears increased to an uncontrollable sobbing.

Eunice immediately became maternal.

"William, I raised my sons to be more attentive to a woman's needs than other men. Courtesy, sensitivity, tenderness and compassion in a man are foreign to today's woman because of your predecessors' examples. More often than not, these are construed as weaknesses, but I think they're assets. From birth, women are taught to believe that fairy tales do come true." Seeing the befuddlement on her son's face through his sniffles, she continued. "Some of our women still believe that a prince riding in on a white horse is supposed to sweep their problems away. The children's stories that are read to us, such as 'Cinderella' and 'Sleeping Beauty' illustrate this. The toys we played with distort the picture further. Women grow up looking for that man to cherish them, to protect them, to provide for them with that happily ever after ending. Hell, I was looking for that my whole life." She sighed. "When you become an adult, you're disheartened and frustrated when you find out it's all a lie.

"Angry from the disillusionment, women today condition themselves to believe that nothing, including happiness with black men, comes without a struggle. While being taught independence—to become doctors, police officers and lawyers—women learn that men aren't always dependable, and the few that are play too many games because they feel they've earned that right. It's either that or they become stoic and ruthless in that they look for 'Mr. Right Now' to fulfill temporary needs such as sex because they're tired of the insensitivity of our men.

"Then a guy like you emerges, one who has a heart, who is sensitive, kind and groomed to do anything to give them the world on a silver platter. Unaccustomed to dealing with a guy like you, women have no clue how to react. Instead of appreciating your tender, heartfelt nobleness, they are confused with the treatment. Or, the tendency to take you for granted surfaces. It's either that, or they sit around figuring sooner or later you'll be like all the others, constantly waiting for the other shoe to drop. With the track record of our men, can you blame them?"

"How can we, as black men, change that way of thinking?"

Eunice lowered her head. "You can't. Not in this generation with people falling in love for all the wrong reasons and expecting so much in relationships while giving so little. I'm afraid it's impossible. But I will say this: You still have a good heart, son. Don't ever change, William."

Affected by her son's emotions, she wiped her own eyes as she rose from her chair. "I feel I have to apologize for not making you aware of some of the games women play, about making you guys easy prey. Sometimes, I wish I could have done a better job with my issues so that I could have helped you."

"You can't fault yourself, Ma. You raised six of us alone and you did the best that you could. And as much as a woman does, she just can't teach us how to be men."

"Maybe you need to use that number in your desk drawer, son."

"I'll think about it, Ma."

For the remainder of the visit William and his mother perused through old photos and watched television while conversing about world events, both avoiding the subject of Della until it was time for him to leave. While retrieving his coat from the hall closet, Eunice returned to the matter.

"Do you have any plans on seeing Della again?"

"I'm not sure. I care about her, Ma."

"Caring is not good enough, son. You cared about your ex-wife and look how that ended up. You've got to love her. If you don't love her, don't even bother contacting her. Women want to be loved, son."

"Everyone wants to be loved, Ma. Even some of the most messed-up men."

That made her smile as she opened the door. "You're right, son. You're right." Eunice kissed William on his cheek as he walked past her into the hallway. "Thanks for coming by. I love you, son."

"I love you, too, Ma."

She closed the door on the stench of the natural world.

Two things stood out in William's mind during his trip home. His mother had emphasized the word love in regards to a possible reconciliation with Della. In order for him to go back this time he had to answer a difficult question. *Do I love this woman enough to commit to her?* When he'd met her for drinks that snowy evening the week before, he was unsure as to how he felt. He cared for her, yes, but did he love her?

Another interesting point his mother had touched upon was in a startling admission. She wondered if she'd raised her sons to be too nice in relationships with black women. To resolve that issue, William would take another trip back in time.

After finally conveying his message to Gladys, William decided the best way to cure his preoccupation with Andrea was by keeping busy. On his way home from work one evening in April he saw an ad in the *New York Daily News* regarding paralegal training. Detouring from his homeward route, he looked into it and enrolled on the spot.

By channeling his loneliness and energy for the remainder of the spring, and deep into the hot New York summer, he excelled in his classes. When grades of final exams were posted after each course of law was completed, William's name always appeared at the top of the list. Fancying the idea that he was reinventing himself, he maintained the laser-like focus into his studies.

Still, memories of Andrea loomed over him. On many warm evenings after class when he arrived home, his thoughts would flash to a moment when they had been together. It had been almost a year since he had last communicated with her, and he wondered how her life was going. On a Thursday evening in mid-July, he found out.

After completing a rigorous legal research session at the NYU Law Library, William walked through Washington Square Park before going home. He hung out at the center circle for fifteen minutes watching a group of Jamaican acrobats do their thing. When he rose to leave, someone grabbed his notebook from his left hand. He turned and saw Vikki, Andrea's best friend.

"Oh my God! How are you?" he shouted, pressing a kiss to her cheek.

"Fine. I see you're still in school."

"Paralegal school now. I'm taking a break from college." Both knew what question was next. "So, how's…"

"She had a baby about six weeks ago, a beautiful baby girl named Jasmine."

Although he remained poker-faced, the news tugged at William's heart. "Tell her I said congratulations."

"Why don't you tell her? She still talks about you a lot."

Vikki's reply sent an unexpected rush through him, but William's common sense still ruled. For now.

"I don't know if I should, Vikki."

"Just call her, man. All you would be doing is saying hi."

"I guess that can't hurt."

"It won't. Listen, I gotta meet someone for drinks at Uno's. It was good seeing you."

"Yeah, it was."

They embraced and just like that, she went on her way. And just like that, William's thoughts were divided in two again.

Should he or shouldn't he? That question plagued this young man from the time Vikki made her suggestion to that Sunday night. Missing Andrea intensely, he feared what hearing her voice would do to him. God help him if they were to start reminiscing; he'd want to see her immediately. The mere thought of her presence made his pulse pound. And if they did get together, he would greet her with a hug or kiss. Contact with her soft skin would make him quiver. *Sometimes love does these things to a man.*

That Sunday evening while raiding a bedroom drawer for a pen, he came across a photo of himself and Andrea on their first date. While they were merrily snuggled arm in arm, she held the stuffed Garfield given to her along with a long-stemmed rose. Moved by the sentimentality of the photo, William's emotions took over.

Be cool. Only wish her congratulations on her birth and that's it.

It rang once. Then twice, and then, a third time.

I'll give it five rings. After the fourth ring, he was about to hang up when…

"Hello?" a familiar voice said.

"Andrea?"

During the brief pause, William wiped the sweat from his palms.

"I don't believe it! I don't believe it!" she shouted. "William, how are you?"

"I should be asking you that. Congratulations on the birth of your daughter."

"Thanks. It was a lot of work."

"I know Derrick must be very proud."

"He feels like he has me now, to be truthful."

Ignoring what he'd just heard, William changed topics. "When are you going back to work?"

"I quit the job at Met Life in December. I'll be doing temp assignments until I find something."

"Good luck."

There was another break in their conversation.

"William, I think of you often."

"So, how's your mother doing?" he responded, pretending he hadn't heard her.

"When are you going to come see Jasmine?"

"How's your brother Jarred doing? And the rest of your family?"

"Did you hear what I just asked you?"

Sighing, William came clean.

"I don't think that would be a good idea. I'd feel uncomfortable."

Andrea "tsked" in annoyance. "Oh, you can call me, but you can't see me?"

"I was just calling to make sure everything was okay with you."

"By the way, who told you about Jasmine?"

"I ran into Vikki at Washington Square Park the other day."

There was yet another pregnant pause.

"Well, it was nice talking to you, Andrea."

"Will I be hearing from you soon?"

"I don't know, Andrea. You take care of yourself. And give Jasmine a hug for me, okay?"

With that phone call, he finally found a sense of closure. *Derrick has her where he wants and she seems content*, he thought. Time to move on.

Only Andrea wouldn't let him. Every week, he heard from her. Engaging in trivial conversation, nothing remotely close to the romantic chats of yore, William wouldn't allow it to go there, abruptly ending a phone call on one occasion when he sensed Andrea was about to tell him she missed him. Attempting to tell her in the nicest way possible that he was over her, William was showing strength; at least externally.

In the pit of his stomach, however, feelings of love still possessed, and screamed for release from the gallows they had been banished to. His resistance slowly wore thin with the sound of her soothing voice because deep down he relished the small talk he was having with this woman. The fact she'd called indicated she'd been thinking about him; that she may have even cared for him. Oh, how he longed to fill the emptiness within his heart with her return.

Waging war against this lurking sentiment, he convinced himself that the burning passion for her had been extinguished. I won't see her. No need to, he reiterated time and time again. It's over between us. That's what he thought.

✪✪✪

One Thursday morning in early September, William received another phone call from Andrea. Although he took the call, he found he didn't have much to say. When she informed him of a job interview coming up two blocks away from his company, his demeanor remained imperturbable and apathetic.

"Aren't you excited?" she asked him. "I may be working a couple of blocks from you. That means we could do lunch every day."

"I'm at court during the afternoon," was his response.

"We'll be able to have a quick drink or two after work."

He discouraged that thought also, by saying, "You have a daughter to go home to."

"I'm sure my mother could watch her on occasion."

"I have paralegal school two nights a week. On Tuesdays and Thursdays."

Andrea sighed. "William, why are you being evasive?"

"I'm not. It's just that..."

"Listen, just tell me you don't want me to call you anymore, and I won't."

That was all he had to say and Andrea would have been gone forever.

But love wouldn't let him do it. Breaking out of its shackles, it caused an extended silence on his end. After a deep breath, he yielded to this energy.

"Andrea... When do you want to see me?"

"Tomorrow," she quickly answered.

"Meet me at my job at five-thirty."

"I'm really looking forward to seeing you. It's been a long time, William."

Damn, I love the way she said that.

"I know. I'll see you tomorrow."

"Okay."

A warm, fuzzy feeling William hadn't known in quite some time came over him. For the first time in over a year, he anticipated tomorrow with excitement. He was going to see his Crumbcake again.

Predictably, anxiety wouldn't allow for much sleep that Thursday night. And despite his "things are different now" approach to it all, time crawled along that Friday. During an afternoon court run, he picked up a bouquet of flowers and a stuffed panda bear for her daughter. *If she asks why, they're because I haven't seen her in a while.* He was only fooling himself.

When he arrived back at his job at five o'clock, there was a message that an extremely attractive woman awaited his arrival on the twentieth floor.

"She's a half-hour early," he said in the presence of his boss.

"You can leave now if you want to," he said.

"Thanks." With flowers and panda bear in hand, William left his desk on the twenty-first floor and rang for the elevator. A minute passed. It seemed like five to him. *Better take the stairs*, he decided.

Perspiring by the time he'd walked to the spiral design, knots had tightened his stomach, and nerves were playing tricks on him. Reaching the bottom step, he turned and there she was.

Andrea looked lovely, quite marvelous. With motherhood maturing her beautiful form, her shape looked more womanly, and the long curls she wore over a year ago had been replaced with a short cut, blending perfectly with her thin facial features. Wearing gold, low-hanging earrings, a short black skirt displaying muscular legs, her red silk blouse complemented her red lipstick and nail polish. Her copper skin glowed as if kissed by the sun, and the moony gaze in her eyes quickly spread to her face once she saw him, illuminating the reception area.

As she hugged him, an energy that had been AWOL surged through William. Then she let go. Love completed its emergence from the doldrums.

"Andrea, how are you?"

"Hungry." They both giggled. "Who are the flowers for?"

William placed them on the receptionist's counter. "They're for her." His dry humor was back also.

"And that cute panda bear?"

"That's for Jasmine." He again studied her outfit. "Andrea, you look fantastic."

"Thanks, sweetie. William, I'm really hungry. Where do you want to go?"

"I know just the place." They ended up at Mr. Leo's, a soul food restaurant on the Eastside. En route, Andrea shared with him all the joys of motherhood. She joked that she could have done without the pains of delivery, yet she enjoyed breastfeeding Jasmine and didn't mind getting up at night.

"Does Derrick help you when he's over your mother's house?" he asked during the two-stop train ride.

"He tries. He changes a diaper every now and then."

"Do you plan on marrying him?"

Andrea glanced at him, seeing despondency on his face and taking a deep breath before acknowledging the question.

"Probably. It's been discussed."

Hearing that hurt, but William remained gracious. "Well, at least I got to see you again."

Over dinner, they continued getting reacquainted. Andrea was proud to hear that, in spite of his not attending college, he continued with an educational pursuit of some sort. She mentioned that despite her motherhood, she would attempt to start college again next year. Next came an inquiry into his love life and William proceeded with every detail. Andrea shook her head and called Tracy, Carolyn and Linda idiots for not recognizing a good man.

Then, as he revealed his escapade with Gladys, she broke.

"William, how could you?" she asked repeatedly, sounding like a woman betrayed.

"It was a mistake, Andrea," was all he told her. "I thought it would prove my manhood to her, and I was wrong."

After a brief silence, Andrea smiled. "Was it good?"

William hedged slightly. "To be honest, no."

"Why?"

"For starters, she wouldn't move with me at all. She just laid there. And when we changed positions I still did all the work."

"What did you expect? You were her young stallion, remember?" Andrea paused once again. "Was it nice and tight?"

"You want the truth?"

Andrea nodded.

"Well, let's just say I could have put two hands in and clapped."

"Did you go down on her?"

"Yes. She said I eat pussy like a champ."

"Don't I know it." She giggled. Still possessing the ability to make him blush after the year apart, Andrea was intrigued and aroused by his candor. "Did she return the favor?"

"No. She said that she didn't like to."

"That lazy ass bitch," Andrea mumbled under her breath before moving on. "Did she say if you were big enough for her?"

William took a sip from his rum and Coke before answering that one. "Yes."

"I can imagine," she responded softly, replacing the initial look of anger and envy with one of desire. "Did she ride you properly?"

"No. She wasn't on top at all."

"I would." She cast her line skillfully in front of where he floated in a warm pool of emotion. William clamped on, and she reeled him in. "I know she had a ball, moving the way you do."

"Well... She did say that I was fantastic."

"Did you go back for any more after that weekend?"

"No."

"Why?"

He lowered his head after a pause. "It wasn't you," he murmured.

"And what if it were me?"

"Don't ask me that." Like a man in the middle of the Sahara desperate for a glass of water, the way William pined for Andrea sent him crashing through the STOP signs of reason constructed in her absence. He was still in love.

"Could we get off the subject, please?"

"Okay," Andrea consented. "But I still want to know what would happen if we made love."

Seeing Andrea reach into her purse as the check came, William stopped her.

"Don't you have a daughter?" he asked.

"Yeah, but…"

"But, nothing. I got this."

"William, you are so thoughtful." She paused. "Damn, I've missed you. I've missed you so much, William."

Her sincerity forced him to inhale deeply while rising from the table, and as they turned toward the restaurant's exit, he swept her into an embrace.

"I've missed you, too, Crumbcake," he said, his words an understatement. Then he kissed her.

✪✪✪

As the returning ferry docked in Manhattan, William McCall had his answer. *No, Mom, I'm not too nice. Deep down, I'm a sucker for love who hasn't learned a thing from his mistakes.* Looking into a bag he'd brought with him and pulling out his Discman, he put in a CD he'd borrowed from a colleague and pushed the PLAY button. It seemed fitting that the Isley Brothers' "Here We Go Again" came from the headphones, and the irony of it all was noticed by a man frustrated with his choices in love. *Out of all the women in the world, I went back to her.*

Chapter Thirteen

DROPPIN' THE BALL

Reaching his Brooklyn apartment that Tuesday afternoon after deciding that it was more practical to cook than order Chinese food, William immediately headed to the kitchen, took some chicken legs from the freezer, and placed them in water to thaw. I'll fry them later.

Then, after plopping on his sofa, he turned the television on. ESPN was in the midst of its Super Bowl drive, showing highlights from past games to promote the upcoming contest between the Oakland Raiders and the Tampa Bay Buccaneers.

Got them on tape.

Channel surfing through the talk-show circuit and finding nothing interesting, he tried HBO. *Waiting to Exhale* was on for the umpteenth time. After watching the scene where the four women are celebrating Gloria's birthday, getting drunk and listing all the faults in African-American men, he sighed. *In order to solve a problem, sometimes you have to see that it exists on two sides. It's hard for us, as well.*

Why can't you see that sometimes your frustration may cause you to pass over or push away some really good men? Why can't you see that every man that is sensitive isn't weak, and sometimes we need you to help us be the men we are capable of being? Why won't you unfold your arms for a second and see that we're in this struggle together? You want me to lead, but if I make the occasional mistake, my character is assaulted with the sharp words of your mouth. Help me understand, because as a work in progress, I really want to.

Wishing he could pass through the television and present these issues to the women on the screen who represented the plight of his sisters, he sighed once more. Flicking to the classic movie station, he found *Imitation of Life* was almost over.

William tuned in when Annie, the black maid played by Juanita Moore, was lying on her deathbed. With her last breath, she told Lana Turner to fulfill her white-horse funeral vision. Additionally, she wanted her to find and take care of her daughter, a racially mixed woman who refused to acknowledge her mother because of her ethnicity. William gave this segment his undivided attention; partly in appreciation of the film, but mostly in tribute to Della, the person who'd introduced him to this classic.

As Mahalia Jackson sang during the funeral, William ran to the bedroom for his cordless phone and dialed Della's number. Remembering their impasse as the phone rang, he changed his mind and disconnected the call.

He recalled the various old movies they'd seen together. There was the time they took in six hours of Dorothy Dandridge movies at a film festival in lower Manhattan. Then there was the day they staged a mock gunfight with bananas after watching *Shane* on television, with the loser having to be a servant for a day to the other's needs. They shot at each other and simultaneously fell to the carpet, both wanting to lose so that they could accommodate the other later. When they both opened their eyes, they laughed and indulged in highly pleasurable and passionate love-making right where they were.

Later on that evening, Della surrounded her queen-sized bed with candles and allowed him to pour honey all over her sculpted frame.

Damn, that was fun, William mused. He missed intimate moments like that.

Turning off the television, he flicked on his stereo to listen to Rachelle Farrell's latest disc. Going to his coffee table, he picked up Christopher John Farley's *My Favorite War*, a book Lisa had turned him on to when he mentioned he hadn't read a good novel in ages. He reached a point in the book where Thurgood Brinkman, an Ivy League reporter for a

Washington newspaper and the novel's principal character, referred to sex for men as being localized and mundane. He also identified a woman's orgasm as a culmination of a long, pleasurable campaign consisting of shared confidences, long strolls at dusk and holding hands at the breakfast table.

William had a problem with that. *Some brothers know that lovemaking starts with the mood. It's not all about pumping for a while, feeling good, and then going to sleep afterward. It's about mental and emotional stimulation as well.* That point made him analyze his recent actions.

Until the day Della had called his house and heard Barbara's voice, William was having sex regularly. But was he making love? Did he really care about the women he shared his nights with? And if not, when was the last time he'd put another person's gratification before his own? When was the last time he'd created this mystical, magical, mysterious ambiance before intercourse? When was the last time he'd experienced a fusion of heart, mind, spirit, body and soul and used this energy to unselfishly satisfy a black woman? Had he ever done this? And if so, why was he so gun-shy about exerting that kind of effort again?

✪✪✪

October 1988

Andrea was back, and William's fading hope was reborn. Acting as if she'd never left, when she got the job working two blocks away from his office, he sent her a dozen roses on her first day. Sometimes, William would take the long express bus ride to Sheepshead Bay just to keep her company. He finally met her mother on one occasion, and there was an immediate chemistry between the two of them. When William saw little Jasmine, a warm sensation gripped him. *She's like my own*, he thought.

Not everyone was thrilled to see Andrea on the scene again. Electing not to warm up to her this time around, William's grandparents never extended a welcome invitation to their home, continually telling their grandson to find someone for himself or the pain would be even worse this time.

Steve also thought he was crazy. Every now and then, he tried talking sense into his boy's head, telling him that he was still the number two guy. William didn't care. Feeling a completeness with her return, he'd told Steve all about that steamy dinner at Mr. Leo's, and confessed a desire to make love to her.

"You sure you want to do that, Black?" Steve asked.

"Yeah, man. It feels like we were never apart. I love her, man."

William heard a sigh from the other end.

"Are you a masochist, Black?"

"Nah, man. I just know what's out there, and I'd rather take my chances with her."

"You never gave yourself the chance, man. Just because you've had bad experiences doesn't mean there's no one for you. You keep tryin', Black. You're twenty-two. They'll be plenty of time to go crazy over that special someone. Me? I'm not pressed like that."

Steve's argument fell on deaf ears.

"You want to know why you're not pressed? It's because you have them lined up in your stable down there in Delaware. I don't have that luxury here. It's like girls up here don't respect what I'm offering, Steve. They don't want to be treated like young ladies. That's why I'd rather take my chances with Andrea. At least she cares."

Steve laughed. "I can't believe it! She's got you pussy-whipped before givin' you the pussy! On the real, I guess you'll have to ride this out, if she has you in love with her. All I can say now is be prepared for anything. Just remember this; she has his child."

"I know, Steve. I know."

With that phone call, William came to the realization that he was going to allow whatever he had with Andrea to run its course. Conjuring up a bad taste of what his other options were, he decided that he would hang in there, no matter what hardships he would endure. *Love, true love*, he surmised, *will win in the end.*

✪✪✪

Fall arrived, and the R&B group Guy dominated the airwaves with a new sound called the New Jack Swing. Luther Vandross was on tour with Anita Baker, serenading crowds with ballads off a new album entitled *Any Love*. And William was about to progress to another level with Andrea.

With the seeds planted and watered at Mr. Leo's, and judging from the steamy phone conversation during which "it" was hinted at, both knew consummation was imminent.

Wanting to be sure this time, on a Monday morning in mid-October William sent a floral arrangement to Andrea at work along with a note carrying "The Question."

Her answer came that afternoon while they shared a turkey sandwich in an empty conference room at his workplace.

"Yes, I would love to make love to you," she said over lunch.

William was startled, pleased and discomfited, all

in the same moment; a moment that he had lived for, seemingly forever.

"Are you sure you want to do this? I mean I was just..."

"Just tell me the time and place," she replied, locking him into a deep, heated kiss before leaving. "Mmm. I can't wait."

Neither could William. That evening, he made reservations at the Penta Hotel, setting a tentative date two weeks from that Saturday and giving himself ample time to set the perfect stage.

During this period he traveled all over the city, frantically searching for any and everything that would enhance the romantic atmosphere. Noticing Andrea's fondness for Cabernet Sauvignon wine, he purchased a bottle. He found a place called the Unique Boutique in Greenwich Village that made air-brushed designs on T-shirts.

She needs another one, he decided.

Outdoing himself with this design, he selected a long aqua shirt and had a large red heart with an arrow running through it placed dead center in the front. Over it was an inscription in black: *My Heart Forever Belongs to...* It continued on the back. *My Crumbcake... I Love You.*

Two words came to mind once he saw the finished product. "It's priceless."

The artist agreed. "You must really love her."

"I do." William handed him the money for his work, plus a ten-dollar tip. "It's for a special occasion."

"Good luck," the designer said as William exited.

The last thing needed took courage for him to purchase. Out on a midnight run to the Playland Arcade, he passed an adult sex store. Smiling mischievously, curiosity set in and he entered.

He deliberated over buying porno movies to view with her.

Too forward, he surmised. He breezed by them, as well as dildos, beads, breast clamps and penis rings. Right before he approached the private booth section, a section of G-strings caught his attention.

Nope, I'm not going to war, he thought while spying a pair that emulated army camouflage fatigues.

There was another with the label, "The Big Whopper," patched on the front.

Talk about vain, he said, shaking his head. *I'm not that big.*

Then he saw it, a tiger-print garment with a big, black zipper in the front. He snatched the display model and smiled.

That Sunday night, William decided to model his G-string. Waiting until midnight when he thought his grandparents were asleep, he locked his room door, and for the first time in some months, put in the red light. Off came his flannel pajamas. Pausing with trepidation, he sighed while slipping out of his black nylon boxers and donned the seductive outfit. He closed his eyes timidly and walked over to the mirror dresser by the room door before opening them.

I think she'll like this, he thought after taking a deep breath.

Because of a nonexistent love life during the summer months, William had saved eight hundred dollars and treated himself to a new stereo system, a black component stack with a high-speed, dual cassette deck, surround sound, and a compact disc player. Into the CD player went Bobby Brown's *Don't Be Cruel*. He searched for song number five and turned the volume down a bit. "Rock Witcha" filled the room, and William, wanting to entertain Andrea as well as make love to her, was feelin' it.

Time moved in slow motion as William danced to the pulsating rhythms of the song, much like a stripper in a male revue. Envisioning Andrea lusting for him while watching him do this, then fantasizing about the moment their two dripping bodies would finally collide, his body ripples turned sensual, the gyrations erotic. Drifting deeper into his fantasy, he kept thinking how that Saturday he wanted to be

Andrea's superman; her chivalrous knight-in-shining-armor over dinner; a gentleman during the movie he planned on taking her to see; her private stripper during the wine and intimate prelude; and lastly, the most breathtaking, exhilarating lover she had ever experienced.

On that evening, he would make love to Andrea in every way imaginable. He would lower himself to her soaked triangle, smother it orally with all the affection he could muster, then, enter Andrea's flowing channel with a stiffness craving to love her the best it could. With sensuously seductive slow strokes, then long hard ones that would propel her to prolonged passion, his motion would drive her to heights she never before reached, culminating in a continuous chain of climaxes. Then, when she thought it was over, he would make her shudder again in orgasmic release with more of him in all of her. On that evening, all the love that had been rampaging through his soul for so long would escape bondage, be let out in its entirety, and she would gladly receive every bit of it.

Suddenly, William was startled out of his zone by three hard knocks on his room door. Forgetting that the door was locked, he yanked a blanket from the bed and covered himself.

"Boy, turn that music down!!"

"Sorry, Grandma!" he yelled back, and as she went back downstairs, he buried his face in a pillow and laughed.

✪✪✪

Talk about almost gettin' caught out there, William remembered as he placed the novel beside him. *If that room door had been unlocked...* Turning the television back on, ESPN2 was now showing clips from Super Bowl XIII between the Dallas Cowboys and Pittsburgh Steelers. Although the result of the game had been decided more than twenty years ago, he rooted for the Cowboys as if he were in the Miami Orange Bowl that Sunday.

With about four minutes to go in the third quarter, the Steelers had a 21-to-14 lead. Dallas had the ball on the Pittsburgh ten-yard line, apparently headed toward a game-tying touchdown.

Then it happened, Verne Lundquist, now a multi-talented broadcaster for Turner and CBS Sports, but then the voice of Cowboy radio, made the classic call:

"So now it's third down. Staubach back to throw. Caught! Touchdown! DROPPED! DROPPED! JACKIE SMITH! Oh bless his heart. He's got to be the sickest man in America!"

John Facenda, the legendary narrator of NFL Films, finished the horror with his own commentary adding, "A catch by Smith would have tied the score." Dallas had to settle for a field goal, which turned out to be the difference as their furious fourth-quarter rally fell four points short. Final score: Pittsburgh 35, Dallas 31.

Every time William saw this highlight, he felt bad for Jackie Smith, a tight end who in the twilight of a brilliant career that landed him in Pro Football's Hall of Fame, longed to contribute to a championship team. His big chance came in that Super Bowl and he failed to come through. The window of opportunity closed on Smith, and his playing days ended shortly afterward without a chance at redemption.

Sadly, William had experiences in his everyday life that enabled him to identify with this football player. *You only get a handful of moments to make a lasting impression*, he thought. *And when these occasions come, you must capitalize on them. You can't let them slip from your grasp.* He turned off the television and headed to his bedroom, reflecting on his squandered chance in time.

William told Andrea about his hotel reservations that Tuesday. Attempting to feed her some crap about always wanting to stay in a hotel in Manhattan at least once in his lifetime, she saw right through his charade.

"Do you plan on having me there as a guest?"

"You're welcome to come if you want to."

"Good. I can't wait."

Neither could he. For the remainder of the week, time crept slowly toward Saturday as making love to Andrea became an obsession, his every thought, his sacrificial offering, a testimony of love. That excited him.

It also worried him, for he fretted about satisfying her. This wasn't Rhonda, his first romance. Nor was it Gladys, with whom he shared nothing more than a screw. This was the woman of his dreams, the love of his life. He had to make it perfect.

"Man, I've never been so scared to have sex in my life," he confessed to Steve the night before his planned tryst.

"Does that mean you'll be quick on the draw, McGraw?" Steve joked, poking fun at every man's worst fear.

"You're funny, man. The only time I was a 'preemie' was the first few times with Rhonda, and that was because I didn't know what to expect. I was a virgin."

Steve paused briefly.

"I can't believe you admitted that to me."

"It happens to the best of 'em, Black."

"I would never tell anyone something like that. My ego won't allow me to."

"The male ego stands in the way of many things, Black. Would you admit that women are superior sexually? They are, you know. Look at the ways our orgasms differ. After a couple, if we're lucky, men are ready to go to sleep, we're so damn exhausted. Whereas with women, each climax they experience is more intense, more enjoyable than the one that preceded it. That's why we have to pace ourselves, man."

"Or become proficient with our tongues," Steve added.

"Tell me about it. We have to be five-tool all-stars."

Steve chuckled.

"Five-tool all-stars, Black?"

"Yeah, Steve, five-tool players."

Steve laughed even harder.

"You're going to have to break that one down for me."

"Steve, we brothas have to be these things in order to please a woman. While you may be deficient in one of these components, you can compensate by utilizing the others in its place."

"Like size, right, Black?"

"That's number one, Steve. We have to be amply endowed. Women often say that size doesn't matter, but believe me, it helps to have a package."

"Tell me about it. So, what's number two?"

"Good hip motion, Black. We must be able to move our hips like an ocean and have the ability to change the speed and the rhythm of our strokes. Intercourse is not all about banging a woman into submission. It's all about mutual pleasure, and that comes with good hip motion. Circular gyrations, V-strokes, figure-eight movements... You follow me, Black?"

"I guess I better do my sit-ups, huh?"

"Which leads me to point number three. We must have a reasonable amount of endurance and stamina. It means being in decent sex shape, Steve. Push-ups and running helps, as well as possessing an 'I want her completely satisfied' mentality."

"I can guess what number four is, Black. Eating pussy, right?"

"Yup. We must know how to eat pussy. Not only that, but, learning to enjoy the taste of it."

"Tell me about it, Black! I use my tongue, mouth, nose, face, lips, and my bald head."

William laughed. "So do I, Steve, so do I. I remember getting caught by my aunt practicing how to flutter my tongue in a mirror. I was so embarrassed."

"What's number five?"

"The last thing in being a five-tool player is the most important. Men must care about sistas enough to realize that their mind is their aphrodisiac; that lovemaking starts outside of the bedroom. Treating them like the queens that they are, making them feel special at all times. Then once you get there..."

"Everything falls into place."

"Exactly. All it takes is a single rose; that, or a pleasant phone call during the day to set the mood. Not many of us want to take the time to satisfy a woman."

"Preach on, Good Doctor, preach on!"

"I get so much joy in putting a woman's gratification before my own. And there's nothing like tasting her cold tongue after an intense orgasm." William joked, then paused. "Sure, I want to get off, too. But, there's nothing like seeing a woman start reaching for shit that's not on the bed when you're downtown munchin' on her coochie, and find that man in the boat. They either do that, or they start pushing your head away because it feels too good. That woman Gladys actually hit me."

Steve laughed. "That's true, Black. That's so true."

"You never hear us admit it, though. All we do is brag about how we knocked a hole in it. That or how many times she called it our pussy after we forcefully asked. I was always under the impression once you know your sexual capabilities, you don't ask, she'll tell you."

"Now that I agree with."

"That's why I'm so scared. I love her so much, and I want to be everything she ever imagined."

"Stop burdening yourself with expectations and enjoy. You're anxious right now. Just relax and let the evening flow. You're in love with her. Everything will be fine." Steve paused. "Get in a couple of strokes for me while you're at it."

William couldn't help but laugh.

"Fuck you, Black."

"Seriously, call me Sunday."

"I will, Black. I will."

He's right, William thought as he hung up. Everything will be fine. Throwing on his stereo headphones, he drifted into his sleep with "Rock Witcha." I hope she enjoys my striptease.

For the first time in recent memory, William got a good night's sleep. He awakened Saturday morning in a peaceful calm, brimming with confidence. The wait was finally over.

Up and about at nine-thirty, the first thing he did was run downstairs to his grandmother's house to get her cassette player. After doing this, he placed a newly made romantic tape containing Bobby Brown's jam into the tape deck. Next, he slowly packed his large blue duffel bag, placing her T-shirt in first, then some baby oil. She may need a massage, he thought. In went a change of clothes for himself, then the bottle of Cabernet, and lastly, five condoms. He prayed he would use them all.

After wolfing down a plate of scrambled eggs for breakfast, he noted the time. It was ten-thirty. It's time to make that call.

While dialing, he tried to keep his mind from turning to her birthday a year and a half ago, where his feelings were left to dry like yesterday's laundry. The swagger he awoke with turned to anxiety.

"Hello?"

"Andrea?"

He breathed easier now.

She's there this time.

"Hi, William. I just changed Jasmine." He heard the rustling of a four-month-old infant. "Say hi to William, honey."

Damn. Should we do this?

"She's so adorable," Andrea gushed.

"Yeah, she is something. Listen, Andrea..."

"You know, I'm really looking forward to tonight. I told my mother all about it."

"You what?"

"Relax. I'm teasin'. She knows all about the dance."

William seemed befuddled.

"You told her we were going dancing?"

"No. I don't lie to her. I told her we were going out, that's all."

"What time do you have to be home?"

"Whenever I get there. What time do we meet at Fourteenth Street?"

"Let's try seven. I'm checking in between twelve and one. I figure I'll take a nap…"

"You're not going to have any hoochies up there, are you?"

William laughed. "Crumbcake, you know me better than that."

"I'm just kidding."

"Do you wanna go eat?"

"Not really. We can get something and bring it back to the room."

"I wanted to check out a movie. How about you?"

"William, I just want to be with you." Hearing that made him squirm with anticipation. "Listen, I gotta feed my daughter. So, I'll see you at seven, right?"

"Right. Goodbye." Punching the air with a clenched fist, Andrea's confirmation left William supercharged. All that was left was the deliverance.

✪✪✪

William went through the revolving doors that led to the spacious lobby of the Pennsylvania Hotel, looking like a lost puppy as he noticed the elegant chandeliers and maroon and gold paisley carpet. *Why do all these places look like you just entered Buckingham Palace?* he wondered as he reached the registration desk. An African-American desk clerk immediately came to his assistance.

"Welcome to the Penta Hotel. Are you checking in, sir?"

"Yes. I have reservations."

"Okay, can you give me your credit card for a moment?"

Uh-oh.

"Um... Can I pay cash?"

The female attendant, an attractive, coffee-colored woman in her forties, smiled knowingly.

"Let me guess. Your cards are full."

William nodded yes.

"Do you have any identification?"

"A non-driver's ID."

He searched his wallet and pulled it out.

After reviewing it, the clerk began punching in reservation information in the computer system on the counter.

"Twenty-two, huh?"

"Yes, ma'am."

"Is 1424 Hancock Street your present address?"

"Yes."

"Do you live alone?" the woman flirted.

William blushed. "No. I live with my grandparents."

"Oh, I see. Will you be staying the weekend?"

"No. Just tonight."

Finished with her information requests, she reached behind her for a beige pamphlet. "Would you like to pay now?"

"Yes."

"That'll be one hundred eighty-eight dollars."

William did a double take.

"Really?"

"Yes, sir."

"It's a good thing I got paid yesterday," he mumbled while handing her four crisp fifty-dollar bills.

"What was that, sir?"

"Nothing."

She made his change, handed him the pamphlet, which contained two white plastic card keys and a small bottle of hotel-sponsored bubble bath. "Enjoy your stay, sir."

"For one hundred eighty-eight dollars, I plan to." While he was shuffling away with his luggage, the attendant called him back.

"Did I forget something?" he asked.

"No. I just wanted to tell you to make your girlfriend feel like the queen she probably is."

Startled by her candor, he remained unflappable. "I'll try. Have a good one."

Walking to the elevator, William was nervous. Wondering what spending the night with Andrea would be like, another self-inquiry filtered through his mind as the elevator opened. *Would she feel awkward if I asked her to spend the night? Will she feel comfortable in an intimate environment other than my room? Do I chill wine, or do I let it breathe?*

He rode the elevator to the twenty-seventh floor. Walking briskly down the dimly lit hallway, he barely observed the maroon and beige floral-patterned wallpaper. At door number 2706, he inserted the card key into a silver-plated slot under the door handle. The light just above the handle turned green as he turned it, gave the door a good push and…

"I think she'll like this," he declared, dropping the duffel bag on the king-sized bed. Examining the decent-sized room, he noticed the walls were a simple beige, yet the brass, adjustable wall lamps gave the room a cozy feel. Placing the Cabernet Sauvignon and the cassette player on a table beside the twenty-seven-inch television, he turned left and went into the bathroom.

He loved the blue and beige striped designs. Adorning the opaque shower curtains were blue flowers, on the sink lay four plastic cups, and the silver soap dish above had blue Penta Hotel soap bars. In William's opinion, the place was a palace; his opinion obviously slanted because of his Crumbcake's impending arrival.

After unpacking his bag, he stretched out on the bed and flicked on the tube. Clicking through the channels, he came across the Notre Dame-USC college football game on ABC. It had just started.

"Oh, Nellie. It's going to be a hot one tonight," William announced, poorly imitating the legendary voice of college football, Keith Jackson, while looking at his watch. Two-thirty. Four and a half hours till Crumbcake. Smiling at the thought, by the end of the first quarter a lazy wave of sleepiness had washed over him.

Awakened by the roar of the television, Stanford had scored the go-ahead touchdown in its game against UCLA.

Stanford? What happened to the Fighting Irish?

William looked at his watch once more.

Six forty-five.

Shit! Dashing into the bathroom, he showered quickly. Minutes later, he was flying into the bedroom to don his black jeans and red and black peppered sweater. Sweating profusely from all the rushing around, he would need another shower once he arrived with Andrea. Finished dressing, he ran out the room and returned with ice buckets; just in case, he stopped for another beverage. Placing them on the table next to the wine bottle, he reached behind the table and plugged in the radio. Next, he went into the dresser drawer and pulled out Andrea's shirt, then the G-string and spread her shirt along the head of the bed. Darting back into the bathroom to wrap his outfit in a towel and place it on the blue toilet seat, he was finally ready. *No, not yet.* He dimmed the lights to the room. *There, now I'm set,* he thought, grabbing the card key off of the night table adjacent to the bed and heading out. Seconds later, he came back in. *One more thing.* Back into the drawer he went, this time getting the prophylactics and the baby oil. After putting the oil on the dresser with mirror, with slight apprehension he placed the condoms between the mattress and box spring. There. After a deep breath, he departed.

Getting off the downtown B train at the Union Square station, the looseness and confidence William displayed earlier in the day had been replaced by his taut nerves. They were tighter than the tightest Marine; and to make matters worse, construction on the downtown express tracks congested the local tracks. When he finally arrived at seven-thirty, a half-hour after their arranged meeting time, there was no sign of Andrea as he crossed over to the uptown platform. He hoped he hadn't missed her.

He hadn't. A half-hour passed with William sitting on a group of wooden chairs near the back of the platform. Suddenly, an uptown D rolled into the station. The doors opened and out of the back car came Andrea, excitement evident on her face as she hugged him.

"Baby, I'm sorry I'm late."

"That's okay. I got here a little late myself."

Andrea detected his nervousness.

"Do you want to get some air, William?"

"Sure."

Instead of taking the train back uptown, the two went upstairs and began the walk to the hotel in silence, both anticipating things to come. Noticing a deli, William asked Andrea if she was hungry.

"I ate before I left," she responded.

He pointed to an adjacent liquor store. "Should I pick up a bottle of champagne?"

"Don't you have something at the room?"

"I have a surprise for you. As a matter of fact, I have three surprises."

"Really?"

"You'll see." Hearing his response accelerated Andrea's feet. It took them ten minutes to complete the trip to the hotel, stopping briefly at a store for William to buy a single red rose.

Going through the revolving doors, she was taken aback by the lobby's presence.

"Wow. This looks so..."

"Regal," William commented.

At the elevator bank, she became inquisitive.

"So, Mr. McCall, how much was the room?"

"None of your business."

"I don't know, with a lobby like this..." The elevator door opened and once they boarded it, William looked her dead in her eyes.

"Andrea, it doesn't matter how much it cost. If I'm with you and I can afford it, I'll give you the best of everything."

She kissed him on the cheek. "That's so sweet. Then again, I don't expect anything less from you. You're one of kind. Don't ever change."

"If I hear that again, I'll..."

The elevator doors opened on the twenty-seventh floor. Ambling slowly down the hallway, William's knees trembled as he approached his room. Reaching into his pocket and pulling out the card key, he slid it in the slot and gave the door a gentle push.

"Ooh, this is nice," Andrea said, entering the posh room before him.

"I'm glad you like it."

She saw her T-shirt unfolded on the bed and went crazy.

"This is beautiful!" He grabbed her hand and showed her the wine. "Mmm, tasty."

"Do you want to pop the cork on it now?"

"Sure. Why not?"

While he retrieved cups from the bathroom, Andrea turned on the television and seated herself on the edge of the bed. He returned to her seductive stare.

"The bed is firm. Just the way I like it," she cooed.

William blushed as he popped the cork. "I bet you do." He handed her a cup. "Let's make a toast. Here's to..."

"Tonight."

"Yeah, tonight." Instead of joining her on the bed, he positioned himself in a guest chair by the table.

"William, you seem uptight. Why don't you relax?" Andrea got up and headed toward him. "Let's put on some music."

"No! Not yet," he said, stopping her in her tracks.

"Why not?"

Giving her a knowing smile, William was transformed back into the person he was that morning. "You'll see."

As she sat back down on the bed, Andrea did a calculation while picking up the green shirt. "Let's see. The wine makes one surprise, and this beautiful shirt makes two. That means you have one more."

William nodded. "I saved the best one for last."

"Mmm, I hope it's big."

"Believe me, it is." He moved to a spot along the bed beside her.

"I like 'em big, William. Big and thick."

He wasn't blushing as he pecked her wine-stained lips. "I think I have enough for you, Crumbcake."

For the next half-hour or so, they watched Nick at Nite while drinking the rest of the wine. Soon, their attention drifted from the television. After rubbing Andrea's thighs, William's wandering hands went to her crotch. With the seat of her black pants already moist, she eagerly spread her legs wider so he could operate more freely. As he slowly stroked her womanhood, Andrea groaned and moved her hips slowly to the timing of his skilled fingers. Next, he moved them under her red blouse in an attempt to undo her bra from behind.

There were no hooks. Andrea giggled.

"The clasp is in the front," she said, undoing it. Pressing her back against his chest, Andrea purred as he massaged her breasts from behind.

"Mmm... That feels so good."

As she turned to face him, William suddenly sprang up.

"We'll finish this later. I need a shower."

"We can shower together."

"No, I think I can do this alone."

Andrea looked disappointed as he grabbed the rose and went into the bathroom.

Ten minutes passed. After splashing down, William

intentionally kept the water running so she would think he was still bathing. Taking the towel from the toilet seat, he dried off and put on the G-string. Carefully removing the thorns from the rose stem, he turned off the shower and went to the bathroom mirror. Wiping away the steam, he gave himself one last look.

I think she'll like this.

Wrapping the towel around his waist, he put the rose in his mouth and headed out.

"Ooh, you look so sexy," Andrea declared as he strode to her and gave her the rose.

"I love you, Crumbcake." He shut off the television and pressed the PLAY button on the cassette deck. A familiar drumbeat filled the room. The music followed.

Dancing slowly, William began to lip-sync, only this time, it was not for amusement. So many nights he had fantasized about this moment and how she would beg him to be a part of her forever. His lips could taste the dew of her succulent flesh. His dick craved the warmth of her paradise. He wanted to make love to all of his Crumbcake, her mind, her body, her heart and her soul. And he delivered this message in song.

Watching with intrigue as he danced his dance, the look on Andrea's face turned to total astonishment as William removed the towel at the second verse. Zoned in to a vision turned reality, during that section he pushed her back on the bed and assumed the missionary position while doing a body-waving pushup over her. Aroused now, a pillar of heat developed in his outfit, curling his manhood to the side as he continued his sensuous maneuvering. Placing the towel between his legs while rotating his midriff slowly in a circular motion, at the musical interlude he camped over her once more and kissed down her clothed body while doing a hip grind. Pulling her from the bed to his arms near the song's end, he gave her a gentle smooch at its conclusion and ran back to the bathroom.

As she raced behind him, the door shut in her face before she could join him.

"William, please come out."

After collecting himself, seconds later he opened the door to an embrace from a glowing Andrea.

"I didn't know you had it in you." She playfully slapped his butt. "You look so cute."

"The love I have for you brings out these things in me."

"Stay in that outfit, sweetie. I want to put lotion on you after my shower." As she grabbed her T-shirt and headed into the bathroom, William went to the bed and stretched out.

Fifteen minutes passed and Andrea came out from the bathroom, her beautiful body draped by the T-shirt. As she walked by the dresser mirror and grabbed the baby oil, William admired the design on her back, and saw no panty lines. Walking to him, her breasts jiggled just enough to reveal she wore no bra.

"Turn over, mister," she said aggressively, dimming the lights while sitting on him. "I want to thank you for the striptease."

"You should have put a dollar in my G-string."

"Very funny, you." She poured baby oil on his back, then massaged his shoulders. William's body tingled as she went from his shoulders to the small of his back, then between his legs.

"You have such a cute ass, baby," he heard her moan while erotically kneading his buttocks. Feeling her soft, delicate lips kiss each cheek, a wonderful sensation rushed through him.

"Could you raise up just a little bit, honey?"

William obliged and Andrea, while wrapping her arms around him, gently pinched his nipples.

"Mmmm," he moaned as he closed his eyes.

"Turn over, sweetie," she ordered between her own deep breaths. The massage turned Andrea on as well, especially when she noticed his manhood pressing against the G-string.

"I think he needs a little air," she cooed, carefully undoing the zipper.

Once freed, his swollen protrusion stood like a flagpole.

"You think he tastes good?" she asked, grinning deviously.

"Andrea, no," William cried meekly.

Andrea lowered herself to his groin, and then he felt a wet, warm feeling. As she encircled his erection with her tongue, she went up and down his shaft, causing the immediate collapse of all his defenses. Slowly pushing her mouth farther and farther down his veined pole, she relaxed her throat and easily accommodated his desires. His tool throbbed with each flick of her hungry tongue along his stiff shaft, and each stroke of her eager lips. Next she moved to his swollen bulb, hungrily slurping as if it were her favorite lollipop. Panting heavily as she suctioned a liquid drop of salty pre-cum from him, William was torn between this pleasure and wanting something more pleasurable.

He pulled her head up to his and kissed her deeply, pausing only to remove her T-shirt. "My turn," he announced, then turned her over onto her back.

Feeling her nipples erect in his mouth as he lapped her bosom, Andrea squirmed uncontrollably as she pushed her right breast deeper and deeper in.

William swallowed like he was an eager infant.

"Yes, darling. Just like that," Andrea moaned as his tongue moved in a circular motion around her areolas. Then, he tugged at her nipples with his lips.

"Sss... damn, this feels too, too good," Andrea responded.

"May I have something to eat? Something like... crumbcake?"

"You're too much."

"I guess that means yes." Making his way down her slim torso, he intentionally kissed around her scented heaven; each affectionate tap sent tingles all through her. After a couple of slow, tantalizing ice cream licks, he decided she wasn't ready.

Andrea lost it.

"Baby, please don't stop!" she gasped impatiently, pushing his head back down in a forceful manner.

"I'll get back to that," he assured. He went down her legs, his lips seductively surveying her thighs, kneecaps and her ankles. Trailing a stiff tongue from the sole of her foot, a gentle squeal escaped Andrea as he sucked and teased her toes. Moments later, he made his way back to her center, isolating his hunger in her salty-sweet nest.

Her thighs clamped around his head firmly as his tongue engulfed her, William did a dance of a different kind to the rhythm of Prince's "Adore" and

Andrea followed his lead. Primitive sensations ran through her quivering frame, she captured his mouth with powerful thrusts.

"Oh God. Oh God...Yes, baby, yes... William... please don't...stop. Please don't... Ooh...Ooh..."

Hearing her moan inflamed his excitement as he upped the intensity of his oral stimulation. French kissing her furnace, on this night more so than any other, he wanted the liquid Andrea expelled at her apex.

"Sss... ooh..."

Turned on by his munching sounds, Andrea wrapped her legs tight around his neck, and her hands pushed his face closer, then deeper, as her womanhood contracted around him like a powerful fist. Feeling her body tense up in preparation for an orgasm, William slowed the tempo slightly, making her labia tingle while sending a tremor shooting through her with his playfulness.

"Please make me come, baby," Andrea begged.

William complied, pecking and licking every corner, every sensuous nook and cranny of her vagina. Caressing her clitoris gently with his mouth, he hummed, sending splendid vibrations through her. Then he stroked her outer lips with his bald dome.

Alternating between heat and chills, Andrea's body tensed once more.

"William, I'm about to... I'm about to... I'm about to..."

She couldn't finish her sentence, for she raised her hips off the bed and experienced a violent, yet pleasurable spasm.

"William!" she screamed. "Oh, God, oh... oh..." she said between short breaths.

A second later, William's face met hers once more, kissing her lovingly.

"Andrea, I never loved anyone more than I love you right now."

She stared at him through the darkness.

"I love..." Pausing quickly, she kissed him to cover up her words. William was too heated to pursue the issue. As her tongue probed deeper and deeper into his mouth, she slowly brushed his organ.

"It feels so good in my hand," she whispered softly. "Can I put him in?"

"Did you dress for the occasion?"

William reached between the mattresses with his left hand and pulled out the condoms.

Andrea chuckled when she saw the connected blue Trojan wrappers. "You think you have enough?"

"I guess so." He rolled from atop her and pulled the packets apart, neatly placing four of them on an adjacent night table.

Andrea took the fifth one from him.

"Let me do this for you," she insisted. William covered his eyes as she lowered herself onto his solid strength. Feeling the erotic sensations of her mouth to his member once more, he moaned as he felt her cover his manhood with the condom. That she did it with the ever-warm wetness of her mouth almost made him come.

"Oh, shit, Andrea..."

"Mmm, that was better than tying a knot in a cherry stem." She giggled softly. "It just made it. I'm impressed."

That appreciative comment made him even harder. William returned to his previous position above her and kissed her tenderly. A couple of minutes passed. Andrea parted her legs slowly. And, from there...

✪✪✪

William's eyes filled with tears as he lay in his cold, lonely bed. In the years that followed, he'd become adept at running from the truth about what happened next. Excuses ranging from the excitement and emotion of the moment to loving her too much served as legitimate buffers. On this night however, he ended his self-denial.

"I dropped the ball," he stated simply. "I dropped the ball."

Remembering for a moment, a brief spectacular moment, how perfect everything had been. Andrea's sweetness was narrow and well-preserved, and he felt her contract around him immediately. She could not believe how good he felt inside of her. An unspoken symmetry took over as they began moving together. At last, the two melded into one.

Alas, it was not for long. William released his love too soon. While disappointed with himself, Andrea was very soothing. To him it was an aberration.

Fate wasn't in accordance, however. It would keep happening; later that night, the next morning, and subsequent attempts thereafter over the span of a month or so. Other than his experiences as a virgin with Rhonda, William had never experienced a premature ejaculation with anyone. Soon, doubts about his intimate abilities beget fear and he would not ask Andrea to try again after all of those failures.

Amazingly, with every other woman since, he'd heard wonderful things about his sexual prowess. *There were never any complaints*, William thought while reflecting on additional liaisons. He came to the conclusion that, after Andrea, he would never put pressure on himself to perform. But he also decided he wouldn't put so much feeling, so much emphasis, so much passion into his sex. The reason why? William felt his defining moment came years ago with Andrea. She was the love of his life, the woman he yearned to share everything with, the one who brought only the best out of him. And during crunch time, when it mattered the most, he was left with this one haunting memory—he had dropped the ball.

Chapter Fourteen
CAUGHT

Day Six

Sleep eluded William once more that night. At six that morning, his phone rang.

"William? It's Lisa. Are you awake?"

"How dare you call my house this early, Miss Strickland!" he answered, faking annoyance while wincing at the hazy, winter daylight seeping in through white Venetian blinds. "What's up, pal?"

"We gotta talk. Check this out. I went out with that motherfucker Augustus again last night…"

"I thought after he came on to you…"

"I know. I did, too. But I had nothin' better to do, and…"

"And, what? Don't tell me you gave him some of your kitty."

"No, stupid, let me finish! We went to Emily's, you know, the soul food joint on One Hundred Eleventh and Fifth, and guess who's sitting up there posturing with some high-yellow heifer? That bastard Roland! You should have seen the look on his face when he saw me with Augustus. He kept staring, like I was in the wrong or somethin'. And when I got home there was a message from him on my machine."

"Lisa, I'm detecting a little jealousy on your part. Are you still carrying a torch for him?" The pause that ensued gave him his answer. "You are, aren't you?"

"I was with him four years, so you can't expect me not to be affected."

"Lisa, he hadn't called you in over a month, and when you see him again he's having dinner with another woman. That's kind of bad, pal. What do you think?"

"I agree, but you can't stop your heart from caring."

"Did you tell Augustus? I would have introduced them if I were you."

"No. He was too busy trying to get my cookies. I'm through with his simple ass, too. He slipped up and called me Wanda."

"Who the fuck is that?"

"His girlfriend."

"His what?"

"His girlfriend. After calling me that bitch's name, I read him the riot act. Quietly, of course, because I didn't want Roland and his Lil' Kim wannabe girlfriend in my biz. And after threatening to leave, he owned up to his error. Pretty fucked-up evening, huh?"

William sighed. "Well, find solace in the fact that he didn't say it while on top of you."

"And to think, I actually thought about letting him meet my cat," Lisa cracked.

William chuckled as well.

"Back to Roland. What did that message on the answering machine say?"

"That he wants to see me and work things out."

"Lisa, you can't keep allowing him back into your life. The only reason he called is because he saw you with the next man. If you take him back, he won't respect you. And the pain you'll feel if it doesn't work out will be even worse. I know from experience."

"I know. You told me about that Andrea chick once. Let me ask you something. When she was still with that other dude, did you ever see them together?"

William sighed. "Yes."

"How'd you feel?"

"Lisa, the situation was weird to begin with..." With that, he elaborated on what had happened.

✪✪✪

Despite his sexual inadequacy when with her, William and Andrea continued into 1989 with their clandestine relationship. But there were changes. Because of Andrea's responsibilities to both Jasmine and Derrick, William saw her less frequently. Although he went through his usual frustration when dealing with the circumstances, his disenchantment was under control, for he reluctantly accepted his position as the number two man.

Becoming more a friend to her at this juncture, William graciously put aside his emotions and told her to make it work whenever she voiced problems with Derrick.

"Does he let you know how much he loves you every day?" he asked her one Wednesday evening in February on the express bus to her neighborhood.

She hesitated slightly before responding. "No. He's not like you. He's very possessive. He wants me to spend all my time with him."

"Possessiveness is a sign of insecurity, you know," he countered.

Andrea nodded. "Tell me about it. Just the other day a guy I grew up with named Terrence walked me from the store to my door. Derrick opened the door for my mother, saw us together and lost it. He actually thought I had something going on with this guy."

"I guess he had the wrong one," William joked.

"I guess so."

They both laughed.

Returning home that evening, William received some good news. His first credit card, a MasterCard with a two thousand-dollar limit had come in the mail. He knew exactly what to do to break it in. Overnight it had snowed heavily, approximately seven inches. Andrea went to work, and about ten that morning she had three dozen assorted roses delivered to her with a simple message: On a snowy day, you know that you can count on me. Let's make love tonight.

"Oh, William, I'd love to, but I can't," she replied later during a phone conversation. "Aunt Flo is in town for five days."

"Tell her I said hi."

"William, my period is Aunt Flo."

"Oh, okay. I never heard it described like that."

"I still want to see you though."

"Okay, I'll arrange something. Can you meet me at Fourteenth Street tomorrow night at eight-thirty?"

"Sure, sweetie. I'll see you then."

She still gives me goose bumps, he thought.

Those goose bumps quickly subsided that Friday evening as Andrea stood him up. He wouldn't bother to ask for an explanation, either.

"Goes with the territory," he deduced sadly while playing pinball at the arcade. His heart was crushed again.

✪✪✪

As winter turned to spring and spring to summer, William focused more on finishing his paralegal studies than on Andrea. Since that day in early September when their romance rekindled, his B+ average in the program had slipped to C+. Two courses remained in the program, contracts law and litigation, and he wanted to finish strongly.

Andrea misinterpreted his sudden remoteness. Thinking his love for her was dying, she became more attentive, increasing the phone calls on her end and demanding more and more of his time. Suspicious whenever he declined, she thought he had met someone else.

"If you're seeing someone, just let me know," she said in a June phone discussion.

William tried to be reassuring. "It's not someone. I want to finish this program on a high note. My grades have fallen off slightly and..."

"It's someone in the program, isn't it?"

"No, baby. I love you more than life itself. You're the best thing that has ever happened to me."

Still, Andrea was disbelieving.

"Yeah right, you probably called that woman Gladys and..."

Agitated with her probing, he interrupted. "Andrea, I'm not fucking anybody!" William shouted. "You know what? Tomorrow, I'll prove it to you."

So the very next day over dinner at their favorite barbecue joint, he handed her a red book. It was his diary for 1988 and 1989.

"How long have you been keeping a diary, William?" she asked.

"Ever since high school. They're more like journals, because I don't write in them every day. But since I met you it's been more of a diary."

"I'm flattered."

"You should be. I've thought about you every day since February of 1987."

"That's when we met, huh?"

William nodded. "You never forget the impact true love has on your life." He reached over the table and kissed her. "I love you, Crumbcake."

"William, don't ever change."

✪✪✪

"So, what did a diary have to do with seeing those two together?" Lisa asked.

"I'm getting to it," William answered.

"You better make it quick. It's a quarter to seven and we both have to get ready for work."

"I'm getting to it, Lisa." He continued with his story.

✪✪✪

There is a benefit and detriment to every decision we make in life; a positive and a negative; a pro and a con. We should never kid ourselves into thinking anything else.

William McCall learned this the hard way when he gave Andrea Richmond his journal that summer evening in June. Nobody knew about his diary, not his mother, his grandmother, nor his brothers and sisters or closest friends. It was the ultimate key to his soul, and the only person he trusted enough to share its subject matter with was Andrea. *After she reviews it, she'll know how deep my love is for her,* he thought. That was the positive spin.

The thought of someone else seeing it never crossed his mind as he gave it to her. He assumed Andrea would guard it as if it were hers, that she and only she would know the contents. Little did he know his old antagonist, his nemesis, his enemy—some powerful and fickle guy named Fate—had other ideas.

Fate commenced his cruel machinations shortly after another one of Andrea's no-shows. A month after his completion of the paralegal program, William purchased tickets to a boat ride featuring the music of Angela Bofill. It was to take place on a Saturday in early August, and he gave Andrea ample notice.

"I'll definitely be there," she announced during a phone call a week before.

"Please don't let me down again, Andrea. This means a lot to me," he replied.

"I won't, William." Those words lingered in his mind as he waited at the Forty-Sixth Street pier off the West Side Highway. As the eight p.m. boarding deadline neared, a resigned calm encompassed him.

She's doing it again.

When one of the crew assistants came to him and asked if he was getting on, he politely declined, not wanting to go alone, especially after seeing numerous black couples boarding the vessel with love in their eyes. Many of the sisters had red roses in their hands, and the glows coming from their male counterparts expressed adoration as they embarked on a night of romance. The love in the air reminded William of the Luther Vandross concert, and how alone he felt then, too.

Finally, eight o'clock came and as the vessel set

sail into the beautiful summer evening, William wiped a tear from his eye and, for the umpteenth time, began the depressing task of putting another disheartening evening behind him. Crossing the intersection in a zombie-like trance, he was almost blindsided by a passing Volvo. Wondering what excuse Andrea had for him this time, he wondered if she ever concerned herself with his feelings after sadistic stunts like this. He wondered if she cared. As he approached Tenth Avenue, something Steve had told him came to mind. He'd said, "When you finally get tired of dealing with an unpleasant situation, you stop complaining and get out of it. No words are usually said to anyone. You just decide that enough is enough."

William had finally reached that point.

He'd grown tired. Tired of all the abuse, tired of all the "I'm sorrys," tired of all the "don't ever changes," tired of the sleepless nights wondering if she was fucking Derrick or not, tired of the lost appetites, tired of being scarred by this woman, period. *Besides, the woman never told me she loved me. She can't even say that to me. I'll never call her again.* He meant it this time.

For a week, there was no communication. Then one Monday night in late August, he arrived home to hear the following message on his answering machine.

"William? William? *(sigh)* It's Andrea. We have to talk. It's urgent. Please call me. It's very important."

What's there to talk about? Fuming, he picked up the phone. "Operator, whom do I speak to about getting my phone number changed?"

That move stopped her phone calls to his home. Two days later, she started leaving messages for him with his boss at work. For a week, William ignored them. Then the messages multiplied to two and three a day.

"Now I know how England felt during World War II when Germany was bombing them every hour on the hour," he cracked after receiving his third message on Thursday.

"You should call her," his boss said. Still he would not acknowledge her existence.

One Monday in September, William relented after his boss threatened to fire him because she had called four times.

Message delivered.

He called her from a conference room on the twenty-first floor.

"Andrea Richmond speaking. How may I help you?"

"Hello, Andrea."

"William? Hold on. Let me go in my boss' office."

He heard a door shut on Andrea's end. "What the

hell is wrong with you? You changed your home number; you don't return calls..."

"Shouldn't that tell you something? I don't want to be fucked with. It's over. Don't ever..."

"Derrick knows about us," she interjected softly.

William was stunned by this news announcement.

"He what? How? I haven't been seeing you."

"I left the diary out at the house and he saw it. Two weeks ago. He knows everything."

"That's private, Andrea! That's private!" He paused. "Andrea, how in the world could you be so careless?"

"He was in my room one day while I was at the store and he looked under my bed."

"Why would he do that?"

"He was playing catch with Jasmine and the..."

"C'mon, Andrea, you can come up with a better one than that."

"I'm serious."

"A fifteen-month-old child can't catch."

"That's what he says. And the ball rolled under the bed..."

"Don't even finish. I don't even want to hear any more. It's your problem. Deal with it. Good..."

"William, all of a sudden you're going to act like you don't care?"

"Did you care when you left me on the pier by myself stuck with those boat ride tickets?"

Andrea paused. "William, I'm sorry about that."

"I'm tired of hearing that from you. I deserve better than this."

"You're right. And after you help me get Derrick back..."

"Help you do what?!" He couldn't believe what he'd heard. "That's your problem. Don't get me involved in that..."

"You're already involved." Andrea sighed. "Listen, he stopped seeing his daughter because he doesn't believe it's his. He wants a blood test done."

"Andrea, did you tell him we slept together after you had her? Did you tell him I protected myself?"

"He's just trying to be difficult. The child looks exactly like him."

"Why do you want him back?"

"Every daughter should have their father play an active part in their lives."

"He can do that and not be with you." Suddenly, William could see an image, one he found to be unconscionable. "You love him, don't you?"

Andrea hesitated. "Yes. I do love him."

During the pause that ensued, a pain all too familiar seared through him once again. Having longed to hear her say those words to him, his hopes were once again dashed. Taking a deep breath, he decided to show her what love meant to him.

"Andrea, what can I do to help?"

✪✪✪

"You were stupid, William. You should have let that bitch swim in her own shit!" Lisa exclaimed.

"I figured if I couldn't have her, I'd like to see her happy. And if being happy meant being with Derrick, then..."

Lisa paused.

"You loved her that much?"

"Yes. I did."

"So, what happened next?"

William proceeded to tell her the rest, including how they met at their favorite spot, the barbecue joint. Noticing Andrea had his diary in hand, he quickly took it from her, sifted through the book, and found the only pages that were missing were ones that told about them making love.

"Ouch," Lisa said.

"Ouch is right. The guy called me a freak just because of things he read."

"You don't hear about guys keeping a journal, you know."

"Don't I know it."

"How'd you help her?"

"She told me he didn't look through the whole thing,

so I put at the end of it that nothing had happened between us."

Lisa was shocked.

"You lied about your shit with her to save her relationship with him?"

"Yes."

"That was…"

William didn't let her finish. "The most idiotic thing I've ever done in my life. I lost what little respect that woman had for me, if there was any to begin with. I also lost a lot of respect for myself."

"So when did you see them together?"

"About two weeks later, I asked her to call me to let me know how everything went…"

✪✪✪

Performing the task of demeaning his love for Andrea left William despondent while sitting under a blue light in his room. Two weeks had passed, and he hadn't heard from her. He accepted the fact that their tryst had run its course; however, after emasculating himself the way he did in order to salvage her relationship with Derrick, he felt that he deserved a phone call, at the very least.

The Jacksons' "Find Me a Girl" blared from his audio system as he took a swig from his champagne cooler. He had always enjoyed the jazzy melody of the tune, but on this night, the fantastic harmony of Michael and his brothers was drowned out by the pain in William's heart.

His mind went back to that snowy evening when Andrea grabbed hold of his life for the first time. *Could it be you?* he remembered thinking as Michael scatted. *Could you make my dreams come true?* For a fleeting moment, she had. But now, almost three years later, the remnants of his crushed spirit lay in a crumpled heap beside him. Those wishes of finding someone soft and warm Michael sang so tenderly, the ones William identified with, were never realized for him. *Being alone never hurt more than it does right now*, he pondered sadly.

It would get worse.

Like a shark smelling blood, fate sensed his vulnerability at that juncture and quickly moved in for the kill. The very next day, he was bypassed for a promotion on his job. For three months his boss had been interviewing candidates for a position as an assistant managing clerk until administration suggested he choose one of his court clerks. Although William was the most experienced at the time and seemed the logical choice, the phone controversy with Andrea stood out in his boss' mind when deciding whom to hire as the new assistant.

Hearing the announcement, William excused himself from the midday meeting. Knowing why his boss hadn't appointed him, he shook his head. Even after she leaves my life, she still fucks me over.

The rest of the day passed without incident, a pleasant surprise to William. Reeling from the day's tension and needing an escape from his snake-bitten fortune, he decided to treat himself to a movie. He would have to get a newspaper to select one, so at five-thirty he headed out the exit of his building. Walking east, he crossed Lexington Avenue, turned left, and entered a small magazine stand next to a fifty-cent hot dog vendor. Handing the merchant thirty-five cents, William buried himself in the newspaper as he left.

His head was still down, reviewing the movie times, when he approached the northeast corner of Forty-Fifth and Lexington. Looking up, he noticed the light was red, glanced straight ahead, and went back to reading the paper. Suddenly, he closed the paper and looked straight once more, this time with instant recognition. There she was.

Andrea hadn't noticed him, for she was affectionately gazing into the eyes of the man holding her hand. Tall, about six-four, William guessed, having a streamlined yet muscular build, his creamy complexion, well-groomed goatee, black double-breasted suit and well-shined Bostonians gave him the look of affluence, his appearance alone telling William who he was.

Andrea complemented his attire in a provocative, snug-fitting black and white dress, looking extremely sexy. William never saw her look like this, even on their dates. As the light turned green, Andrea looked straight ahead and saw him. Her face remained unchanged as they walked toward him, and William concealed his pain as he slowly walked by. And as he passed, he gave Derrick the once-over that lasted seconds in his mind yet was merely the span of a blink.

On the other side of the street, he looked back. Andrea went to use a phone on the corner while Derrick stood nearby. He looked in William's direction, then, as his girlfriend finished her call, he grabbed her hand and they continued their trip up Lexington Avenue.

William crossed the street, this time west, toward Park Avenue. Number two always loses to number one, he thought, depositing the newspaper in the corner wastebasket. There would be no movie for him that night.

"Damn, that's fucked up," Lisa said. She heard no response from William. "You there, pal?"

"Yeah," he said in a low voice.

"That whole thing with her really hurt, huh?" She heard a muffled sniffle. "You're not crying, are you?"

"No, Lisa, just blowing my nose."

"For a second there I thought I'd have to clown on you. But on the real, you're a very special person, and I know there'll be better days. For both of us. William, don't..."

"Ever change," he said, finishing her sentence.

Lisa paused.

"How'd you know I was going to say that?"

"Lucky guess, Lisa. Lucky guess."

Chapter Fifteen

PASSED OVER

"Betty, I gotta go. Someone's coming."

The receptionist at Goetz, Gallagher & Green, the one who had enthusiastically called to inform William of Della's delivery of bleached clothes last Friday, noticed his arrival that Wednesday morning and quickly ended her conversation. "Good morning, Mr. No... I mean Mr. McCall," she giggled as he passed by.

William shielded his embarrassment.

"Good morning, Roxanne. Any messages?"

"Yeah. Mr. Gallagher wants to see you in his office at ten-thirty."

"Thanks." As he headed to his office, William wondered what Gallagher wanted to see him about. The minute he reached his office and closed his door, a premonition of something bad hit him. *Shit! I hope it's not about that Della fiasco on Friday.*

The sixty minutes passed slowly as William thought of what else he could have done to initiate the meeting, and prepared an apology for allowing his personal life to be displayed at work. Thinking he faced termination of his job, five minutes before the scheduled meeting William called the supply department to request a delivery of large boxes, just in case.

Walking down the dimly lit hallway to Mr. Gallagher's office, William wore the look of a convict walking the final mile to the gas chamber. What else can go wrong? he thought while passing the portrait of the only deceased partner of the firm, Hollis Green. Knocking on Gallagher's closed door, William told himself, "No matter what, everything will be okay."

"William, is that you?" the voice asked.

William opened the door slightly and popped his head in. "Come in, son."

To his surprise not only did William find the pale, gray-haired, distinguished-looking partner who was Mr. Gallagher, the senior principal at the firm, but also, his tall, heavy-set supervisor.

"Have a seat," Mr. Gallagher said from behind his huge oak desk. William complied, sitting in one of the matching guest chairs next to his boss.

"We were just discussing how long you've been here," his supervisor began. "It's been what, about four years since you left Robinson, Burton & Luftkow, am I correct?"

"Yes, and I'm glad I did. I've learned so much working under Michael." William was trying to score brownie points.

"I see," Mr. Gallagher said. "I see." A pause ensued, during which William searched the facial expressions of both parties for answers, not finding any. The atmosphere wasn't hostile, so he couldn't judge from that, either. *What's up?* he thought. Finally the suspense ended.

"Should I tell him?" Michael asked his superior.

"Yeah, he can handle it," Mr. Gallagher replied.

Handle what? Handle losing my job? It's bad enough Della doesn't want me. Now this. Does the bad karma ever wear off? William was sure he was a goner now.

"I'm leaving in two weeks," Michael Garvey announced. "I'm kind of tired of the everyday grind of being a managing clerk."

William looked flustered. "What are you going to do?"

"Write horror novels." William shot him this "you've got to be shittin' me" look. "Seriously, I've been discussing book deals with my agent and Random House is interested."

"Well, good luck," William countered.

Finally, Mr. Gallagher intervened. "Mr. McCall, shouldn't you be more concerned with the future of the Attorney Support Department?"

"Don't get me wrong, Mr. Gallagher. I am. I'm sure I can support whoever you bring in to run the department."

"Who said he was bringing anyone in?" Garvey asked with a smile. "I recommend that you take over as Managing Clerk."

William's facial expression changed, and Gallagher recognized it immediately.

"Yes, you, William McCall. You know your stuff. And ever since you've gotten here, Mr. Garvey over there has been singing your praises to me. He loves the way you never say no to responsibility. And from what I hear, your interface with the attorneys is superb."

"I had a good teacher," William said, chuckling with relief.

"Thanks," Mike Garvey responded.

"You know the position will come with a significant salary increase," Mr. Gallagher added. "As of January first, your salary was thirty-one, five. Starting February first you'll be getting a ten thousand-dollar raise, retroactive to January first. We'll be giving you an additional check at the end of this month to cover January."

Wide-eyed, William looked at his soon-to-be ex-boss.

"You've earned it," Mike Garvey stated.

Mr. Gallagher rose from his chair and extended his hand to William. "Congratulations, William. Keep up the good work in your new position. Now if you'll excuse us, we have some other business to tend to."

"Thank you. Oh, of course." As William got up and walked toward the door, Mike and Mr. Gallagher began discussing plans for later in the evening, namely, the Knicks game they would be attending.

Racing down the hall, he could barely suppress the elation he felt over his promotion. Zipping into his office, he closed the door, let out a resounding, "Yes!" as he punched the air à la Tiger Woods. Wanting to share this good news with someone, he thought of Della first, instinctively dialing her work number. After the phone rang twice, he quickly hung up. She didn't want to hear from him again, he remembered.

But hadn't he shared all of his accomplishments with her, no matter how small they were? Shortly after they had met, his Lower East Side touch football team had won the championship game in ten-degree weather. Who was there shivering by the East River as William scored the winning touchdown, greeting him with a congratulatory kiss, and a Thermos of hot chocolate afterward? Della. Whenever his firm's basketball team won in the Lawyers League, she invited him to her house, where he'd receive a triumphant dinner, hot bath, and a sensuous massage. Shit, Della even exchanged high-fives while watching boxing fights on HBO. And while he was accruing job-related commendations, she always boosted his confidence, telling him that he'd be running his own show soon. Her prediction proved true and the fact that he couldn't share his greatest achievement with her persecuted him.

God, I miss her. He felt alone, just as he had some time ago.

✪✪✪

February 1990

A new decade had begun, and William McCall was determined not to have it begin the way the last one had ended. Andrea had been gone about four months, and although his memories remained constant, he was bent on finding a replacement.

He had dates with Constance and Karen, and was turned off by the actions of Sonia. Constance had passed the bar exam that summer and she thought that dating William, who was just a court clerk, was beneath her. Her birthday was around Christmastime, and despite the fact that he barely knew her, he had taken her on a dinner cruise around Manhattan. Through- out the entire boat ride, she spoke to him in a bourgeois, condescending fashion, as if he was a minion because her new salary was four times as much as his.

William arrived home from this date scratching his head.

Love and the almighty dollar don't mix very well, he reflected sadly.

He met Sonia at a housewarming party, after hearing her complaints about how there were no good brothers. After striking a conversation with her, he thought about leaving his phone number with her. He dismissed the idea a couple of hours later, however, when he saw her on the couch, legs spread eagle and up in the air. Between them was a man simulating cunnilingus.

"She just met him," William mumbled as he put his pen away. "How can I respect you if you can't respect yourself?"

His date with Karen was a little better. Not only did he find her butterscotch complexion, hazel eyes and heavenly curvaceous body enchanting—she looked like a model fresh from the *JET* centerfold page—but her personality was pleasant. There seemed to be a smoldering interest building as they casually ate dinner at Serendipity's, a quaint little eatery on Manhattan's Upper East Side. However when it came to making future plans, the light mood changed considerably when she mentioned that she was kind of seeing someone.

"How can you be kind of seeing someone?" William asked as the waitress brought the check.

"I have this friend I see a lot," was her response.

"Are you romantically involved with this friend?" The sad look he received from Karen's eyes told it all. "What are you, out lookin for a better friend to replace this one?" Sighing at her silence, he continued. "Karen, why are you out here with me if you have a boyfriend?"

"He's not my boyfriend."

"Then what is he?"

"He's a friend, that's all." Seeing William shake his head in disgust caused her to continue confessing. "I'm not sure what he wants. I mean, things go on between us and..."

"What type of things, Karen?"

She wouldn't answer that one, so he did.

"I understand, Karen. You're just testing the waters. Let's just have a good time for the rest of the evening."

They did, too, going to Club Savage on the Lower West Side and dancing the night away. When they arrived at Karen's apartment building in the Jamaica

Estates section of Queens at two in the morning, she asked if he was coming upstairs for a nightcap.

"Nope. You won't be seeing me anymore after tonight."

"But I had a nice time..."

"Have your friend with benefits take you out next time."

"But we never go out. All he wants to do is come over and have sex."

William sighed, then struggled to maintain his composure.

"Karen, I had a nice time. Have a nice life." Turning his back on her with disgust and beginning his trek to the train station, he was bewildered. *Every man who fucks a woman isn't a friend*, he thought. They're just fucking her. Why do women confuse casual sex with friendship? *Because he fulfills a temporary need? What happens when she really needs him? He's never around. But he'll make himself available for that pussy.*

Continuing to wallow in frustration over another deflated evening, William sat on the Manhattan-bound F wondering if sisters had any idea what a nice guy goes through.

I hope that sincerity and generosity win me over, but they don't. These women out here expect me to wait around for them while they constantly have fun with suckers they know aren't worth shit. Then, after they get tired of being abused by the bad boys, they run to my type for protection and security, because they're wiser, and I'm good for them all of a sudden. Am I supposed to wait around for that?

Until then I'm wasting time. And money. If I shower them with affection, then I'm perceived as a wimp for being gullible. If I purchase trinkets from my heart, then they'll tell their girlfriends how much of a fool I am in their hen-clucking sessions. But I'm the nice guy, and I'm expected to pick up the tab on that first date, to always reach in my pocket, no matter how much money they're making. And as long as I'm paying, some of these trifling bitches couldn't care less.

Then to top it all off, they expect me to be ready-made by the time they realize these unstable thug niggas aren't who they want to have their children with. I'm expected to be financially secure, have the nice car, steady cash flow, expensive suits, fit whatever image they have of a good black man and, most importantly, all of this must be accomplished before I meet them. What do I need you for if I have to do it all alone? It doesn't make sense.

How can I have anything when I spend all of my money dating, tryin' to find you? Why can't you, black woman, take me out for a change? Shit, have you ever thought that I might like flowers, too?

He returned home to a message from Constance

on the answering machine, wanting to see him again.

Instead of feeling validated, he thought, she wants another free meal. *She needs to get a life*, he decided while listening to the message.

William knew he needed a life as well. Not that he wasn't trying, but things just weren't right without Andrea. Missing her youthful, yet sensual effervescence, he wondered how things were going with her and Derrick. *I wonder if he's regained trust in her*, he brooded as his head hit the pillow early that dawn.

The things William was asking for…

✪✪✪

William was jolted from his reminiscence by a knock on his office door. "Come in," he answered, and in came a familiar face from the Supply Department. "What's up, Tim?" As the young brother set the unmade boxes flat on the carpet floor behind his interview chair, William came from behind his desk and greeted him with a friendly embrace.

"Congratulations, Will. We heard about your promotion downstairs. It's your shit now, baby! I always told you you're the man."

"Nah, Tim, I'm applying for a green card in your world, baby." Laughing, they gave each other a pound. "I try, young bruh, I try."

"Nah, Will, you're doin' more than trying. You're blowing up! On the real, Will, you're doing this shit while keeping it real with the peeps. You act just like one of the fellas. You don't be tryin' to dis us supply niggas, just because you got an office. We're all proud of you, dawg."

"I'm struggling just like you, bruh, but only from a different level. Just remember what I said about using the N-word. If you don't use it, others won't."

Tim nodded his head in agreement as he headed toward the door.

"My bad, Will."

"How's school, Tim?"

"It's kicking my ass. But I always remember what you said about success never coming easy and it pushes me on. Good lookin'." Tim paused. "Yo, when are you gonna come uptown and play ball with the fellas again? After seeing you do your thing in the Rucker tournament last summer, they're all wondering if you've still got game."

"Of course, I've still got it, man! Listen, tell Darryl to put an order in for a jump shot. If he doesn't, tell him I'll go to the deuce and buy one for him."

Closing the door to confine his amusement to the office, Tim laughed. "You're a trip, man. Peace."

"Peace."

Good news travels fast, William realized as his office door shut. Taking pride in Tim's assessment, he always strived to be the best person he could be in an occupational environment without sacrificing too much of himself. *It's almost as if black men have to be bilingual sometimes*, he mused.

The fact that Michael Garvey had recommended him as his replacement left him giddy, as well. For six years William had toiled dutifully at Robinson, Burton & Luftkow as a court clerk, only to be passed over on numerous occasions for promotions he deserved. Undeterred and undiscouraged, he had studied the civil and federal procedures on many a late night, with the hopes that someone would appreciate his diligence. No one at his old firm had. Having reached the financial ceiling in that position, he realized someday he would have to leave that firm to utilize skills he'd honed for an assistant managing clerk.

Now, in two weeks, he would be in charge of coordinating the court runs he'd been doing for so long. When attorneys had questions regarding statutes of limitations, they would come to him for answers. He would represent New York's fourth largest law firm at client-affiliated luncheons and holiday dinners with administrative judges, chief court clerks and officials. *All of the holiday gifts from potential out-of-state court services would come to me*, he amusedly mused. Instead of feeling burdened by the new responsibilities that would come with the new position, he relished the challenge of keeping the department ship sailing ahead. All this newness had him beaming.

His jovial mood was interrupted by a phone call.

"William? It's Jerry."

What the fuck does this asshole want from me?

"I tried calling you yesterday afternoon to reschedule and..."

"Well, you should have left a message," William replied stonily. "You could've called me at home, like you did Monday night to tell me what's up." Hearing Jerry pause caused a short circuit in William's political correctness switch as he continued. "Your stupid ass didn't have the decency to come downstairs to let me know you couldn't make it."

"I was in a meeting." Jerry sighed. "Listen, William, there's something I have to tell you."

"No, Jerry, you've got nothing to say to me. Lose my number." Upon slamming down the receiver, William raged, *prime time asshole. It's bad enough I miss Della, now I gotta listen to this jerk tell me how much he wants to be with my*... Sadly, he didn't finish the sentence.

She'd be so proud of me, he reflected while picking up his phone again. He dialed her job number. This time the call was answered after the second ring.

"Hello?"

William didn't respond.

"Hello?"

Nothing.

"Hello?"

Still, nothing. She finally hung up.

Damn! I should have said something! Mulling over the idea of trying again a few minutes later, he decided against it. *She needs her space*, he concluded.

Or does she? While sitting in the upstairs cafeteria a couple of hours later, another bad feeling came over him. The thought of giving Della her space surely didn't sound as good as it had earlier, for he recalled a time in his past when giving someone ample space proved extremely costly.

✪✪✪

As the trees budded anew in spring, Angela Johnson entered William's life. She had been a receptionist at Robinson, Burton & Luftkow for about a year, though William had never paid attention to her beauty. Constantly bickering with her about numerous political issues, she'd always gotten the last word in their animated spats. One day when a fellow employee suggested he ask her out on a date, he brushed him aside.

"Not Angela," William said. "She's too difficult. And she's bossy."

"That's only because she likes you, man," the colleague assured him. "She thinks you're very intelligent and that you have a lot going for you."

Hearing Angela's positive comments made William smile. *If she thinks that I'm intelligent, she can't be all bad.* So he arranged a date with this woman.

Scheduled to meet her at ten o'clock on a Friday night in early April in front of the business school she attended, William got off the L train at the Union Square station at nine-thirty and searched frantically for the school for half an hour. Pessimism again reared its head. *She gave me a phony address. That's a new one,* he thought, walking past Washington Irving High School. *All she had to do was say that she wasn't interested, that's all.* He headed to the Palladium, which was one block from the train station. As he was about to give the doorman money with which to enter the club, Angela called out to him. Getting out of line, he greeted her with the flowers he was about to discard.

"I thought you said your school was around the corner," he insisted, pointing toward Irving Place.

"It is," she responded in her usual arbitrary tone. Grabbing his hand, she took him around the left corner, to Fourth Avenue, and sure enough, big, bold, black letters spelling out Blake's Business School faced him.

Duh.

Angela smiled.

So, they went to the Shark Bar, a quaint, dimly lit, black-owned establishment uptown. Surprisingly, William had a nice time. Behind Angela's sassiness he found a deeply sensitive woman who, like himself, had been injured many times in the game of love. At twenty-seven, she had experienced two broken engagements, plus more than her share of cheating boyfriends.

"That explains your no-nonsense attitude," William commented while leaving the bar area with her to be seated upstairs for dinner.

"Don't start no shit, won't be no shit," she replied.

She's a tough cookie, William thought, *tough, but very pretty*. Finally awakening to her beauty he noticed that the woman was also built. Her complexion was ebony, even darker than his, and her breasts jutted out proudly, looking full and firm. Strong, sturdy legs complemented her compact curves and cute face, and her round black eyes widened beautifully whenever she got excited. Her medium-size nose brought out her Jamaican ancestry, although she lacked the heavy accent.

"You're a very attractive woman, Angela," he told her as if just realizing it.

"You're kind of cute yourself. I like my men lean. That means they're packin'," she responded, causing him to blush. Smiling like she amazed herself with the statement, she got bolder. "What size shoe do you wear?"

"Twelve D," William responded.

"Just curious, man." He was warming to her aggression. It reminds me of Andrea, he thought. After dinner and a cab downtown, Angela suggested that the two walk across the Brooklyn Bridge. Once in Brooklyn, they walked to the Kings County Supreme Court. There, William explained to her the commencement of motion practice in the sometimes fair, often not New York State Judicial System. Angela seemed impressed.

"You mean it'll cost one hundred and seventy dollars to start any sort of action here?" she asked.

William nodded. "That's how much it costs for a plaintiff or petitioner to file a complaint. In order to get a judge assigned to your case, you have to file what is called a Request for Judicial Intervention

Form. That costs an additional seventy-five dollars."

They stopped on Adams Street, in front of the building.

"So when does this motion thing get started?"

"First off, let me explain what the word motion means legally. When you petition the court for a particular relief, the adversary of the plaintiff in any sort of action is called the defendant. Suppose the defendant wants to dismiss the complaint filed by the plaintiffs. He has to request, or move to the court, that he wants to dismiss the plaintiff's claims as described in their complaint. The way he does that is by serving a 'Notice of Motion' on his opposition. You follow me?" Angela nodded, and he continued.

"After he serves such documents on his opponent, he files those documents, as well as any documents supporting his course of action, with the court along with that form I was talking about..."

"I'll call that the RJI form. That's short for all that mumbo jumbo you guys call it," she said.

"We call it that, as well." They laughed. "So anyway, we file those papers. They're called motion papers because the defense is moving to the court with the hopes that they may grant its request. It can get much deeper than that. You get to respond to motion papers by filing opposition papers. You respond to opposition papers by filing what are called reply papers in further support, and so on, and so on..."

"You mean to tell me you have to remember all of that?"

"Yep. Not only do I have to know how to file all of that, but I'm starting to gain knowledge of the timetables for all of that. These are things called calendared diary dates which attorneys base all their filings and response times by."

"Sounds like a lot of paper pushing to me," Angela said as they resumed their walk.

"We call it due process, Angela."

"Whatever." They approached Atlantic Avenue, where William left the sidewalk to hail a livery cab to take her home. "So that's why you're always at the office so late studying?"

Shocked, he turned back to her.

"You paid attention to that?"

"Sure did. Actually, I felt kind of sorry for you. There you were, a handsome, intelligent, ambitious young man always staying late at work. You know what I thought?" At that instant, a blue cab pulled up to them. William opened the back door for her.

"That this brother should be coming home to someone like you?" he inferred.

He guessed wrong.

"No. I thought that you needed a life." Smiling,

Angela climbed into the cab and shut the door without giving him even a handshake. "Sorry, I don't kiss on the first date. Good night, William."

Just like that, the cab sped off into the night. The cliffhanger left William puzzled. *Did she enjoy herself?*

His answer would come three weeks later, as Janet Jackson's *Rhythm Nation* tour invaded Madison Square Garden one weekend in April. William attempted to charge tickets for the Friday show, but was unsuccessful in trying to get through to Ticketmaster.

On the night of the concert, Angela found him studying procedural books in the law library.

"C'mon, let's go," she asserted, closing the red CPLR manual he was reviewing. "We've got half an hour."

"For what? Where are we going?"

"You'll see."

So, William played good soldier and followed. Angela grabbed her coat, rushed the two of them outside the Helmsley Building, and hailed a cab.

"You still haven't told me where we're going."

She looked at him and flashed a grin. "It's a surprise."

Seconds later, a cab pulled up. "Take us to Thirty-Third and Seventh," she ordered the driver as they climbed in.

William's doe-shaped eyes widened in amazement. "Angela, are we going..."

"Shut up! I remember how you freaked every time they played a Jackson song at the last Christmas party. I figured you might want to go."

They did go, and William enjoyed himself to the fullest. As Janet and her dancers glided across the stage throughout her performance, he mimicked all their moves from his tenth-row seat. Angela kept staring at him, seemingly mesmerized by his movements.

"I see you also study dance moves," she quipped.

"Yeah, I guess so," he replied, sheepishly.

After the show, William offered to take her to dinner. She had a better idea. "Let's go to your place and chill."

Stunned by her straightforwardness, he paused.

"What's the matter, William? You can't bring a woman home with you?"

"No, it's not that. It's just..." Up to that point, only one woman had accompanied him home to his grandmother's house. Unable to share his apprehension with Angela, he did the expected.

"C'mon. Let's go."

When they arrived at his home, William went to open the door to his grandparents' house and found it locked.

"I'm sorry. They must have gone away again. I wanted you to meet them."

"There'll be another time for that. Let's go upstairs."

As she started to climb the steps, he grabbed her hand.

"Can I tidy up the place a little bit? I wasn't expecting any company tonight."

"Sure."

Taking a good ten minutes to straighten up his room, William was just about finished when he noticed two messages on his answering machine. The first was from Steve. He was, "just calling to see what's going on with your black butt."

He was smiling at that message when the next one almost made his heart stop.

"Hey, William. It's me, Andrea. I hope you haven't forgotten about me. I realize it's been a while, but I've been sorting through some things. My daughter is getting very, very big. You've gotta see her. Anyway I was thinking about you, and I wanna hear from you soon. Call me."

"Damn," he muttered. All it took was that one message, and like someone sniffing from a bottle of ammonia, his nose, eyes, and even his heart were wide open again. He couldn't wait to call her.

He had to, though. Angela was downstairs. Shit!

Treating him to the concert was a hint and a half to him that she liked him, and that blossoming feeling left William between a rock and a hard place.

As he came downstairs, Angela detected his indecision.

"Is there something wrong, William?"

"No." *How do women do that?* he asked himself as they climbed the stairs.

Upon entering his room, Angela was impressed.

"Well, isn't this special?" she commented after seeing his AIWA audio system and his overflowing music collection. "You think you have enough music?"

"Yeah," William replied, screwing in a blue light. Then he sat down on the edge of his bed. Angela took a seat in his guest chair.

"So, do you want to hear anything special?"

"Do you have anything by Nat King Cole? He's one of my favorites."

Nat King Cole?

By shaking his head, to Angela he was saying no; to himself he was still saying *Nat King Cole?* "How about Roberta Flack?" he suggested.

"Sure."

Rising, he reached into his CD collection and pulled out Roberta's *Greatest Hits* collection. Instantly, the room was filled with the haunting sounds of "Killing Me Softly." For the first couple of minutes, the two sat in silence. Then Angela broke the ice.

"You think she had something going with Donny Hathaway?"

"You know, it sure sounded like it. The chemistry they had while singing together was awesome. She couldn't find it with anyone else after his death. She'd collaborated with Peabo Bryson on some stuff, but it wasn't the same. Just like after Tammy Terrell passed on. Marvin Gaye didn't have that same feel with Diana Ross or anyone else he'd sung duets with. Sometimes, you can only have that kind of inspiration once."

"You didn't answer the question, William."

"Yes, I think so. Listen to 'Where is the Love' or 'The Closer I Get To You.' They had an innate feel for each other, as if their sole purpose in life was to blend their voices together. You could feel their love for each other through their music." Choosing an appropriate segue, he programmed the selections into his CD system. "Listen."

And for the next two tunes, neither of them spoke.

William's solitude was dominated by thoughts not of the chemistry of the two singers, but of what he had with Angela, or the lack thereof. The message from Andrea stripped the momentum away from getting to know her. Although he enjoyed Angela's company, he only allowed himself to admire her but so much. Andrea still had him feelin' like making love.

His confusion was interrupted by a bold question.

"William, do you find me attractive?" Angela came and sat beside him on his bed.

"Why do you need to ask?" *Where'd that come from?* he thought.

"Well, you're sitting there like you're ashamed to look at me. Do you have another woman on your mind?"

"Of course not!" he asserted loudly as he again asked himself, *how do women do that?* "I'm just feeling the music." He paused. "Angela, do you like Luther Vandross?"

"Of course."

"Let's put his music on." Rising from the bed, William went to his CD collection, pulled out Luther's *Best of Love* two-disc compilation and put in CD number two. "Superstar/Until You Come Back To Me" started playing.

Angela smiled. "Ooh, that's one of my favorites."

"I have all of his music. When I got this system, I purchased all his solo albums on disc. I have them all on vinyl, as well, along with the album he made with the group Change." William paused once more. "Angela, do you have a record player?"

"Yes. Why do you ask?" Instead of responding verbally, William reached behind his bed and pulled out two plastic shopping bags. After making a double bag, he got up and went to the record crate closest to Angela. He pulled out Luther's first five solo LPs and placed them in the double bag.

"Don't forget to take these when you go," he said, placing the bag in his guest chair. Returning to his position beside her, Angela's warm embrace swallowed him, and she gave him a peck on the cheek.

"Thank you, William. That's so sweet of you."

Looking down, William noticed that Angela's arms were still wrapped around him. He lifted his head and fired a yearning look into her eyes. Closing his own, he moved to kiss her. Not one to shy away, Angela's tongue immediately darted into his mouth, sending a chill through him.

As they fell back on the bed, their passion increased. Then just as suddenly, the flicker of flame descended slightly.

"Wait," Angela murmured tenderly. "It's been so long. I want to enjoy this. Hiking her black-leather miniskirt above her waist, she pulled William back atop of her and tasted his lips slowly. "Please make love to me."

William tried his best to oblige, but his desire waned, though no fault of Angela's physical beauty.

Her anatomy was appetizing and enchanting. He removed her silk floral blouse and blue brassiere and nibbled attentively on her luscious breasts. Her nipples were large and sensitive, as William found out by running his tongue across them.

"Make me climb walls tonight, honey," she moaned in a low, sexy whisper. Molding their semi-clothed bodies together and moving their hips together slowly, their chemistry was apparent. William followed suit when her hips moved in a circular motion, and he felt her tremble.

"Ooh, baby," she moaned.

A storm built inside of Angela, causing her to suck hard on his neck. Worked up to the point of frenzy, Angela asked William to remove some of his clothing. He wouldn't. Finally, after a half-hour, she caught on to his reluctance.

"William, don't you want me?"

Hearing the disappointment in her voice caused him to take a deep breath as he looked up from her breasts.

"Angela, I'm sorry… It's not you. It's me."

Proceeding with the history of the woman who still had a firm hold of his heart, William told Angela everything; how he'd found Andrea's beauty both enchanting and intoxicating, how she brought out the best in him and how he had never stopped loving her. He even told her about the love triangle with Derrick and how, despite feeling sorry for falling in love with an unavailable woman, his passion for her remained unabated, even to the point of thinking he was insane for still loving her.

"I think a part of me is always going to love her. I'll probably go to my grave feeling this way," he concluded.

Hearing this story made Angela cry, not in disappointment of the evening's events, but, ironically, in joy. Unaccustomed to hearing a black man express his unyielding, unending love for a woman despite hardly ever being with her, she encouraged William through her tears not to give up on his true love.

"One day, she'll see what I see already. I respect you more than you'll ever know. Don't ever change."

Sighing after hearing that phrase once more, William helped her straighten up, and walked her downstairs. After calling a cab for her, he asked if he could continue to see her on a platonic basis.

"Definitely," came her swift response. As they awaited the cab's arrival, he kissed her again, this time on the cheek.

"Thanks for not hating me."

Angela's brazen attitude returned.

"Please. I got some Luther albums without givin' it up," she joked, returning the kiss on his cheek.

"Thanks for a wonderful time." As she bounced down the stairs, and out the front door, into the cab, William beamed. Not only had he remained a gentleman and not taken advantage of Angela, but his love for Andrea remained intact.

Anxious to find the reason for her sudden phone call, he barely slept that night. Promptly at ten the next morning he placed the call.

"Hey, you," he said after Andrea picked up.

"What? I don't believe it! You're still alive."

William laughed.

"Alive and kicking. How's Jasmine doing?"

"She's fine. She's with her father this weekend."

"How are things going with that? Is he trusting you again?"

"We broke up about six weeks ago." She waited for his response. There was none, for William didn't know what to say. So, she continued. "He asked me to marry him."

"In spite of everything that happened?"

"Yes. Over dinner at the Sea Grill. You know, the place at..."

"Rockefeller Center," William interrupted. "I always wanted to eat there, but it's a little steep for my pockets. One day I'll go there. So anyway..."

"Anyway, we're sitting there by the ice skating window and he pulls out this big diamond ring, gets on his knees and proposes to me. I felt weird."

"I guess he likes theater," William cracked.

"I guess so. William, it was crazy. People skating by stopped once they saw what was going on, and they made a spectacle of the proposal. They were all pulling for me to say yes."

"Talk about pressure. So what happened next?"

"I told him that I'd think about it. A couple of days later I told him no."

"Did he ask for a reason why?"

"No. He kept muttering 'that fucking William' over and over again. Then about a week later, we broke up. He said he couldn't trust me anymore. He felt that if I married him, that would validate his trust."

William shook his head. "I don't understand his logic. Married people cheat."

"I know. But I told him a long time ago that once I say those vows, I plan to stick to them. He remembered that, so he tried to use it against me."

"Do you think you would have married him if…"

"If you never appeared on the scene? To be honest, I don't know. I was with him almost six years. I still can't believe it's over." She paused. "So, how are things with you?"

"Well, I date."

"You haven't met anyone special?"

Desperately trying to forget the events of the night before, William hesitated slightly after hearing that question. "Not really."

"As special as you are? That's hard to believe."

William felt compelled to confess.

"Well, I did have a date last night. She took me to see Janet Jackson and we came back here afterward."

"Oh, so that's why you didn't call me back last night!"

With Andrea sounding as though he had cheated on her, William again felt the need to explain.

"Andrea, I didn't sleep with her. In fact I told her all about you and the love I have for you. It moved her to tears. She thought the love I had for you was the most beautiful thing…"

"Is that what really happened? You know, you could tell me if you loved her down."

"That's what really happened, Crumbcake."

"God, I miss hearing that. You know when Derrick heard that you called me that, he ridiculed it in every way possible."

"You remember what I said about possessiveness and insecurity, right?"

"Yeah. I do." There was another break. "William, I miss you."

"I miss you, too, Crumbcake. Listen, why don't you come over tonight and listen to some music. I'll meet you at Fourteenth Street, just like we used to do. We can have a nice dinner and…"

"Now you know what'll happen if I do that, don't you?"

"My point exactly." Chuckling a bit, William became serious. "Andrea, it's been a very long time since I've held the woman I love."

"Ooh, I know, honey," Andrea said, as if warding off temptation was a struggle between life and death. "But I don't want to confuse what would happen if we hooked up tonight with us gettin' together as boyfriend and girlfriend."

William hadn't entertained that idea up to now, but it didn't sound bad at all. Mulling it over in a few precious seconds, he agreed with her. If he slept with her now, he would want her as his woman.

"You're right, Crumbcake. I love you too much and there would be a conflict. I'll tell you what. Whenever you're ready to see me, in any way, give me a call. If we do go out and something happens, I'll know that you're ready to commit. Right now, it's too soon for you to be thinking about gettin' with me. I'll need to know that Derrick is completely out of your system. It's not that I don't trust you; I'll always trust you. It's just that I'll know when you step to me, it'll be because you want to be with me. All I can do now is hope that I've shown you enough over the years to have the honor of being your man one day. I'll always love you, Crumbcake, and I'll be waiting."

"Wow!" Andrea said. "You are incredible. Don't ever change."

"I won't, Andrea. I won't."

After hanging up the phone that day, William was feeling exhilarated. He just knew Andrea would be his. Realizing that she needed time and space to move on with her life now, he made the right call in giving her this, although he fought the decision to say the right thing every step of the way. His conscience applauded loudly. *True love always wins in the end.*

He never saw the land mine he stepped on.

✪✪✪

Four months went by and William hadn't heard a peep from Andrea. True to his word, he never called her. For once he wanted her to take the same steps to his heart that he'd taken to hers numerous times over; just one time he wanted her to act on her own accord to show him love. One time.

For the most part William kept busy. Bragging to his boy Steve that he would "have a dope crib in New York by twenty-four," he began making strides to fulfill his dream. Instead of squandering money on unsatisfying dinner dates, he limited himself to movies in an effort to save money.

Angela was often his escort. Becoming his friend and confidante during the summer months, the two were inseparable. On Wednesday nights after work they zipped to the Slave Theater in Brooklyn to listen to lectures by Haki Madhubuti, Jawanza Kunjufu, and C. Vernon Mason concerning important issues of cultural awareness. On Thursdays there were trips to Harlem to attend New Alliance Party meetings with Lenora Fulani. Angela heightened his awareness further by constantly buying him books.

"You need to learn more about your people," she always said while passing him one book after another to read. During those months he devoured *Seize the Time* by Bobby Seale, *Soul On Ice* by Eldridge Cleaver, *Before the Mayflower* by Lerone Bennett Jr., *Black Man—Single, Desperate & Obsolete* by Haki Madhubuti, and *The Autobiography of Malcolm X* as told to Alex Haley. Feeling embarrassed when confessing to Angela that he had never read the last one, he received it as a twenty-fourth birthday present.

Saturday nights or Sunday afternoons were movie days, either at the theater or at her apartment in Crown Heights. William always made sure there was enough distance between them on her white leather sofa, for he didn't want to give her mixed signals. Angela respected that.

Whenever Andrea was brought up in conversation, a sparkle appeared in William's eyes, like a kid anticipating a new toy for good behavior. He told

Angela all about the April phone call, and how he'd handled the scenario.

She winced. "Bad move," she commented over drinks one Tuesday after work in mid-August. "You should have been more persistent in finding out how she felt about you."

"Why do you say that?"

"William, don't you think if she wanted to be with you, she would have done so then? So what she broke up with that dude six weeks prior to calling you. It doesn't matter."

Still, he defended her.

"Maybe she needs to make sure this guy is completely out of her system. When you have a child by someone that you've been with for six years, sometimes it takes a little longer to get that person out of your system."

Angela lost it. "I can't believe someone so intelligent can be so stupid sometimes! Has the woman called you? Has she?"

"No," William answered softly. "She's probably still confused."

"Doesn't that..." She stopped herself and began to cry.

Seeing the tears, William realized why she was crying.

She has feelings for me.

His thought was right on target. After composing herself, Angela confessed that she had fallen for him. She had tried not to, but the more time they spent around each other, it had become a forgone conclusion for her that it would happen.

"You're such a special guy, and this woman is stringing you along. You deserve so, so much better. I love you, William, and I don't want to see you hurting over her."

That was the first time a woman uttered those precious words to him. But it wasn't Andrea, the one from whom he wanted desperately to hear those words.

On the way home that evening, he thought about a closing remark Angela had made before saying good-bye. "Love can be strange, William, loyal to the point of blindness to reality." Andrea still had not called. Not one message on his answering machine, not one message at his job to call him. He worked only two blocks from her, and she couldn't even hook up with him for lunch? Alarmed now, he began a self-imposed seclusion.

In the last two weeks before she finally did call, he kept Angela at a distance, not because of her growing feelings for him, but for fear her call on Andrea was right on target. Following his cue, Angela, knowing what was about to happen, respectfully gave him his space.

Steve knew also. During a phone conversation in late August he all but blew "Taps" in his friend's ear.

"Black," he said with restraint in his tone, "I want you to be happy."

"I will be happy. Andrea couldn't have forgotten all those wonderful moments we shared. She couldn't have, Steve."

"I'm quite sure she didn't, William, but..."

Steve hadn't called William by his first name since eighth grade, when as captain of the school basketball team, he'd had the dubious honor of telling his best friend—the one he'd sat next to in five classes that year; the one he'd had to console following his elimination from an English class spelling bee after Steve had cheered his defeat; and the one he'd spent hours with at the hospital when William broke his arm between seventh and eighth grades—he hadn't made the team. Seeing the anguish on William's face that day, years ago when he'd broken the news to him, Steve vowed to never bring him to those depths again. He came awfully close during this conversation.

He sighed, then continued, "Keep hangin' in there, Black."

During that last week before she called, William regressed to the one-meal-a-day, sleepless-night pattern he had previously overcome. Never wondering if she was with someone else, he simply thought, *Why hasn't she called?*

She finally did on the first Thursday in September. Taking the liberty to make reservations at Cavanaugh's, an after-hours restaurant in Times Square, she announced, "This one's on me."

William's eyes glistened with the prospect that she was finally meeting him halfway.

En route, the fantasy of them leaving the restaurant as one after all this time caused his feet to barely touch the ground as he walked west, across Forty-Second Street. Recalling all the lonely nights thinking of her endlessly, he remembered the extreme patience and perseverance he had displayed during hardships endured, and now he was on the precipice of the moment of his life because of it. *She'll finally be mine. I know it! I feel it!*

Arriving, he found Andrea alone at a table in a strangely deserted area at the rear of the dusky restaurant, nursing an Absolut Sea Breeze. When she stood as he approached her, he noted her appearance. The black, calf-length dress she wore had a 1920s' appeal to it with fringes around the bottom of it. Her curvaceous, perfectly shaped body brought out its elegance, and the matching black pumps she wore enhanced the appearance of her long, toned legs. In his eyes, she had never looked better.

She has no right to look this good, he thought. That she stood once she saw him only added to his heart-pounding, breathtaking captivation.

"It's been a long time, Crumbcake," he said, greeting her with a kiss and proffering a dozen red roses he'd purchased along the way.

"It has been, William."

He seated her, then himself.

"What are you having to drink?" she asked.

"I'll have a soda."

Wanting to remain as sober as possible for the moment where she finally called him "my man," his "I love you smile" never was brighter as he continued, "So, how has the summer treated you?"

"It's been fine. And yours?"

"Pretty cool, Andrea. I've learned a lot about myself and my people."

"Really?"

"Yeah."

There was a pause during which they locked eyes. Andrea seemed aloof, uptight, and her conversation to that point seemed strained. The lively, mobile facial expressions he was accustomed to seeing in her were replaced with tension.

Cold feet, William concluded. *I'll take care of that*, he thought, giving her a love-filled look of reassurance.

"How's Jasmine doing?"

"William, she's fine. She's got a big mouth for a two-year-old. She's very bright."

"She got all that from you, big mouth," he joked.

Andrea smiled weakly. "Nah, the smarts are from me. The big mouth is from her father."

She finally opened the door and William wasted no time striding through it. "How are things going there? Have you been seeing him?"

"Every other weekend when he gets his daughter."

William paused, as if he were holding his breath before preparing to go underwater.

"Are you and he... Do you guys still..."

"No, William. It's over."

Hearing that made his heart soar, but he had to go further.

"Do you still love him, Andrea?"

Again, there was a quick reply. "I care about him. We have a daughter together, but I couldn't see myself with him anymore. I can't believe I stayed with him for so long. We never would have made it. He's too damn possessive and self-centered."

"Even if..."

"Even if there weren't a William, I don't think I would have married him."

William was never more relieved in his life than in hearing the statement that cleared his conscience, eliminating a sordid memory. Despite his love for her, shame and guilt ate at him like acid over the fact that she had been another man's woman while they were dating, especially once his feelings grew. That "no rings...fair game" statement had kicked his ass a million times over during their tenure. Now exonerated, he knew what Nixon must have felt in 1974 when, after resigning his presidency because of the Watergate scandal, he was pardoned by Gerald Ford. There was one more question to ask and now, with Derrick out of the picture, his confidence increased.

"Andrea, do you love me?"

Just as after *Dreamgirls*, she wouldn't respond. As she lowered her head, William calmly waited for a response. Seconds passed. Then Andrea did something she hadn't done when he asked her on that summer night three years prior. She spoke.

"William, I don't deserve you. You're too good to be true."

With deep definition in his eyes, and a face contorted in emotion, this man who loved his hopeful queen reached across the table, and firmly grabbed her left hand.

"Andrea, I've been this way to you and only to you. You bring out the best in me. My soul is alive only when I'm in your presence. Then, nothing is unattainable. The feeling you give me when I hold you defies description. There are no words for the overwhelming, overflowing love my soul possesses for you. I've been in love with you since I first set eyes on you. It's never died. I would give the world to make you and Jasmine part of a family...my family. I've been waiting my whole life for someone like you to come along. Andrea, I love you and it would be my honor to call you my woman. Please be my woman, Crumbcake." His declaration of love came powerfully, with a conviction he'd never articulated before, a conviction only the strongest of emotions can evoke. *Sometimes love does these things to a man. A Black man.*

She lowered her head again; this time, her silence lasted for minutes. Too nervous to bear the quiet, William went outside.

Leaving her alone at the table, he seemed perplexed that she hadn't jumped into his arms after he'd poured his soul out to her. Then, with the late-summer sun causing beads of perspiration to form on his bald pate, he began feeling nauseated; not from the humidity, but from a horrific thought.

Oh no, I've lost her.

Fighting queasiness, he stormed back inside and returned to the table. Andrea's head was raised, her hands folded. A couple of tissues lay on the table next to the roses and her eyes were red from crying.

"Andrea, is it too late?"

"Yes."

Suddenly, William couldn't stop his ears from ringing. Shaking his pounding head while tapping his left foot on the floor, as if he had a painful toothache, his whole body hurt. Fighting off the tears now forming in his eyes, he was losing control of his emotions in front of her. Somehow, he pulled it together just enough to ask one more question.

"Andrea, why? Why?"

✪✪✪

Because of his fractured emotions, the rest of the evening remained a blur to William, even as he sat in that cafeteria years later. Thinking he must have experienced a nervous breakdown that day, somehow he'd survived the traumatic moment.

Through it all, he served up this unpleasant memory. Andrea told him about Terrence, the guy who walked her from the store and incurred Derrick's wrath.

He recalled her exact words that day, and the great pain he'd concealed.

"He always said he was going to marry me and I used to laugh at him. I also avoided him and took him for granted. Everyone in the neighborhood growing up said we would end up together. And, like a fairy tale, we did. As a matter of fact, he sends me roses and everything, just like you.

"After I reached the decision to leave you alone, I knew what type of person I would end up with. And, who I would end up with. Over the summer, it just happened. I'm in love with him, William, and he makes me so happy. I'm lucky to have found him."

She continued talking about Terrence and her newfound joy, but William was in such an emotionally bewildered state he excused himself from the table twice to go outside, so she wouldn't see tears and the terrible pain of a hopeful heart.

It was as if she'd ripped his heart out of his chest, placed it on the ground and stomped on it. That was the same thing he'd done to Della.

On the way home that painful evening William conceded that Angela, the woman who actually loved him at the time, had predicted this would happen.

Getting up from that cafeteria table in a hurry, he knew what needed to be done. He had to call Della. He loved her and he wanted her to be his woman. There could be no delay. Fate, he concluded, had given him a second chance at true love; and up to now, he had blown it. If he continued to stall, he would miss the opportunity again.

Chapter Sixteen

SHOULD I CALL?

C'mon, Della, pick up the phone. C'mon, baby. After her phone rang three times, someone picked up, but it wasn't the voice he'd hoped to hear.

"Ms. Montgomery's line," the unfamiliar voice answered.

"Is Del... I mean, Ms. Montgomery available? It's extremely urgent."

"I'm sorry, sir. She's left for the day and won't be returning until Monday. Can I help with anything?"

William became agitated.

"Did she say where she's going today?"

"No, she didn't make me privy to that information, sir. I'm sorry."

After a pause and a sigh, "Thanks. Thanks for your help."

"I hope everything's okay," the woman responded, detecting his panicked state.

Hanging up the phone, William looked at his watch, a quarter to two. He tried dialing her home number. After it rang three times, her answering machine came on. He placed the receiver down without leaving a message, then looked in his desk drawer for her cell number. Instead, the digits discovered made him stop in his tracks.

Should I call?

Every time he'd come across that number over the past two years, the deliberation process had been agonizing. He had wanted to call his father and tell him that it was okay that they had been out of touch for two years, but he couldn't. Although utilizing diplomacy in front of his mother, William couldn't push his feelings aside this time, for his store of patience with Wilford McCall was filled with years of simmering hostility.

In William's youth, there had been many times in which he'd suppressed disappointment and frustration: so many nights when he'd curled up next to his mother and cried for his father; so many basketball games he'd wished he could have gone to when his neighborhood buddies had gone with their dads; so many school plays and choir performances where neither of his parents had been in attendance; so many father-son talks that might have proved beneficial, especially with regard to women; so many times he'd needed a man in his life to show him how to fix things, help him overcome his fear of driving, teach him how to use a condom, help him with anything.

On those rare occasions when they had gotten together, brewing resentment for his absence had been miraculously transformed into love. He enjoyed his father's tales and wished he were around to tell more. He gave him belated Father's Day cards months later; even sent him clippings from the local paper concerning school performances. Yet every time he tried to call him at the dry cleaners he owned in the Cobble Hill section of Brooklyn, he could never reach him, for he was always busy. Then, there were times when he and his older brother, Andrew, had traveled to their father's job. Not only was the elder McCall unavailable, but they had to endure being called Mason and Marlon by his employees, the twins from his second marriage.

Still, the love he felt for his father was unconditional, even as William struggled to find his way through his teens and twenties. All that changed two years ago in early December when he got a call from his father telling him that he'd suffered a series of heart attacks and was convalescing in Brooklyn Hospital. Immediately rushing to his side, he had never been braver when upon arrival, he saw tears from the strong, muscular man he'd taken his looks from; the man he wished he'd known growing up.

"I'm going to have a quadruple bypass tomorrow, son," Wilford told him through tears.

Those words brought immediate action. William took care of all the pre-surgery arrangements with doctors and family, made sure he had power-of-attorney to oversee his affairs, and stayed with him through the procedure. When he found out that Wilford was between insurance coverage plans, he secured Medicare coverage for him, then performed the responsibilities of nurse's aides when the lapse was revealed to all.

"The hospitals treat you like a leper when you aren't insured," he told his weakened father while helping him wash himself. Whenever Wilford battled post-operative depression, William became his father's drill sergeant, demanding that he do the necessary exercises so he could leave the facilities.

"I can't believe you washed me up and shaved me," Wilford said from his wheelchair on the day he left the hospital.

"I'm your son, Pop," William responded.

It was more than washing the backside of his father, however. Through his love, he thought a connection had finally been made, a harmonious union he wished they'd shared years ago. After making sure he was okay for the next few weeks, William gave his father the necessary healing space, only asking for a call every now and then.

He'd made a fool of himself once more. Although he had gone on with his everyday life, the hope of a little boy had surfaced, and with the childlike feeling brought the need for a simple hello from his sixty-one-year-old father. He had put aside more pressing issues to be there for him, despite the fact that his own life was slowly unraveling. He'd put resentful feelings of abandonment aside to do what a dutiful son was supposed to do.

That's what enraged him. What made it worse was that this wasn't a woman who'd been ignorant of his struggles with his own vulnerabilities. It was his father, Wilford McCall, his own flesh and blood. That he couldn't even trust him with his heart brought it all back.

Warring with the toxic mix of anger and confusion for an hour, William asked for a sign from above.

He got one when his phone suddenly rang.

"Son, how are you?" the masculine voice intoned.

"Pop?"

"Yeah." Wilford sighed. "It's me."

A pregnant pause filled the air between phone lines, during which William fought emotional confusion. Wanting to curse his father's being, he couldn't pull the trigger. Eunice McCall had taught him to love and forgive everyone, as if he'd never been hurt before. And his recent treatment of Black women indicated the derailment of his original train of compassion. He would begin to put his beliefs and virtues back on track, right here, right now. An edifice of trust in people had to be reconstructed, and it would start with this phone call.

"How are you?" William asked. "Are you still on all that medication?"

"For a while I was, but I'm fine now. I almost lost a leg, son."

"Really?"

"Yeah. I had circulation problems after they took the arteries. The doctors thought I was beginning to heal, but when they saw that my medication wasn't reducing the swelling, they ran more tests and found out I was a diabetic."

"Are you taking insulin shots?"

"Every morning."

"Hang in there, man." William paused to look at his caller ID. Wilford wasn't calling from New York City. "So, where are you living now?"

"I've relocated to Norfolk, Virginia, with Charene. You remember her, right?"

"The retired judge you've been dating, right?"

"Yeah, son. She'd been trying to get me down here for quite some time now and I fought it for a long time. It took getting sick like I did to make me realize some things, William."

He wanted to believe his father this time, however, cynicism reared its ugly head once more. *Realize what? That you have never been there for your first two children? That your life revolved around your selfish needs? That you gave your next three kids everything, and Andrew and me nothing? Even after you took ill and I nursed you to health, you couldn't even call me to say "Hey, dawg, let's have breakfast?" And you realize some things? Realize what?! Give me a freakin' break!* Rather than say this to the man whose sperm had produced him, he let the measured, meaningful, minute-long silence speak for him.

The silence was deafening, doubting and defining. The message that emanated from the break in their conversation traveled hundreds of miles, through all the telephone cables and computer systems, out the receiver, and into the heart and mind of Wilford McCall, who noted this as he continued.

"William, I want to tell you how sorry I am for not being in touch. When I looked up at you from the wheelchair the day we left that hospital, I felt so much guilt for not being the father to you that I should have been."

"Then you should have said that, Pop. What made you think that I wouldn't understand?"

"I just don't open up like that. Men never do. We acknowledge our mistakes silently, then we go forward."

"But you didn't even do that with your actions! Give me a fuckin' break, Pop! Do you have any idea of what I've gone through over the years? Do you?" Wilford's silence indicated he didn't. "Well, Pop, let me take you inside the wonderful world of William McCall.

"When I was young, I prayed for you to show more interest in me, to show me how to be a decent man. You couldn't even do that. So you know what? I'm doing the best I can with what I learned from Ma, especially with dealing with some of these confused women out here. And you know where it's gotten me? Nowhere!

"Over the years, I've been stood up on dates, rejected and passed over by women who thought I wasn't good enough. Then, they found people just like me to settle down with. I've been labeled as weak and soft by women when I open up and show them some sensitivity. Some have even called me gay, Pop. Gay!

"I've had one failed relationship after another, a sorry attempt at marriage because of my pain from all this bullshit, and as we speak, a duffel bag of clothes with bleach on them is at my apartment courtesy of a woman that I didn't open up to in time. Now, I'm not blaming you for all my problems, but you could have at least taken time out to give me a balance that I'm still trying to learn. At thirty-four, I'm still trying to learn how to be a man."

Wilford responded with a startling confession. "How could I have done that when I wasn't balanced, William? I know your mother has told you about the lies I told her, as well as some of the bad things I've done."

"Yes, Pop. Your transgressions are well-documented."

"I was a womanizer, son; a man with a weakness for pussy. And I used to do anything to get it. I was having kids by other women while still married to your mother and I cheated on my second wife as well. It wasn't until I lost my third wife, Carol, to cancer, that the gongs went off in my head. After she died, I spent many years alone, beating myself up over the things I've done."

"I do that now, Pop," William answered.

"I'm here to tell you, son, that you can't do that to yourself. Ask for God's forgiveness, change what you can change, son, and go from there." Wilford sighed. "You know, your grandfather and great-grandfather were alcoholics, and I used to always tell myself that I would never be like them. I would go out of my way to ensure this, by drinking in moderation and knowing my limitations.

"William, you know my history, and I'm asking you not to make the same mistakes I've made. Thanks to your mother, I know you won't. Someone will come along, and you'll know it. Now, about us..."

William sighed.

"Pop, we can't change any of our past. My issues are not your issues and I have to deal with them the best way I know how. But what you and I can do right now is make a promise to go from here and try to establish some sort of relationship. Can we do that, Pop? Let me know if we can't, because we can end this phone call and continue on with our lives as if we never existed. I know one thing. I won't lose any sleep, because I made an effort. But will you be able to live with yourself after this conversation? Can you honestly go to sleep at night and say that you did everything in your power to get to know me? You'll have to live with that guilt, not me."

There was another awkward pause as the chilling truth of William's words boarded Amtrak's Express service to Norfolk, Virginia, knocked on his father's door, and with no questions asked, bludgeoned him with brutal candor, then for good measure, punched him in the mouth. The terms put in front of him poured salt into open wounds, and left Wilford with an ultimatum as it traveled back to New York. If not complied with, the reality of this executioner's hit, William leaving his father's life with a clear conscience, would be much worse than the warning of words just received.

Wilford McCall got the message loud and clear. "William, I will keep in touch. I promise."

"Are you sure, Pop? Because I'll understand if I'm asking too much from you."

"William, I got the message."

William exhaled as another pause captured the moment.

Then, from his father's lips came the words that haunted his very existence. "Son, don't ever change."

"You know, Pop, I've heard those exact words all my life."

"I can't speak for everyone that has said that to you, but I like who you are, son. You're as strong-willed as your mother. By the way, how is she?"

"She says wonderful things about you all the time."

"Yeah. Right."

They both laughed.

"Pop, you should try giving her a call again. Just to tell her what you just told me."

"I'll think about it. So, what woman poured bleach on your clothes?"

"Her name is Della. She was good to me and I took

too long to realize it. Then after I was given the opportunity to make amends, I fucked up again."

The senior McCall sighed.

"That sure sounds familiar. William, do you love this woman?"

"Yes, Pop. I do."

"Then you gotta make it right. Don't be like me, son. When I was your age, I was trying to get so much pussy that I broke the hearts of many women. Too many. Man, I used to leave one house, then go to another and lay up, then another. Sure, it was good for my ego. But you know what happened? When I got sick, the only one I could call was you."

"What about my other brothers and sisters?"

"They're still mad at me because things didn't work out with their mothers and me. Why do you think they're so spread out all over the place? Son, if you love this woman, make it right. Have you tried calling her?"

"Yes, Pop. Right before I called you."

"And?"

"She's not at work. And not at home."

"Then you gotta go to her. Find her and tell her the truth. Go to her house if you need to. And do it quick, because from the way it sounds, you may have hung yourself."

Hearing those words made William grab his neck

and feel the noose that threatened to end his life. The horse was about to pull away and leave him hanging, a limp lifeless shell of the man he could have been to Della. He had to remove the rope of emotional baggage that weighed him down, and there was only one way he could do this.

"Pop, you are so right. I better go save this thing."

"I'll be in touch, son."

"I love you, Pop."

"I love you, too, William."

After hanging up, he decided to take the drastic measure his father suggested.

"I'm going up there right now. This can't wait," he muttered.

Unfortunately, it would have to, for at that second Michael Garvey entered his office. "William, I need you to do me a solid. It's a rush."

William couldn't help but smile when he heard his supervisor refer to a favor as a solid. His influence must have rubbed off on his boss.

"Mike, after what you just did for me, I owe you the world." He came from behind his desk and gave Mike a heartfelt hug. "Good looking out."

"I try, William, but save the syrup for my last day. I need you to go to Brooklyn for me. Have you ever been to the Unemployment Insurance Appeals Board at One Main Street?" William nodded. "Good. They have a record room there that closes at four and I need you to see if you can get access to a file for me. It's for my cousin. He has something on appeal and wants to take a look at a related case. The reason..."

"He can't get it is because of his pending case, right? That's why he's using you to retrieve it on the DL."

"Exactly. What does DL mean?"

Laughing, William reached behind his office door for his leather coat.

"DL means on the down-low, boss. Acting with discretion."

"You gotta write me an urban vernacular dictionary before I leave, so I can relate to my teenage nieces and nephews."

"Sure thing, Mike. So I gotta get there by four, huh?"

"Yeah. Speak to Ed Mahoney, one of the chief clerks there. He said I could hold it for a day or two," Garvey announced. "Just think, in two weeks you'll have that type of pull with clerks."

"I sure hope so, Mike. I hope so." They both looked at their watches and realized the time. "Five after three. I better go."

William placed his black Coach briefcase on his shoulder and headed out.

Walking to the Eighth Avenue subway line, William

noticed the cloudy skies and suddenly balmy air. *Snow is on the horizon*, he thought.

On the downtown C train, his mind shifted to Della. Remembering the many times during their year together when she told him that she was falling in love with him, he winced when he thought of his constant, "I just got divorced" response. At the time he met her, he'd been divorced for a little more than a year. Despite his stalling, she grew to love him and all she ever wanted from him in return was love, respect and most importantly, a commitment. She wanted William to become a man. Up to this point, William ascertained, he had let her down.

Not anymore, he vowed as the C train entered a station in downtown Brooklyn. Coming out the train station, he just missed the special bus that took people to the Unemployment Appeals building. Looking around now, he saw that the forecast he had made in Manhattan had come true. The shopping area in downtown Brooklyn was littered with post-holiday Christmas lights, and it was snowing. He had about twenty-five minutes to walk to the building, which was south of the Brooklyn Bridge and near the river.

Walking briskly, he arrived there in fifteen minutes.

After receiving the file and reviewing the documents, he made a call to his boss.

"Leave it on my desk. I'll be gone by the time you get back," Mike instructed. Hearing that also let him know that he didn't have to rush back; Michael would have indicated as much.

His mind already made up when he stepped outside, William wasn't walking back through the maze of side streets to return to the train; he would wait for the bus. With the snow circling down from the heavens at a blizzard-like pace, and because of the location of the building-near the river-the sudden weather change was blistering. As the afternoon turned to nightfall, the scenario seemed eerily familiar to William. The snowy evening reminded him of six days ago when he'd messed up. Perhaps fate had decided to smile on him for a change, give him a chance at redemption. Time would tell. For now, he just wanted a bus to come.

Ten minutes passed and he now had company at the bus stop. A tall, distinguished-looking black man wearing a long, wool overcoat came out of One Main Street, and stood beside him.

"Have you been waiting long?" he asked.

"About ten minutes. I wish it would come. It's taking too long." Pivoting right, William pointed to a barren building next to One Main Street. "What ever happened to the seafood restaurant that was there?"

"It closed down about two or three years ago," the man responded. "The owner lost business because it was by the water. A lot of people thought it was out of the way." He sighed, then continued. "I sure miss Parker's Lighthouse. Ever been there?"

"Twice," William answered. "Once I went with my older brother for dinner. It was summertime and I couldn't really appreciate the place." Turning to face the brother, he now had a look of melancholy on his face. "The second time I was there…" His voice trailed off and he refused to finish the sentence. He wouldn't have to because at that second, the bus arrived, ending their chat.

"Yeah, that's cool, man," the man responded the way New Yorkers do when the small talk has run its course. "Listen, try to stay out of this snow tonight. They say a foot of snow is headed our way." Boarding the bus quickly, he headed to the back.

William seated himself in the middle. As the vehicle pulled away, he took one last look at the vacant space that used to be Parker's Lighthouse and his mind went back to that second visit.

✪✪✪

February 1992

Gutted. Empty. Those two words described the

year and a half that followed Andrea's stunning announcement. People who are in love never know when the guillotine of truth will come down on them, although everyone around them can see what's about to happen. Too naive to see it coming, William was quickly beheaded.

His spirit destroyed, his pride decimated, every time he tried to rationalize why Andrea wasn't his, his analysis ended in tears. He thought long and hard about things he could have done differently, yet the fact that he found nothing made everything harder to accept. *Nothing hurts more than to give everything you have and still be overlooked*, he thought repeatedly.

Hadn't he bent over backward being understanding to this woman, sensitive to her every need and compassionate to a fault? Hadn't he been benevolent, chivalrous, and patient? Hadn't he been creative, fun-loving and affectionate?

There were so many things he had planned to do once they'd become one. Because of William's lengthy pursuit of Andrea, they never talked about a future together. Wanting to share all of his dreams and all of his fears with her, the thought of leaving New York with all of its hustle and bustle to help raise Jasmine even entered his mind.

Although there would be many phone conversations between the two during those eighteen months, he respected her new man and never sought her company. And although he still loved her, he knew things would never be the same.

During their dialogue William couldn't understand why Andrea now encouraged him to date other women.

All of a sudden she's acting like nothing ever happened between us, he thought. *How can you just shut down like that?* She could because she was in love with Terrence, and not with William. *Had she ever loved me?* he often wondered. Fate knew the answer, and presented it to William through one more heartbreaking event.

✪✪✪

Coming home to his new apartment in Flatbush after another unsuccessful date, William had a message on his answering machine from Andrea, mentioning that she had to see him. It was important, she'd stressed. She told him to meet her at Honeysuckle, a swank restaurant with live jazz on Manhattan's Upper West Side. Tomorrow at seven, the message concluded. William looked at his calendar. Tomorrow was Thursday, February sixth, the fifth anniversary of the night his life had changed.

A lot of things have happened since that night, he

ruminated. *A lot of bad things.* He thought of standing her up as he went to his living room and turned on the television. Surfing through the channels, he came across MTV. The station was premiering Michael Jackson's new video off the *Dangerous* album. He couldn't catch the name of the short film, but liked what he saw. At its inception, he saw Eddie Murphy and supermodel Iman sitting on a throne in Egyptian garb. Then appeared Magic Johnson, who had recently announced his retirement from the Los Angeles Lakers because of his HIV-positive infection, in the role of a palace guard. Michael appeared as a magician who made himself disappear into particles of sand. Fusing himself back together, Michael did his trademark spin and the music began. The song? "Remember The Time."

Captivated by the video, William got up and started dancing like him. MTV played the video four successive times, with William increasing the volume on his television during each showing. By the second showing, he had the intricate choreography mastered. *Too bad I can't go into Bentleys doing this,* he joked, referring to a trendy midtown club where wannabe executives and high-post honeys did more profiling than dancing. *People will think I've lost my mind.* Bored after the third showing, he sat down and merely watched. Suddenly, his bedroom phone rang.

"I bet I know what you're doing right now," the caller said.

It was Andrea.

"Yeah, I'm watching the video," he responded nonchalantly. "I got your message. So, what do you want to talk about?"

"I have some news for you that I thought you might want to know." The calm, delicate tone in which she spoke had William thinking he was not going to like what she was about to say, so during the slight pause he put on his coat of armor.

Hearing Andrea sigh, he grew impatient.

"So, what is it?" There was another pause during which he sensed that she was collecting herself. This must be something, he thought, so he abandoned his defenses for a brief moment. "Crumbcake, just blurt it out."

"I'm leaving New York this weekend. I'm leaving Sunday night. For good."

All it took was that second out of his cloak and he felt pain all over again. With blood rising to his temples, his head felt like it was going to explode, it hurt that bad. He couldn't understand why he still cared deeply for her.

"You're what?!" he shouted into the phone, like some crazed person. "You can't... I mean..." He paused again to gather himself. Still shaken, he continued. "Where are you going?"

"Terrence has family in Dallas and he's found a job there as a social worker..."

Again feeling an agonizing pounding in his head, William interrupted her. "Dallas? Dallas? What the fuck is in Dallas other than the Cowboys, the Texas Book Depository and the grassy knoll? It's hot and muggy down there. Why do you want to go there? Where are you going to live? What are you going to do there?"

"Well, today he found a place for us in North Dallas, on Preston and Arapaho. And he's looking into finding a day care center for Jasmine so that I can finish school," she replied softly. "There's more," she added.

"Let me guess. I know. You're marrying him, right? RIGHT?"

There was another pause before, "Yes, William. We're engaged to be married this summer."

Again, there was stunned silence on William's end. He had never hated being right about something more than now. "Married," he muttered silently over and over again.

"What was that, William?"

"Congratulations, Andrea," he responded. Finally accepting the news bulletin that hammered his senses, he continued. "I know you're going to be a beautiful bride. You deserve the best in your future and I hope you, Terrence, and Jasmine receive that in your new life as a family."

"That was so sweet, William."

"I might as well die with my boots on."

"What does that mean?"

"Nothing, Andrea. Nothing." He sighed. "So, now that you've shared your wonderful news with me, do you still want to see me?"

"Yes, I do. I didn't want to leave New York without saying goodbye to you. Have you ever been to Honeysuckle? It's a nice place on Columbus Avenue between Eighty-Fourth and Eighty-Fifth. It's pretty cool."

"I've never been there," he replied somberly.

"You'll enjoy it. I'm sorry if I disrupted your mood. It's just that I was watching the video and I felt like I had to call..."

"Listen, Andrea, I'm really tired now so I'm going to cut this short."

"Are you okay with what I told you?"

"Yes, Andrea. I have to go now. I'll see you tomorrow, okay?"

"Sure."

Hanging up the phone, William sat on his bed, blankly staring through the darkness at his bedroom ceiling, murmuring the word married over and over again for nearly five minutes. Eighteen months had passed since he'd last seen her smile, heard the melody of her laugh; it had been even longer since their last kiss. She had gone on living and so had he, despite his current futility in the dating arena. It shouldn't have mattered to him that she was moving away, but it did. He shouldn't have cared that she was getting married, but he did. *Sometimes love does these things to a Black man.*

He felt sick and helpless. In just three days, his Crumbcake would be gone for good. That's all he could think of. Through the night, the thought of her imminent departure tortured him, causing one last sleepless night. Holding his pillows tight, he relived every moment they had shared together. Laughing, crying, smiling, gnashing his teeth in anger, he realized one thing, through it all, he still loved her and he had to let her know this while there was still time.

Throughout that Thursday, he made ample preparations. Purchasing five roses, each one signifying a year she had been in his life, William also bought five red, heart-shaped balloons. With a lump in his throat, he inscribed in a blank card:

Though we now embark onto different roads,
Our parting should not be filled with sorrow,
For part of the journey through life we traveled together.

Thank you, Crumbcake, for the experience...

I'll always love you...

En route to their designated meeting place, he read that card at least a dozen times. After getting off the No. 1 train at Eighty-Sixth Street, he remembered one last thing. *I've got to know if she ever loved me.*

Reaching the restaurant at a quarter to seven, he punched in five dollars' worth of love ballads into the jukebox. Passing the stage area where live jazz musicians performed after ten, he was seated by the hostess near the back of the restaurant.

To his surprise, Andrea was only forty-five minutes late. While removing her brown leather coat, he couldn't help but notice the glittering gold and diamond object adorning her left ring finger. William wished he could crush it with his bare hands as he held it lightly while kissing her cheek.

"You could have put the kiss elsewhere," she said, taking a seat across the table.

"That's a ring I respect, Andrea. Congratulations, again," he muttered solemnly while reaching under the table for her parting gifts.

Suddenly, out of the jukebox came Gregory Abbott's "Shake You Down." They both shared a look expressing the song's significance.

"Our first slow dance," she remembered, beaming.

"Really? I forgot," William blatantly lied.

Andrea looked appalled.

"William, how could you forget? You never forget anything. That's why… Forget it."

"I'm just teasing. I remembered. I remember everything, Andrea." He handed her the roses, the balloons and the card.

Visibly moved after reading the card, she reached across the table with her left hand. William's hand met hers halfway and just as he was about to latch on to her, he saw the engagement ring and pulled back. Lowering his head, he dabbed at his eyes.

"William, you are so special. I'm really going to miss you."

"I'm going to miss you, too, Crumbcake."

The next couple of hours slowly drifted by as Andrea talked excitedly about her relocation and future with Terrence over dinner. Referring to her daughter, Andrea also mentioned how she wanted to raise her outside of New York. Terrence had found a nice two-bedroom house that he could rent for half of what an apartment would cost here, she'd declared.

When William asked about Derrick supporting his daughter, Andrea's gaiety waned.

"You know I had to take that bastard to court. He gets three hundred and fifty dollars a month taken directly out of his check," she revealed. "All I wanted was two hundred dollars a month from him and he gave me less than that or nothing at all for months at a time. He was doing that out of spite."

"Can you blame him?" William responded, not siding with Derrick, but understanding his hostility. "You did cheat on him, and to add insult to injury, you ended up with someone else. If I met him tomorrow, I'd apologize to him."

"I can't believe you agree with..."

"No, I'm not saying I do. You should never shirk from your parental responsibilities. But you've gotta understand, this guy never did anything to deserve what we did to him. I feel bad about that, especially knowing you didn't end up with me, either."

Caught off guard by his candor, Andrea paused.

"So, you regret having anything to do with me, don't you?" she demanded, her voice rising slightly.

"In some aspects, yes," William replied, annoying her further.

"You know, I don't know why I came out here tonight. I don't deserve this."

Andrea rose from the table and put on her coat. At first, William watched her in silence. Then as she reached for her gifts, he grabbed her hand.

"Take off your coat, Andrea, and sit down," he ordered aggressively, with just enough force not to create a scene. With her mouth agape and not knowing how to react to this newly commanding tone, she obeyed.

"Let me tell you something. If there's anyone that should be leaving this table this evening, it should be me. I've sat here for two hours with the hope that you would say something to me that I've never heard from you, yet all that's come out your mouth is Terrence, Dallas, Jasmine and Derrick. What about me, damn it! What about me?

"For five years, I put up with this shit! I had sleepless nights thinking about... no, knowing exactly what you were doing with other people, fucking 'em! I starved myself because food wouldn't stay down while I was worrying about you. I put up with you standing me up and mistreating me. You used me to save a hopeless relationship and then passed me over like I didn't even count. And you know what? I'm still having dinner with you today. You wanna know why? Because I love you! I love you with all my heart and soul, Andrea! You'd think even a person like you would notice that by now, but you haven't, even as I leave your life.

"Think about it. You showed everyone your heart except me. You can't even bring yourself to admit the real reason why you invited me out. Because you love me! You can't even tell me that. You never could. You loved me more than Derrick, didn't you? Didn't you?"

His bluntness prompted nothing from her but a stupefied look. So, he continued. "And you probably love me as much, if not more than this guy you're marrying, right?"

Still, there was no response.

"Yeah, I may not have everything you may get from other guys, but you know what I have that they don't have?" He pounded his chest. "Heart! Others may love you, but they don't and never will love you the way I did. It wasn't about cars or expensive dinners, nor was it about having some cool, Rico Suave persona, or the fancy wardrobe. It wasn't about being a hard nigga, either. I may not have been the coolest, most exciting man you met, and at times I acted foolishly, but I loved you with all my heart! *My* heart, Andrea! It's a shame you didn't see that or refused to. And because your selfish, greedy ass failed to recognize, I don't give a fuck how you feel at this point!"

When he was finally done unloading a half decade of pent-up frustration, the waitress came over, right on cue. Watching as she placed the check on the table before quickly walking away, he again directed his attention to Andrea. "Don't look at me. I'm not paying for shit tonight."

Rising from the table, he put on his black blazer, then his overcoat. "Now if you'll excuse me, I'd like to get on with the rest of my life."

Leaving those words behind him, he stormed from the restaurant.

By the time he walked across Eighty-Sixth Street to Broadway, William felt bad about his outburst, but knew it was the right thing to do.

I should've done that a long time ago, he thought, nearing the train station.

Suddenly feeling a tap on his shoulder, he turned to see Andrea, out of breath, coatless and crying.

"Where's your coat?" he asked, forgetting his anger and showing genuine concern.

"I left it behind."

Immediately, he whipped his off and placed it around her shoulders. Then they headed back in the direction of Honeysuckle. "The other customers will think I'm crazy when I go back in there."

Andrea stopped suddenly and as she hugged William the coat fell to the ground. William didn't care about that as he heard her say, "But I couldn't let you leave my life without letting you know that I love you. I love you so much, William McCall."

Trembling with emotion, William kissed her pliant lips slowly and she reciprocated passionately. When finished, both shed tears as they locked hands tightly.

Returning to the restaurant, they were embarrassed by applause from patrons who sensed the drama between the two. One of the sisters adjacent to the table they were at yelled out, "You go, girl! Get your man!"

"They never should have put *Martin* on the air," William joked, assisting her with her coat and gifts. "C'mon, Andrea. This evening can't end like this, especially if this is the last time we'll ever see each other."

"Where do you want to go?" They took a taxi through Central Park, down the FDR Drive and across the Brooklyn Bridge into Brooklyn. William instructed the driver to leave the bridge via the Cadman Plaza West exit, which he did. Then William guided him through dark streets and past a series of warehouses, and onto Main Street.

"What's down here?" Andrea asked.

"A restaurant my brother and I ate at a long, long time ago." Once in front of Parker's Lighthouse, the two exited the cab and William looked at his watch. It was ten forty-five. "What time do you have to be home, Andrea?"

Looking at him incredulously, she glared as if she'd been insulted.

"William, I don't want this night to end."

Hearing that almost brought tears to his eyes once more, but he remained composed as they walked to the edge of the water on the pier where the restaurant was located.

"What a view!" Andrea exclaimed. Separated by about a mile of water lay the spectacular iridescence of the brightly lit South Street Seaport. Farther north they could see the brilliance, beauty and majesty of the Manhattan skyline, and the illuminated bridges that connected it to other boroughs. Although the buildings surrounding them were darkened, the roads barren, bricked and bumpy, the panoramic sights across the water more than made up for the desolate environment.

William thought of saying, "I love you," once more to Andrea, but was beaten to the punch when he turned to her.

"I love you, William McCall."

"I love you, too, Andrea Richmond."

They shared another deep kiss, and grabbed hands tightly once more, ignoring the fact that one of them was wearing a diamond ring. Then, they headed inside for drinks.

The time spent in this restaurant was a dream to William as Andrea spent the next two hours pouring out her soul to him. Confessing to him that her love for him was like no other, she admitted, "You were more than a friend and you were more than a lover. You were like a prince. Too good to be true. Sweet. Sensitive. Compassionate. Handsome. Intelligent. Diverse. I've never known anyone like you and I probably never will." Eyes damp with tears, devoid of shame, the sad salty waters flowing freely let William know that she wasn't making this up.

"Were you ever in love with me, Andrea?"

"I'll never tell," she responded with the widest smile William had ever seen from her. On she went singing his praises, as she told him about her favorite day together, the day she'd fallen for him. Just as he assumed, it was the day spent at Central Park. "It was like you were my protector. We even shared a hot dog," she added. She even mentioned how painful it was for her to see him walk off the express bus the day they'd initially tried to say good-bye.

"That night it rained so hard. I kept wondering how you made it home," she admitted.

"Andrea, if all of this is true, then why did I suffer so much? You should have let go."

"I couldn't. I still can't," she retorted, quivering and summoning all her will to keep it together. "I was greedy for your love, William. Some parts of me still are." She paused. "I'm so confused. I was on a table in the delivery room of Brookdale Hospital, having Derrick's baby, and all I thought about was you. I'm about to start a new life and you're still on my mind every day. I love you so much, William. Please believe me when I tell you that I never meant to cause you so much pain."

"But you kept hurting me, Crumbcake. Over and over again."

"That's why I know I could never be with you. There's already been too much damage done. You didn't deserve all of the things I did to you. And deep down, you're probably thinking I'm lying to you now. But I'm not, William. I do love you."

Whether or not he believed she was being honest at this juncture was irrelevant; with that statement came the truth. After being passed over the way he had been, William realized he could never be with her and have complete peace of mind. He could never trust her the way she deserved to be trusted. He would have sleepless nights with her beside him, still unsure as to whether she wanted to be with others. *Timing is everything*, he pondered through tears. *She wasn't the right one.* As painful as the truth was on that day, he stared it down.

"You're right, Andrea," he said after an extended lull. "You are so right. That's what makes this night all the more agonizing. We still have to say goodbye, no matter what happens."

At that instant a waiter came over and informed them that it was last call at the bar.

William glanced at Andrea and knew exactly what she was thinking.

"I know. We have one more stop to make."

His Crumbcake smiled approvingly.

"William, whatever you do from this point on in life, please don't ever change."

"I'll try not to, Andrea," he responded, helping her into her coat.

Outside again, the two held hands once more as they trudged silently through the darkness of the cold early Friday morning, walking all the way to Atlantic Avenue, where William flagged a cab.

Once in the car, Andrea asked him a question. "Are you sure you want to do this? The night's been draining enough."

"Andrea, no matter what happens now, it doesn't matter. I'll have a broken heart anyway, so I might as well die with my boots on."

Andrea laughed nervously. "So, that's what that means."

The cab driver motored up Flatbush Avenue, past Grand Army Plaza and Church Avenue, and then to Cortelyou, where he turned right, letting them out at the corner of Sixteenth Street.

Andrea turned to William. "My God, you're so close..."

"Yet so far away," he interrupted. "C'mon, let's go upstairs."

Inside, Andrea took a seat on his sofa after he removed her coat. Turning on the stereo, William put in the *Dangerous* CD. He found song thirteen and pressed the REPEAT button for the selection entitled "Gone Too Soon." Although the song was a moving tribute to Ryan White, an 11-year-old who had died of AIDS, it had a dual meaning for him, a point expressed to his Crumbcake before leaving her alone in his living room.

When he came back five minutes later, tears again streamed down her face.

"The song is beautiful," she said, collapsing into his arms. Their relationship was, as Michael put it, like a comet, blazing cross the evening sky; like a rainbow, fading in the twinkling of an eye. And, like a sunset dying with the rising of the moon, his love would leave at the onset of dawn. Andrea would be gone, *Gone Too Soon*.

The song played repeatedly with the two clinging to each other like they were passengers going down on the Titanic, both fearful of letting go.

Finally pulling apart, Andrea managed a brave smile while wiping a tear away.

"Let's go to bed, William," she said.

Turning off the stereo, he again ignored the jewel on her left hand. Leading her to his bedroom, he lowered his mouth to hers and pecked her slowly, thoughtfully and tenderly. Then as the two realized the finality of their actions, their kisses became desperate, ardent and ferocious.

Licking away the salty droplets that slid down her cheeks, and using a strength he didn't know he possessed, William picked her up and carried her to his bed. Quickly undressing her, and then himself, he turned her over and seductively caressed her nape. Proceeding downward, his mouth went across her shoulder blades, then her spinal column. Andrea moaned as he returned a favor from years ago and kissed her soft buttocks. Then turning her over, he inhaled her scent with a peck on her forehead, then started on her fingers one at a time, engulfing them with the comfort and warmness of his mouth.

Losing her composure both emotionally and physically, Andrea couldn't take it.

"Please, William. Please don't stop."

She spoke those words in ragged, labored breaths as William brought his mouth to her navel and abdomen. Running his tongue in circles along them, soft, seductive sounds left his Crumbcake as she made an uncharacteristic request.

"Mmm, I need something to suck on."

Now entwined side by side, the two unspokenly positioned themselves for mutual stimulation. Mewling softly as a familiar warm, wet feeling engulfed his erection and had him floating, a certain nectar muffled William's utterance. Warring with conflicting emotions, the love he had for his Crumbcake wouldn't allow him to stop pleasing her, even as the dam holding his emotional tear ducts broke, resulting in a waterfall of crystal liquid that ran down his cheeks. Bravely, he fought off those uncontrollable tears as he loved her orally.

Warmth and pleasure radiated through Andrea's body as his lips probed her womanhood, then trickled along her vaginal lips. The heat spreading outward with each delicious flicker of his tongue, Andrea was experiencing one last ride to heaven. William, using his hands to steady her quivering frame, settled into a rhythm as he buried his mouth, then nose into her womanhood. As she began grinding against his face, the combination of her arousal, the taste of his saliva and her elixir, and her soft thighs against his cheeks upped the intensity of William's performance as he let Andrea's pleasure and pressure build in unison.

"Baby, please make me come hard."

Knowing that she would reach her peak with the explosion of a firecracker, he wet two of his fingers, slowly inserting one in her already drenched canyon, and after tickling the rim of another place, slowly, seductively pushed it inside.

Andrea reached the point of no return. Minutes later, as her firm body lurched forward, a scream pierced the air. "Ooh, baby!" she shouted, wrapping her legs around his neck as best she could.

William held her close through the tremors of acute pleasure.

Gravitating slowly to earth, Andrea repositioned herself and fell into his arms, bawling unashamedly. Already stretching her loyalty to Terrence to its limit, she knew William's penetration of her would render her commitment to her fiancé moot. Apologizing to him profusely for not being able to go further, she was crestfallen.

"I understand," was all William could say.

He, too, stopped short, finally acknowledging the engagement ring that rested on her left hand.

"William, I love you so much."

"I love you, too, Crumbcake."

"Please don't ever change..."

✪✪✪

Don't ever change, she said.

It was probably supposed to end that way, William thought, placing the file retrieved from the Unemployment Appeals Board on the desk of his outgoing supervisor. During the trip back to work, he recalled how they'd held each other and watched their shadows along his bedroom walls, weeping until seven the next morning when the sun rose. Realizing she had stayed much longer than expected, he put his emotions aside and facilitated her departure. Holding her hand one last time after walking her to a cab, they shared one last kiss. As their lips touched that last time, he felt something leave his body. Someone shut out the lights to the room that contained his heart.

Once again she said to him, "William, don't ever change," while entering the taxi.

Then she was gone.

William also thought of a few of the landmarks they had visited. Although Dallas BBQ's, their favorite barbecue spot, remained at the corner of Eighth and University, the Hawaii Kai had closed down. So did Honeysuckle, Mr. Leo's, Cavanaugh's, and Parker's Lighthouse. Even the Copacabana, the place where it all started, had closed down in a way. In actuality, the club moved cross-town, to West Fifty-Seventh Street and Eleventh Avenue. Fate was giving him signs, he thought. It was time to move on and love again. *A broken heart is a motherfucker,* he concluded. *I lived with one for a long time. It's time to show someone else I know how to love.*

That someone was Della.

Chapter Seventeen

SNOWY MOONLIT EVENINGS

William didn't know which was worse, the snowy, moonlit January evening he now walked into or the fact that he had not allowed himself to love for so long. Making his way to the D line at Fifty-Third and Broadway, he purchased a dozen roses. Della's going to love these, he thought. Even more so, she's going to love what I'm about to tell her. Although six days had passed since the incident, William felt reborn. Finally ready to become what his sisters wanted—a secure black man of strength—he was ready and willing to prove this to Della—that is, if she would forgive him.

The wait for the train seemed endless, during which he rehearsed in his mind what he would say to her. Realizing that Della was through with him, he knew the only way he stood a chance was by telling her the truth, that he was in love with her and had fought it every step of the way; that because of a broken heart, he had never opened himself up to feel this for any woman since Andrea. When the metal horse finally arrived, William seated himself and analyzed this revelation.

✪✪✪

Before the series of heartbreaks and dates culminating with the Andrea Richmond saga, William McCall used to think that a black man who displayed respectful mannerisms and a pleasant demeanor would come out ahead in his pursuit for happiness and tranquility with his mate. Selling himself on the notion that having chivalrous qualities and exhibiting generosity and sensitivity would endear himself to his sisters, he'd brainwashed himself with the belief that doing right by the person he loved would ensure success in his relationships. All those principles slowly died once Andrea went away.

Although he'd never envisioned it or done it intentionally, William began the negative distillation process men normally undergo when shielding themselves from emotional devastation. That warm sensation leaving his soul years ago was the hope that black men feel when they've given their all and have nothing to show for their effort. The loss of Andrea propelled him into a downward spiral.

Shortly after Andrea left for Texas, William began

a relationship with Angela, his companion and confidante. After she left the firm they worked at together, their friendship turned to romance, but on her side only. Instead of behaving impulsively and giving from the heart, William acted on compulsion throughout, dually trying to appease her increasing demands and divert his attention from past hurts.

Thinking matrimony would cure all ills, he married her three years later, despite pleas from his best friend, Steve; Steve's brother, Darren; and all other family members who questioned his readiness.

It was over in three years.

Increasingly miserable because of the failure to mend his broken heart, he frequented the local nightclubs and mastered the game of seduction. Utilizing a phony charm, he became a predator for the unsuspecting. Successful at satisfying his needs while sleeping with women at will, he would then dismiss them with an iciness rivaling that of the despicable Hannibal Lecter, removing a victim's heart, then devouring it. Arriving home in the wee hours, he would feed Angela the usual bullshit about hangin' out with the boys. Tolerant at first—she knew her man was suffering—she could put up with it no longer when she found out that her husband was bringing home other women's panties, a revelation she discovered when looking for a pen in William's briefcase.

After a year and half of separation, Angela found love elsewhere and the divorce was brutal, leaving William with exactly what he'd entered the relationship with—his Brooklyn apartment, a stack of bills, a feeling of failure, and no self-confidence. Carrying that feeling like a sack of potatoes, it was after almost multiplying the number of women he'd slept with by ten, that he met Della.

Untrusting and figuring she was going to be like all the others, he slept with her after their first date. Despite her flaws, something inside told him she might be someone special. Even as she was being pursued by others, he continued to see her, and despite being tempted by what others were offering, she always made William her priority, never giving in to anyone else.

Slowly, his feelings for her began to grow. Unlocking shreds of material Eunice McCall had instilled in him, he began sewing his heart together again. He could talk to Della about work, his dreams, his nightmares and future goals. He laughed with this woman, cried while watching sentimental movies without traces of ridicule, and was loved for the flawed man he was.

Still, he was afraid to commit to her. Every time

she mentioned her male pursuers, his insecurities resurfaced. He retreated into a protective shell, going almost two weeks at a time without seeing her. On that last occasion he met Barbara.

When things went too far with her, William felt guilty. So after that infamous morning in late November, he stopped seeing her. Not if it meant losing Della, he recalled thinking after giving Barbara the news over the phone.

The evening he sent Della the holiday package, he remembered the special feeling that enveloped him while he picked out the teddy bear. He knew she would love holding it. Also recalling how it took him three nights to compose the tape that was enclosed, he remembered how he wanted it to be just so, as if he were delivering a message directly from his heart. He also thought of the tears that had welled in his eyes six days prior when she had called him a "fucking dog, like so many of you sorry ass black men."

Despite the recent cavalier attitude he had displayed toward black women, William felt an uncomfortable feeling pass through him when she uttered the D-O-G word. A long way from the "don't ever change" testimony he'd heard repeatedly through the years, for so long his personality traits had been synonymous with all the adjectives relevant to a nice guy. While cognizant of the fact that most of his brothers didn't like identification with the positive label for fear of also hearing words such as "weak" and "syrupy," William missed being called that. He was still a good black man, but through heartbreak and single-mindedness he'd transformed himself into something he was not proud of. Through love, he hoped he would be afforded the opportunity to find redemption with Della.

✪✪✪

Getting off the train at the Fordham Street station, William felt ready to reclaim his love life, although he wished he could do it on a better day. Snow continued to fall and by the time he reached Della's neighborhood, he gingerly crossed icy, unsalted pathways, much like the evening when it all started.

Finally reaching her apartment on University Avenue, he saw the door to her lobby had been left open. Moving quickly through it, he glanced right, saw a broken elevator and went to a nearby staircase.

Reaching the second floor, anxiety enveloped him, causing him shortness of breath. The importance of the situation stalled him. For fifteen minutes he deliberated at the top of the stairs. Drifting through each experience that shaped his negative spiral,

William battled his insecurities one last time. This reminded him of the night when his life changed, when he gave his heart for the last time. It had been years since that snowy evening in February, so many years since he had given himself unconditionally to a black woman.

It's time to give my all again, he announced.

William went to apartment 2B and knocked hard. There was no answer. He knocked again even harder. Still, there was only silence. Pressing his left ear against the door, he heard a faint sound, like someone slipping into slippers. About a minute elapsed. Then, the door opened.

Della, in her pink bathrobe and open-mouthed, looked stunned.

"William! What are you doing here? I thought I told you..."

"Della, before you go any further, please let me explain," he implored, handing her the bouquet of roses.

"I can't believe you're doing this to me. William, don't do this..."

"I've got to, Della, I've got to! There's something I have to say, and I won't leave before I say it."

"I don't want to hear your shit anymore! I gave you a year of my life and all I received in return is a pile of bullshit. There's nothing you have to say to me." She dropped the flowers to the floor. "And you can keep your damn roses!"

As she tried closing the door, William wedged a foot in.

"Della, please. This can't wait. I love you!" Miraculously, she opened the door. "That's right, Della Montgomery, I love you." His eyes glazing with tears, he picked up the roses and extended them to her once more. "I know I should have said this to you a long time ago, but I've been fucked up for a long time...a very long time. I want to give you everything, Della. Everything you ever wanted from a man. I'm ready. Scared, but ready."

Hearing the sincerity and desperation in his voice, she allowed herself to be drawn in once more.

"How do you know you love me? Just the other day as I surrendered my heart to you once more, you called me Barbara. How am I supposed to feel all the things a woman is supposed to feel when you keep stepping on me? How do I know it won't happen again?"

"Della, you've gotta believe me, it won't. The problem was much deeper than Barbara. I'd been hurt a long time ago, and I allowed the wounds to remain open. I couldn't give myself to anyone. Anyone!

"I allowed myself to be swallowed up by my insecurities. I couldn't trust anyone with my heart. I was that scared to love again. And as my feelings for you grew, so did my fears. You kept talking about what other guys wanted to do for you, so I figured you were giving them some play."

Wiping her eyes now, Della began shaking her head.

"No, William. I chose you and was committed to loving you, no matter what. I'm not going to say that it was easy, because from what you showed me, it wasn't. But I loved you, William. I loved you."

"What's stopping you from loving me now? Della, I love you and I'm ready to be your man, everything you ever wanted. Please be my woman."

Dropping to his knees, he clasped his hands together.

"Della, please…"

During the pause that followed, he looked into Della's lovely brown eyes. Although teary, they looked beautiful to him. In fact, despite wearing no makeup (not that she wore a lot, anyway) and being robed, she had never looked better to him. He was in love again.

"Della, please…"

Della's tears turned into a cry. "I'm… I'm…" Stopping to compose herself, she tried to speak again, but couldn't. Sobbing, she fell.

Springing to his feet, William caught her as she

fell into his waiting embrace. "Baby, what is it? What is it?"

Just as suddenly as she fell, she pushed him to the wall behind. "I'm sorry, William. I can't. I just can't..." Hurrying into her apartment, Della tried to close the door. William quickly pushed the door open and stepped into the apartment.

"Della, wait! I love..."

William's legs almost buckled when he realized what he had obviously interrupted. He saw a bearded, middle-aged man about forty, he guessed, rising off her sofa, bare-chested, in boxer shorts and with a hard-on that formed a miniature tent. The look on his face was not only of surprise, but one telling William that a certain, familiar type of groove had been disrupted. Della ran into his hairy chest.

"I'm sorry, William," the man said, the look on his face turning into a despicable smirk as if he'd won some sort of Olympic competition.

With his body trembling and his head throbbing like never before, William summoned strength he never knew he possessed. Going quickly to the door, he reached outside, picked up the roses and brought them inside, laying them at the couple's feet.

"Congratulations, Jerry," he said. "I hope you give this beautiful woman everything she needs. She deserves the best, you know."

With those words he staggered out of the apartment.

Numbly walking through the bitter cold, William knew why he'd been directed there on this humiliating evening. *There's always a price to pay when you play with someone's heart*, he reflected sadly, as he slid his MetroCard through the turnstile at the Fordham Road station.

Dazed, barely coherent of his surroundings, William stumbled to a seat and waited for a D train home. *Get a hold of yourself, partner*, he exhorted, fighting insensibility. *You've been through tough times before. You'll get over it.* When the train came, the voice became his spirit, somehow guiding him homeward.

Sitting down in the last car, he reached into his coat pocket for his Walkman. Pressing the PLAY button filled his ears with Phyllis Hyman's "When I Give My Love (This Time)." Hearing the words Phyllis sang—*No more mistakes, that's my resolution. Lord knows I've been through so many changes*—thawed his numbness, causing him to bawl uncontrollably. Again experiencing the price one has to pay for his actions, fate, as it had done so many times in his past, delivered the pain straight, no chaser.

This final lesson, although excruciating to William's senses, had a positive effect. In realizing the pain was still the same, he decided he'd rather take his chances being the sensitive, benevolent man he once was, and could be again.

Additionally, he came to the conclusion that he wasn't a dog, his reason being that a dog can evolve, but it can't change. *I can change*, he concluded. The proof was in the pudding. Having transformed himself in a short time into a woman's worst nightmare, now he would revert to his sensitive nature.

With the train nearing his stop at Cortelyou Road, he made another pact with himself; this one, he planned to uphold for the rest of his days. He would be the William McCall many people knew as someone special; the gentleman who loved and gave freely from his heart without expectation or remuneration; the man who would display the positive traits Eunice McCall had instilled in him. Taking his time, he would look steadily for his soul mate. Once he found her, he would show her the strength and resolve acquired through experience, not to mention diversity, intelligence, tenderness and compassion.

Yes, that included making love again. If and when opportunities arose, he planned to engage in foreplay with her mind, taking his time during lovemaking and letting her know repeatedly how much he loved her afterward. *This approach might not always be successful, but it won't be because I didn't give my all*, he concluded, turning the key in his apartment door.

Directly going to his answering machine without removing his coat, he hoped to find a message, a miracle actually, from Della. There were two messages. The first was from Lisa, relaying the news of a possible reconciliation with Roland, asking him to pray for her because it would be the last time.

"Not a problem," he mumbled while retrieving his second message.

Message received 8:05 p.m. "William this is Janet, the woman you met at Justin's a couple of days ago. I guess you succeeded in making a lasting impression since you've been on my mind constantly. Hopefully, that Della woman sees what I see. If not, then I just wanted to let you know that my coffee offer is still on the table." (sexy giggle) "If you want some, then call me. My number is 718-555-3690. Hope to hear from you soon."

Mulling over the invitation, and the events of the past six days, William picked up his cordless phone. There would be change, but it wouldn't occur this night. *Just this last time*, he thought while dialing Janet's number. *Just this last time...*

REAL LOVE

Are you there, God? It's me, William again. I humbly come to You, my creator, with so much to be grateful for. Thank You so much for giving me the strength to rise this morning, and for blessing me with such a beautiful daughter. Thank You for allowing the air to pass through my lungs another day. With each passing day, I continue to praise You, hoping You keep the wondrous light shining down upon me. You have given me a talent that I cherish daily, and the fact that my words touch others means so much. The endless cupboard of energy and strength that I have been blessed with drives people crazy, but my intentions are good, Lord. The sole purpose of the breath You have given me is to make a difference.

Recently, I was told that sometimes we have to specifically ask for what we need. So today, I come before Your incredible spirit asking for the one thing that has evaded me: A REAL LOVE.

It was so hard rising from bed this morning, as I

needed every bit of the strength You provide to will me to this computer. The other day, I said goodbye to love again. Tears met at my chin as another love boarded the train of heartbreak. Her destination: out of my life for good. Lord, I didn't want her to go, but she said we're not in the same place and time of our lives, that our destiny is to be friends. How can you accept that after giving your heart in a sacred way?

You indicated in Proverbs that man cannot direct his own steps, and You were right, Lord; oh, You were so right. That is why I now leave the most treasured piece of my existence in Your hands: my heart. I apologize for its battered and bruised state, missing pieces and frayed at the edges; please forgive its present condition. Twenty-plus years of excess baggage can do that. The favor I ask from You is to mend it this one last time, for I am a man that truly wants to love unconditionally, wholeheartedly, and completely.

Sometimes, I feel like I have nothing left, Lord. Each heartbreaking experience takes something from me. I realize that You created me very different from most men in that I am in touch with my emotions, but it doesn't make me weak. Because of You, I am both lamb and lion simultaneously. Through Your love, You have given me insight on love that most fail to possess, and for that alone, I feel whole. Sadly, when it comes to Your beautiful energy and its correlation with my life, it seems to be allergic to my heart.

Lord, You have instructed us to always love as if the first time, however, after each bout with the residue a failed love leaves behind, when awry, has done something to me; it takes longer and longer to open my soul to the goodness I know You have in store for me. Fear can paralyze the warmest of them, and I am frightened of the pain that accompanies hurt, and frustration. But, agony is what I feel right now. Alone. Again.

The feeling of love was once so strong in me, but I'm losing hope, Lord; I'm losing hope. That is why I need You to guide me, with Your wondrous strength, to help me find that real love, that true love, that lasting love. The shared energy that starts with nothing and ends up with something, the mutual adjoining of spirits where worlds are complete as hearts, minds, bodies, souls and spirits fuse to one. The positive radiance that illuminates the darkest of skies, that makes the meek move mountains. The passion that never stays away when things go awry, the communal that prays together to stay together, the heavenly union that goes through the rain to appreciate your glorious sun.

I want it so bad, Lord, I've tasted its beauty at times. I've held it, fought the good fight for it, longed for it during lonely nights, cherished it and appreciated when given rations of it, worked alone to salvage what appeared on the surface to be it, pushed it away in fear and because of the pain it often caused, abused it at times; please forgive my imperfections. I keep trying, Lord, and I'm running into walls everywhere.

Tears are flowing from my eyes right now as the meditation of my words transfer to screen, and paper. Heavenly Father, I call upon You to reconstruct my soul yet again. I place all my faith in You, Lord, that You may build my tattered heart into an indestructible edifice once more. Please replenish my faith in love once more, one last time, Lord, so that when it comes I'll embrace it with everything I have, endlessly, fearlessly and totally. You are love, so I know that it can't be wrong when I tell people that Love conquers All. Please help me find it.

In Jesus' name…Amen.
William "FREDRICK" Cooper
Copyright 2003

ACKNOWLEDGMENTS

November 12, 2003—10:18 a.m.

My Goodness, where do I begin? Well, I'm not rushing to meet a Federal Express deadline because I haven't blown up like nitro…yet. *(Smile)* That gives me ample time to write the longest list of acknowledgments in history. My apologies for the length of this in advance; there are so many people to thank. Lord knows, this has been an incredible journey.

Heavenly Father, I never knew I had so much inside, so much courage and strength I never knew I possessed. Thank You for providing the vision, focus and determination, as well as bringing me to Reverend Calvin Butts and the Abyssinian Baptist Church. To the family of the late Phyllis Hyman: I cannot begin to thank you enough for encouraging her to develop such a magnificent instrument. Her music was my companion, my lover, and my "Old Friend" during all those lonely nights working on a dream. I hope I kept her spirit alive.

Zane: Thank you so much for not forgetting about me. Nobody in the publishing industry believed in this story, except for you. (Does that sound familiar, or what?) With Sistergirls.com, I finally got a computer at home, and, with *Six Days*, I hope to make a major statement about Black Men and their hearts. I owe all of this to you, and I won't let you down. Wayne Stewart: You are so crazy! Charmaine Parker, Pamela Crockett and Destiny Wood: That our family at Strebor has your loving support is a blessing from the Most High.

I want to thank all the book clubs and readers who took time out to read the self-published version of the novel. Trust me, it was not easy hearing some of the criticism, but it truly made a difference, and I only hope the revisions answered all questions.

Henri Forget, my first editor, you were the bomb, and I can't wait to work with you again. To Cheryl Faye Smith: Now, I realize that if I said this to you in person, I would get the twisted look and the "I never really cared" response in return. So, I'll do it in print: I never liked the fact that you have made me a better writer, and, with some real tough love, a stronger, more focused man. I never liked the endless support you have given me through our journey of up and downs. I loved all of these things, and I Love You, for being you. Don't Ever Change. David McGoy: From the very beginning you were there, improving my skills with difficult exercises, possessing the patience to deal with my emotions, keeping me grounded, never letting me become puffed up and most of all, believing in me in times when I doubted myself. Your talent and intelligence inspires me more than you'll ever know. I love you, bro. To Steven McGoy, Christian Davis, Allen Brown, Askia Farrell, Darrell Sargent, Kevin Walton, Stacey and Tad Spencer, Darren McCalla, David M. Dore, Bobby Moore, Daniel Marks, N'Dea and Owen Lake, Josephine A. E. Tucker, Baruiti Tucker, Wayne Dorsey, Richard Gibbs and Cody "Mr. Baldhead" Fugate: Let's open some doors together.

My Family: Stephanie, Adrian, Jeffrey, Gerald, Janessa, Allan, Alvin & Darlene: I did it! I did it! I'm a published author! To L'il Ivory Meyers: Big brother wishes you were here. Rest in peace, little guy. To the Proskauer/Pryor Cashman Posse: Michael Cooper, Anthony Lopez, Roger McLean, Ronnie Garvey, James Bethea, Jesus Hernandez, Richard Randig, Allen F. Healy, Mary Jane McAleavy, Jennifer Robinson, Theresa Allison, Cynthia Mondesir, Rodney Felder, John Fleming, Jeffrey Widen, Harvey Hylan, Sharon Livingston, Omar Brunson, Emerson Moore, Jeremy Feinberg, Larry Silfen, and the Cagers, Lahai Johnson, Gregory (ROCKY) Lachaga, Lisa Funk, John Braatz,

Yvonne Montgomery, Don Reese, Clifton Brathwaite, Debbie Botie, Sirocco Wilson, Marybeth Hare, Tammy-Figueroa-White, Frances Figueroa, Velanica (Nikki) Donaldson, and Nereida Foxworth: You guys are wonderful. Tammy Taylor, Rosalyn Lewis, Timothy Chappelle, Christopher Burns, Jeannette Sangster, Ramona Seay, Frederick Manigault, Letitia Cofer, Katrina Spicer, Anita Turner, Joyce Powell, Yolanda Chatham, Ms. Atherline Smith, Cassandra Solomon, Theodosia Barrerio, Brenda Colon, Tanika McCray, Veronica Curet, Germaine Lee, Reginald Orcel, George Ruge, and Azailia Wynter: Thanks for keepin' the faith. Elizabeth Morgan, Lisa Carr, Bryan Block, Marc D. Coleman, Sylvester James, Roberto Jourdan, Austin and Denise Wilkinson, Reese Walker, Antoine Francois, Anthony M. Pabon, Frank S. Pezella, Valorie Smith, Patricia Mack, Sonja Oden, Rosie Harvey, Brenda T. Wilson, Marlaina B. Moses, Sharon Gethers, Dorothy M. Williams, Ingrid and Albert Morgan, Karen Williams, Venetta Williams, Elaine DiBartolo, Deborah Holmes, Barbara Reaves, Jayne Coleman, Rita Rippy, Sandi Broughton, and Darlene James: Your continued support, and never-ending encouragement mean more to me than you'll ever know. To My Barber "Lo": Keep givin' a brotha the bangin' Jordan cuts, yo. To James (Rhino) Harris and the Falcons: Forgive me for not being the ultimate teammate during this process, however, you guys are close to me always. Hopefully, we won't have to worry about sponsorship for a while. Let's win a football championship, y'all.

To the Court Clerks: Juan Roldan, Jamel Summers, Darren Hunter, Duane Grant, Iscom/Krista Jones, Gerri Parker, Sandra Somerville, Onika McClean, Lynn Little, Richard Montanez, Brian Simpson, Jahjaira Santiago,Greg Tomey, Jonathan Wilson, Jonah Perry, Samuel DeLeon and "'Crazy" Hector/ Martha Gonzalez: I cannot begin to thank you guys for showing me I can be an OG and have fun. Now, let's pop the Cristal, yo. To Lawrence Shapiro, Lenny Goldfaden, Sharmaine Haughton, Tara "Fabulous" Atherly, Jasmeen Smith, Patricia Kinard, Anita Fecunda, Sharon Davis, Lana Browne, Theresa Braxton, Daryl and Debbie Elliot, Patrick Boone and Lynn Boone (thank you so much for those buddy passes. A struggling author always needs the hook-up—wink.), Ira Wortham, Cydney Rax, and "DA FAM"- Jamal Sharif, Tia Shabazz, Tanya (Journey) Allen, Judith Middlebrooks, Lawanne (L.D.) Stewart, Angela Ray, Kim Alexander, Monica Blache, Deborah Maisonet, Tonya Evans, Susan Border Evans, Karla Drain, Martina C. Royal (RAWSISTAZ), Carol Mackey (Black Expressions), Clara Villarosa (Hue-Man Bookstore). Thank you so much for everything!) Rhonda and Terence Gipson, Davida Davis, Emma Wisdom, Ms. Jackie Perkins, Tia Shabazz, Melonie Payne, and Memphis Vaughan, Jr: I wish I could give you all individual shout-outs. I hope this is suffice. Nicki Lancaster: That final phone conversation touched me. If I pull this off, it'll be because of your tough critique. Harlem Hosptital's (TAP) Mentors: Edna Chandler, Carol Roberts-Matthews, Mark Moodie (you are da man!), Laticia Mitchell, Kwame Christian, Takira Reed, Lawrence (Poppa Smurf) Brown, Kenneth Moodie, Hisham Tawfiq, and Claude Collins: We are doing this.

To Charene Thornton: ZeDiva, I cannot thank you enough for everything you've done for me. Continue to be the special person that you are. Love, Little bro. Glendon Cameron: Man, you are one funny dude. I only hope that I tell this tale as well as I know you would. Tony Smith: From Paralegal School to the Doubletree, you've always been there, like another brother to me. To Lisa Solomon-Jackson: Keep that positive energy flowin'. Patrice Waldron: Thank you for pushing my books, baby. Gail Carr: You know how we do, baby.

PHEW! Now, for my author friends: Nancey Flowers, Joylynn Jossel, Marlon Green (Thanks so, so much for allowing me to Water Cherry's Garden—wink), Jacque Bamberg Moore, Leslie Esdaile, Brian

Egeston, Toschia, Allison McVey, Steven Barnes (you are so cool!), Frederick Williams (Little Fred loves your passion!!!), Mary B. Morrison (you, my dear, have a heart of gold!!!), Toni Staton Harris (my dance partner), Scott Haskins, Darrien Lee, Bernice McFadden, Shonell Bacon, JDaniels, Tracy Price-Thompson, Vanessa Morman, Travis Hunter, Timm McCann (Yoda, wherever you are, Luke can't do this alone) and my Strebor Brothers: Jonathan Luckett (thank you so much for your last-minute insight), DV Bernard, Franklin White, V. Anthony Rivers (thanks, Vaughn—smile), Nane Quartay and Rique Johnson: We are all in this together. Special Big-ups to Eric E. Pete, Chet "C. Kelly" Robinson, Earl Sewell, Vincent "One In A Million" Alexandria, Victor McGlothin (I thought I had a lot of heart, man), Kwame Alexander (you are a deep brotha!!), and lastly, my partner in crime, Tracy Grant: You guys are not only an inspiration as talented writers, but as Black Men.

My heart is with these next group of ladies. God is Love, and one of his manifestations of this is in the romance novel. Gwynne Forster, Loure Bussey, Dee Savoy, Jacquelin Thomas, Tee Garner, Evelyn Palfrey, Sharmaine Henry and Brenda Jackson: I am grateful to be an acquaintance. My writing mentors, Donna Hill (thank you so much.), Andree Michelle (you are so special), Nathasha Brooks-Harris (my gurl!!), and, Rochelle Alers (you are THE TRUTH, da WHOLE TRUTH, and nothin' but DA TRUTH! Continue to drop it like it's hot!): Thank you so much for candor and wisdom. I'm so glad you ladies are a phone call away and love you all very much.

To Gigi Roane and Willie Jennings: You were the only ones who invested in me when I was POD (Print On Demand), and I will never forget those hot summer days we sweated our asses off. From the bottom of my heart, I say thank you. To the Ebony Erotica Lounge, Ebony Thick N BBW, Voluptuous Angels, Platinum Thick Dymez, and Voluptuous Women: FullFigureDiva, Pretty Brown Eyes, OnTyme Girl, Platinum Cherry, Star, Black Princess, Dsire1Luv, KaramelQtee, Antoinette, Paul Yarde, Bonita and Trina, Chrome, Ced, Seo, Tim Dawg, Playa, Chocolate City, Cocoa B, Patt M, (You are crazy!!!) and lastly, Sxulstimulation: Ya'll know I love you, and Doctor Fredrick (Fredneb) Cooper sends his love. To Rosa-Parker Holland, D.V. Moore, Sandra Bell, Ayokari Hoyes, Beverly Robinson, and, Candace Putman: All of you are very, very special to me, and I'm hoping all of you continue to shine under such a positive light. God bless each of you.

To Audra P. Wooten: It took some time, but I finally realized what it was. There is something about me, something very special. Thanks for lighting the fire, baby. To Audrey T. Cooper: By admission, you deserved a better husband and I apologize for the pain you endured at the hands of a man unprepared for marriage. Thanks for the wonderful job on our daughter. She's really something, isn't she? To Staci Shands and Ms. Jackie Perkins: There's something about a Delta Sigma Theta woman that makes a man stronger. Thanks for entering my life and showing me a better way of doing things. My dreams and beliefs carry a lot of power because of your existence. Brenda Woodbury: You are an incredible woman. I'm sure glad to have sent that E-mail back in the day. Thank you, for being you. Jo-Ona Danois: "99," there was "an edge" missing, a certain ingredient (toughness) missing in my maturation as a man. You forged this in me, and for this alone you'll always have a special place in my heart. Allegra Maple: Your loving support and friendship means so much to me, baby. You are an incredible, resilient woman. POP: Please take better care of yourself. I love you. Dr. Eyvonne T. Wilton: The embodiment of strength. Thank you so much for bringing order to my love life with your words of wisdom, your spirituality, and wonderful heart. I have so much peace with life's decisions because of knowing you. I love you. GRANDMA: Thanks for everything. I only hope to accomplish a little of what you have. MOM: All your son wants to do is make a difference. To my lovely daughter, Maranda: I LOVE YOU, HONEY, DON'T EVER FORGET THAT!

Lastly, to my hopeful readers: Some of us write for the green paper. Others, like myself, write to make a difference. As black scribes, all of us write for the support and love of our people as well as our heritage. There are so many stories to tell, so many books to read by us. All of the pebbles we throw in this ocean of African-American literature would not be possible without your eagerness to support all of us, and from the bottom of my heart, I want to thank you.

ABOUT THE AUTHOR

William Fredrick Cooper is an ordinary guy who is trying to make a difference in life. Born in Brooklyn and reared on Staten Island, he presently resides in the Bronx in New York City. A legal assistant at the law firm of Pryor, Cashman, Sherman & Flynn, he is the proud father of a lovely daughter named Maranda. Mr. Cooper is a teen mentor with the Brother 2 Brother Mentorship Program in conjunction with Harlem Hospital; a member of Harlem Abyssinian Baptist Church; a co-coordinator of the Well Read Reading group, a Brooklyn-based literacy initiative that connects with African-American teenagers; and a member of the Board of Directors with Brother 2 Brother Symposium, Inc., a program that encourages men and young adults to read fiction.

Affectionately known as "Mr. Romance," Cooper is also a contributing author to several anthologies: "Legal Days, Lonely Nights" in *Sistergirls.com*; "Watering Cherry's Garden" in *Twilight Moods: African American Erotica*; and "Snowy Moonlit Evenings" in

Journey to Timbooktu, a collection of poetry and prose as compiled by Memphis Vaughnes. Future stories include "Corbin Mantra," a story for young adults in *Book of Rhymes*, the Brother 2 Brother children's anthology; and for an Ebony Lounge erotica collection and sequel to *Twilight Moods*. His follow-up to *Six Days in January* is scheduled for publication in March 2007.

Excerpt from

There's Always a Reason

by William Fredrick Cooper

Strebor Books International

March 2007

"Yes, yes, don't stop, hurt this pussy so good!" the woman screamed as the flesh slapping with her chiseled lover reached a fever pitch.

"That's right! You better take all *of this dick!"*

Over the past year, he survived many things that would break the spirit of any man. Somehow, he brought a semblance of order to a world that was FUBAR: Fucked Up Beyond All Recognition.

But the genesis of it all tortured him. Remembering the mind-blowing image, the memory still jolted his senses like a sledgehammer blow to his temple. His bald dome throbbing intensely, all attempts to still the pounding headache were futile, continuing his concussive state.

A year later, the torment of the nightmare remained.

Riding across the Manhattan Bridge on a crowded "Q" train in a punch-drunk stupor, still unsure of his surroundings, William McCall stared at the downtown skyline of New York City through red, sleepless eyes.

The hub of concrete skyscrapers lacked a familiar accent without the Twin Towers. This particular morning, the majestic view seemed even emptier, for if anything, mirroring the loss of the magnificent World Trade Center, it was the gaping hole in his heart.

Rolling the dice of love for the umpteenth time, once more he crapped out. All his dreams of a future with Anna Daniels—his exclusive, exquisite love, the woman he would grow old with—were shattered by an unforgettable sight.

"It's all yours, baby..."

"That's right, you greedy bitch! This is my shit here."

"Ooh, I love it when you fuck me doggy-style...Harder, Dammit! Harder!"

It wasn't supposed to happen again. He thought he had figured the damn thing out; the crazy masculine force that embodied strength, yet made them vulnerable to the desires when surrendering to that special woman. Praising its workings during its prosperity, William McCall wouldn't allow the jaded world of contemporary dating to bring about negativity.

Acknowledging and correcting mistakes of yore, his past demons were in the rear-view mirror of distant memories, having been replaced with confidence and restored trust. Coming of age, he reached the stage in his life where wisdom met self-worth, only adding to substance. Someone would come along, appreciate his virtues while strengthening his flaws, help him grow as he would her, and love would conquer all.

What he saw shattered all conventional thinking.

"Does he hit it like this?"

Trembling, Anna's sinuous back arched like a jungle cat as she succumbed to the powerful sensations of his in-out movements.

"No...he...doesn't...mmph."

Churning against his abdomen while squealing, her hips rolled and her backside wobbled as she met her lover's vicious thrusts with equal vigor.

"That's right. You better cum!"

✪✪✪

Repeatedly replaying the scene, *she never responded to me like that*, William thought. Lovemaking with Anna was always pleasurable: addictive, affectionate, exciting and ecstatic, spellbindingly sensual. He loved the way she said "take me there" when he explored each curve and crevice, every single pore of her copper skin.

Her orgasms always drenched our sheets, he recalled. Remembering how he always wanted her to cum before him, he enjoyed investigating the core of her with his mouth, face, and nose. Licking her labia like an starved cat, then tickling her triangle the way Ray

Charles tuned the ivory, his singular purpose after midnight was to make her chest hurt from the ragged breaths of a climax. Then, as she recovered from his oral performance, he pleased her with the deep digging and seductive stirring of something hard and stiff. Taking delight in the fact that she pursed her lips while squirting climatic satisfaction from his action, living for her sigh of contentment that came from her sexual surrender, *there was no equal to the loving I gave her,* he believed.

Assumptions can be a motherfucker. His performance paled in comparison to those five minutes of unwanted voyeurism.

"Baby, let me suck you. I wanna taste you."

"Damn, girl, you're out of control," the baritone announced as Anna swept her tongue along his erection. Pumping her head like a piston, up, down, and all around on his oiled shaft, she proceeded to seal her lips around the meaty spot where cockshaft meets cockhead, and sucked relentlessly. Connecting with the male version of the G-spot, her lover's knees sagged ever so slightly.

"Damn, baby, you got skills!"

Peering upward from his groin, Anna's facial expression was of a famished woman willing to do anything to please.

"You like that? Do you like the way I suck it?"

"Oh, hell yeah!!"

"Cum in my mouth," Carla begged during slurps. "I want to taste your babies."

Moaning like a wounded animal, her lover had no choice but to submit.

Seeing the woman you love roll another man's semen around in her mouth, mixing salty-sour masculine juice with her saliva can devastate a man; especially when watching the events with an engagement ring in hand. But the simultaneous loss of love and your livelihood, and the recollection of such, can drive him to insanity.

✪✪✪

Approaching midlife matured William McCall. A couple of years before his world collapsed, his responsibilities as a managing clerk at Goetz, Gallagher and Green quintupled, for the New-York based law firm merged with smaller ones in Seattle, Philadelphia, Chicago, Dallas, and Los Angeles. Having complete confidence in his abilities, Mr. Gallagher, the senior principal of the country's third-largest law firm, met with William and other partners from the additional cities. He recommended William oversee the implementation and progress of various computer databases in the newer venues.

The promotion was not without resistance, from an elderly, seventy-something Dallas partner.

"Are you sure he is the best man for the job?"

Singed by the heat of corporate racism, a wrinkled

pair of indifferent pupils bore a hole through William.

Surprisingly, Gallagher's response was immediate.

"I wouldn't be too concerned," he announced. "I can assure you that Mr. McCall is the best man for the job."

"I must say, his credentials stand out," the Seattle partner added.

"But he doesn't have a bachelor's degree," the Dallas attorney countered.

Somehow, he felt like Vivien Thomas, the dexterity-gifted craftsman turned "Baby Blue" surgeon revolutionary, in that his natural abilities and experience were being downplayed.

"At this point, I don't think that has any relevance," a Chicago partner, a fifty-something black man stated. "I mean, his longevity in the New York office speaks for itself."

The Philadelphia-based partner agreed. "He's the right man for the job," he boomed.

"He'll need an assistant to supervise the New York offices in his absence," Gallagher added.

"I'm sure I'll find someone," William uttered.

"Okay, then it's settled. Congratulations, William," Gallagher said. "You will be the managing supervisor of all the offices. It is your responsibility to make sure Pacer, Courtlink, Database, Legal-key docketing, and additional court search components are implemented and functioning effectively. You will be visiting all offices, instructing the staff at each venue; and your salary, as of today, is seventy thousand dollars a year."

William beamed.

That's a long way from the twelve thousand a year I made doing messenger work back in the eighties.

"Gentleman, I assure you that you selected the right man for the position," he boasted.

Now it was up to him to find a suitable assistant.

He thought he secured such in Markham Chandler, whose alluring chestnut tone accompanied broad shoulders and bedroom eyes. A single-breasted, five-button black suit, complete with white cotton shirt and knotted red power tie, complemented a compact physique and an ambitious, model-like smile. Articulate and handsome, his zealous energy reminded William of himself at thirty.

The screening was conducted over steak dinner at Houston's, a swank midtown restaurant located in the Citicorp building. Noticing and admiring his confidence from their initial handshake, *we had so much in common*, William recalled. Both were born in Brooklyn's King's County Hospital, came from large families, had college education from NYU, and, as was revealed later, acquired their degrees from the same hard-knocks school concerning issues of the heart. Additionally, Mark, as he preferred to be called, paid rough dues in his occupational field, a point William noted while surveying his resume.

"So, I see that you're presently working for National Clerical Services, Mr. Chandler," he observed.

Mark nodded.

"I enjoy working with—"

"Hector Roldan."

"You know him?"

"Very well, Mark. He's like a brother to me, and I try to support his business by sending him my legal business for the other offices. You know, like out-of-state document retrieval, filings, and service of process. I'm so proud of him." William paused. "Since I know everyone that's employed by him, I find it rather odd that he never mentioned you."

For the first time, he saw a tiny crack in the veneer of Mark's self-assurance.

"Mr. McCall, I was always busy, handling his court work in Westchester, Suffolk, and Orange counties."

An awkward moment ensued, during which William fought confusion. A novice at conducting interviews, he wanted to be professional, yet easygoing and approachable. Unlike his interactions with superiors who fancied their reputations as taskmasters, he decided to be a "cool boss," one who could chill after-hours with his employees, yet maintain the bridge that separates manager from staff member.

The process would start with a simple request.

"Mark, please call me William. Whenever I hear Mr. McCall, I look over my shoulder for my father."

Seeing the calmed smile from across the table, he eased the pressure that came with the attempt of leaving an impression.

"Are you familiar with the local and federal rules?"

"I sure am."

"Can I give you an exam?"

"I'm ready whenever you are."

"Okay then. Let's count the days on state court pleadings. Can you do that for me, Mark?"

"Sure. On a Summons with Notice, it's twenty days from the date of personal service that a defendant must serve a Notice of Appearance and demand for complaint. A Summons with the Complaint, if personally served, defendant has twenty days to answer. Am I correct?"

Smiling, William remained silent.

"I guess you want more, huh?"

"Yup."

"If served in any fashion other than personal, then the defendant has thirty days from the completion of service to answer or file a motion."

"What constitutes a completion of service?"

"Service is perfected when the proof of service has been filed with the court."

The probing continued for an additional half-hour,

with the statutory and procedural inquiry growing increasingly difficult. Yet, the answers came easy for Mark, William noticed. Dazzled by his future employee's zeal, he remained coy with his findings. After discussing the firm's benefits package and incentives, he was comfortable enough to shift to a lighter dialogue.

"Come to think of it, Mark, you do look familiar."

"I've seen you play basketball," Mark noted as he sipped a Coke.

Nothing like talking sports to raise an eyebrow.

"So you ball, huh?"

"Very well," he responded.

"Our firm team could use help at shooting guard."

"I play the point, William. I love comin' down, shakin' the crap out of a dude with a killer crossover, and laughing at him as I score."

"But will your team win? All that matters to me is the 'W,' Mark. And that comes from making your teammates better. "

"I make *my team* better by scorin' buckets."

Smiling, William couldn't help but notice the arrogance Mark exhibited, not to mention the articulacy transfer to street vernacular.

He'll learn a lot from me if he can suppress the swagger.

"See, now with that attitude, you couldn't play the point here." William laughed. "You get everyone else involved first. Only when necessary do you take over games."

Smirking, the competitor in Mark surfaced, albeit slightly.

"I take it you're the point."

"Yes, Mark. I've been the lead guard for years now."

"I know. I remember you torching some teams in the Corporate League games."

"I'm kind of old now."

"But you can still hoop. That championship game at Baruch College last year, you hit about thirty, right?"

Smiling, William nodded.

"But I can take you."

Shooting Mark an *oh really?* look only hardened competitors recognize, William yearned to pull the sweaty asphalt of a summer blacktop beneath him, and the spirit of a gym battle into his bloodstream. In his youth, the pill would have been at the table, and just a sniff of conceit from an opponent would be sufficient fuel to wax the ass of any trash-talker.

But he was older now.

"I pace myself now and hope that I conserve enough energy in the tank to see my teams through adversity." He sighed while making a concession to Father Time.

"C'mon, man. You mean to tell me you don't keep track of your points?"

"That's for you young guys. When you near forty, all the individual stuff becomes irrelevant."

They would argue the point for five minutes: Mark, from his And 1 mix-tape point of view; and his future employer, from the *been-there, done-that* perspective. During the banter, and the ensuing back-to-business conversation, William McCall smiled. Reminding him of an impetuous little brother, he relished the opportunity of having a protégé; for a previous authority, Michael Garvey, had done the same to him.

That his skin was bronze and his origins were of the same impoverished roots he rose from only strengthened the bond. In loving his fellow black man, he made a pact with his maker that whenever the opportunity presented itself to be his brother's keeper, his actions would be swift. Like in the famous Young portrait, he reached over the wall for his brother.

No further candidates would be interviewed, no credit report or references checked. The next day, the office manager made Mark an offer of thirty-eight thousand a year—*More than I ever made as an assistant*, William quipped—and he had his running mate, both professionally and socially.

Having a pupil, he recanted, *meant letting him know he was appreciated.*

Acting on those thoughts, he always sprung for dinner during the after-hour training sessions, as well as drinks whenever they ventured to 40/40, the fantastic Jay-Z-owned sports bar Mark had introduced to him.

"What about Justin's?" William contended, referring to a familiar watering hole four blocks south.

"Man, Diddy's spot is A.P.O."

William was baffled.

"A.P.O.?"

"Yeah, man. A.P.O.: All Played Out."

"Oh. I knew that."

"Yeah, right."

Together, they chuckled.

They would find that same chemistry in the Lawyer's League basketball skirmishes. Finding his desire for the game rekindled by his younger, more gifted backcourt mate, together they led their firm to consecutive seasonal championships. Realizing the oomph of his colt-like partner, William relinquished the point guard position and flourished at shooting guard.

A year later, he was still rewarding his pupil, for they watched Yankee games from first-base box seats and endured the "what are they doing here" stares given to token minorities seated close to the historic playing field. One particular evening, the fabled Pinstripes had opened up a 10-2 can of whoop-ass on the hated Red Sox.

"Yo, this game sucks," Mark announced as A-Rod launched another lame fastball from Curt Schilling toward the right-field bleacher bums. "The Yankees are killin' 'em."

"Tell me about it," William responded as he scanned the historical landmark. Hundreds of fans headed toward the exits; they, too, would not stay for Frank Sinatra's "New York, New York" victory serenade.

"We're outta here, Mark."

Leaving the House that Ruth Built, William dialed his cell.

"Hey, baby. I know it's late, but do you want me to come out? Cool. I'll see you later."

Mark sighed. "Are you still dealin' with that correction officer? I keep telling you to leave her alone."

"Mark, what do you know about women?"

"Man, I have a K I.S.S. philosophy."

"K.I.S.S.?"

Mark nodded. "The 'Keep It Simple, Stupid' philosophy. No woman's pussy is worth more than my dick, William."

Shaking his head while sliding his metrocard through the train turnstile, William sighed. To a lesser degree, he understood Mark's resentment. Five years earlier, Mark was engaged to his high school sweetheart, Clarissa Stevens, and found out that Douglas, the three-year-old boy he fathered, was the child of Stan, an older brother.

Distraught over the revelation, he almost landed in jail; he pummeled his sibling so bad. Clarissa was to fend for herself from that point forward. He even attempted to recoup the monetary support given from his heart in judicial proceedings, but his efforts were futile when the judge dismissed the case.

He might have fared better had he not beat up his brother, William thought. Seeing a remorseless stare in his eyes every time Mark recounted the events that damaged his heart, he removed the employer hat.

"Sometimes, they're too young to appreciate a man with good qualities," he argued. "Most women in their twenties are still finding themselves. Experiencing life, a lot of their actions are self-centered. It's an 'all about me' stage. They grow out of that with maturity." Hearing his own tone reminded him of the many times Steve Randall, his old Delaware buddy, tried to fill his head with logic when it came to his dating beliefs. "Have you healed completely?"

"Yeah, man. Fuck these bitches."

"They're not bitches, Mark."

"You should be saying the same thing. Anna guarded her heart for a year before submitting. How do you know she's worth marrying? The times we watched prize fights at her house, she seemed rude to me, like she didn't respect you."

Crossing the line, William became stern.

"Mark, you should stick to resolving your own issues. I got this. Besides, I think she's ready."

"I sure hope so."